A FISTFUL
OF CHARMS

By Kim Harrison

DEAD WITCH WALKING
THE GOOD, THE BAD, AND THE UNDEAD
EVERY WHICH WAY BUT DEAD

A FISTFUL OF CHARMS

KIM HARRISON

HARPER
Voyager

Harper*Voyager*
An Imprint of HarperCollins*Publishers*
77–85 Fulham Palace Road,
Hammersmith, London W6 8JB

www.harpercollins.co.uk

Published by Voyager 2006

5

A catalogue record for this book
is available from the British Library

ISBN-13 978 0 00 723613 8
ISBN-10 0 00 723613 1

Printed and bound in Great Britain by
Clays Limited, St Ives plc

*To the man who invariably says, "Really? Okay,"
instead of, "You want to do what?"*

Acknowledgements

I'd like to thank Gwen Hunter for helping me with the med stuff on the bridge, and TB, who read through my diving sequences. If anything doesn't jive, it wasn't from these two ladies but me pushing the envelope. And of course, a very large thank you to my agent, Richard Curtis, and to my editor, Diana Gill, without whom the Hollows would have stayed in my imagination alone.

A FISTFUL OF CHARMS

One

The solid thud of David's car door shutting echoed off the stone face of the eight-story building we had parked beside. Leaning against the gray sports car, I shaded my eyes and squinted up at its aged and architecturally beautiful columns and fluted sills. The uppermost floor was golden in the setting sun, but here at street level we were in a chill shadow. Cincinnati had a handful of such landmark buildings, most abandoned, as this one appeared to be.

"Are you sure this is the place?" I asked, then dragged the flat of my arms off the roof of his car. The river was close; I could smell the oil and gas mix of boats. The top floor probably had a view. Though the streets were clean, the area was clearly depressed. But with a little attention—and a lot of money—I could see it as one of the city's newest residential hot spots.

David set his worn leather briefcase down and reached into the inner pocket of his suit coat. Pulling out a sheaf of papers, he flipped to the back, then glanced at the distant corner and the street sign. "Yes," he said, his soft voice tense but not worried.

Tugging my little red leather jacket down, I hiked my bag higher on my shoulder and headed to his side of the car, heels clunking. I'd like to say I was wearing my butt-kicking boots in deference to this being a run, but in reality I just liked them. They went well with the blue jeans and black

T-shirt I had on; and with the matching cap, I looked and felt sassy.

David frowned at the chunking—or my choice of attire, maybe—steeling his features to bland acceptance when he saw me quietly laughing at him. He was in his respectable work clothes, somehow pulling off the mix of the three-piece suit and his shoulder-length, wavy black hair held back in a subdued clip. I'd seen him a couple of times in running tights that showed off his excellently maintained, mid-thirties physique—yum—and a full-length duster and cowboy hat—Van Helsing, eat your heart out—but his somewhat small stature lost none of its presence when he dressed like the insurance claims adjuster he was. David was kind of complex for a Were.

I hesitated when I came even with him, and together we eyed the building. Three streets over I could hear the shush of traffic, but here, nothing moved. "It's really quiet," I said, holding my elbows against the chill of the mid-May evening.

Brown eyes pinched, David ran a hand over his clean-shaven cheeks. "It's the right address, Rachel," he said, peering at the top floor. "I can call to check if you want."

"No, this is cool." I smiled with my lips closed, hefting my shoulder bag and feeling the extra weight of my splat gun. This was David's run, not mine, and about as benign as you could get—adjusting the claim of an earth witch whose wall had cracked. I wouldn't need the sleepy-time charms I loaded my modified paint ball gun with, but I just grabbed my bag when David asked me to come with him. It was still packed from my last run—storming the back room of an illegal spammer. God, plugging him had been satisfying.

David pushed into motion, gallantly gesturing me to go first. He was older than I by about ten years, but it was hard to tell unless you looked at his eyes. "She's probably living in one of those new flats they're making above old warehouses," he said, heading for the ornate stoop.

I snickered, and David looked at me.

"What?" he said, dark eyebrows rising.

I entered the building before him, shoving the door so he could follow tight on my heels. "I was thinking if you lived in one, it would still be a warehouse. Were house? Get it?"

He sighed, and I frowned. Jenks, my old backup, would have laughed. Guilt hit me, and my pace faltered. Jenks was currently AWOL, hiding out in some Were's basement after I'd majorly screwed up by not trusting him, but with spring here, I could step up my efforts to apologize and get him to return.

The front lobby was spacious, full of gray marble and little else. My heels sounded loud in the tall-ceilinged space. Creeped out, I stopped chunking and started walking to minimize the noise. A pair of black-edged elevators were across the lobby, and we headed for them. David pushed the up button and rocked back.

I eyed him, the corners of my lips quirking. Though he was trying to hide it, I could see he was getting excited about his run. Being a field insurance adjustor wasn't the desk job one might think it was. Most of his company's clients were Inderlanders—witches, Weres, and the occasional vampire—and as such, getting the truth as to why a client's car was totaled was harder than it sounded. Was it from the teenage son backing it into the garage wall, or did the witch down the street finally get tired of hearing him beep every time he left the drive? One was covered, the other wasn't, and sometimes it took, ah, creative interviewing techniques to get the truth.

David noticed I was smiling at him, and the rims of his ears went red under his dark complexion. "I appreciate you coming with me," he said, shifting forward as the elevator dinged and the doors opened. "I owe you dinner, okay?"

"No problem." I joined him in the murky, mirrored lift, and watched my reflection in the amber light as the doors closed. I'd had to move an interview for a possible client, but David had helped me in the past, and that was far more important.

The trim Were winced. "The last time I adjusted the claim of an earth witch, I later found she had scammed the company. My ignorance cost them hundreds of thousands. I appreciate you giving me your opinion as to whether she caused the damage with a misuse of magic."

I tucked a loosely curling lock of red hair that had escaped my French braid behind an ear, then adjusted my leather cap. The lift was old and slow. "Like I said, no problem."

David watched the numbers counting up. "I think my boss is trying to get me fired," he said softly. "This is the third claim this week to hit my desk that I'm not familiar with." His grip on his briefcase shifted. "He's waiting for me to make a mistake. Pushing for it."

I leaned against the back mirror and smiled weakly at him. "Sorry. I know how that feels." I had quit my old job at Inderland Security, the I.S., almost a year ago to go independent. Though it had been rough—and still was, occasionally—it was the best decision I'd ever made.

"Still," he persisted, the not unpleasant scent of musk growing as he turned to me in the confined space. "This isn't your job. I owe you."

"David, let it go," I said, exasperated. "I'm happy to come out here and make sure some witch isn't scamming you. It's no big deal. I do this stuff every day. In the dark. Usually alone. And if I'm lucky, it involves running, and screaming, and my foot in somebody's gut."

The Were smiled to show his flat, blocky teeth. "You like your job, don't you?"

I smiled right back. "You bet I do."

The floor lurched, and the doors opened. David waited for me to exit first, and I looked out onto the huge, building-sized room on the top floor. The setting sun streamed in the ceiling-to-floor windows, shining on the scattered construction materials. Past the windows, the Ohio River made a gray sheen. When finished, this would be an excellent apartment. My nose tickled at the scent of two-by-fours and sanded plaster, and I sneezed.

David's eyes went everywhere. "Hello? Mrs. Bryant?" he said, his deep voice echoing. "I'm David. David Hue from

Were Insurance. I brought an assistant with me." He gave my tight jeans, T-shirt, and red leather jacket a disparaging look. "Mrs. Bryant?"

I followed him farther in, my nose wrinkling. "I think the crack in her wall might be from removing some of those supporting members," I said softly. "Like I said, no problem."

"Mrs. Bryant?" David called again.

My thoughts went to the empty street and how far we were from the casual observer. Behind me, the elevator doors slid shut and the lift descended. A small scuff from the far end of the room sent a stab of adrenaline through me, and I spun.

David was on edge too, and together we laughed at ourselves when a slight figure rose from the couch set adjacent to a modern kitchen at the end of the long room, the cupboards still wrapped in plastic.

"Mrs. Bryant? I'm David Hue."

"As prompt as your last yearly review claims," a masculine voice said, the soft resonances sifting through the darkening air. "And very thoughtful to bring a witch with you to check your customer's claim with. Tell me, do you take that off your end-of-the-year taxes, or do you claim it as a business expense?"

David's eyes were wide. "It's a business expense, sir."

I looked from David to the man. "Ah, David? I take it that's not Mrs. Bryant."

His grip on his briefcase shifting, David shook his head. "I think it's the president of the company."

"Oh." I thought about that. Then thought about that some more. I was getting a bad feeling about this. "David?"

He put a hand on my shoulder and leaned in. "I think you should leave," he said, the worry in his brown eyes running right to my core.

Recalling what he'd said in the elevator about his boss gunning for him, my pulse quickened. "David, if you're in trouble, I'm not leaving," I said, boots thumping as he hustled me to the lift.

His face was grim. "I can handle this."

I tried to twist from his grip. "Then I'll stay and help you to the car when it's over."

He glanced at me. "I don't think so, Rachel. But thanks."

The elevator opened. Still protesting, I was ill prepared when David jerked me back. My head came up and my face went cold. *Crap.* The lift was full of Weres in various levels of elegance, ranging from Armani suits and sophisticated skirt and top combos to jeans and blouses. Even worse, they all had the collected, confident pride of alpha wolves. And they were smiling.

Shit. David had a *big* problem.

"Please tell me it's your birthday," I said, "and this is a surprise party."

A young Were in a bright red dress was the last to step from the elevator. Tossing her thick length of black hair, she gave me a once-over. Though sure of herself, I could tell by her stance that at least, she wasn't an alpha bitch. This was getting weird. Alphas never got together. They just didn't. Especially without their respective packs behind them.

"It's not his birthday," the woman said cattily. "But I imagine he's surprised."

David's grip on my arm twitched. "Hello, Karen," he said caustically.

My skin crawled and my muscles tightened as the Weres ringed us. I thought of the splat gun in my bag, then felt for a ley line, but didn't tap it. David couldn't pay me to leave now. This looked like a lynching.

"Hi, David," the woman in red said, satisfaction clear in both her voice and in her stance behind the alpha males. "You can't imagine how overjoyed I was to find you had started a pack."

David's boss was now there too, and with quick and confident steps he moved between us and the elevator. The tension in the room ratcheted up a notch, and Karen slinked behind him.

I hadn't known David long, but I'd never seen this mix of anger, pride, and annoyance on him before. There was no fear. David was a loner, and as such, the personal power of an alpha held little sway over him. But there were eight of them, and one was his boss.

"This doesn't involve her, sir," David said with a respectful anger. "Let her leave."

David's boss lifted an eyebrow. "Actually, this has nothing to do with you."

My breath caught. *Okay, maybe I was the one with the problem.*

"Thank you for coming, David. Your presence is no longer needed," the polished Were said. Turning to the others, he added, "Get him out of here."

I took a heaving lungful of air. With my second sight, I reached for a ley line, latching onto the one that ran under the university. My concentration shattered when two men grabbed my arms. "Hey!" I shouted as one ripped my shoulder bag off and sent it spinning to land against a stack of lumber. "Let go of me!" I demanded, unable to twist easily from their twin grips.

David grunted in pain, and when I stomped on someone's foot, they shoved me down. Plaster dust puffed up, choking me. My breath whooshed out as someone sat on me. My hands were pulled behind my back, and I went still. "Ow," I complained. Blowing a red curl from my face, I gave another squirm. Crap, David was being dragged into the elevator.

He was still fighting them. Red-faced and wrathful, his fists lashed out, making ugly sounding thumps when he scored. He could have Wered to fight more viciously, but there was a five-minute downtime when he would be helpless.

"Get him *out of here!*" David's boss shouted impatiently, and the doors shut. There was a clunk as something hit the inside of the elevator, and then the machinery started to lower the lift. I heard a shout and the sounds of a fight that slowly grew muffled.

Fear slid through me, and I gave another wiggle. David's boss turned his gaze to me. "Strap her," he said lightly.

My breath hissed in. Frantic, I reached for the ley line

again, tapping it with a splinter of thought. Ever-after energy flowed through me, filling my chi and then the secondary spindle I could keep in my head. Pain struck through me when someone wrenched my right arm too far back. The cool plastic of a zip-strip was jammed over one wrist, snugged tight with a quick pull and a familiar ratcheting sound to leave the end dangling. My face went cold as every last erg of ever-after washed out of me. The bitter taste of dandelions was on my lips. *Stupid, stupid witch!*

"Son of a bitch!" I shouted, and the Weres sitting on me fell away.

I staggered to my feet and tried to wedge the flexible plastic-wrapped band off me, failing. Its core was charmed silver, like in my long-gone I.S. issue cuffs. I couldn't tap a line. I couldn't do anything. I seldom used my new ley line skills in defense, and I hadn't been thinking of how easy they could be nullified.

Utterly bereft of my magic, I stood in the last of the amber light coming in the tall windows. I was alone with a pack of alphas. My thoughts zinged to Mr. Ray's pack and the wishing fish I had accidentally stolen from him, and then me making the owners of the Howlers baseball team pay for my time doing it. *Oh . . . crap.* I had to get out of there.

David's boss shifted his weight to his other foot. The sun spilled over him to glint on the dust on his dress shoes. "Ms. Morgan, isn't it?" he asked companionably.

I nodded, wiping my palms off on my jeans. Plaster dust clung to me, and I only made things worse. I never took my eyes from him, knowing it was a blatant show of dominance. I had dealt a little with Weres, and none of them but David seemed to like me. I didn't know why.

"It's a pleasure to meet you," he said, coming closer and pulling a pair of metal-rimmed glasses from an inner pocket of his suit coat. "I'm David's boss. You can call me Mr. Finley."

Perching the glasses on his narrow nose, he took the stapled papers that Karen smugly handed him. "Forgive me if I'm a little slow," he said, peering at them. "My secretary usually does this." He looked over the papers at me, pen clicking open. "Your pack number is what?"

"Huh?" I said intelligently, then stiffened as the ring of Weres seemed to close in. Karen snickered, and my face warmed.

Mr. Finley's slight wrinkles bunched as he frowned. "You're David's alpha. Karen is challenging you for your place. There is paperwork. What is your pack number?"

My mouth dropped open. This wasn't about the Rays or the Howlers. I was the sole member of David's pack, yeah. But it was just a paper relationship, one designed so I could get my overly inflated insurance cheap, cheap, cheap, and David could keep his job and buck the system to continue working alone and without a partner. He didn't want a real pack, being a confirmed loner and good at it, but it was nearly impossible to fire an alpha, which was why he had asked me to start a pack with him.

My gaze darted to Karen, smiling like the queen of the Nile, as dark and exotic as an Egyptian whore. She wanted to challenge me for my position?

"Oh, hell no!" I said, and Karen snorted, thinking I was afraid. "I'm not fighting her! David doesn't want a real pack!"

"Obviously," Karen scorned. "I claim ascension. Before eight packs, I claim it."

There weren't eight alphas there anymore, but I thought the five that were left were more than enough to force the issue.

Mr. Finley let the hand holding the sheet of papers fall. "Does anyone have a catalog? She doesn't know her pack number."

"I do," sang out a woman, swinging her purse around and digging to bring out what looked like a small address book. "New edition," she added, and thumbed it open.

"This is nothing personal," Mr. Finley said. "Your alpha has become the topic of interest at the water cooler, and this is the simplest way to get David back on track and end the disturbing rumors that have been reaching me. I have invited the principal shareholders in the company as witnesses." He smiled without warmth. "This will be legally binding."

"This is crap!" I said nastily, and the surrounding Weres either chuckled or gasped at my temerity to swear at him. Lips pressed tight, I glanced at my bag and the splat gun halfway across the room. My hand touched the small of my back, looking for my nonexistent cuffs, long gone with my I.S. paycheck. God, I missed my cuffs.

"Here it is," the woman said, her head lowered. "Rachel Morgan. O-C(H) 93AF."

"You registered in Cincinnati?" David's boss asked idly, writing it down. Folding the pages over, he fixed on my eyes. "David isn't the first to start a pack with someone not of, ah, Were descent," he finally said. "But he is the first in this company to do so with the sole intent to save his job. This is not a good trend."

"Challenger's choice," Karen said, reaching for the tie to her dress. "I choose to Were first."

David's boss clicked the pen shut. "Then let's get started."

Someone grabbed my arms, and I froze for three heart-beats. Challenger's choice, my grandmother's ass. I had five minutes to subdue her while she Wered, or I was going to lose this.

I silently twisted, going down and rolling. There were several shouts when I knocked the feet out from whoever held me. Then my breath was crushed out of my lungs as some-one else fell on me. Adrenaline surged painfully. Someone pinned my legs. Another pushed my head into the plaster-dust-covered plywood.

They won't kill me, I told myself as I spit the hair out of my mouth and tried to get a decent breath. *This is some asi-nine Were dominance thing, and they won't kill me.*

That's what I was telling myself, but it was hard to con-vince my trembling muscles.

A low snarl far deeper than it ought to have been rumbled thorough the empty top floor, and the three men holding me let me up.

What in hell? I thought as I scrambled to my feet, then stared. Karen had Wered. She had Wered in thirty seconds flat!

"How . . ." I stammered, not believing it.

Karen made one hell of a wolf. As a person she was petite, maybe 110 pounds. But turn that same 110 pounds into snarling animal, and you get a wolf the size of a pony. *Damn.*

A steady growl of discontent came from her, lips curling from her muzzle in a warning older than dirt. Silky fur reminiscent of her black hair covered her except for her ears, which were rimmed in white. Beyond the circle were her clothes, discarded into a pile on the plywood floor. The faces ringing me were solemn. It wasn't a street brawl but a serious affair that would be as binding as a legal document.

Around me, the Weres were backing up, enlarging the circle. *Double damn.*

Mr. Finley smiled knowingly at me, and my gaze darted from him to the surrounding alphas in their nice clothes and five-hundred-dollar shoes. My heart hammered, and I figured it out. I was in deep shit. They had bound themselves into a round.

Frightened, I eased into a fighting stance. When Weres bound themselves together outside their usual packs, weird stuff happened. I'd seen this once before at a Howlers' game when several alphas had united to support an injured player, taking on the player's pain so he could go on to win the game. Illegal, but wickedly hard to prove since picking out the alphas responsible in a huge stadium was next to impossible. The effect was temporary since Weres, especially alphas, couldn't seem to work under anyone's direction for long. But they would be able to hold it together long enough for Karen to hurt me really, really bad.

I settled my feet more firmly in their boots, feeling my fists begin to sweat. This wasn't fair, damn it! They took my magic away, so the only thing I could do would be to try to beat her off, but she wasn't going to feel a thing! I was toast. I was dog chow. I was going to be really sore in the morning. But I wasn't going to go down without a fight.

Karen's ears went back. It was the only warning I got.

Instinct overpowered training, and I backpedaled as she lunged. Teeth snapping where my face would have been, we went down, her paws on my chest. The floor slammed into me, and I grunted. Hot dog breath hit my face, and I kneed her, trying to knock her breath away. There was a startled yip, and dull claws raked my side as she scrambled up and back.

I stayed down, rolling to my knees so she couldn't push me over again. Not waiting, she jumped.

I cried out, stiff-arming her. Panic struck me when my fist went right square into her mouth. Her paws, the size of my hands, pushed at me as she frantically backed off, and I fell backward. I was lucky she hadn't twisted her head and taken a chunk out of my arm. As it was, I was bleeding from a nasty gash.

Karen's echoing, racking coughs turned into an aggressive growl. "What's the matter, grandma," I panted, flipping my braid out of the way. "Can't get Little Red Riding Hood down your throat?"

Ears pinned, hackles raised, and lips curled to show her teeth, she came at me.

Okay. Maybe that wasn't the best thing to say. Karen slammed into me like a flung door, rocking me back and sending me down. Her teeth went around my neck, choking. I grabbed the foot that was pinching me, digging my nails into it. She bit down, and I gasped.

I made a fist and punched her in the ribs twice. My knee came up and I got her somewhere. There was silky hair in my mouth, and I reached up and pulled an ear. Her teeth gripped harder, cutting off my air. My sight started to go black. Panicking, I went for her eyes.

With no thought but survival, I dug my nails into her eyelids. That, she felt, and yelping, she jerked off me. I took a ragged breath, levering myself up on an elbow. My other hand went to my neck. It came away wet with blood.

"This isn't fair!" I shouted, mad as hell as I scrambled up. My knuckles were bleeding, my side hurt, and I was shaking from adrenaline and fear. I could see Mr. Finley's excitement—smell the rising musk. They were all getting off on the chance to see one of their own "legally" maul a person.

"Nobody said it was supposed to be fair," the man said softly, then gestured to Karen.

But her impetus to attack hesitated at the ding of the elevator.

Despair crept over me. With three more alphas, she wasn't going to feel anything. Not even if I cut something off.

The doors slid open to show David leaning against the back of the lift. His face had a bruise that was likely going to turn his eye black, and his sport coat was torn and filthy. Slowly, he lifted his head, a murderous look in his brown eyes.

"Leave!" his boss said sharply.

"I forgot my briefcase," he said, limping forward. He took in the situation in a glance, still breathing heavily from escaping the three Weres who had dragged him off. "You challenge my alpha, I'm damn well going to be here to make sure it's a fair fight." Shambling to his briefcase, he picked it up, dusted it off, and turned to me. "Rachel, you doing okay?"

I felt a flush of gratitude. He wasn't coming to my rescue, he wanted to make sure they were playing fair. "I'm doing okay," I said, voice cracking. "But that bitch isn't feeling any pain, and they took away my magic." I was going to lose this. I was going to lose this so bad. *Sorry, David.*

The surrounding Weres glanced uneasily at each other now that they had a witness, and Mr. Finley's complexion darkened. "Finish it," he said roughly, and Karen came at me.

Her nails scraped on the plywood floor as they scrambled for purchase. Gasping, I fell to my back before she could push me down. Pulling my knees to my chest, I planted my feet against her as she landed on me and flung her over my head.

I heard a startled yip and thump and David shouting something. There were two fights going on.

I spun on my butt to face her. My eyes widened and I flung up an arm.

Karen smashed into me, pinning me to the floor. She covered me, and fear stabbed deep. I had to keep her from getting a grip on my throat again, and I cried out when she bit my arm.

I'd had enough.

Making a fist, I smashed it into her head. She jerked her muzzle up, raking my arm and sending a pulse of pain through me. Immediately she was back, snarling and more savage. But a ribbon of hope rose in me and I gritted my teeth. She had felt that.

I could hear thumps and cries in the background. David was interfering, breaking their concentration. The round was falling apart. I couldn't best Karen, but sure as hell she was going to walk away remembering me.

The anger and excessive adrenaline wouldn't be denied. "You stupid dog!" I shouted, slamming my fist into her ear again to make her yelp. "You're a foul-breathed, dung flop of a city-bred poodle! How do you like this? Huh!" I hit her again, unable to see from the tears blurring my vision. "Want some more? How about this?"

She latched onto my shoulder and picked me up, intending to shake me. A silky ear landed in my mouth, and after failing to spit it out, I bit down, hard.

Karen barked and was gone. Taking a clean breath, I rolled over onto all fours to see her.

"Rachel!" David cried, and my splat ball gun slid to within my grasp.

I picked the cherry-red gun up, and on my knees, aimed it at Karen. She sat back, her forelegs scrambling to halt her forward motion. Arms shaking, I spit out a tuft of white fur. "Game over, bitch," I said, then plugged her.

The puff of air from my gun was almost lost in someone's cry of frustration.

It hit her square in the nose, covering her face with a sleepy-time potion, the most aggressive thing a white witch would use. Karen went down as if strings were cut, sliding to land three feet from me.

I rose, shaking and so full of adrenaline I could hardly

stand. Arms stiff, I aimed my gun at Mr. Finley. The sun had gone behind the surrounding hills across the river, and his face was shadowed. His posture was easy enough to read. "I win," I said, then smacked David when he put a hand on my shoulder.

"Easy, Rachel," David soothed.

"I'm fine!" I shouted, pulling my aim back to his boss before the man could move. "If you want to challenge my title, okay! But I do it as a *witch,* not with my strength washed out of me! This wasn't fair, and you know it!"

"Come on, Rachel. Let's go."

I was still aiming at his boss. I really, *really* wanted to plug him. But in what I thought was a huge show of class, I lowered the gun, snatching my bag from David as he handed it to me. Around me, I felt an easing of tension from the watching alphas.

Briefcase in hand, David escorted me to the elevator. I was still shaking, but I turned my back on them, knowing it would say more clearly than words that I wasn't afraid.

I was scared, though. If Karen had been trying to kill me, not just cow me into submission, it would have been over in the first thirty seconds.

David hit the down button, and together we turned. "This was not a fair contest," he said, then wiped his mouth to make his hand come away red with blood. "I had a right to be here."

Mr. Finley shook his head. "Either the female's alpha shall be present, or in the case of his absence, six alphas may serve as witness to prevent any . . ." He smiled. ". . . foul play."

"There weren't six alphas here at the time of the contest," David said. "I expect to see this recorded as a win for Rachel. That woman is *not* my alpha."

I followed his gaze to Karen lying forgotten on the floor, and I wondered if someone was going to douse her in saltwater to break the charm or just dump her on her pack's doorstep unconscious. I didn't care, and I wasn't going to ask.

"Wrong or not, it's the law," Mr. Finley said, the alphas

moving to back him. "And it's there to allow a gentle correction when an alpha goes astray." He took a deep breath, clearly thinking. "This will be recorded as a win for your alpha," he said as if he didn't care, "provided you don't file a complaint. But David, she isn't a Were. If she can't best another with her physical skills, she doesn't deserve an alpha title and will be taken down."

I felt a stab of fear at the memory of Karen on top of me.

"A person can't stand against a wolf," Mr. Finley said. "She would have to Were to have even a chance, and witches can't Were."

The man's eyes went to mine, and though I didn't look away, the fear slid to my belly. The elevator dinged, and I backed up into it, not caring if they knew I was afraid. David joined me, and I gripped my bag and my gun as if I'd fall apart without them.

David's boss stepped forward, his presence threatening and his face utterly shadowed in the new night. "You are an alpha," he said as if correcting a child. "Stop playing with witches and start paying your dues."

The doors slid shut, and I slumped against the mirror. *Paying his dues? What was that supposed to mean?*

Slowly, the lift descended, my tension easing with every floor between us. It smelled like angry Were in there, and I glanced at David. One of the mirrors was cracked, and my reflection looked awful: braid falling apart and caked with plaster dust, a bite mark on my neck where Karen's teeth had bruised and broken my skin, my knuckles scraped from being in her mouth. My back hurt, my foot was sore, and damn it, I was missing an earring. My favorite hoops, too.

I remembered the soft feel of Karen's ear in my mouth and the sudden give as I bit down. It had been awful, hurting someone that intimately. But I was okay. I wasn't dead. Nothing had changed. I'd never tried to use my ley line skills in a pitched fight like that, and now I knew to watch out for wristbands. Caught like a teenager shoplifting, God help me.

I licked my thumb and wiped a smear of plaster dust off my forehead. The wristband was ugly, but I'd need Ivy's bolt cutters to get it off. Removing my remaining earring, I dropped it in my bag. David was leaning into the corner and holding his ribs, but he didn't look like he was worried about running into the three Weres he had downed, so I put my gun away. Lone wolves were like alphas that didn't need the support of a pack to feel confident. Rather dangerous when one stopped to think about it.

David chuckled. Looking at him, I made a face, and he started to laugh, cutting it short as he winced in pain. His lightly wrinkled face still showing his amusement, he glanced at the numbers counting down, then pulled himself upright, trying to arrange his torn coat. "How about that dinner?" he asked, and I snorted.

"I'm getting the lobster," I said, then added, "Weres never work together outside their packs. I must have really pissed them off. God! What is their problem?"

"It's not you, it's me," he said, discomfited. "They don't like that I started a pack with you. No, that's not true. They don't like that I'm not contributing to the Were population."

The adrenaline was fading, making me hurt all over. I had a pain amulet in my bag, but I wasn't going to use it when David had nothing. And when in hell had Karen scored on my face? Tilting my head, I examined the red claw mark running close to my ear in the dim light, then turned to David when his last words penetrated. "Excuse me?" I asked, confused. "What do you mean, not contributing to the Were population?"

David dropped his gaze. "I started a pack with you."

I tried to straighten, but it hurt. "Yeah, I got the no-kids part there. Why do they care?"

"Because I don't have any, ah, informal relations with any other Were woman, either."

Because if he did, they would expect to be in his pack, eventually. "And . . ." I prompted.

He shifted from foot to foot. "The only way to get more

Weres is by birth. Not like vampires who can turn humans if they work at it. With numbers come strength and power. . . ." His voice trailed off, and I got it.

"Oh, for crying out loud," I complained, holding my shoulder. "This was political?"

The elevator chimed and the doors opened. " 'Fraid so," he said. "They let subordinate Weres do what they will, but as a loner, what I do matters."

I trooped out before him, looking for trouble, but it was quiet in the abandoned lobby, apart from the three Weres slumped in the corner. David had sounded bitter, and when he opened the main door for me, I touched his arm in a show of support. Clearly surprised, he glanced at me. "Uh, about dinner," he said, looking at his clothes. "You want to reschedule?"

My feet hit the pavement, the cadence of my boots telling me I was limping. It was quiet, but the stillness seemed to hold a new threat. Mr. Finley was right about one thing. This was going to happen again unless I asserted my claim in a way they would respect.

Breathing deeply of the chill air, I headed for David's car. "No way, man. You owe me dinner. How about some Skyline chili?" I said, and he hesitated in confusion. "Go through the drive-through. I have to do some research tonight."

"Rachel," he protested as his car gave a cheerful chirp and unlocked. "I think you deserve at least one night off." His eyes narrowed and he looked at me over the roof of his car. "I am really sorry about this. Maybe . . . we should get the pack contract annulled."

I looked up from opening my door. "Don't you dare!" I said loudly in case someone was listening from a top floor. Then my expression went sheepish. "I can't afford the rider everyone else makes me take out on my health insurance."

David chuckled, but I could tell he wasn't satisfied. We slipped into his car, both of us moving slowly when we found new pains and tried to find a comfortable way to sit. *Oh God, I hurt all over.*

"I mean it, Rachel," he said, his low voice filling the small car after our doors shut. "It's not fair to ask you to put up with this crap."

Smiling, I looked across the car at him. "Don't worry about it, David. I like being your alpha. All I have to do is find the right charm to Were with."

He sighed, his small frame moving in his exhalation, then he snorted.

"What?" I asked, buckling myself in as he started the car.

"The right charm to Were?" he said, putting the car into gear and pulling from the curb. "Get it? You want to be my alpha, but have nothing to Were?"

Putting a hand to my head, I leaned my elbow into the door for support. "That's not funny," I said, but he just laughed, even though it hurt him.

Two

Dappled patterns of afternoon light sifted over my gloved hands as I knelt on a green foam pad and strained to reach the back of the flower bed where grass had taken root despite the shade of the mature oak above it. From the street came the soft sound of cars. A blue jay called and was answered. Saturday in the Hollows was the pinnacle of casual.

Straightening, I stretched to crack my back, then slumped, wincing when my amulet lost contact with my skin and I felt a jolt of pain. I knew I shouldn't be working out there under the influence of a pain amulet, lest I hurt myself without re-alizing it, but after yesterday I needed some "dirt time" to reassure my subconscious that I was alive. And the garden needed attention. It was a mess without Jenks and his family keeping it up.

The smell of brewing coffee slipped out the kitchen win-dow and into the peace of the cool spring afternoon, and I knew that Ivy was up. Standing, I gazed from the yellow clapboard add-on behind the rented church to the walled graveyard past the witch's garden. The entire grounds took up four city lots and stretched from one street to the other be-hind it. Though no one had been buried here for almost thirty years, the grass was mown by yours truly. I felt a tidy grave-yard made a happy graveyard.

Wondering if Ivy would bring me coffee if I shouted, I nudged my knee pad into the sun near a patch of soft-stemmed black violets. Jenks had seeded the plot last fall, and I wanted to thin them before they got spindly from competition. I knelt before the small plants, moving my way around the bed, circling the rosebush and pulling a third of them.

I had been out there long enough to get warm from exertion, worry waking me before noon. Sleep hadn't come easily either. I'd sat up past sunrise in the kitchen with my spell books in search of a charm to Were into a wolf. It was a task whose success was slim at best; there were no spells to change into sentient beings—at least no legal ones. And it would have to be an earth charm since ley line magic was mostly illusion or physical bursts of energy. I had a small but unique library, yet for all my spells and charms, I had nothing that told me how to Were.

Inching my pad down the flower bed, I felt a band of worry tighten in me. As David had said, the only way you could be a Were was to be born that way. The bandage-covered tooth gashes on my knuckles and neck from Karen would soon be gone with no lingering effects but for what remained in my memory. There might be a charm in the black arts section of the library, but black earth magic used nasty ingredients— like indispensable people parts—and I wasn't going to go there.

The one time I had considered using black earth magic, I came away with a demon mark, then got another, then managed to find myself said demon's familiar. Lucky for me, I had kept my soul and the bargain was declared unenforceable. I was free and clear but for Big Al's original demon mark, which I'd wear along with Newt's mark until I found a way to pay both of them back. But at least with the familiar bond broken, Al wasn't showing up every time I tapped a ley line.

Eyes pinched from the sun, I smeared dirt over my wrist and Al's demon mark. The earth was cool, and it hid the upraised circle-and-line scar more reliably than any charm. It covered the red welt from the band the Weres had put on me, too. God, I had been stupid.

The breeze shifted a red curl to tickle my face, and I tucked it away, glancing past the rosebush to the back of the flower bed. My lips parted in dismay. It had been trampled.

An entire section of plants had been snapped at their bases and were now sprawled and wilting. Tiny footprints gave evidence of who had done it. Outraged, I gathered a handful of broken stems, feeling in the soft pliancy their unstoppable death. *Damn garden fairies.*

"Hey!" I shouted, lurching up to stare into the canopy of the nearby ash tree. Face warm, I stomped over and stood under it, the plants in my hand like an accusation. I'd been fighting them since they'd migrated up from Mexico last week, but it was a losing battle. Fairies ate insects, not nectar, like pixies did, and they didn't care if they killed a garden in their search for food. They were like humans that way, destroying what kept them alive in the long term in their search for short-term resources. There were only six of them, but they had no respect for anything.

"I said hey!" I called louder, craning my neck to the wad of leaves that looked like a squirrel's nest midway up the tree. "I told you to stay out of my garden if you couldn't keep from wrecking it! What are you going to do about this!"

As I fumed on the ground, there was a rustling, and a dead leaf fluttered down. A pale fairy poked his head out, the leader of the small bachelor clan orienting on me immediately. "It's not your garden," he said loudly. "It's my garden, and you can take a long walk in a short ley line for all I care."

My mouth dropped open. From behind me came the thump of a window closing; Ivy didn't want anything to do with what was to follow. I didn't blame her, but it was Jenks's garden, and if I didn't drive them out, it would be trashed by the time I convinced him to come back. I was a runner, damn it. If I couldn't keep Jenks's garden intact, I didn't deserve the title. But it was getting harder each time, and they only returned the moment I went inside.

"Don't ignore me!" I shouted as the fairy disappeared inside the communal nest. "You nasty little twit!" A cry of outrage slipped from me when a tiny bare ass took the place of the pale face and shook at me from the wad of leaves. They thought they were safe up there, out of my reach.

Disgusted, I dropped the broken stems and stalked to the shed. They wouldn't come to me, so I would go to them. I had a ladder.

The blue jays in the graveyard called, enjoying something new to gossip about while I struggled with the twelve-foot length of metal. It smacked into the lower branches as I maneuvered it against the trunk, and with a shrill protest, the nest emptied in an explosion of blue and orange butterfly wings. I put a foot on the first rail, puffing a red curl out of my eyes. I hated to do this, but if they ruined the garden, Jenks's kids would starve.

"Now!" came a loud demand, and I cried out when sharp pings pinched my back.

Cowering, I ducked my head and spun. The ladder slipped, crashing down into the very flower bed they had destroyed. Ticked, I looked up. They were lobbing last year's acorns at me, the sharp ends hard enough to hurt. "You little boogers!" I cried, glad I had on a pain amulet.

"Again!" the leader shouted.

My eyes widened at the handful of acorns coming at me. "*Rhombus,*" I said, the trigger word instigating a hard-learned series of mental exercises into an almost instinctive action. Quicker than thought, my awareness touched the small ley line in the graveyard. Energy filled me, the balance equalizing in the time between memory and action. I spun around, toe pointing, sketching a rough circle, and ley line force filled it, closing it. I could have done this last night and avoided a trouncing, but for the charmed silver they had put on me.

A shimmering band of ever-after flashed into existence, the molecule-thin sheet of alternate reality arching to a close over my head and six feet under my feet, making an oblong bubble that prevented anything more obnoxious than air to pass through. It was sloppy and wouldn't hold a demon, but the acorns pinged off it. It worked against bullets too.

"Knock it off!" I exclaimed, flustered. The usual red sheen of energy shifted to gold as it took on the main color of my aura.

Seeing me safe but trapped in my bubble, the largest fairy fluttered down on his mothlike wings, his hands on his narrow hips and his gossamer, spiderweb-draped hair making him look like a six-inch negative of the grim reaper. His lips were a stark red against his pale face, and his thin features were tight in determination. His harsh beauty made him look incredibly fragile, but he was tougher than sinew. He was a garden fairy, not one of the assassins that had almost killed me last spring, but he was still accustomed to fighting for his right to live. "Go inside and we won't hurt you," he said, leering.

I snickered. What were they going to do? Butterfly kiss me to death?

An excited whisper pulled my attention to the row of neighborhood kids watching from over the tall wall surrounding the graveyard. Their eyes were wide while I tried to best tiny little flying things, something every Inderlander knew was impossible. Crap, I was acting like an ignorant human. But it was Jenks's garden, and I'd hold them off as long as I could.

Resolute, I pushed out of my circle. I jerked as the energy of the circle raced back into me, overflowed my chi and returned to the ley line. A shrill cry came to ready the darts.

Darts? Oh swell. Pulse quickening, I ran to the far side of the kitchen for the hose.

"I tried to be nice. I tried to be reasonable," I muttered while I opened the valve and water started dripping from the spray nozzle. The blue jays in the graveyard called, and I struggled with the hose, jerking to a halt when it caught on the corner of the kitchen. Taking off my gloves, I snapped the hose into a sine wave. It came free, and I stumbled backward. From the ash tree came the high-pitched sounds of organization. I'd never hosed them off before. Maybe this would do it. Fairy wings didn't do well when wet.

"Get her!" came a shout, and I jerked my head up. The

thorns they held looked as large as swords as they headed right for me.

Gasping, I aimed the hose and squeezed. They darted up and I followed them, my lips parting when the water turned into a pathetic trickle to arch to the ground and die. *What in hell?* I spun at the sound of gushing water. They had cut the hose!

"I spent twenty bucks on that hose!" I cried, then felt myself pale as the entire clan fronted me, tiny spears probably tipped with poison ivy. "Er, can we talk about this?" I stammered.

I dropped the hose, and the orange-winged fairy grinned like a vampire stripper at a bachelorette party. My heart pounded and I wondered if I should flee inside the church, and subject myself to Ivy's laughter, or tough it out and get a bad case of poison ivy.

The sound of pixy wings brought my heart into my throat. "Jenks!" I exclaimed, turning to follow the head fairy's worried gaze, fixed beyond my shoulder. But it wasn't Jenks, it was his wife, Matalina, and eldest daughter, Jih.

"Back off," Matalina threatened, hovering beside me at head height. The harsh clatter of her more maneuverable dragonfly-like wings set the stray strands of my damp hair to tickle my face. She looked thinner than last winter, her childlike features severe. Determination showed in her eyes, and she held a drawn bow with an arrow at the string. Her daughter looked even more ominous, with a wood-handled sword of silver in her grip. She had possession of a small garden across the street and needed silver to protect it and herself since she had yet to take a husband.

"It's mine!" the fairy screamed in frustration. "Two women can't hold a garden!"

"I need only hold the ground I fly over," Matalina said resolutely. "Get out. Now."

He hesitated, and Matalina pulled the bow back farther, making a tiny creak.

"We'll only take it when you leave!" he cried, motioning for his clan to retreat.

"Then take it," she said. "But while I am here, you won't be."

I watched, awed, while a four-inch pixy stood down an entire clan of fairies. Such was Jenks's reputation, and such was the capabilities of pixies. They could rule the world by assassinations and blackmail if they wanted. But all they desired was a small plot of ground and the peace to tend it. "Thanks, Matalina," I whispered.

She didn't take her steely gaze off them as they retreated to the knee-high wall that divided the garden from the graveyard. "Thank me when I've watered seedlings with their blood," she muttered, shocking me. The pretty, silk-clad pixy looked all of eighteen, her usual tan pale from living with Jenks and her children in that Were's basement all winter. Her billowy green, lightweight dress swirled in the draft from her wings. They were a harsh red with anger, as were her daughter's.

The faire of garden fairies fled to a corner of the graveyard, hovering and dancing in a belligerent display over the dandelions almost a street away. Matalina pulled her bow, loosing an arrow on an exhale. A bright spot of orange jerked up and then down.

"Did you get him?" her daughter asked, her ethereal voice frightening in its vehemence.

Matalina lowered her bow. "I pinned his wing to a stone. He tore it when he jerked away. Something to remember me by."

I swallowed and nervously wiped my hands on my jeans. The shot was clear across the property. Steadying myself, I went to the faucet and turned off the spraying water. "Matalina," I said as I straightened, bobbing my head at her daughter in greeting. "Thanks. They almost filled me with poison ivy. How are you? How's Jenks? Will he talk to me?" I blurted, but my brow furrowed and my hope fell when she dropped her eyes.

"I'm sorry, Rachel." She settled upon my offered hand, her wings shifting into motion, then stilling as they turned a dismal blue. "He . . . I . . . That's why I'm here."

"Oh God, is he all right?" I said, suddenly afraid when the pretty woman looked ready to burst into tears. Her ferocity had been washed away in misery, and I glanced at the distant fairies while Matalina struggled for her composure. *He was dead. Jenks was dead.*

"Rachel . . ." she warbled, looking all the more like an angel when she wiped a hand under her eye. "He needs me, and he forbade the children to return. Especially now."

My first wash of relief that he was alive spilled right back to worry, and I glanced at the butterfly wings. They were getting closer. "Let's go inside," I said. "I'll make you up some sugar water."

Matalina shook her head, bow hanging from her grip. Beside her, her daughter watched the graveyard. "Thank you," she said. "I'll make sure Jih's garden is safe, then I'll be back."

I looked to the front of the church as if I could see her garden on the opposite side of the street. Jih looked eight, but in pixy years she was old enough to be on her own and was actively searching for a husband, finding herself in the unique situation of being able to take her time as she developed her own garden, holding it with silver given to her by her father. And seeing that they had just evicted a clan of fairies, making sure there was no one waiting to jump Jih when she returned home sounded like a good idea.

"Okay," I said, and Matalina and Jih rose a few inches, sending the scent of green things to me. "I'll wait inside. Just come on in. I'll be in the kitchen."

In a soft clatter, they flitted up and over the tall steeple, and I watched, concerned. Things were probably tough for them while Jenks's pride kept them out of their garden and they struggled to make ends meet. What was it with small men and oversized pride?

Checking to see that my bandages hadn't come off my knuckles, I stomped up the wooden steps and wedged my gardening sneakers off. Leaving them there, I went in the back door and into the living room. The smell of coffee was almost a slap. A set of masculine boots clattered on the linoleum in the kitchen across the hall, and I hesitated. That wasn't Ivy. *Kisten?*

Curious, I padded to the kitchen. Hesitating in the open archway, I scanned the apparently empty room.

I liked my kitchen. No, let me rephrase. I loved my kitchen with the loyalty of a bulldog to his favorite bone. It took up more space than the living room and had two stoves—so I never had to stir spells and cook on the same flame. There were bright fluorescent lights, expansive counter and cupboard space, and sundry ceramic spelling utensils hanging over the center island counter. An oversized brandy snifter with my beta, Mr. Fish, rested on the sill of the single blue-curtained window over the sink. A shallow circle was etched in the linoleum for when I needed the extra protection for a sensitive spell, and herbs hung from a sweater rack in the corner.

A heavy, antique farm table took up the interior wall, my end holding a stack of books that hadn't been there earlier. The rest held Ivy's precisely arranged computer, printer, maps, colored markers, and whatever else she needed to plan her runs into boredom. My eyebrows rose at the pile of books, but I smiled because of the jeans-clad backside poking out from the open stainless-steel fridge door.

"Kist," I said, the pleased sound of my voice bringing the living vamp's head up. "I thought you were Ivy."

"Hi, love," he said, the British accent he usually faked almost nonexistent as he casually shut the door with a foot. "Hope you don't mind I let myself in. I didn't want to ring the bell and wake the dead."

I smiled, and he set the cream cheese on the counter and moved to me. Ivy wasn't dead yet, but she was as nasty as a homeless bridge troll if you woke her before she thought she should be up. "Mmmm, you can let yourself in anytime so long as you make me coffee," I said, curving my arms around his tapering waist as he gave me a hug hello.

His close-cut fingernails traced an inch above the new bruises and tooth marks on my neck. "Are you okay?" he breathed.

My eyes slid shut at the concern in his voice. He had wanted to come over last night, and I appreciated that he hadn't when I asked him not to. "I'm fine," I said, toying with the idea of telling him that they hadn't played fair, five alphas binding into a round to give their bitch the advantage in an already unfair fight. But it was so unusual an occurrence that I was afraid he would say I was making it up—and it sounded too much like whining to me.

Instead, I leaned my head against him and took in his scent: a mix of dark leather and silk. He was wearing a black cotton tee that pulled tight across his shoulders, but the aroma of silk and leather remained. With it was the dusky hint of incense that lingered around vampires. I hadn't identified that particular scent with vamps until I started living with Ivy, but now I could probably tell with my eyes closed whether it was Ivy or Kisten in the room.

Either scent was delicious, and I breathed deeply, willingly taking in the vampire pheromones he was unconsciously giving off to soothe and relax me. It was an adaptation to make finding a willing source of blood easier. Not that Kisten and I were sharing blood. Not me. Not this little witch. No how or ever. The risk of becoming a plaything—my will given to a vampire—was too real. But that didn't mean I couldn't enjoy the mild buzz.

I could hear his heartbeat, and I lingered while his fingers traced a yummy path to the small of my back. My forehead came to his shoulder, lower than usual, since he was in boots and I was in socks. His exhaled breath stirred my hair. The sensation brought my head up, and I met his blue eyes squarely from under his long bangs, reading in the normal-sized pupils that he had slaked his blood lust before coming over. He usually did.

"I like it when you smell like dirt," he said, his eyes half-lidded and sly.

Smiling, I ran a fingernail down his rough cheek. He had a small nose and chin, and he usually kept a day's worth of stubble to give himself a more rugged cast. His hair was dyed blond to match his almost-beard, though I had yet to catch him with darker roots or a charm to color it. "What's the real color of your hair?" I asked impulsively as I played with the wispy strands at the nape of his neck.

He pulled away, blinking in surprise. Two slices of toast popped up, and he shifted to the counter, bringing out a plate and setting the bread on it. "Ah, it's blond."

My eyes roved over his very nice backside, and I slumped against the counter, enjoying the view. The rims of his ears were a faint red, and I pushed into motion, leaning to run a finger along his torn ear where someone had ripped out one of the twin diamond studs. His right ear still held both studs, and I wondered who had the missing earring. I would have asked, but was afraid he'd tell me Ivy had it. "You dye your hair," I insisted. "What color is it, really?"

He wouldn't look at me while he opened the cream cheese and spread a thick layer on the toast. "It's sort of brown. Why? Is that a problem?"

Dropping my hands to his waist, I turned him around. Pinning him to the counter, I leaned until our hips touched. "God, no. I just wondered."

"Oh." His hands went about my waist, and clearly relieved, he inhaled slowly, seeming to take my very soul in with him. A spark of desire jumped from him to me, going right to my core to catch my breath. I knew he was scenting me, reading in the slight tension of my body pressing into him my willingness to turn our embrace into something more. I knew our natural scents mixing was a potent blood aphrodisiac. I also knew Ivy would kill him if he broke my skin even by accident. But this was all old news, and I'd be a fool if I didn't admit that part of Kisten's allure was the mix of deep intimacy he offered along with the potential danger of him losing control and biting me. Yeah, I was a stupid, trusting girl, but it made for great sex.

And Kisten is very careful, I thought, pulling coyly away at the low growl rumbling up through him. He wouldn't have come over if he wasn't sure of his control, and I knew he teased himself with my off-limits blood as much as I tested my will against the supposedly better-than-sex carnal ecstasy that a vampire bite could bring.

"I see you're making friends with your neighbors," he said, and I eased from him to reopen the window and wash my hands. If I didn't stop, Ivy would sense it and be out here glowering like a shunned lover. We were roommates and business partners—that was all—but she made no attempt to hide that she wanted more. She had asked me once to be her scion, which was sort of a number-one helper and wielder of vampire power when the vamp in question was limited by sunlight. She wasn't dead yet and didn't need a scion, but Ivy was a planner.

The position was an honor, but I didn't want it, even though, as a witch, I couldn't be turned vampire. It involved an exchange of blood to cement ties, which was why I had flatly refused her the first time she'd asked, but after meeting her old high school roommate, I thought she was after more than that. Kisten could separate the drive for blood from the desire for sex, but Ivy couldn't, and the sensations a blood-lusting vamp pulled from me were too much like sexual hunger for me to think otherwise. Ivy's offer that I become her scion was also an offer to be her lover, and as much as I cared for her, I wasn't wired that way.

I turned off the tap and dried my hands on the dish towel, frowning at the butterfly wings drifting closer to the garden. "You could have helped me out there," I said sourly.

"Me?" Blue eyes glinting in amusement, he set the orange juice on the counter and shut the fridge. "Rachel, honey, I love you and all, but what do you think I could have done?"

Tossing the dish towel to the counter, I turned my back on him, crossing my arms while I gazed out at the cautiously approaching wings. He was right, but that didn't mean I had to like it. I was lucky Matalina had shown up, and I wondered again what she wanted.

A warm breath touched my shoulder and I jerked, realizing Kisten had snuck up on me, unheard with his vamp-soft steps. "I would have come out if you needed it," he said, his rumbly voice going right into me. "But they were only garden fairies."

"Yeah," I said with a sigh. "I suppose." Turning, my eyes went over his shoulder to the three books on the table. "Are those for me?" I asked, wanting to change the subject.

Kisten reached past me to pluck an early daisy from the vase beside Mr. Fish. "Piscary had them behind glass. They look like spell books to me. I thought you might find something to Were in them. They're yours if you want them. I'm not going to tell him where they went."

His eyes were eager for the chance to help me, but I didn't move, standing beside the sink with my arms crossed, eyeing them. If the master vampire had them under glass, then they were probably older than the sun. Even worse, they had the look of demon magic, making them useless since only demons could work it. *Generally.*

Uncrossing my arms, I considered them again. Maybe there *was* something I could use. "Thanks," I said, moving to touch the top book and stifling a shudder when I felt a slight sponginess, as if my aura had gone from liquid to syrup. My torn skin tingled, and I wiped my hand on my jeans. "You won't get in trouble?"

The faint tightening of his jaw was the only sign of his nervousness. "You mean in more trouble than trying to kill him?" he said, flicking his long bangs from his eyes.

I gave him a sick smile. "I see your point." I went to get myself a cup of coffee while Kisten poured a small glass of orange juice and set it on a tray he pulled from behind the microwave. The plate of toast went on it, shortly followed by the daisy he'd taken from the windowsill. I watched, my curiosity growing when he gave me a sideways smile to show his sharp canines and hustled into the hallway with it all. Okay, so it wasn't for me.

Leaning against the counter, I sipped my coffee and listened to a door creak open. Kisten's voice called out cheerfully, "Good afternoon, Ivy. Wakey, wakey, eggs and bakey!"

"Shove it, Kist," came Ivy's slurred mumble. "Hey!" she cried louder. "Don't open those! What the hell are you doing?"

A smile curved over my face and I snickered, taking my coffee and sitting at the table.

"There's my girl," Kisten coaxed. "Sit up. Take the damn tray before I spill the coffee."

"It's Saturday," she snarled. "What are you doing here so early?"

As I listened to Kisten's soothing voice rise and fall in an unrecognizable patter, I wondered what was going on. From families of wealth, Kisten and Ivy had grown up together, tried the cohabitation thing, and parted as friends. Rumor had it Piscary planned for them to get together and have a passel of children to carry on his living-vamp line before one of them died. I was no expert in relationships, but even I could tell that wasn't going to happen. Kisten cared deeply for Ivy, and she for him, but seeing them together always gave me the feeling of a close brother/sister relationship. Even so, this breakfast in bed thing was unusual.

"Watch the coffee!" Kisten exclaimed, shortly followed by Ivy's yelp.

"You aren't helping. Get out of my room!" she snarled, her gray-silk voice harsh.

"Shall I lay out your clothes, love?" Kisten said, his fake British accent on full and laughter in his voice. "I adore that pink skirt you wore all last fall. Why don't you wear that anymore?"

"Get out!" she exclaimed, and I heard something hit the wall.

"Pancakes tomorrow?"

"Get the hell out of my room!"

The door clicked shut, and I met Kisten's grin with my own when he came in and went to the coffeemaker. "Lose a bet?" I guessed, and he nodded, his thin eyebrows high.

I pushed out a chair kitty-corner from me with my foot and he settled in with his mug, his long legs going out to encircle mine under the corner of the table.

"I said you could go on a run with David and come home without turning it into a slugfest. She said you couldn't." He reached for the sugar bowl and dumped two spoonfuls in.

"Thanks," I said, glad he had bet against her.

"I lost on purpose," he said, crushing my vindication before it had taken its first breath.

"Thanks a lot," I amended, pulling my feet from between his.

Setting his mug down, he leaned forward and took my hands in his. "Stop it, Rachel. How else could I find an excuse to come over here every morning for a week?"

I couldn't be mad at him *now,* so I smiled, dropping my gaze to our twined hands, mine thin and pale beside his tan, masculine fingers. It was nice seeing them there together like that. The past four months he had not lavished attention on me, but rather was there and available whenever the mood struck either of us.

He was incredibly busy running Piscary's affairs now that the undead master vampire was in jail—thanks to me—and I was occupied with my end of Ivy's and my runner firm, Vampiric Charms. As a result, Kisten and I spent spontaneous snips of intense time together that I found both extremely satisfying and curiously freeing. Our brief, nearly daily conversations over coffee or dinner were more enjoyable and reassuring than a three-day weekend backpacking in the Adirondacks dodging weekend-warrior Weres and slapping mosquitoes.

He felt no jealousy about the time I spent pursuing my career, and I felt only relief that he slaked his blood lust elsewhere—it was a part of him I was ignoring until I found a way to deal with it. There were problems brewing in our future, as blood-chaste witches and living vampires were not known for making long-term commitments. But I was tired of being alone, and Kisten met every emotional need I had raised and I met all of his but one, allowing someone else to do that with no distrust on my part. Our relationship was too good to be true, and I wondered again how I could find comfort with a vampire when I'd never been able to hold onto it with a witch.

Or with Nick, I thought, feeling the expression leave my face.

"What?" Kisten said, more aware of my mood shift than if I had painted my face blue.

I took a breath, hating myself for where my thoughts had gone. "Nothing." I smiled thinly. "Just thinking how much I like being with you."

"Oh." His bristly face creased into a worried smile. "What are you doing today?"

I sat back, pulling my hand from his and putting my sock feet to either side of his lap so he wouldn't think I was drawing away. My eyes drifted to my shoulder bag and my checkbook. I wasn't desperate for money—wonder of wonders, since the calls for my services had dropped dramatically after the six o'clock news last winter had featured me being dragged down the street on my ass by a demon. And because I was heeding David's advice to take a few days off to mend, I knew I ought to spend the time in research, or balancing my bank account, or cleaning my bathroom, or doing something constructive.

But then I met Kisten's eyes, and the only idea that came to me was . . . ah, not the least bit constructive at all. His eyes were not calm. There was the faintest rising of black in them, the faintest thinning of blue. Gaze riveted to mine, he reached for one of my feet, bringing it onto his lap and starting to rub it. The intent behind his action strengthened when he sensed my pulse quickening, and his massage took on a rhythm that spoke of . . . possibilities.

My breath came and went. There was no blood lust in his eyes, only a desire that made my gut tighten and a tingle start at my demon scar.

"I need to . . . do my laundry?" I said, arching my eyebrows.

"Laundry." He never looked from me as his hands left my

foot and started creeping upward. Moving, pressing, hinting. "That sounds like it involves water and soap. Mmmm. Could be slippery. And messy. I think I have a bar of soap somewhere. Want some help?"

Uh-huh, I thought, my mind pinging over the possible ways he could "help" me, and how I could get Ivy out of the church for a few hours.

Seeing my—well . . . willingness might be too weak a word—enthusiasm in my inviting smile, Kisten reached out and pulled my chair bumping and scraping around the corner of the table, snuggling it up to his with a living vampire's strength. My legs opened to put my knees to either side of him, and he leaned forward, the blue of his eyes vanishing to a thin ribbon.

Tension rising, I put my lips beside his torn ear. The scent of leather and silk crashed over me, and I closed my eyes in anticipation. "You have your caps?" I whispered.

I felt him nod, but I was more interested in where his lips were going. He cupped a hand along my jaw and tilted my face to his. "Always," he said. "Always and forever with you."

Oh God, I thought, just about melting. Kisten wore caps on his sharp canines to keep from breaking my skin in a moment of passion. They were generally worn by adolescent living vampires still lacking control, and Kisten risked a severe ribbing should anyone find out he wore them when we slept together. His decision was born from his respect for my desire to withhold my blood from him, and Ivy's threat to stake him twice if he took my blood. Kisten claimed it was possible to be bound and not become a vampire's shadow, but everything I had seen said otherwise. My fear remained. And so did his caps.

I inhaled, bringing the vamp pheromones deep into me, willing them to relax me, wanting the tingling promise that was humming in my demon scar to race through my body. But then Kisten stiffened and drew away.

"Ivy?" I whispered, feeling my eyes go worried as his gaze went distant.

"Pixy wings," he said, pushing my chair out.

"Matalina," I answered, sending my gaze to the open archway to the hall.

There was a distant thump. "Jenks?" came Ivy's muffled call from her room.

My lips parted in surprise. She had heard Matalina's wings through a closed door? Great. Just freaking great. Then she'd heard our conversation, too.

"It's Matalina!" I shouted, not wanting her to burst out thinking it was Jenks.

But it was too late, and I stood awkwardly when her door thumped open. Matalina zipped into the kitchen a heartbeat before Ivy staggered in, halting in an undignified slump with one hand supporting herself against the open archway.

She was still in her skimpy nightgown, her black silk robe doing next to nothing to hide her tall lanky build, trim and smooth-limbed from her martial arts practice. Her straight black hair, mussed from sleeping, framed her oval face in an untidy fashion. She'd had it cut not too long ago, and it still surprised me to see it bumping about just under her ears. It made her long neck look longer, the single scar on it a smooth line, now faint from cosmetic surgery. Wide-eyed from being jerked from her bed, her brown, somewhat almond-shaped eyes looked larger than usual, and her thin lips were open to show small teeth.

Head cocked, Kisten spun in his chair. Taking in her lack of clothes, his grin widened.

Grimacing at her less than suave entrance, Ivy pulled herself straight, trying to find her usual iron hold on her emotions. Her pale cheeks were flushed, and she wouldn't meet my eyes as she closed her robe with an abrupt motion. "Matalina," she said, her voice still rough from sleep. "Is Jenks okay? Will he talk to us?"

"God, I hope so," Kisten said dryly, turning his chair so he didn't have his back to Ivy.

The agitated pixy flitted to perch on the center island counter. A glittering trail of silver sparkles sifted from her, slowly falling to make a temporary sunbeam, clear evidence of her flustered state. I already knew her answer, but I couldn't help but slump when she shook her head, her wings stilling. Her pretty eyes went wide and she twisted the fabric of her silk dress. "Please," she said, her voice carrying a frightening amount of worry. "Jenks won't come to you. I'm so scared, Rachel. He can't go alone. He won't come back if he goes alone!"

Suddenly I was a whole lot more concerned. "Go where?" I said, crowding closer. Ivy moved in too, and we clustered before her, almost helpless as the tiny woman who could stand down six fairies started to cry. Forever the gentleman, Kisten carefully tore a tissue and handed her a piece the size of his thumbnail. She could have used it for a washcloth.

"It's Jax," Matalina said, holding her breath between sobs. Jax was her oldest son.

My fear quickened. "He's at Nick's apartment," I said. "I'll drive you over."

Matalina shook her head. "He's not there. He left with Nick on the winter solstice."

I jerked upright, feeling as if I'd been kicked in the stomach. "Nick was here?" I stammered. "At the solstice? He never even called!" I looked at Ivy, shocked. The freaking human bastard! He had come, cleared out his apartment, and left; just like Jenks said he would. And I thought he cared for me. I had been hurt and half dead from hypothermia, and he just left? As I fumed, the betrayal and confusion I thought long gone swelled to make my head hurt.

"We got a call this morning," Matalina was saying, oblivious to my state, though Kisten and Ivy exchanged knowing glances. "We think he's in Michigan."

"Michigan!" I blurted. "What the Turn is he doing in Michigan?"

Ivy nudged closer, almost coming between Matalina and me. "You said you think. You don't know for certain?"

The pixy turned her tear-streaked face to Ivy, looking as tragic and strong as a mourning angel. "Nick told Jax they were in Michigan, but they moved him. Jax doesn't know for sure."

They moved *him?*

"Who moved him?" I said, bending close. "Are they in trouble?"

The tiny woman's eyes were frightened. "I've never seen Jenks so angry. Nick took Jax to help him with his work, but something went wrong. Now Nick is hurt and Jax can't get home. It's cold up there, and I'm so worried."

I glanced at Ivy, her eyes dark with widening pupils, her lips pressed into a thin angry line. Work? Nick cleaned museum artifacts and restored old books. What kind of work would he need a pixy for? In Michigan? In the springtime when most pixies were still shaking off hibernation at that latitude?

My thoughts went to Nick's confidant casualness, his aversion to anything with a badge, his wickedly quick mind, and his uncanny tendency to be able to get ahold of just about anything, given time. I'd met him in Cincy's rat fights, where he had been turned into a rat after "borrowing" a tome from a vampire.

He had come back to Cincinnati and left with Jax, without telling me he was here. Why would he take Jax with him?

My face went hot and I felt my knees go quivery. Pixies had *other* skills than gardening. *Shit. Nick was a thief*.

Leaning hard against the counter, I looked from Kisten to Ivy, her expression telling me that she had known, but realized I'd only get mad at her until I figured it out for myself. God, I was so stupid! It had been there all the time, and I hadn't let myself see it.

I opened my mouth, jumping when Kisten jabbed me in the ribs. His eyes went to Matalina. The poor woman didn't know. I shut my mouth, feeling cold.

"Matalina," I said softly. "Is there any way to find out where they are? Maybe Jax could find a newspaper or something."

"Jax can't read," she whispered, dropping her head into her hands, her wings drooping. "None of us can," she said,

crying, "except Jenks. He learned so he could work for the
I.S."

I felt so helpless, unable to do anything. How do you give
someone four inches high a hug? How do you tell her that
her eldest son had been misled by a thief? A thief I had
trusted?

"I'm so scared," the tiny pixy said, her voice muffled.
"Jenks is going after him. He's going all the way up north.
He won't come back. It's too far. He won't be able to find
enough to eat, and it's too cold unless he has somewhere
safe to stay at night." Her hands fell away, the misery and
heartache on her tiny features striking fear in me.

"Where is he?" I asked, my growing anger pushing out
the fear.

"I don't know." Matalina sniffed as she looked at the torn
tissue in her grip. "Jax said it was cold and everyone was
making candy. There's a big green bridge and lots of water."

I shook my head impatiently. "Not Jax. Jenks."

Matalina's hopeful expression made her look more beautiful than all of God's angels. "You'll talk to him?" she
quavered.

Taking a slow breath, I glanced at Ivy. "He's sulked
enough," I said. "I'm going to talk to the little twit, and he's
going to listen. And then we'll both go."

Ivy straightened, her arms held tight at her sides as she
took two steps back. Her eyes were wide and her face carefully blank.

"Rachel—" Kisten said, the warning in his voice jerking
my attention to him.

Matalina rose three inches into the air, her face alight even
as the tears continued. "He'll be angry if he finds out I came
to you for help. D-Don't tell him I asked you."

Ignoring Kisten, I took a resolute breath. "Tell me where
he's going to be and I'll find him. He isn't going to do this
alone. I don't care if he talks to me or not, but I'm going
with him."

Three

The coffee in my cup was cold, which I didn't remember until I had it to my lips. Sharp and bitter, the taste of it puckered my face an instant before I let it slip down my throat. Shuddering, I held another dollop on my tongue. A soft thrill lifted through me as I tapped the line in the grave-yard and set my pencil down on the kitchen table.

"From candle's burn and planet's spin," I whispered awkwardly around the coffee, my fingers sketching out a complex figure. "Friction is how it ends and begins." Rolling my eyes, I brought my hands together to make a loud pop, simultaneously saying, *"Consimilis."* God help me, it was so hokey, but the rhyme did help me remember the finger motions and the two words that actually did the charm.

"Cold to hot, harness within," I finished, making the ley line gesture that would use the coffee in my mouth as a focal object so I wouldn't warm up . . . say . . . Mr. Fish's bowl. *"Calefacio,"* I said, smiling at the familiar drop of line energy through me. I tightened my awareness to let what I thought was the right amount of power run through me to excite the water molecules and warm the coffee. "Excellent," I breathed when the mug began to steam.

My fingers curled about the warm porcelain, and I dropped the line entirely. *Much better,* I thought when I went to take a sip, jerking back and touching my lip when I found it too hot. Ceri had said control would come with practice, but I was still waiting.

I set the mug down, pushing Ivy's maps farther out of my space and into hers. The robins were singing loudly, and I squinted, trying to read in the early dusk of the developing rain clouds as I leafed through Kisten's borrowed books. I'd have to leave in half an hour to accidentally run into Jenks on his run, and I was getting antsy.

Ivy was in one of her moods, and Kisten had hustled her out shortly after Matalina left so she wouldn't drive me crazy all afternoon. I'd find out soon enough what was bothering her, and maybe Kisten could take care of it for me instead.

My spine cracked when I straightened, arching my back and taking a deep breath. I pulled my fingers off the dusk-darkened print, feeling the tingle of disconnection strike through me like a reverse static shock. Kist's books were indeed demon texts. I'd quickly gotten used to the numb feeling of the pages, lured into exploring them when I realized every curse mixed earth and ley line magic, utilizing both to make more than the sum of the parts. It made for fascinating reading, even if my Latin sucked dishwater, and I was only now starting to remember I was supposed to be afraid of this stuff. It wasn't what I had expected.

Sure, there were the nasty spells that would turn your neighbor's barking dog inside out, strike your fourth-grade teacher with agony, or call down a flaming ball of hell to smack the guy tailgating you, but there were softer spells too. Ones I couldn't see harm in, spells that did the same things many of my eminently legal earth charms did. And that's what scared me the most.

Mood going introspective, I flipped the page and found a curse that would encase someone in a thick layer of air to slow their movements as if they were in molasses. I suppose one could use it to gain the advantage in a fight and kill them with a blow to the head or knife thrust, but would it tarnish one's soul if all you did was slow them down so you could slap a pair of cuffs on them? The more I looked, the harder it was to tell. I had assumed demon curses were black as a matter of course, but I truly couldn't see the harm here.

Even more worrisome was the potential power they all had. The curse detailed before me wasn't the illusion of molasses that black ley line witches used to give people bad dreams in which they were unable to escape something or to help a loved one. And it wasn't the earth charm that had to be laboriously cooked and targeted to a specific person, which resulted in slower reactions, not this almost complete immobility. The demon curse took the quick implementation and wide range of application of a ley line charm and harnessed it in a pair of "polarized" amulets, thereby giving it the reality and permanence of earth magic. It was a mix of both. It was the real thing. It was demon magic, and I was one of two people who could both walk under the sun and kindle it.

"Thanks, Trent," I muttered as I turned the page, my fingertips prickling. "Your dad was a peach."

But I wasn't complaining. I shouldn't have lived to puberty. The genetic aberration that I was afflicted with killed every witch born with it before they were two. I truly believed that Trent Kalamack's father hadn't known that the same thing that was killing me had made it possible for me to kindle demon magic, accidentally circumventing a genetic checks-and-balances. All he knew was his friend's daughter was dying of an ancient malady and he had the wisdom and technology—even if it was illegal—to save my life.

So he had. And it kinda worried me that the only other witch Trent's father had fixed was now suffering a living hell as the demon Algaliarept's familiar in the ever-after.

Guilt assailed me, quickly quashed. I had told Lee not to give me to Al. I'd warned him to get us the hell out of the ever-after when we had the chance. But no-o-o-o-o. The wicked witch from the West thought he knew everything, and now he was paying for his mistake with his life. It had been either him or me, and I liked where I lived.

A freshening gust of wind blew in, carrying the hint of rain and shifting the curtains. I glanced at the book before me and turned the page to find a curse to pull out someone's intelligence until they had the brain of a worm. Blinking, I closed the book. Okay, so it was easy to figure out that some of them were black, but was there such a thing as a white curse?

The thing was, I knew earth magic was powerful, but giving it the speed and versatility of ley line magic was frightening. And the mixing of the two branches of magic was in every curse. In the few hours I had been sitting here, I found curses that shifted mass to line energy or vice versa, so you could actually make big things little and little things big, not just project the illusion of a size change, as with ley line magic; and since it also involved an earth magic potion, the change was real—as in "having viable offspring" real.

Nervous, I pushed myself away from the table. My fingers tapped the old wood in a quick rhythm, and I glanced at the clock. Almost six. I couldn't sit here any longer. The weather was shifting, and I wanted to be in it.

Surging to my feet, I snatched the book up and knelt at the low shelf under the center island counter. I didn't want to shelve it with my usual library, but I certainly didn't want the three of them under my pillow, either. Brow creasing, I moved a mundane cookbook to serve as a buffer between my spell books and the demon tomes. So I was superstitious. So sue me.

The last two books slid into place, and I straightened, wiping my hands on my jeans while I looked at them sitting oh so nicely between the *Country Farm's Cookie Cookbook* I'd swiped from my mom and the copy of *Real Witches Eat Quiche* I had gotten from the I.S.'s secret Santa three years ago. You can guess which one I used the most.

Grabbing my bag, I headed out, boot heels clunking as I went down the hallway past Ivy's and my bedrooms and bathrooms and into the sanctuary. The pews were long gone, leaving only the faded reminder of a huge cross above where the altar once stood. Stained-glass windows stretched from knee height to the top of the twelve-foot walls. The open raftered ceiling was dusky with the early twilight from the clouds, and I would use my panties as a sun hat if I could hear the whispered giggles of pixies plotting mischief up there again.

The large room took up half the heated space in the church, and it was empty but for my plant-strewn desk on the ankle-high stage where the altar had stood and Ivy's baby grand piano just past the foyer. I'd only heard her play it once, her long fingers pulling a depth of emotion from the keys that I only rarely saw in her face.

I snatched my keys from my desk in passing, and they jingled happily as I continued into the dark foyer. Squinting, I plucked my red leather jacket and cap from the peg beside the four-inch-thick, twin oak doors. At the last moment, I grabbed Ivy's umbrella with the ebony handle before wedging the door open. There was no lock—only a bar to lower from the inside—but no one on this side of the ley lines would dare steal from a Tamwood vampire.

The door thumped shut behind me, and I flounced down the steps to the cracked sidewalk. The spring evening was balmy, the humidity of an approaching storm shifting the air pressure to make the robins sing and my blood quicken. I could smell rain and imagine the distant rumble of thunder. I loved spring storms, and I smiled at the fresh green leaves shifting in the rising breeze.

My steps quickened when I saw my car tucked in the tiny carport: a bright red convertible with two seats up front and two unusable seats in back. Across the street and a few houses down, our neighbor Keasley was standing at the edge of his front porch, his spine bent from arthritis and his head up as he tasted the changing wind. He raised a gnarly hand when I waved, telling me everything was fine with him. Unseen preschool-age kids were shouting, responding to the air pressure shift with less restraint than I was managing.

Up and down the street, people were coming out of their Americana middle-class homes, heads up and eyes on the sky. It was the season's first warm rain, and only three days out of a new moon. The I.S. would have a busy night trying to rein everyone in.

Not my problem anymore, I cheerfully thought as I settled in behind the wheel of my car and took the time to put the top down so I could feel the wind in my hair. Yeah, it was going to rain, but not for a few hours yet.

Saucy little red cap on my head, and wearing a snappy leather jacket to block the wind, I drove through the Hollows at a modest pace, waiting until I crossed the bridge and got on the interstate before I opened her up. The damp wind beating on my face brought every smell to me, sharper and more vivid than it had been for months, and the rumble of tires, engine, and wind muffling everything else was like freedom itself. I found myself inching past eighty when I saw the cruiser parked on an entrance ramp. It had the Federal Inderland Bureau emblem on it, and waving merrily, I tunked it down and got a headlight blink in return. Everyone in the human-run FIB knew my car—heck, they had given it to me. The FIB wouldn't stop me, but the Inderland run I.S. would, just out of spite for having quit their lame-ass, nationwide police force.

I tucked a strand of blowing hair behind my ear and warily checked behind me. I'd only had my car a couple of months, and already the entire fleet of I.S. flunkies doing street duty knew me by sight, taking every opportunity to help me rack up points on my license. And it wasn't fair! The red light I ran a month ago was for a darn good reason—and at five in the morning, no one had even been at the intersection but the cop. I still don't know where he had come from—my trunk maybe? And I'd been late for an appointment the time I got pulled over for speeding on 75. I hadn't been going *that* much faster than everyone else.

"Stupid car," I muttered fondly, though I wouldn't trade my little red ticket magnet for anything. It wasn't its fault the I.S. took every chance they could to make my life miserable.

But "Walkie Talkie Man" was cranked, Steriogram singing so fast only a vamp could keep up, and it wasn't long before the little white hand crept up to eighty again, pulling my mood along with it. I even found a cute-looking guy on a cycle to flirt with while I made my way to Edgemont where Jenks had his run.

The cessation of wind as I came off the interstate was

almost an assault, and when a rumble of real thunder rolled over me, I pulled to the side of the road to put the top up. My head jerked up when the guy on the cycle whizzed past, his hand raised in salute. My faint smile lingered for a moment, then vanished.

If I couldn't get Jenks to talk to me, I was going to kill the little twit.

Taking a deep breath, I turned my phone to vibrate, snapped off the music, and pulled into traffic. I jostled over a railroad track, peering into the coming dusk and noting that the pace of the pedestrian and bike traffic had changed from casual to intense as the threat of rain increased. It was a business district, one of the old industrial areas that the city had thrown a lot of money at to turn it into a themed mall and parks to attract the usual outlying shops and apartments. It reminded me of "Mrs. Bryant's flat," and I frowned.

I drove past the address to evaluate the multistoried sprawling building. By the art deco and the mailbox drive-through, it looked like a manufacturing complex turned into a mix of light commercial and upscale apartments. I hadn't seen Jenks, but that wouldn't be unusual if he was tailing someone. Matalina said he was on a smut run to build up money to buy an airline ticket.

My brow was furrowed in worry when I turned the corner and got a lucky spot at the curb in front of a coffeehouse, jerking the parking break up and shifting the stick to neutral. Pixies couldn't fly commercially—the shifting air pressures wreaked havoc with them. Jenks wasn't thinking straight anymore. No wonder Matalina had come to me.

Snatching up my bag, I timed my move with traffic and got out. A quick look at the lowering clouds, and I reached for Ivy's umbrella. The smell of coffee almost pulled me inside, but I dutifully went the other way. A quick glance, and I slipped into the alley of the building in question, walking so my feet were silent in my vamp-made boots.

The scent of garbage and dog urine was strong, and I wrinkled my nose and pulled my jacket closer, looking for a spot where I could stay out of sight and watch the front door of the complex. I was early. If I could catch him before he went in, it would be all the better. But then I froze at the sound of a familiar wing clatter.

Face going still, I looked up the narrow passage to find a pixy dressed in a black body stocking rubbing a clean spot to see through on a dirt-grimed, bird-spotted, upper-story window.

Shame stilled my voice. God, I had been so stupid. I didn't blame him for leaving, for thinking I hadn't trusted him. The ugly truth was, I hadn't. Last solstice I had figured out that Trent Kalamack was an elf, and getting the wealthy son of a bitch to not kill me for knowing that the elves weren't extinct but had gone into hiding had taken a pretty piece of blackmail. Finding out what kind of Inderlander Trent was had become the holy grail of the pixy world, and I knew the temptation for Jenks to blab it would be too much. Even so, he deserved better than my lies of omission, and I was afraid he might not listen to me even now.

Jenks hovered, intent on whatever was inside. His dragonfly wings were invisible in his calm state, and not a hint of pixy dust sifted from him. He looked confident, and a red bandanna was tied about his forehead. It was protection against accidentally invading a rival pixy's or fairy's territory, a promise of a quick departure with no attempt at poaching.

I nervously gathered my resolve, glancing at the wall of the alley before I leaned against it and tried to look casual. "So, is she cheating on her husband?" I asked.

"Nah," Jenks said, his eyes focused through the glass. "She's taking an exercise class to surprise him on their twenty-fifth anniversary. He doesn't deserve her, the mistrusting bastard."

Then he jerked, slamming back six feet to nearly hit the adjacent building.

"You!" he cried, pixy dust sifting like sunbeams. "What the hell are you doing here?"

I pushed myself off the wall and stepped forward. "Jenks—"

He dropped like a stone to hover before me, finger point-ing as the pixy dust he had let slip slowly fell over us. Anger creased his tiny features to make him grim and threatening. "She told you!" he shrilled, his jaw clenched and his face red under his short blond hair.

I took a step back, alarmed. "Jenks, she's only worried—"

"The hell with you both," he snarled. "I'm outta here."

He turned, wings a blur of red. Ticked, I tapped a line. En-ergy flowed, equalizing in the time it takes for a burst bubble to vanish. "Rhombus," I snapped, imagining a circle. A sheet of gold hummed into existence, so thick it blurred the walls of the surrounding alley. I staggered, my balance ques-tionable since I hadn't taken even the time to pretend to draw a circle in the air.

Jenks jerked to a stop a mere inch in front of the circle. "You sorry stupid witch!" he shrilled, seeming at a loss for something worse. "Let me out. I ought to kill your car. I ought to leave slug eggs in your slippers! I ought to, I ought to . . ."

Hands on my hips, I got in his face. "Yeah, you ought to, but first you're going to listen to me!" His eyes widened, and I leaned forward until he shifted back. "What is wrong with you, Jenks? This can't just be about me not telling you what Trent is!"

Jenks's face lost its surprise. His eyes touched upon the bandages and bruises on my neck, then dropped to my pain amulet. Seemingly by force of will, his eyes narrowed with an old anger. "That's right," he said, hovering an inch before my nose. "It's about you lying to me! It's about you not trust-ing me with information. It's about you pissing all over our partnership!"

Finally, I thought. Finally. I gritted my jaw, almost cross-eyed with him so close. "Good God! If I tell you what he is, will that make you happy?"

"Shut your mouth!" he shouted. "I don't care anymore, and I don't need your help. Break your circle so I can get the hell away from you, or I'll jam something where it shouldn't go, witch."

"You stupid ass," I exclaimed, warming. "Fine!" Furious, I shoved a foot into the circle. My breath hissed in when the circle's energy flowed into me. At the end of the alley the passing people gave us a few curious looks. "Run away!" I said, gesturing wildly, not caring what they thought. "Leave, you cowardly ball of spider snot. I've been trying to apologize for the last five months, but you're so preoccupied with your stinking little hurt feelings that you won't listen. I think you like being slighted. I think you feel secure in your down-trodden pixy mentality. I think you get off on the 'poor little pixy that no one takes seriously crap' that you wrap yourself in. And when I believed in you, you got scared and ran away at the first sign that you might have to live up to your ideals!"

Jenks's mouth was hanging open and he was slowly loosing altitude. Seeing him floundering, I surged ahead, thinking I might have finally shaken him loose.

"Go on and leave," I continued, my legs starting to shake. "Stay in your stinking little basement and hide. But Matalina and your kids are coming back to the garden. You can shove a cherry up your ass and make jam for all I care, but I need them. I can't keep those damn fairies out to save my dandelions, and I need my garden as much as I need backup on a night with a full moon. And your bitching and moaning don't mean crap anymore because I've been trying to apologize and all you've done is shit on me. Well, I'm not apologizing anymore!"

Still he hung in the air, his wings shifting to a lighter shade of red. He didn't seem to know what to do with his hands, and they tugged his bandanna and fell to his sword.

"I'm going to find Jax and Nick," I said, my anger lessening. I had said what I wanted, and all that was left was hearing what he thought. "Are you coming with me or not?"

Jenks rose. "My going north has nothing to do with you," he said tightly.

"Like hell it doesn't," I said, hearing the first heavy drop of rain hit the nearby Dumpster. "He may be your son, but it was my old boyfriend who got him in trouble. He lied to you. He lied to me. And I'm going up there so I can kick Nick's ass from here to the ever-after." Even I could hear my sullen tone, and Jenks gave me a nasty smile.

"Be careful," he goaded. "Someone might think you still like him."

"I do *not*," I said, feeling a headache start. "But he's in trouble and I can't just let whoever it is kill him."

A bitter, saucy look returned to Jenks's face, and he flitted to the end of a two-by-four sticking out of a can. "Yuh-huh," he said snidely, hands on his hips. "Why are you really going?"

"I just told you why," I snapped, hiding my bitten hand when he looked at it.

His head bobbed up and down. "Yada yada yada," he said, making a get-on-with-it gesture with one hand. "I know why you're going, but I want to hear you say it."

I fumbled, not believing this. "Because I'm as mad as all hell!" I said, the rain falling steadily now. If we had to continue this conversation much longer, we were going to get soaked. "He said he was going to come back, and he did, just long enough to clear out his apartment and take off. No good-bye, not even an 'it was great, babe, but I gotta go now.' I need to tell him to his face that he crapped all over me and I don't love him anymore."

Jenks's tiny eyebrows rose, and I wished he was bigger so I could wipe the smirk off his face. "This is some female closure thing, isn't it?" he said, and I sneered.

"Look," I said. "I'm going to get Jax and pull Nick's sorry ass out from whatever mess he's in. Are you coming with me, or are you going to waste your time taking smut runs for a paycheck you will only waste on a plane ticket that will leave you hospitalized for three days?" I slowed, thinking I could chance appealing to his love for Matalina without him flying away. "Matalina is scared, Jenks. She's afraid you won't come back if you go alone."

His face emptied of emotion, and for a moment I thought I'd gone too far. "I can do this on my own," he said angrily. "I don't need your help."

My thoughts went to his iffy food supply and the cold

northern nights. It could snow in May in Michigan. Jenks knew it. "Sure you don't," I said. I crossed my arms and eyed him. "Just like I could have survived those fairy assassins last year without your help."

His lips pursed. He took a breath to tell me something. His hand went up, finger pointing. I made my eyes wide and mocking. Slowly his hand fell. Still standing on the two-by-four, Jenks's wings drooped. "You're going?"

I fought to keep my surge of hope from showing. "Yes," I said. "But to even have a chance, I need a security bypass expert, reconnaissance, and someone I trust to watch my back. Ivy can't do it. She can't leave Cincinnati."

Jenks's wings hummed into motion, then stilled. "You hurt me bad, Rachel."

My chest clenched in guilt. "I know," I whispered. "And I'm sorry. I don't deserve your help, but I'm asking for it." I pulled my head up, pleading with him with my eyes. For the first time, his face showed the hurt I'd given him, and my heart broke again.

"I'll think about it," he muttered, taking to the air.

I took a faltering step after him. "I'm leaving tomorrow. Early noon."

Wings clattering, Jenks flew a swooping path back to me. I nearly raised my hand for him to land on, but it would hurt too much if he shunned it. "I suppose that's early for a witch," he said. The pitch of his wings rose until my eyeballs hurt. "Okay. I'll come with you, but I'm not coming back to the firm. This is a one-shot deal."

My throat closed and I swallowed down a lump. He'd come back. He knew it as much as I did. I wanted to shout an exuberant, "Yes!" I wanted to whoop to make the passing people stare, but what I did instead was smile shakily at him. "Okay," I said, so relieved I was almost crying.

Blinking profusely, I followed him to the head of the alley. Though Jenks would have snugged under my hat before, to get out of the rain, it was too much to ask just yet. "Can you meet me tonight at the church after midnight?" I asked. "I have a few charms to prep before we head out."

We left the alley together, the lighter gloom making me feel as if we had come out of a black hole. We were both walking on eggshells; the patterns were familiar, but the sensitivities were so very fragile.

"I can do that," Jenks said apprehensively, glancing up at the rain.

"Good. Good." I listened to my feet hit the sidewalk, the thumps jarring up my spine. "Do you still have your half of the phone set you gave me?" I could hear the hesitancy in my voice, and I wondered if Jenks could too. I had kept the phone he'd given me for the solstice. Hell, I had almost made it into a shrine.

I popped open Ivy's black umbrella, and Jenks flew under it. Five months ago he would have sat on my shoulder, but even this small show of trust caught at me.

"David brought it over," he said stiffly, keeping to the distant corner.

"Good," I said again, feeling stupid. "Can you bring it with you?"

"It's a little big for me to slip into my pocket, but I'll manage." It was sarcastic and biting, but he was sounding more like the Jenks I knew.

I glanced at him, seeing he was trailing the faintest wisp of silver sparkles. My car was just ahead, and I wondered whether he'd take offense if I offered him a ride home.

"Cowardly ball of spider snot?" Jenks said when I opened the door and he darted inside.

Swallowing hard, I stared across to the sidewalk and the people running for cover as the clouds opened and it began to pour. He was back. I had gotten him back. It wasn't perfect, but it was a start. Breath shaking, I folded the umbrella and ducked inside. "Give me a break," I said as I started the car and turned the heat on full to warm him up. "I was pressed for time."

Four

I held up the black lace top in consideration. Sighing, I decided against it, folding it up and jamming it back into the third drawer down. Sure, I looked good in it, but this was a rescue run, not spring break. Taking the short-sleeve peach-colored cotton shirt instead, I set it atop the jeans already packed in the suitcase my mom had given me for graduation. She insisted it hadn't been a hint, but I reserved my doubts to this day.

Moving to my top drawer, I grabbed enough socks and undies for a week. The church was empty since Ivy was out getting Jenks and his brood. The rain pattered pleasantly on my small stained-glass window propped open with a pencil, getting the sill wet but little else. From the dark garden came the trill of a toad. It mixed well with the soft jazz from the living room.

In the back of my closet I found the red turtleneck sweater I'd stored last week. I shook the hanger from it, carefully folded it, and set it with the rest. I added a pair of running shorts and my favorite black tee with STAFF on it that I'd gotten while working Takata's concert last winter. The temp could hit eighty as easily as thirty-five. I sighed, content. Midnight rain, toad song, jazz, and Jenks coming home. It didn't get much better.

My head rose at the creak of the front door. "Hey, it's me," came Kisten's voice.

And now it was better still. "Back here," I called, taking

two steps to the hall, one hand on the doorframe as I leaned out. The lights were dim in the sanctuary, his tall silhouette mysterious and attractive as he shook the rain from his full-length slicker.

I ducked back inside and shut my underwear drawer just before Kisten came in, the soft and certain steps of his dress shoes distinct on the hardwood floor. The scent of pizza and someone else's perfume hung about him, and by his carefully styled hair, clean-shaven cheeks, expensive dress slacks and silk shirt, I knew he had come from work. I liked the respectable, financially successful club manager aspect of Kisten as much as his rougher, bad boy image. He could do both equally well.

"Hi, love," he said, hitting his fake British accent hard to make me smile. A rain-spotted paper grocery bag was in his hands, the top rolled down. I padded forward in my sneakers, having to reach to give him a hug. My fingers played with the damp tips of his hair as I drew away, and he smiled, enjoying the tease.

"Hi," I said, reaching for the bag. "Is that them?"

Nodding, he gave it to me, and I set it on the bed, opening it and peering inside. As I had asked, there was a pair of sweatpants and a soft flannel sweatshirt.

Kisten looked at the bag, clearly wanting to know why, but all he said was, "Ivy's out?"

"She went to get Jenks because of the rain." Pensive, I opened a lower drawer and packed another T-shirt. "She missed him as much as me," I finished softly.

Looking tired, Kisten sat at the head of my bed, his long fingers rolling the top of the bag down. I closed my suitcase but didn't zip it. It was unusual for him to leave Piscary's club mid-hours. Clearly something was bothering him. I straightened, arms crossed, and waited for it.

"I don't think you should go," he said, his voice serious.

My mouth fell open, surprise shifting to anger when I pieced it together. "Is this about Nick?" I said, turning to my dresser to pack the ungodly expensive bottle of perfume that kept my natural scent from mixing with a vampire's. "Kisten, I'm over him. Give me some credit."

"That's not why. Ivy—"

"Ivy!" I stiffened, glancing into the empty hall. "What about her? Is Piscary . . ."

His slowly moving head said no, and I relaxed a notch. "He's leaving her alone. But she relies on you more than you know. If you go, things might shift."

Flustered, I jammed the perfume into a zippy bag and dropped it into a pocket in my vanity case. "I'm only going to be gone for a week, maybe two. It's not as if I'm her scion."

"No. You're her friend. And that's more important than anything else to her right now."

Arms crossed, I leaned back against my dresser. "This isn't my responsibility—I have my own life," I protested. "Gods, we share rent. We aren't married!"

Kisten's eyes were dark in the dim light from my table lamp, his brow pinched with worry. "You have coffee with her every day when she wakes up. You're across the hall when she shuts the curtains before going to sleep. That might not mean much to you, but it's everything to her. You're her first real friend in . . . Damn, I think it's been over ten years."

"You're her friend," I said. "And what about Skimmer?"

"You're her only friend not after her blood," he amended, his eyes sad. "It's different."

"Well, just crap on that," I said, picking up my last favorite earring but not knowing what to do with it. Disgusted, I threw it away. "Ivy hasn't said anything to me about not leaving."

"Rachel . . ." He stood, coming to take my elbows in his grip. His fingers were warm, and I felt them tighten and relax. From the living room, jazz rose and fell. "She won't."

I dropped my head, frustrated. "Never once did I tell her I'd be anything but what we are now," I said. "We aren't sharing a bed or blood or anything! I don't belong to her, and keeping her together isn't my job. Why is this all on me, anyway? You've known her longer than I."

"I know her past. You don't. She leans on you more because of your ignorance of what she was." He took a hesitant breath before he continued. "It was ugly, Rachel. Piscary warped her into a viciously savage lover who couldn't separate blood from lust or love. She survived by becoming something she hated, accepting the pattern of self-abuse of trying to please everyone she thought she loved."

I didn't want to hear this, but when I tried to move, his grip tightened.

"She's better now," he said, his blue eyes pleading for me to listen. "It took her a long time to break the pattern, and even longer to start to feel good about herself. I've never seen her happier, and like it or not, it's because of you. She loves Skimmer, but that woman is a big part of what Ivy was and how she got there, and if you leave . . ."

My jaw tightened and I stiffened, not liking this at all. "I am *not* Ivy's keeper," I said, gut twisting. "I did not sign up for this, Kisten!"

But he only smiled, soft and full of understanding and regret. I liked Ivy—I liked her, respected her, and wished I had half her willpower—but I didn't want anyone relying on me that heavily. Hell, I could hardly take care of myself, much less a powerful, mentally abused vampire.

"She won't ask more than you can give," he said. "Especially if she needs it. But you did move in with her, and more telling, you stayed when your relationship began to evolve."

"Excuse me?" I said, trying to pull away. He wouldn't let go, and I jerked from him, falling two steps back.

Kisten's expression had a hint of accusation. "She asked you to be her scion," he said.

"And I said no!"

"But you forgave her for trying to force you, and you did it without a second thought."

This was crap. He had heard all of this. Why was he making such a big deal about it? "Only because I jumped on her back and breathed in her ear when we were sparring!" I said. "I pushed her too far, and it wasn't her fault. Besides, she was scared that if she didn't make me her scion, Piscary was going to kill me."

Kisten nodded, his calm state helping to dissipate my anger. "It was a no-win situation," he said softly. "And you both handled it the best you could, but the point is, you did jump on her knowing what it might trigger."

I took a breath to protest, then turned away, flustered. "It was a mistake, and I didn't think it was right to walk out because *I* made a mistake."

"Why not?" he insisted. "People leave all the time when someone makes a mistake."

Frightened, I went to push past him. I had to get out of there.

"Rachel," he said loudly, jerking me into him. "Why didn't you leave right then? No one would have thought any less of you."

I took a breath, then let it out. "Because she is my friend," I said, eyes down, and keeping my voice low so it wouldn't shake. "That's why. And it wouldn't be fair for me to leave because of my mistake, because she . . . relies on me."

My shoulders slumped, and Kisten's grip on me eased, pulling me closer.

"Damn it, Kist," I said, putting my cheek to his shirt and breathing in his scent. "I can hardly take care of myself. I can't save her too."

"No one said you had to," he said, his voice rumbling into me. "And no one says it's going to stay this way. Helping to keep you alive and unbound with that scar of yours makes Ivy feel worthwhile—that she's making the world a better place. Do you know how hard that is for a vampire to find? She leans on you harder than me because she feels responsible for you and you owe her."

There is that, I thought, remembering how vulnerable my unclaimed vampire scar made me. But my debt to Ivy wasn't why I hadn't left. Nick had said I was making excuses to stay in an unsafe situation, that I had wanted her to bite me. I couldn't believe that. It was just friendship. Wasn't it?

Kisten's hand across my hair was soothing, and I put my arms around his waist, finding comfort in his touch. "If you leave," he said, "you take her strength."

"I never wanted this," I said. How had I become her lodestone? Her savior. All I wanted was to be her friend.

"I know." His breath moved my hair. "Will you stay?"

I swallowed, not wanting to move. "I can't," I said, and he gently pushed me back until he could see my face. "Jenks needs me. It's just a quick run. Five hundred miles. How much trouble could Nick and Jax be in? They probably just need bail money. I'll be back."

Kisten's face was creased, his elegant grace marred by sorrow. The caring he felt for me and for Ivy were mixed together and somehow beautiful. "I know you will. I just hope Ivy is here when you do."

Uncomfortable, I went to my closet and pretended to shuffle for something. "She's a big girl. She'll be fine. It's only a day's drive."

He took a breath to say something, then stopped, shifting from foot to foot as he changed his mind. Going back to the bed, he opened the crinkling bag of sweats and looked inside. "What do you want these for anyway? A disguise? Or is it to remember me by?"

Glad at the shift in topics, I turned with my butt-kicking boots in hand and set them by the bed. "Remember you by?"

A faint flush rimmed his ears. "Yeah. I thought you wanted them to put under your pillow or something. So it was like I was there with you?"

Taking the bag from him, I peered into it in speculation. "You wore them already?"

He rubbed a hand across his smooth chin, discomforted. "Ah, just once. I didn't sweat in them or anything. I dated a girl who liked wearing one of my shirts to bed. She said it was like I was holding her all night. I thought it was a, uh, girl thing."

My smile blossomed. "You mean, like this?" Feeling wicked, I pulled out the sweatshirt and slipped it on over my top. Holding my arms about myself, I shifted back and forth, my eyes closed and breathing deeply. I didn't care that the reason he smelled good was from a thousand years of evolution to make it easier for him to find prey.

"You wicked, wicked witch," Kisten whispered. The sudden heat in his voice pulled my eyes open. He took a slow breath, his entire body moving. "Oh God, you smell good."

"Yeah? What about now?" Grinning, I did jumping jacks, knowing the mixing of our scents would drive him slightly nuts.

As expected, his eyes dilated with a sudden blood lust, flashing to black. "Rachel," he said, his voice strained. "Don't."

Giggling, I evaded his reaching hand. "Wait! Wait!" I gasped. "I can make it worse."

"Stop," Kisten said, his voice low and controlled. There was a hint of threat in it, and when he reached for me again, I shrieked, darting around the end of the bed. With vampire quickness he followed, my back hitting the wall with a breath-stealing thump as he pinned me.

Eyes crinkled and smiling, I wiggled and twisted, enjoying pushing his buttons. After only a token show of resistance, I stopped, letting him find my mouth.

My breath left me in a slow sound as I eased against him, my arms crunched between us. His grip on my shoulders was firm and dominating. Possessive. But I knew he'd let go if I made one real motion to break free. Soft jazz completed my mood.

His fingers clenched and released, his lips moving lower until his mouth brushed my chin, following the line of my jaw to the hollow under my ear. My heart pounded and I tilted my head. In a surprised sound, my breath escaped when the tingling at my scar surged. With the quickness and sudden shock of a flag snapping in the wind, heat scoured me, following my veins and settling into an insistent pounding—demanding I follow it through to its natural end.

Kisten felt it, and as his breath quickened, I pulled my hands from between us, sending my fingers to the nape of his neck. My eyes closed as I felt his need, his desire, beat on mine to make it stronger. A sound escaped me as his lips gently worked my old scar. My body rebelled at the surge of passion, and my knees gave way. He was ready for it, holding me firm to him. I wanted this. God, how I wanted it. I should have tried wearing something of his ages ago.

"Rachel," he whispered, his breathing harsh and heavy with desire.

"What?" I panted, my blood still humming though his lips weren't on my scar anymore.

"Don't ever—wear anything of mine—again. I can't . . ."

I froze, not understanding. I made a motion to break free, but he held me firm. Fear scoured painfully where passion once ran. My eyes flicked to his, seeing them lost and black, then to his mouth. He wasn't wearing his caps. *Shit, I had pushed him too far*.

"I can't let go of you," he said, his lips not moving.

Adrenaline surged, and a drop of sweat formed at his hairline. *Shit, shit, shit. I was in trouble*. My gaze flicked to the glint of fang at the corner of his mouth. From one breath to the next, the coin of desire had flipped from sex to blood. Damn, the next ten seconds were going to be really dicey.

"I think I can let go if you aren't afraid," he said, fear and blood lust mixed in his voice.

I couldn't look away from his black eyes. I could *not* look from his eyes. While Kisten unconsciously dumped pheromones into the air to make my vampire scar send wave after wave of passion through me in time with my hammering pulse, my gut twisted.

Mind racing, I forced my breathing to be slow and even. Fear would trip him over the edge. I'd pulled Ivy down once, and I knew if he was still talking, then the odds were highly in my favor. "Listen," I said, the ecstasy from my vampire scar mixing with my fear in an unreal slurry. It felt good. It was a rush, the thrill of skydiving and sex all at the same time, and I knew that letting him bite me would triple the sensation. And I was going to let go of him and push him away. "I'm going to close my eyes because I trust you," I said.

"Rachel?"

It was soft and pleading. He truly wanted to let go. Damn it, this was my fault. Tension made my head hurt, and I closed my eyes on the black orbs his gaze had become. It made the fear ten times harder to surmount, but still, I trusted him. I could tap a line and send him flying into the wall—and if push came to shove, I would—but it would change our relationship utterly, and I loved him. It was a quiet, tentative love with the frightening promise that it would grow if I didn't screw it up. And I wanted a love based on trust, not who was stronger.

"Kisten," I said, forcing my jaw to unclench. "I'm going to let go of you, and you are going to let go of my shoulders and step back. Ready?" I could hear him breathe, harsh and insistent. It struck a chord inside me, and we both shuddered.

It would feel so damn good to let him bite me, his teeth sinking deep, pulling me to him, the pain twisted to pleasure, scouring through me like fire and stealing my breath, taking me to imagined heights of ecstasy. It would be incredible, the best thing I'd ever felt. It would change my life forever. *And it was not going to happen.* For all the promised pleasure, I knew it hid an equally ugly reality. And I was afraid.

"Now, Kisten," I said, eyes still closed, forcing my fingers to move.

My hands fell from him and he stepped away. My eyes flashed open. He had his back to me, a hand on the waist-high post at the foot of my bed. His free hand shook. I reached out, then hesitated. "Kisten, I'm sorry," I said, voice trembling, and he bobbed his head.

"Me too." His husky voice ran through me like water through sand, leaving me warm and tingly. "Do me a favor and don't do that again."

"You bet." Crossing my arms in front of me, I took off his sweatshirt and let it fall to the bed. The tingle at my neck faded, leaving me shaking and sick at heart. I had known mixing our scents was a blood aphrodisiac, but not how potent it was or that it could come on that fast. I was still making mistakes. Almost a year at this and I was *still* making mistakes.

Kisten's head came up, and I wasn't surprised to hear the front door open. In three seconds flat six streaks of silver and gold whizzed by my door at head height. Two more seconds and they raced back.

"Hi, Ms. Morgan!" came a high-pitched voice, and a pixy girl came to a short stop at the door, peering in with her dress fluttering about her ankles. Her face was flushed and her fair hair was swirling in the draft from her wings. There was a crash from the living room, and she darted off, shouting so high that my head hurt. The music blared, then cut out.

I took a step to the door, jerking to a stop when Matalina halted before me.

"I'm sorry, Rachel," the pretty pixy woman said, looking frazzled. "I'll take care of it. I'll get them out to the stump as soon as it stops raining."

Smoothing the rough edges of my bandaged knuckles, I tried to wash away the last of my runaway passions and the fear from Kisten. He hadn't moved, clearly still trying to regain control. "Don't worry about it," I said. "I didn't have time to pixy-proof the church." There was another crash, this time from the kitchen. A handful of pixies flowed by, all talking at once, and Matalina followed, admonishing them to stay out of my cupboards.

My worry deepened when Ivy strode past. Jenks was on her shoulder, and he gave me an unsure look and a nod of recognition. Ivy caught sight of Kisten and she backpedaled, her shorter hair swinging. Her gaze went to his shirt on the bed, then took in my soft guilt and the tremor in my hands. Nostrils flaring, she scented the vamp pheromones and my fear, realizing in seconds what had transpired. I shrugged helplessly.

"We're back," she said dryly, then continued to the kitchen, the new loudness of her steps and the slight tension in her body the only sign that she knew I had pushed Kisten too far.

Kisten didn't meet my gaze, but my shoulders eased at the returning ring of blue in his eyes. "You okay?" I asked, and he gave me a closed-lipped smile.

"I shouldn't have given you a pair I already wore," he said, taking the shirt and stuffing it in the bag. "Maybe you should wash them."

I took the bag when he extended it, embarrassed. He followed me into the hallway, turning to the kitchen while I went the other way to get the washer going. The sharp scent of the soap ticked my nose, and I dumped in a full measure, then added a little more. I closed the lid and stood with my hands on the washer as it filled, my head bowed. My gaze fell on my bitten hand. Sometimes I thought I was the stupidest witch ever born. Straightening, I forced a pleasant expression onto my face and headed to the kitchen, anticipating Ivy's mocking look.

Unable to met anyone's eyes, I went straight to the coffeemaker to get a mug to hide behind. All the pixy kids were in the living room, and the sound of their play mixed with the soft hush of the rain past the open kitchen window. Ivy gave me one wry look before returning to her e-mails, having parked herself at her computer, out of the way in the corner. Jenks was on the sill, his back to me as he looked into the wet garden, and Kisten was sitting in my chair, his legs stretched to poke out past the corner of the table. No one was saying anything.

"Hey, uh, Kist," I stammered, and he pulled his head up. "I found a spell to Were with in one of the books you gave me."

He seemed to have found his calm, and though I was wire-tight, his eyes were weary. "No kidding," he said.

Encouraged, I brought out the book and thumped it open before him.

Jenks flitted over, nearly landing on my shoulder but choosing Kisten's at the last moment. He glanced down, his wings stilling before his head jerked up to mine. "Isn't that—"

"Yeah," I interrupted. "It's demon magic. But see? I don't have to kill anything."

Kisten blew out his breath, meeting Ivy's blank expression before easing away from the book. "You can do demon magic?" he asked.

I nodded and tucked a curl behind my ear. I didn't want to tell him why, and though Kisten was too much of a gentleman to ask when others could hear, Jenks was another story. Wings clattering, he put his hands on his hips and frowned at me in his best Peter Pan pose. "How come you can do demon magic and no one else can?" he asked.

"I'm not the only one," I said tightly, and then the metallic bong of the pull bell Ivy and I used for a doorbell vibrated through the damp air.

Ivy and Kisten both straightened, and I said, "It's probably Ceri. I asked her to come over to help me with my spells tonight."

"Your *demon* spells?" Jenks said bitingly, and I frowned, not wanting to argue.

"I'll let her in," Kisten said as he stood. "I've got to go. I—have an appointment."

His voice was strained, and I backed up, feeling like dirt when I saw his rising hunger. Crap, he was having a hard time staying balanced tonight. I was *never* going to do that again.

Kisten smoothly reached out, and I didn't move when he put his hands lightly on my shoulder and gave me a quick kiss. "I'll call you after we close. You going to be up?"

I nodded. "Kisten, I'm sorry," I whispered, and he gave me a smile before walking out with slow, measured steps. Riling him up without being able to satisfy his hunger wasn't fair.

Jenks landed on the table beside me, his wings clattering for my attention. "Rachel, that's demon magic," he said, his belligerent attitude not hiding his worry.

"That's why I asked Ceri to look at it," I said. "I've got this under control."

"But it's demon magic! Ivy, tell her she's being stupid."

"She knows she's being stupid." Ivy closed her computer down with a few clicks. "See what she did to Kist?"

I crossed my arms. "All right, it's demon magic. But that doesn't necessarily make it black. Can we hear what Ceri says before we decide anything?" *We. Yeah, we. It was we again, and it was going to stay that way, damn it.*

In a surge of motion, Ivy rose, stretching for the ceiling in her black jeans and a tight knit shirt. She grabbed her purse and shouted, "Wait up, Kist!"

Jenks and I stared at her. "You're going with him?" I asked for both of us.

Ivy's look, rife with disapproval, was aimed at me. "I want to make sure no one takes advantage of him and he ends up hating himself when the sun comes up." She shrugged into her jacket and put on her shades though it was dark out. "If you pulled that on me, I'd pin you to the wall and have at it. Kist is a gentleman. You don't deserve him."

My breath caught at the memory of my back to the wall and Kisten's lips on my neck. A spike of remembered need raced from my neck to my groin. Ivy sucked in her breath as if I'd slapped her, her heightened senses taking in my state as easily as I could see the sparkles sifting from Jenks. "I'm sorry," I said, though my skin was tingling. "I wasn't thinking."

"That's why I gave you the damn book," she said tightly. "So you wouldn't have to."

"What did she do?" Jenks asked, but Ivy had walked out, boot heels clunking. "What book? The one about dating vampires? Tink's panties, you still have that?" he added.

"I'll bring back a pizza," Ivy called, unseen from the hallway.

"What did you do, Rache?" Jenks said, the wind from his wings cooling my cheeks.

"I put on Kisten's shirt and did jumping jacks," I said, embarrassed.

The small pixy snorted, going to the windowsill to check on the rain. "You keep pulling stunts like that and people will think you want to be bitten."

"Yeah," I muttered, taking a sip of my cooling coffee and leaning against the center island counter. I was still making mistakes. Then I remembered what Quen had once told me. *If you do it once, it's a mistake. If you do it twice, it's not a mistake anymore.*

Five

I looked up when the soft conversation in the sanctuary gave way to clipped steps and Ceri peered hesitantly around the corner of the archway. Pulling the rain hood from her, she smiled, clearly pleased to see Jenks and me back on speaking terms. "Jenks, about Trent . . ." I said, seeing his wings turn an excited red. He knew that whatever Trent was, Ceri was the same.

"I can figure this out myself," he said, focusing on Ceri. "Shut your mouth."

I shut my mouth.

I stood and extended my hands to give Ceri a hug. I wasn't a touchy-feely person, but Ceri was. She had been Al's familiar until I stole her in the breath of time between her retirement and my attempted installment. Glancing briefly at my neck and bandaged knuckles, she pressed her lips disapprovingly, but thankfully said nothing. Her small, almost ethereal stature met mine, and the hand-tooled silver crucifix Ivy had given her made a cold spot through my shirt. The hug was brief but sincere, and she was smiling when she put me at arm's length. She had thin, fair hair that she wore free and flowing, a small chin, delicate nose, large pride, short temper, and a mild demeanor unless challenged.

She took off her rain cape and draped it over Ivy's chair, the self-proclaimed "throne" of the room. Al had dressed her commensurate to her earthly status while in his service—treating her as a favored slave/servant/bed warmer as well as an adornment—and though she now wore jeans and a sweater in her usual purple, gold, and black, instead of a skin-tight gown of shimmering silk and gold, the bearing was still there.

"Thanks for coming over," I said, genuinely glad to see her. "Do you want some tea?"

"No, thank you." She elegantly extended a narrow hand for Jenks to land on. "It's good to see you back where you can help the people who need you the most, master pixy," she said to him, and I would swear he turned three shades of red.

"Hi, Ceri," he said. "You look well-rested. Did you sleep well tonight?"

Her heart-shaped face went crafty, knowing he was trying to decipher what kind of Inderlander she was by her sleep patterns. "I have yet to take my evening rest," she said, shifting her fingers until he took to the air. Her gaze went to the open book on the table. "Is that it?"

A thrill of adrenaline went through me. "One of them. Is it demon?"

Tucking her long fair hair behind an ear, she leaned to take a closer look. "Oh yes."

Suddenly I was a whole lot more nervous, and I set my mug on the counter while my stomach churned. "There are a couple of charms I might want to try. Would you look at them for me and tell me what you think?"

Ceri's delicate features glowed with pleasure. "I'd love to."

I exhaled in a puff of relief. "Thanks." Wiping my hands on my jeans, I pointed to the curse to Were. "This one here. What about it? Do you think I can do it all right?"

The tips of her severely straight hair touched the stain-spotted, yellow text as she bent over the book. Frowning, she gathered the strands up and out of the way. Jenks flitted to the table as she squinted, alighting on the saltshaker. There was a crash from the living room followed by a chorus of pixy shrieks, and he sighed. "I'll be right back," he said, buzzing out.

"I've stirred this one before," she said, fingers hovering over the print.

"What does it do?" I asked, nervous all over again. "I mean, would it make me into a real wolf, or would I just look like one?"

Ceri straightened, her gaze darting to the hallway as Jenks's high-pitched harangue filtered in, making my eyeballs hurt. "It's a standard morphing curse, the same class that Al uses. You keep your intelligence and personality, same as when you shift with an earth charm. The difference is the blending of you and wolf goes to the cellular level. If there were two of you, you could have pups with a witch's IQ if you stayed a wolf through gestation."

My mouth dropped open. I reached out to touch the page, then drew back. "Oh."

With casual interest, she ran her finger down the list of ingredients, all in Latin. "This won't turn you into a Were, but this is how werewolves got started," she said conversationally. "There was a fad about six millennia ago where demons would torment a human woman in payment for a vanity wish by forcing a demonwolf/human pairing. It always resulted in a human child that could Were."

My eyes darted to her, but she didn't notice my fear. God, how . . . disgusting. And tragic for both the woman and child. The shame of dealing with a demon would never fade, always tied as it was to the love of a child. I'd often wondered how the Weres had gotten started, since they weren't from the ever-after like witches and elves.

"Would you like me to make it for you?" Ceri asked, her green eyes placid.

I jerked, my focus sharpening. "It's okay to use?"

Nodding, she reached under the counter for my smallest copper spell pot. "I don't mind. I could do this one in my sleep. Making curses is what demon familiars do. It will take all of thirty minutes." Seemingly unaware of my bewilderment, she casually moved the curse book to the island counter. "Demons aren't any more powerful than witches," she said. "But they're prepared for anything, so it looks like they're stronger."

"But Al morphs so fast, and into so many things," I protested, leaning against the counter.

Tiny boots clicking, Ceri turned from one of my cupboards, a wad of wolf's bane in her hand. The stuff was toxic in large doses, and I felt a twinge of worry. "Al is a higher demon," she said. "You could probably best a lesser, surface demon with the earth magic you have in your charm cupboard, though with enough prep work a surface demon is as powerful as Al."

Was she saying I could best Al with my magic? I didn't believe that for a second.

With a preoccupied grace, Ceri lit the Sterno flame canister from a taper she started from the gas burner. The stove served as my "hearth fire," since the pilot light was always burning, and it made for a stable beginning to any spell. "Ceri," I protested. "I can do this."

"Sit," she said. "Or watch. I want to be useful." She smiled without showing her teeth, sadness clouding her clear eyes. "Where do you keep your blessed candles?"

"Um, in with the big silver serving spoons," I said, pointing. *Doesn't everyone?*

Jenks swooped in, gold sparkles sifting from him in agitation. "Sorry about the lamp," he muttered. "They will be washing the windows inside and out tomorrow."

"That's okay. It was Ivy's," I said, thinking they could break every light in the place if they wanted. It was more than nice having them back—it was right.

"Al is a walking pharmaceutical," Ceri said, flipping to an index to check something, and Jenks made a hiccup of surprised sound. "That's why demons want familiars experienced in the craft. Familiars make the curses they use, the demons kindling them to life, taking them internally, and holding them until invoking them with ley line magic."

With the first inklings of understanding, I pulled another demon book out and rifled through it, seeing the patterns in Al's magic. "So every time he morphs or does a charm . . ."

"Or travels the lines, he uses a curse or spell. Probably

one that I made him," Ceri finished for me, squinting as she snatched one of Ivy's pens and changed something in the text, muttering a word of Latin to make it stick. "Traveling the lines puts a lot of blackness on your soul, which is why they're so angry when you call them. Al agreed to pay the price for pulling you through the first time, and he wants information to compensate for the smut."

I glanced at the circular scar on my wrist. There was a second one on the underside of my foot from Newt, the demon from whom I'd bought a trip home the last time I found myself stranded in the ever-after. Nervous, I hid that foot behind the other. I hadn't told Ceri because she was afraid of Newt. That she was terrified of the clearly insane demon and not Al made me feel all warm and cozy. I was never going to travel the lines again.

"May I have a lock of your hair?" Ceri asked, surprising me.

Taking the 99.8 percent silver snippers I'd spent a small fortune on that she was extending to me now, I cut a spaghetti-sized wad of hair from the nape of my neck.

"I'm simplifying things," she said when I handed it to her. "And you probably noticed he has a few shapes and spells that he enjoys more than others."

"The British nobleman in a green coat," I said, and a delicate rose color came over Ceri. I wondered what the story behind *that* was, but I wouldn't ask.

"I spent three years doing nothing but twisting that curse," she said, fingers going slow.

From the ladle came Jenks's attention-getting wing clatter. "Three years?"

"She's a thousand years old," I said, and his eyes widened.

Ceri laughed at his disconcertion. "That isn't my normal span," she said. "I'm aging now, as are you."

Jenks's wings blurred into motion, then stilled. "I can live twenty years," he said, and I heard the frustration in his voice. "How about you?"

Ceri turned her solemn green eyes to me for guidance. That elves were not entirely extinct was a secret I had told her to keep, and while knowing her expected life span wouldn't give it away, it could be used to piece the truth together. I nodded, and she closed her eyes in a slow blink of understanding. "About a hundred sixty years," she said softly. "Same as a witch."

I glanced uneasily between them while Jenks fought to hide an unknown emotion. I hadn't known how long elves lived, and while I watched Ceri weave my hair into an elaborate chain that looped back into itself, I wondered how old Trent's parents had been when they had him. A witch was fertile for about a hundred years, with a twenty-year lag on one end and forty at the tail end. I hadn't had a period in two years, since things pretty much shut down unless there was a suitable candidate to stir things up. And as much as I liked Kisten, he wasn't a witch to click the right hormones on. Seeing that elves had their origins in the ever-after, like witches, I was willing to bet their physiologies were closer to witch than human.

As if feeling Jenks's distress, Matalina flitted in trailing three of their daughters and an unsteady toddler. "Jenks, dear," she said, giving me an apologetic look. "The rain has slacked. I'm going to move everyone out so Rachel and Ivy can have some peace."

Jenks's hand dropped to his sword hilt. "I want to do a room-by-room check first."

"No." She flitted close and gave him a hovering kiss on the cheek. She looked happy and content, and I loved seeing her like that. "You stay here. The seals weren't tampered with."

My lower lip curled in to catch between my teeth. Jenks wasn't going to like my next move. "Actually, Matalina, I'd like you to stay, if you could."

Jenks jerked upward, a sudden wariness in him as he joined her, their wings somehow not tangling though they hovered side by side. "Why," he said flatly.

"Ah . . ." I glanced at Ceri, who was muttering Latin and making gestures over my ring of hair at the center of a plate-sized pentacle she had sifted onto the counter with salt. I stifled a feeling of worry; knotting your hair made an unbreakable link to the donor. The ring of twisted hair vanished with a pop, replaced with a pile of ash. Apparently this was okay, since she smiled and carefully brushed it and the salt into the shot-glass-sized spell pot.

"Rachel . . ." Jenks prompted, and I tore my gaze from Ceri; she had tapped a line, and her hair was drifting in an unfelt breeze.

"She might want a say in this next spell," I said. Nervous, I pulled the demon book closer and opened it to a page marked with the silk bookmark Ivy had gotten on sale last week.

Jenks hovered a good inch above the text, and Matalina gave a set of intent instructions to her daughters. With a whining toddler in tow, they darted out of the kitchen.

"Ceri," I prompted cautiously, not wanting to interrupt her. "Is this one okay to do?"

The elf blinked as if coming out of a trance. Nodding, she pushed her sleeves to her elbows and crossed the room to the ten-gallon vat of saltwater I used to dissolution used amulets. As I watched in surprise, she dunked her hands into it, arms coming up dripping wet. I tossed her a dish towel, wondering if I should start a similar practice. Fingers moving gracefully, she dried her hands while she came to peer at the spell book on the table. Her eyes widened at the charm I'd found to make little things big. "For . . ." she started, her gaze darting to Jenks.

I nodded. "Is it safe?"

She bit her lips, a pretty frown crossing her angular, delicate face. "You'd have to modify it with something to supplement bone mass. Maybe tweak the metabolism so it's not burning so fast. And then you'd have to take the wings into account."

"Whoa!" Jenks exclaimed, darting to the ceiling. "No freaking way. You aren't doing anything to this little pixy. No way. No how!"

Ignoring him, I watched Matalina take a slow, steady

breath, her hands clasped before her. I turned to Ceri. "Can it be done?"

"Oh, yes," she said. "Much of it is ley line magic. And you have the earth charm ingredients in your stock. The hard part will be developing the supplemental curses to fine-tune it to limit his discomfort. But I can do it."

"No!" Jenks cried. "*Augmen.* I know that one. That means big. I'm not going to get big. You can forget it! I like who I am, and I can't do my job if I'm big."

He had retreated to where Matalina was standing on the counter, her wings unusually still, and I gestured helplessly. "Jenks," I coaxed. "Just listen."

"No." His voice was shrill as he pointed at me. "You are a freaky, misguided, crazy-ass witch! I'm not doing this!"

I straightened at the sound of the back door opening. The curtains fluttered, and I recognized Ivy's footsteps. The smell of pizza mixed with the rich scent of wet garden, and Ivy came in looking like a frat boy's fantasy in her rain-damp, sex-in-leather coat and a square box of pizza balanced on one hand. Short hair swinging, she noisily dropped the box on the table, taking in the room with a solemn, quiet face. She moved Ceri's rain cape to a different chair, and the tension ratcheted up a notch.

"If you're big," I said while Ivy got herself a plate, "you won't have to worry about the temperature fluctuations. It could snow up there, Jenks."

"No."

Ivy flipped the top open and took a slice, carefully putting it on a plate and retreating to her corner of the kitchen. "You want to make Jenks big?" she said. "Witches can do that?"

"Uh . . ." I stammered, not wanting to get into why my blood could kindle demon magic.

"*She* can," Ceri said, skirting the issue.

"And food won't be a problem," I blurted, to keep the subject to Jenks and off of me.

Jenks bristled despite the gentle hand Matalina put on

his arm. "I've never had a problem keeping my family fed," he said.

"I never said you did." The smell of the pizza was making me feel ill as my stomach knotted, and I sat down. "But we're talking almost five hundred miles, if they are where I think they are, and I don't want to have to stop every hour for you to fight off roadside park fairies so you can eat. Sugar water and peanut butter won't do it, and you know that."

Jenks took a breath to protest. Ivy ate her pizza, scooting down in the chair and putting her heels on the table next to her keyboard, her gaze shifting between Jenks and me.

I tucked a red curl behind an ear, hoping I wasn't pushing our delicate working relationship too far. "And you can see how the other side lives," I said. "You won't have to wait for someone to open the door for you, or use the phone. Hell, you could drive. . . ."

His wings blurred into motion, and Matalina looked frightened.

"Look," I said, feeling uncomfortable. "Why don't you and Matalina talk it over."

"I don't need to talk it over," Jenks said tightly. "I'm not going to do it."

My shoulders slumped, but I was too afraid to push him further. "Fine," I said sourly. "Excuse me. I have to move my laundry."

Covering my worry with a false anger, I stomped out of the kitchen, sneakers squeaking on the linoleum and then the hardwood floors as I went to my bathroom. Slamming the white enameled doors harder than I needed to, I shifted Kisten's sweats to the dryer. Jenks didn't need them anymore, but I wasn't going to give them back wet.

I wrenched the dial to dry, punched the on button, and heard the drier start to turn. Arms shoulder width apart, I leaned over the dryer. Low temperatures would severely limit Jenks after sunset. Another month and it wouldn't matter, but May could be cold in Michigan.

I pushed myself up, resigned to dealing with it. It was his choice. Resolute, I padded toward the kitchen, forcing the frown from me.

"Please, Jenks," I heard Ivy plead just before I turned the corner, the unusual emotion in her voice jerking me to a stop. She never let her emotions show like that. "Rachel needs someone as a buffer between her and any vamp she runs into outside of Cincinnati," she whispered, unaware that I could hear. "Every vamp here knows I'll kill them twice if they touch her, but once she's out of my influence, her unclaimed scar is going to make her fair game. I can't go with her. Piscary—" She took a shaky breath. "He'd be really pissed if I left his influence. God, Jenks, this is just about killing me. I can't go with her. You have to. And you have to be big, otherwise no one will take you seriously."

My face went cold and I put a hand to my scar. *Crap. I forgot about that.*

"I don't need to be big to protect her," he said, and I nodded.

"I know that," Ivy said, "and she knows that, but a blood-hungry vamp won't care. And there might be more than one."

Insides shaking, I slowly backed up. My fingers felt for the knob of my bathroom door and I yanked it closed, slamming it, as if I'd just gotten out. Then I briskly entered the kitchen, not looking at anyone. Ceri was standing by my smallest spell pot with a finger stick in her hand; what she wanted was obvious. Ivy was pretending to read her e-mail, and Jenks was standing with a horrified look on his face, Matalina beside him. "So, I guess we're stopping every hour?" I said.

Jenks swallowed hard. "I'll do it."

"Really, Jenks," I said, trying to hide my guilt. "It's okay. You don't have to do this."

He flitted up, hands on hips while he got in my face. "I'm doing this, so shut the hell up and say thank-you!"

Feeling miserable and vulnerable, I whispered, "Thank you."

His wings clattered as he flitted shakily to Matalina with a little huff. She clutched at him, her beautiful angel face looking scared when she turned him so his back was to me and they started to talk, their words so high-pitched and fast I couldn't follow.

With the practiced silence of a slave, Ceri eased close to set the spell pot with the Were potion beside me. She placed the finger stick next to it with a small click and backed away. Still upset, I fumbled the sterile blade open and glanced at the brew. It looked like cherry Kool-Aid in the miniature copper pot.

"Thanks," I muttered. White or not, using demon magic wasn't what I wanted to be known for. The prick of the blade was a jolt, and I massaged my finger. Three drops of my blood went plopping into the vat, and the throat-catching scent of burnt amber rose as my blood kindled demon magic. *How nice is that?*

My stomach quivered, and I looked at it. "It won't invoke early?" I asked, and Ceri shook her head. Lifting the heavy tome, she moved it in front of me.

"Here," she said, pointing. "This is the word of invocation. It won't work unless you're connected to a line or you have enough ever-after spindled to effect a change. I've seen what you can hold, and it's enough. This one here"—she pointed farther down the page—"is the word to shift back. I suggest not using it unless you're connected to a line. You're adding to your mass on this second one, not removing it, and it's hard to know how much energy to withhold from your spindle to make up for the imbalance. It's easier to connect to a line and let it balance itself. Saltwater won't break demon magic, so don't forget the countercurse."

Nervous, I shifted my grip on the little copper pot. It would be enough potion for seven earth charms, but ley line magic was usually one spell per go. I looked again at the word of invocation. *Lupus.* Pretty straightforward.

"It won't work unless it's inside of you," Ceri said, sounding annoyed.

Jenks flitted close, hovering over the pages. His gaze

moved from the print to me. "How is she going to say the word to shift back if she's a wolf?" he asked, and a flash of angst burned through me until I guessed it must be like any ley line charm that only required you to think it hard enough. Though shouting a word of invocation definitely added a measure of strength.

Ceri's green eyes narrowed. "Saying it in her mind will be enough," she said. "Do you want me to put it in a pentagram to keep it fresh, or are you going to take it now?"

I raised the spell pot, trying to smooth out my brow so I at least didn't look nervous. It was just an elaborate disguise potion, one that would make me furry and with big teeth. If I was lucky, I'd never have to invoke it. I felt Ivy's attention on me, and while everyone watched, I downed it.

I tried not to taste it, but the biting grit of ash and the bitter taste of tinfoil, chlorophyll, and salt puckered my lips. "Oh God," I said while Ivy grabbed a second slice of pizza. "That tastes like crap." I went to the dissolution vat and gave the empty spell pot a quick dunk before I set it in the sink. The potion burned through me, and I tried to stifle a shudder, failing.

"You okay?" Ivy asked as I shivered and the pot rattled against the sink before I let it go.

"Fine," I said, my voice rough. I'd just taken a demon spell. Voluntarily. Tonight I was peachy keen, and tomorrow I would be taking the bus tour of the nicest parts of hell.

Ceri hid a smile, and I frowned at her. "What!" I snapped, but she only smiled wider.

"That's what Al said whenever he took his potions."

"Swell," I snarled, going to sit at the table and pull the pizza closer. I knew it was anxiety that was making me irritable, and I tried to smooth my face out, pretending it didn't bother me.

"See, Matalina?" Jenks coaxed, and he flew to land beside her on the sill next to my beta. "It's fine. Rachel took a demon spell and she's okay. It will be easier this way, and I won't die of the cold. I'll be just as big as she is. It will be okay, Mattie. I promise."

Matalina rose in a column of silver sparkles. She wrung her hands and stared at everyone for a moment, her distress obvious and heartbreaking. In an instant she was gone, out into the rain through the pixy hole in the screen.

Standing on the sill, Jenks let his wings droop. I felt a flash of guilt, then stifled it. Jenks was going whether I was with him or not, and if he was big, he would have a better chance of coming back in one piece. But she was so upset, it was hard not to feel like it was my fault.

"Okay," I said, the bite of pizza tasteless. "What do we do first for Jenks?"

Ceri's slight shoulders eased and she gripped her crucifix with what was clearly an unknowing gesture of contentment. "His curse will have to be specially tailored. We should probably set a circle too. This is going to be difficult."

Six

The harsh smell of low-grade yarn dye didn't mix well with the luscious scent of leather and silk. Through it ran a dusky incense that soaked into me with each slow breath, keeping my muscles loose and slack. *Kisten.* My nose tickled, and I pushed the afghan from my face, snuggling deeper into the sound of his heartbeat. I felt him shift, and a sleepy part of me remembered we were in the living room on the couch, lying like spoons. My head was tucked under his chin, and his arm was over my middle, warm and secure.

"Rachel?" he whispered so softly that it barely stirred my hair.

"Mmmm?" I mumbled, not wanting to move. In the past eleven months I'd found that a vampire's blood lust varied like tempers, dependent upon stress, temperament, upbringing, and when they had slaked it last. I had gone into living with Ivy as a roommate as a complete idiot. Turns out she had been on the extreme end of the hairy-scary scale at the time, being stressed about Piscary wanting her to make me a toy or kill me, acerbated by her guilt at her desire for blood and trying to abstain from it. Three years of abstinence made for a very anxious vamp. I didn't want to know what Ivy had been before going cold turkey to try to remake herself. All I knew was she was much easier to live with now that she was "taking care of business," though it left her hating herself and feeling she was a failure every time she succumbed.

I'd found Kisten to be on the other end, with a laid-back temperament to begin with and no issues about satisfying his blood lust. And though I wouldn't feel comfortable napping in the same room with Ivy, I could snuggle up to Kisten, provided he took care of things beforehand. *And I didn't do jumping jacks in his sweatshirt,* I thought sourly.

"Rachel, love," he said again, louder, with a hint of pleading. I could feel his muscles tense and his breathing quicken. "I think Ceri is ready for you to kindle Jenks's spell, and as much as I'd love to pull blood from you, it might be better if you did it yourself."

My eyes flew open and I stared at the bank of Ivy's electronic equipment. "She finished it?" I said, and Kisten grunted when my elbow pushed off his gut when I sat up. My sock feet hit the rug, and my eyes shot to the clock on the TV. *It was past noon?*

"I fell asleep!" I said, seeing our pizza-crust-strewn plates on the coffee table. "Kist," I complained, "you weren't supposed to let me fall asleep!"

He remained reclining on Ivy's gray suede couch, his hair tousled and a content, sleepy look to his eyes. "Sorry," he said around a yawn, not looking sorry at all.

"Darn it. I was supposed to be helping Ceri." It was bad enough she was doing my spelling for me. To be sleeping when she did it was just rude.

He lifted one shoulder and let it fall. "She said to let you sleep."

Giving him an exasperated sigh, I tugged my jeans straight. I hated it when I fell asleep in my clothes. At least I had showered before dinner, thinking it only fair I get rid of the lingering scent of wearing his sweatshirt. "Ceri?" I said, shuffling into the kitchen. For crying out loud, I'd wanted to have Kisten's borrowed van packed and be on the road by now.

Ceri was sitting with her elbows on Ivy's antique table. Beside her was a pizza box, empty but for a single slice and an untouched container of garlic dipping sauce. Her long, wispy hair was the only movement, floating in the chill breeze from the window. The kitchen was cleaner than I ever managed when I did my spelling: copper bowls stacked neatly in the sink, the grit of salt under my feet from where she had made a circle, and a scattering of ley line magic paraphernalia and earth magic herbs. A demon book was open on the center counter, and the purple candle I burned last Halloween guttered even as I watched.

The early afternoon sun was a bright swath of light coming in the window. Past the drifting curtains, pixies shrieked and played, shredding the fairy nest in the ash tree with a savage enthusiasm. Jenks was sitting on the table, slumped against Ceri's half-empty cup of tea. "Ceri," I said, reaching to touch her shoulder.

Her head jerked up. "*O di immortals,* Gally," she said, clearly not awake. "My apologies! Your curse is ready. I'll have your tea directly."

Jenks took to the air in a clattering of wings, and my attention shot from him to her. "Ceri?" I repeated, frightened. *She called Algaliarept Gally?*

The young woman stiffened, then dropped her head into her hands again. "God help me, Rachel," she said, her words muffled. "For a moment . . ."

My hand slipped from her shoulder. She had thought she was back with Al. "I'm sorry," I said, feeling even more guilty. "I fell asleep and Kisten didn't wake me. Are you okay?"

She turned, a thin smile on her heart-shaped face. Her green eyes were tired and weary. I was sure she hadn't slept since yesterday afternoon, and she looked ready to drop. "I'm fine," she lisped faintly, clearly not.

Embarrassed, I sat before her. "Jeez, Ceri, I could have done something."

"I'm fine," she repeated, her eyes on the ribbon of smoke spiraling up from the candle. "Jenks helped me with the plants. He's very knowledgeable."

Eyebrows rising, I watched Jenks tug his green silk gardening jacket down. "You think I'm going to take a spell without knowing what's in it?" he said.

"Jenks helped you make it?" I asked.

She shrugged. "It doesn't matter who makes it, as long as you kindle it." Pale face smiling tiredly, she nodded to the potion and finger stick.

Moving slowly, I rose and went to Jenks's spell. The crack of the safety seal on the finger stick breaking was loud.

"Use your Jupiter finger," Ceri advised. "It will add the strength of your will to it."

It made a difference? I wondered, feeling ill from more than lack of sleep as I pricked my finger for three drops of blood. Kisten stirred in the living room when they went plopping into the spell pot and the scent of burnt amber rose. Jenks's wings blurred to motion, and I held my breath, waiting for something to happen. Nothing. But I had to say the "magic words" first.

"Done," Ceri said, slumping where she sat.

My eyes went to Kisten's lanky form when he strode into the kitchen, barefoot and rumpled. "Afternoon, ladies," he said, pulling the pizza box closer and dropping the last stiff slice on a plate. He wasn't the first guy to have a toothbrush at my sink, but he was the only one to have kept it there this long, and I felt good seeing him here in his disheveled, untucked-shirt state, content and comfortable.

"Coffee?" I asked, and he nodded, clearly not functioning on all levels yet as he dragged the plate from the table and headed into the hall, scratching the bristles on his jawline.

I jumped when Kisten pounded on Ivy's door and shouted, "Ivy! Get up! Here's your breakfast. Rachel is leaving, and you'd better hurry if you want to see Jenks change."

So much for coffee, toast, juice, and a flower, I thought, hearing Ivy's voice rise in disgust before Kisten shut her door and cut off her complaints. Ceri looked mystified, and I shook my head to tell her it wasn't worth explaining. I went to clean the coffeemaker, turning the water to a trickle when Kisten thunked my bathroom door shut and my shower started.

"So, we going to do this, Jenks?" I prompted while I swirled the water around.

His wings shading to blue, Jenks landed by the shot-glass-sized cup of brew. "I drink it?"

Ceri nodded. "Once it's in you, Rachel will invoke it. Nothing will happen until then."

"All of it?" I asked, eyes widening. "It's like, what, a gallon in pixy terms?"

Jenks shrugged. "I drink that much sugar water for breakfast," he said, and my brow furrowed. If he drank like that, we might be stopping every hour anyway.

My fingers fumbled to unroll the coffee bag, and the dark scent of grounds hit me, thick and comforting. I measured out what I needed into the new filter, then added a smidgen more while I surreptitiously watched Jenks procrastinate. Finally he scuffed his boots on the counter and spooned out a pixy-sized portion with a tiny glass. He downed the dripping cup in one go, making a face when he lowered the cup.

I flipped the coffeemaker on and leaned against the counter, arms crossed. "What does it taste like?" I asked, remembering the demon spell already in me. I was hoping he didn't say it tasted like my blood.

"Uh . . ." Jenks scooped out another cupful. "It tastes like the garden in the fall when people have been burning their leaves."

Dead ashes? I thought. *Gre-e-e-e-eat.*

Chin high, he swallowed it, then turned to me. "For the love of Tink, you aren't going to stand there and watch me, are you?"

Grimacing, I pushed myself from the counter. "Can I make you some tea?" I asked Ceri, not wanting to look like I was watching but not wanting to leave either. What if he had a reaction or something?

With a barely perceptible motion, Ceri regained her upright posture, my offer seeming to turn on an entirely new set of behaviors. "Yes, thank you," she said carefully.

I returned to the sink and filled the kettle, wincing at Jenks's tiny belch and groan. The sound of running water seemed to revive Ceri, and she rose, moving about the kitchen to put things away. "I can do that," I protested, and she watched my eyes go to the clock above the sink. *Crap, it was getting late.*

"So can I," she said. "You have a long way to drive, and all I have to do is—" She looked sourly about the kitchen. "I don't have anything to do but sleep. I should be thanking you. It was exhilarating to craft such a complex curse. It's one of my best efforts."

Her pride was obvious, and after the burner ignited under the kettle, I stood against the counter and watched Jenks belch and recite his ABCs at the same time. Would the man's talents never end? Curiosity finally prompted me to ask, "What was it like, being his familiar?"

Ceri seemed to grow drowsy as she stood in the sun at the sink and washed her teacup. "He is domineering and cruel," she said softly, head down as she watched her thin hands, "but my origins made me unique. He enjoyed showing me off and so kept me well. Once I became pliant, he often gave me favors and courtesies that most remained ignorant of."

My thoughts returned to her embarrassment when speaking of Al's favorite appearance of a British nobleman. They had been together for a thousand years, and there were countless cases of captives becoming enamored of their captors. *And that nickname* . . . I tried to meet her eyes, but she avoided it.

"I'll be back," Jenks said, patting his stomach. "This stuff makes you pee like a toad."

I cringed as he took to the air and flew heavily past Ceri and out the pixy hole in the screen. A glance at the spell pot brought my eyebrows up. It was half gone. *Damn, the man could slam it faster than a frat boy.*

"I made anywhere from thirty to fifty curses a day," Ceri said, taking a rag from the sink and wiping the island counter free of salt, "apart from warming his bed and putting food on his table. Every seventh day he would work in the lab with me, expanding my knowledge. This charm . . ." Eyes distant, she touched the counter beside the remaining brew. "This one we would have spent all day with, going slow so he could explain the complexities of mixing curses. Those days . . . I almost felt good about myself."

Clasping my hands about my middle, I felt cold at the hint of wistfulness to her voice. She nearly seemed to regret she wasn't working in a demon sweatshop anymore. Eyes distant, she took the boiling water from the stove and poured it into a small teapot.

Jenks returned without comment, settling before the brew with his little cup. The hair on the back of my neck pricked, and Ivy came in with a soft scuffing, hands busy tucking her shirt behind her jeans. Not meeting anyone's eyes, she shuffled to the coffeemaker and poured two mugs even as the last drips spilled onto the hot plate to sizzle. I looked up in surprise when she hesitantly set one beside me.

Kisten's words echoed through my thoughts as I watched her sit at her computer, reading the tension in her shoulders when she jabbed the on button and hit the shortcut to her mail. What he'd said about her leaning on me more than him because I didn't know her past tightened my gut. I looked at her as she sat at the far end of the kitchen, distant but a part of the group. Her perfect face was quiet and still, not a glimmer of her savage past showing. A chill went through me at what might lie beneath it, what might come out if I left her. Just how bad had it been?

Ivy looked from her monitor, her eyes fastening on me from under her short bangs. My gaze dropped. *Good Lord. It was only for a few days.*

"Thanks for the coffee," I said, uncurling my fingers and lacing them about the warm ceramic while I steeled my emotions. I had to go. Nick and Jax needed help. I'd be back.

She said nothing, her face showing no emotion. A screen of new e-mails came in one after the other, and she began winnowing through them.

Nervous, I turned to Ceri. "I really appreciate this," I said, thinking of the long drive ahead. "If it wasn't for your help, I wouldn't even try it. I'm just glad it's not a black charm," I added. White or not, using demon magic was not what I wanted to be known for.

In her spot in the sun, Ceri stiffened. "Um, Rachel?" she said, and my heart seemed to skip a beat. My head slowly lifted and my mouth went dry. Jenks stopped with his cup halfway to his mouth. He met my eyes, his wings going absolutely still.

"It's a black charm?" I said, my voice squeaky at the end.

"Well, it's demon magic. . . ." she said, sounding apologetic. "They're all black." She looked between Jenks and me, mystified. "I thought you knew that."

Seven

I took a shaky breath and reached for the counter. *It was black? I had taken a black charm? This just keeps getting better and better. Why in hell hadn't she told me?*

"Hell no!" Jenks rose in a flurry of copper-colored sparkles. "Just forget it. Ivy, forget it! I'm not doing this!"

While Ivy snarled at Jenks that he would or she'd jam him through a keyhole backward, I wobbled to the table and slumped into my chair. Ceri was so odd, seemingly as innocent as Joan of Arc but as accepting of black magic as if she sat at Lucifer's feet and did his nails every other Wednesday. *They were all black, and she didn't see anything wrong with them?* Come to think of it, Joan of Arc had heard voices in her head telling her to kill people.

"Rachel . . ."

Ceri's hand on my shoulder pulled my head up and I stared. "I, uh," I muttered. "I kinda expected they were black, but you didn't seem to be having any problem making them, so . . ." I looked at the remainder of Jenks's potion, wondering if he quit now whether he'd be okay.

"He needs this curse." Ceri gracefully sat so I couldn't see Jenks and Ivy arguing at the far end of the table. "And the smut from one or two is trifling."

Matalina zipped in through the pixy hole in the screen at one of Jenks's sharp squeaks, bringing the smell of the spring noon with her. Her yellow dress swirled prettily about her ankles when she came to a short stop, her expression inquisitive as she tried to figure out what was going on. I couldn't seem to get enough air. *Trifling? Didn't she get it?*

"What if I only use them for good?" I tried. "Will they still stain my soul if I only do good with them?"

Matalina's wings stopped and she dropped three inches to the table, losing her balance and falling, to bend a wing backward. Ceri exhaled in obvious exasperation. "You're severely breaking the laws of nature with these curses," she lectured, her green eyes narrow, "far more than with earth or line magic on their own. It doesn't matter if they're used for good or bad, the smut on your soul is the same. If you mess with nature's books, you pay a price."

My eyes flicked past her to Matalina and Jenks. The small pixy woman had found her feet, and she had a hand on Jenks's shoulder as he hunched over his knees. He was hyperventilating by the look of it, pixy dust shading to red sifting from him to pool and spill onto the floor. It swirled in the draft from the window, and it would have been pretty if I hadn't known that it meant he was severely stressed.

Ivy's lips were a thin line. I didn't understand why she was arguing with him. I didn't expect him to go through with it if it was a black curse. *Damn it, Ceri had been calling them curses all along, and I hadn't been listening.*

"But I don't want my soul to go black," I almost whined. "I just got rid of Al's aura."

Ceri's delicate features went annoyed, and she stood. "Then get rid of it."

Jenks's head came up, his eyes looking frightened. "Rachel is *not* a black witch!" he shouted, and I wondered at his hot loyalty. "She's not going to foster it off on an innocent!"

"I never said she should," Ceri said, bristling.

"Ceri," I said hesitantly, listening to Matalina try to soothe her husband. "Isn't there another way to get rid of the reality imbalance than to pass it to someone else?"

Clearly aware of Jenks ready to fly at her, Ceri calmly went to her brewed tea. "No. Once you make it, the only way to get rid of it is to pass it to someone else. But I'm not suggesting you give it to an innocent. People will accept it voluntarily if you sweeten the deal."

I didn't like the sound of that. "Why would someone voluntarily take my blackness onto their soul?" I said, and the elf sighed, visibly biting back her annoyance. Tact wasn't in her repertoire, despite her kindness and overflowing goodwill.

"You attach it to something they want, Rachel," she said. "A spell or task. Information."

My eyes widened as I figured it out. "Like a demon," I said, and she nodded.

Oh God. My stomach hurt. The only way to get rid of it would be to trick people into taking it. Like a demon.

Ceri stood at my sink, the morning sun streaming about her making her look like a princess in jeans and a black and gold sweater. "It's a good option," she said, blowing at her tea to hasten its cooling. "I have too much imbalance to rid myself of it that way, but perhaps if I forayed into the ever-after and rescued people stolen and still in possession of their souls, they might take a hundred years of my imbalance in return for the chance to be free of the ever-after."

"Ceri," I protested, frightened, and she raised a soothing hand.

"I'm not going into the ever-after," she said. "But if the opportunity ever arose that I could help free someone, will you tell me?"

Ivy stirred, and Jenks interrupted her with a hot, "Rache is not going into the ever-after."

"He's right," I said, and I rose, my knees feeling weak. "I can't ask anyone to take the black I put on my soul. Just forget it." My fingers encircled the remainder of Jenks's potion and I headed for my dissolution vat. "I'm *not* a black witch."

Matalina heaved a sigh of relief, and even Jenks relaxed, his feet settling into a puddle of silver sparkles on the table, only to jerk upward when Ceri slammed her hand onto the counter. "You listen to me, and listen good!" she shouted, shocking me and making Ivy jerk. "I am not evil because I have a thousand years of demon smut on my soul!" she exclaimed, the tips of her hair trembling and her face flushed. "Every time you disturb reality, nature has to balance it out. The black on your soul isn't evil, it's a promise to make up for what you have done. It's a mark, not a death sentence. And you can get rid of it given time."

"Ceri, I'm sorry," I fumbled, but she wasn't listening.

"You're an ignorant, foolish, stupid witch," she berated, and I cringed, my grip tightening on the copper spell pot and feeling the anger from her like a whip. "Are you saying that because I carry the stink of demon magic, that I'm a bad person?"

"No . . ." I wedged in.

"That God will show no pity?" she said, green eyes flashing. "That because I made one mistake in fear that led to a thousand more, that I will burn in hell?"

"No. Ceri—" I took a step forward.

"My soul is black," she said, her fear showing in her suddenly pale cheeks. "I'll never be rid of it all before I die. I'll suffer for it, but it won't be because I'm a bad person but because I was a frightened one."

"That's why I don't want to do this," I pleaded.

She took a breath as if only now realizing she had been shouting. Closing her eyes, she seemed to steady herself. The anger had been reduced to a slow shimmer in the back of her green eyes when she opened them. Her usual mild countenance made it difficult to remember that she had once been royalty and accustomed to command.

Ivy took a wary sip of her coffee, her eyes never moving from Ceri. Kisten's shower went off, and the ensuing silence seemed loud.

"I'm sorry," Ceri said, head down, the sheet of her fair hair hiding her face. "I shouldn't have raised my voice."

I set the copper pot on the counter. "Don't worry about it," I said. "Like you said, I'm an ignorant witch."

Her smile was sour and showed a mild embarrassment. "No, you aren't. You can't know what you haven't been told." She ran her hands down her jeans, soothing herself. "Perhaps

I'm more concerned than I want to admit about the payment I carry," she admitted. "Seeing you worry about one or two curses when I have several million on my soul made me—" She flushed delicately, and I wondered if her ears were a tiny bit pointed. "I was most unfair to you."

Her voice had acquired a noble cadence. Behind me, I heard Ivy cross her legs at her knees. "Forget it," I said, feeling cold.

"Rachel." Ceri hid her hands' trembling by clasping them. "The blackness these two curses carry is so small compared to the benefits that will come from it: Jenks safely journeying to help his son, you using a demon curse to Were so as to retain the title of David's alpha that you deserve. It would be more of a crime to let these things remain undone or slip away than to willingly accept the price to have them."

She touched the pot of remaining brew, and I eyed it with a sick feeling. I was not going to ask Jenks to finish it.

"Everything of value or strength has a price," she continued. "To let Jax and Nick continue to suffer because you were afraid makes you look . . . unconscionably timid."

Cowardly might be a better word, I thought, looking at Jenks and feeling ill, knowing that I had a curse inside me just waiting to be put into play—and I had done it to myself.

"I'll take the black for my curse," Jenks said abruptly, his face hard with determination.

From the table came Matalina's tiny hiccup, and I saw fear in her childlike features. She loved Jenks more than life itself. "No," I said. "You've only got a few years left to get rid of it. And it's my idea, my spell. My curse. I'll take it."

Jenks flew up in my face, his wings red and his face severe. "Shut up!" he shouted, and I jerked back so I could focus on him. "He's my son! I take the curse. I pay the price."

There was the sound of my bathroom door opening, and Kisten ambled into the kitchen, his shirt rumpled and with a sly smile. His hair was slicked back and his damp stubbled face caught the sun. He looked great, and he knew it. But his confidence faltered when he saw Ivy unhappy at her computer, Jenks and Matalina clearly distressed, me undoubtedly looking scared with my hands wrapped around my middle, and of course Ceri's exasperated expression as she once again found herself trying to convince the plebeians that she knew what was best for them.

"What did I miss?" he asked, going to the coffeemaker and pouring what was left into one of my oversized mugs.

Ivy pushed her chair out and looked sullen. "They're demon curses. It's going to leave a mark on Rachel's soul. Jenks is having second thoughts."

"I am not!" the small pixy shouted. "But I'll kiss a fairy's ass before I let Rachel pay the price for my curse."

Kisten slowly tucked his shirttails in and sipped his coffee. His eyes went everywhere, and he breathed deeply, absorbing the scents of the room and using them to read the situation.

"Jenks," I protested, then made a sound of defeat when he flew to the last of the potion and drank it, his throat moving as he gulped it down. Matalina dropped to the table, her wings unmoving. She was a small spot of brightness, looking more alone than I'd ever seen her while she watched her husband put his life in jeopardy for my safety and that of their son.

The kitchen was silent but for the sound of his kids in the garden when he belligerently dropped his pixy-sized cup into the spell pot with a dull clang.

"I guess that's it, then," I said, gathering myself and leaning so I could glimpse the clock above the sink. I didn't like this. Not at all.

Looking as if she was desperately trying not to cry, Matalina rubbed her wings together to make a piercing whistle, which gave us all of three seconds before what looked like Jenks's entire family flowed into the kitchen from the hallway. The sharp scent of ashes came in with them, and I realized they had come in down the chimney. "Out!" Jenks shouted. "I said you could watch from the door!"

In a swirl of Disney nightmare, his brood settled on the

top of the door frame. Shrieks scraped the inside of my skull as they shoved each other, vying for the best vantage point. Ivy and Kisten cringed visibly, and Jenks made another whistle of admonishment. They obediently settled, whispering at my threshold of hearing. Ivy swore under her breath, her face taking on a dark cast. His tall stature graceful, Kisten crossed the kitchen to stand beside her, pouring half his coffee into her mug to try to pacify her. She wasn't at her best until at least sundown.

"Okay, Jenks," I said, thinking that willfully twisting a demon curse was spectacularly stupid and that I'd never hear the end of it if it killed me. What would my mother say? "Ready?"

The pixies lining the door frame squealed, and Matalina flitted to him, her pretty face pale. "Be careful, love," she whispered, and I looked away when they exchanged a last embrace, the two of them rising slowly in a cloud of gold sparkles before they parted. She went to the sill, wings moving fitfully to make glittering flashes of light. This was all but killing her, and I felt guilty even though it was probably the best way to ensure his safety.

Standing beside Matalina in the sun, Ceri nodded confidently. Kisten put a supportive hand atop Ivy's shoulder. Taking a breath, I went to the table, nervously settling myself at my usual spot and pulling the demon book of spells onto my lap. It was heavy, and my blood hummed in my legs, almost as if it was trying to reach the pages. *Oh, there's a nice thought.*

"What's going to happen?" Jenks asked, fidgeting as he landed on the center counter, and I turned sideways in the chair so I could see him.

I licked my lips and looked at the print. It was in Latin, but Ceri and I had gone over it while eating pizza before I fell asleep.

"The Demon Magic for Idiots version, please," he added, and a thin smile crossed me.

"I tap a line and say the words of invocation," I said. "To shift you back, I say it again. Same as with the Wereing charm."

"That's it?"

His eyes were wide, and Ceri sniffed. "You did want the short version," she said, moving everything off the island counter and to the sink. "I did a horrendous amount of prep work to make it that easy, Master Pixy."

His wings drooped. "Sorry."

Ivy held her arms close to her and frowned, her aggression clearly misplaced worry. "Can we get on with this?" she asked, and I dropped my head to the print again.

Exhaling, I stretched my awareness past the clapboard walls of the kitchen, past the flower beds already feeling the light presence of pixies, to the small underused ley line running through the graveyard. Touching it with a finger of thought, I stifled a tremor at the jolt of connection. It used to be that the flow of force into me had been slow and sedate. Not anymore.

The surge of energy coursed through me, backwashing through me in an uncomfortable sensation. It settled into my chi with the warmth and satisfaction of hot chocolate. I could pull out more and spindle it in my head to use later, but I didn't need it, so I let the heavy, resonating wash of energy find its way out of me and back into the line. I was a net through which the ley line ran, flowing free but for what I pulled out.

It all happened in the time between one heartbeat and the next, and I lifted my head, my eyes closed. My hair was moving in the wind that always seemed to be blowing in the ever-after, and I ran a hand over my loose curls to tame them. I thanked God that it was daylight and I couldn't see even a shadow of the ever-after unless I stood right in a line. Which I wasn't.

"I hate it when she taps a line," Ivy whispered to Kisten in the corner. "You ever see anything freakier than that?"

"You should see the face she makes when she—"

"Shut up, Kist!" I exclaimed, my eyes flashing open to find him grinning at me.

Standing with her teacup perched in her fingers and the sun streaming in around her, Ceri was trying to keep a scholarly air about her, but the snicker on her face ruined it.

"Is it going to hurt?" Jenks asked, gold pixy dust sifting from him in a steady stream.

I thought back to the gut-wrenching pain when I had turned into a mink and cringed. "Close your eyes and count down from ten," I said. "I'll hit you with it when you get to zero."

He took a breath, dark lashes fluttering against his cheeks. His wings slowly stilled until he came to a rest on top of the cleared island counter. "Ten . . . nine . . ." he said, his voice steady.

Setting the book on the table, I stood. Light and unreal from the line running through me, I reached out and put a hand over him. My knees were shaking, and I hoped that no one saw it. *Demon magic. God save me.* I took another breath. *"Non sum qualis eram,"* I said.

"Eight—"

Ivy gasped, and I staggered when Jenks was encased in the swirl of gold ever-after that had dropped from my hand to encompass him.

"Jenks!" Matalina cried, flying up into the utensils.

My breath was crushed out of me. Stumbling, I put a hand behind me, searching for support. I gasped when a torrent of line energy slammed into me, and I shoved the helping hands away. My head seemed to expand, and I cried out when the line exploded out of me and hit Jenks with a crack that had to be audible.

I fell, finding myself on the kitchen floor with Ivy's arms under my shoulders as she eased me down. I couldn't breathe. As I struggled to remember how to make my lungs work, I heard a crash in the hanging utensils, followed by a groan and a thump.

"Sweet mother of Tink," a new, lightly masculine voice

said. "I'm dying. I'm dying. Matalina! My heart isn't beating!"

I took a clean breath, then another, propped up in Ivy's grip. I was hot, then cold. And I couldn't see clearly. Looking up past the edge of the counter, I found Kisten beside Ceri, frozen as if unable to decide what to do. I pushed Ivy's hand off me and sat up when I realized what had laid me out. It wasn't the force of the line I had channeled but the shit-load of intent-to-pay-back that I had just laid on my soul. I had it, not Jenks, and it was going to stay that way.

Heart pounding, I got to my feet, my mouth dropping open when I saw Jenks on the counter. "Oh—my—God . . ." I whispered.

Jenks turned to me, his eyes wide and frightened. Angular face pinched, he looked at the ceiling, chest heaving as he hyperventilated. Ceri was at the sink, beaming. Beside me, Ivy stared, shocked. Kisten wasn't much better. Matalina was in tears, and pixy children were flying around. Someone got tangled in my hair, pulling me back to reality.

"Anyone younger than fifteen—out of the kitchen!" I shouted. "Someone get me a paper bag. Ivy, go get a towel for Jenks. You think you'd never seen a naked man before."

Ivy jerked into motion. "Not one sitting on my counter," she muttered, walking out.

Jenks's eyes were wide in panic as I snatched the bag Kisten handed me. Shaking it open, I puffed into it. "Here," I said. "Breath into this."

"Rache?" he gasped, his face pale and his shoulder cold when I touched him. He flinched, then let me hold the bag to his face. "My heart," he said, his words muffled around the bag. "Something's wrong! Rache, turn me back! I'm dying!"

Smiling, I held the bag to him as he sat on my counter, stark naked and hyperventilating. "That's how slow it beats," I said. "And you don't have to breathe so fast. Slow down," I soothed. "Close your eyes. Take a breath. Count to three. Let it out. Count to four."

"Shove it up your ass," he said, hunching into himself and

starting to shake. "The last time you told me to close my eyes and count from ten, look what happened to me."

Ivy returned, draping the first towel over his lap and the second over his shoulders. He was calming down, his eyes roving over the kitchen, darting from the ceiling to the open archway. His breath caught when he saw the garden through the window. "Holy crap," he whispered, and I pulled the bag away. He might not look like Jenks, but he sounded like him.

"Better?" I said, taking a step back.

His head bobbed, and as he sat on the counter and concentrated on breathing, we stood with our mouths hanging open, taking in a six-foot pixy. In a word, he was . . . damn!

Jenks had said he was eighteen, and he looked it. A very athletic eighteen, with wide innocent eyes, a smooth young face, and a blond shock of curly hair all tousled and needing to be arranged. His wings were gone, leaving only wide shoulders and the lean muscles that had once supported them. He had a trim waist, and his feet dangling to the floor were long and narrow. They were perfectly shaped, and my eyebrows rose; I'd seen his feet before, and one had been terribly misshapen.

I silently cataloged the rest of him, realizing all his scars were gone, even the one he'd gotten from fairy steel. His incredibly defined abs were smooth and perfect, making him utterly lanky with the clean smoothness of late adolescence. Every part of him was lean with a long strength. There wasn't a fleck of hair on him anywhere but for his eyebrows and atop his head. I knew. I had looked.

His gaze met mine from under his mussed bangs, and I blinked, taken by them. Ceri had green eyes, but Jenks's were shockingly green, like new leaves. They were narrowed with anxiety, but even the fading fear couldn't hide his youth. Sure, he had a wife and fifty-four kids, but he looked like a college freshman. A yummy college freshman majoring in oh-my-God-I-gotta-get-me-some-of-that.

Jenks rubbed his head where he had hit the overhanging rack. "Matalina?" he said, the cadence of his voice familiar but the sound of it odd. "Oh, Matalina," he breathed when she dropped to land on his shaking hand, "you're beautiful. . . ."

"Jenks," she said, hiccuping. "I'm so proud of you. I—"

"Shhhh," he said, his face twisting in heartache when he found himself unable to touch her. "Please don't cry, Mattie. It's going to be okay. I promise."

My eyes warmed with unshed tears as she played with the folds of her dress. "I'm sorry. I promised myself I wasn't going to cry. I don't want you to see me cry!"

She darted up, zipping out into the hall. Jenks made a move to follow, probably forgetting he didn't have wings anymore. He leaned forward and fell to the floor, face first.

"Jenks!" I shouted when he hit with a dull smack and started swearing.

"Le'go! Let go of me!" he exclaimed, slapping at me as he wedged his legs under him, only to fall back down. His towel fell away, and he struggled to hold it in place and stand up all at the same time. "Damn it all to hell! Why can't I balance right?" His face went ashen and he quit struggling. "Crap, I gotta pee again."

I looked pleadingly at Kisten. The living vamp swung into motion, easily dodging Jenks's flailing arms and hoisting him up off the floor by his shoulders. Jenks was taller by four inches, but Kisten had done bouncer work at his club. "Come on, Jenks," he said, moving him into the hallway. "I've got some clothes you can put on. Falling down is a lot more comfortable when you have something between your ass and the carpet."

"Matalina?" Jenks called in panic from the hall, protesting as Kisten manhandled him to my bathroom. "Hey, I can walk. I just forgot I didn't have wings. Le'me go. I can do this."

I jumped at the sound of Kisten shutting the bathroom door.

"Nice ass, Jenks," Ivy said into the new silence. Shaking her head, she picked up the second towel Jenks had left behind, folding it as if needing to give herself something to do.

My breath came from me in a long exhalation. "That,"

I said to Ceri, "has got to be the most fantastic charm I've ever seen."

Ceri beamed, and I realized she'd been worried, waiting for my approval. "Curse," she said, her eyes on her teacup as she blushed. "Thank you," she added modestly. "I wrote it down in the back with all the supplemental curses worked in on the chance you'd want to use it again. The countercurse is included, just as it's supposed to be. All you have to do is tap a line and say the words."

Countercurse, I thought morosely, wondering if that meant more black on my soul or if I had taken it all already. "Um, thanks, Ceri. You're incredible. I'll never be able to do a charm that complex. Thank you."

She stood in front of the window and sipped her tea, looking pleased. "You returned me my soul, Rachel Mariana Morgan. Making your life easier is a small thing."

Ivy made a rude sound and dropped the folded towel on the table. She didn't seem to know what to do next. *My soul. My poor, tarnished, blackening soul.*

My mouth went dry as the enormity of what I had done fell on me. Shit. I was playing with the black arts. No, not the black arts—which you could go to jail for—but demonic arts. They didn't even have laws for people practicing demonic arts. I felt cold, then hot. Not only had I just put a bunch of black on my soul, but I had called it a good thing, not bad.

Oh God, I was going to be sick.

"Rachel?"

I sank down into my chair feeling shaky. Ceri had her hand on my shoulder, but I hardly felt it. Ivy was shouting something, and Ceri was telling her to sit down and be still, that it was just the delayed shock of taking on so much reality imbalance and that I was going to be okay.

Okay? I thought, putting my head on the table before I fell over. *Maybe.* "Rhombus," I whispered, feeling the eye-blink-fast connection to the line and the protective circle rise around me. Ceri leapt forward, joining me before it finished forming. I had practiced this ley line charm for three months, and it was white magic, damn it, not black.

"Rachel!" Ivy cried as the shimmering band of ever-after wavered into existence between us. I pulled my head up, determined not to spew. I wanted to see what I had done to my soul, and though I couldn't see my aura, I could see a reflection of the damage in the shimmering band of ever-after.

"God help me," I whispered, feeling my face go cold.

"Rachel, it's all right." Ceri was crouched before me, her hand gripping mine, trying to get me to look at her. "You're seeing an artificially inflated shade. It hasn't had a chance to soak in yet. It really isn't that bad."

"Soak in?" I said, my voice cracking. "I don't want it to soak in!" My aura had turned the usually red sheen of ever-after to black. Hidden in it was a shimmer of gold from my aura, looking like an aged patina. I swallowed hard. *I would not spew. I would not spew.*

"It will get better. I promise."

I met her eyes, the panic subsiding. It would get better. Ceri said so; I had to believe her.

"Rachel!" Ivy cried, standing helplessly outside the circle. "Take this down!"

My head hurt and I couldn't get enough air. "Sorry," I breathed, breaking my link with the line. The sheet of ever-after flickered and vanished, and I felt a surge through me when I emptied my chi. I didn't want anything extra in me right now. I was too full of blackness.

Looking embarrassed, Ivy forced the tension from her shoulders. She blinked several times, trying to recapture her usual placid calmness, when I knew what she wanted to do was give me a slap and tell me I was being stupid or give me a hug and tell me it was going to be okay. But she couldn't do either, so she just stood there, looking miserable.

"I gotta go," I said abruptly, surging to my feet.

Ceri gracefully stood and got out of my way, but Ivy reached for me. "Rachel, wait," she protested, and I hesitated, vision swimming as she gripped my elbow.

I couldn't stay there. I felt like a leper in a house of innocents, a pariah among nobles. I was covered in blackness, and this time it was all mine. "Jenks!" I shouted, yanking out of Ivy's grip and heading for my room. "Let's go!"

"Rachel, what are you doing?"

I went to my room, scuffed my shoes on, grabbed my bag, and pushed past her and into the hall. "Exactly what I had planned," I said, ignoring her, pacing far too close behind me.

"You haven't had anything to eat," she said. "You're still reeling from invoking that . . . spell. It won't kill you to sit down and have a cup of coffee."

There was a thump from my bathroom followed by Kisten's muffled exclamation. The door crashed open, and I stopped. Kisten was leaning against the washer, face contorted in pain as he tried to catch his breath. Jenks was holding the door frame, looking casual in Kisten's gray and black sweats, but his green eyes were stressed. "Sorry," he said, sounding as if he meant it. "I, uh, slipped." He ran his eyes up and down my haggard appearance. "Ready to go?"

I could feel Ivy behind me. "Here," I said, extending my suitcase. "Make yourself useful and get this in the van."

He blinked, then grinned to show even, very white teeth. "Yeah. I can carry that."

I handed it over, and Jenks stumbled at the weight. His head thunked into the wall of the narrow hallway. "Bloody hell!" he exclaimed, crashing into the opposite wall when he overcompensated. "I'm all right!" he said quickly, waving off any help. "I'm all right. Sweet mother of Tink, the damn walls are so close! It's like walking in a freaking anthill."

I watched to make sure he was going to be okay, reaching out when he started weaving once he lost the guidance of the walls and was in the open space of the sanctuary. His kids were with him, adding to the noise as they shouted encouragement and advice. Hoping he took the time to walk down the steps instead of trying to jump them, I headed for the kitchen. Ivy was hot on my heels, Kisten close behind, quiet and pensive.

"Rachel," Ivy said, and I stood in my kitchen and stared at

Ceri, trying to remember why I had come in there. "I'm going with you."

"No, you aren't." *Oh yeah. My stuff.* I grabbed my shoulder bag, with its usual charms, then opened the pantry for one of the canvas carry bags Ivy used when she went shopping. "If you leave, Piscary will slip into your head."

"Kisten, then," she said, desperation creeping into her gray-silk voice. "You can't go alone."

"I'm not going alone. Jenks is with me."

I jammed the three demon books into the bag, then bent to get my splat gun from under the counter where I kept it at crawling height. I didn't know what I would need, but if I was going to use demon magic, I was going to use demon magic. My chest clenched and I held my breath to keep the tears from starting. *What in hell was wrong with me?*

"Jenks can hardly stand up!" Ivy said as I ran a hand through my charm cupboard and scooped them all into my shoulder bag.

Pain amulets, generic disguise charms . . . Yeah, those would be good. I pulled myself to a stop, heart pounding as I looked at her distress.

"You're not feeling right," Ivy said. "I'm not letting you walk out of here alone."

"I'm fine!" I said, trembling. "And I'm not alone. Jenks is with me!" My voice rose, and Kisten's eyes went round. "Jenks is all the backup I need. He is all the backup I *ever* needed. The only time I screw up royally is when he's not with me. And you have no right to question his competency!"

Ivy's mouth snapped shut. "That not what I meant," she said, and I pushed past her and into the hall. I almost ran Jenks down, and realized that he'd heard the whole thing.

"I can carry that," he said softly, and I handed the bag of demon texts to him. His balance bobbled, but his head didn't hit the wall like last time. He headed down the dark hall, limping.

Breath fast, I walked into Ivy's room, kneeling on the floor by her bed and pulling her sword out from where I'd seen her tuck it once. "Rachel," she protested from the hallway as

I straightened up, gripping the wickedly sharp katana safe in its sheath.

"Can I take this?" I asked shortly, and she nodded. "Thanks." Jenks needed a sword. So he couldn't walk without running into things. He'd get better, and then he'd need a sword.

Kisten and Ivy trailed behind me as I slung the sword over my shoulder to hang with my bag and stomped down the hall. I had to be angry. If I wasn't angry, I was going to fall apart. My soul was black. I was doing demon magic. I was turning into everything I feared and hated, and I was doing it to save someone who had lied and left me to make my partner's son a thief.

Leaning into my bathroom in passing, I snapped my vanity case shut. Jenks was going to need a toothbrush. Hell, he was going to need a wardrobe, but I had to get out of there. If I didn't keep moving, I was going to realize just how deep into the shit I had fallen.

"Rachel, wait," Ivy said after I reached the foyer, snatched my leather jacket from its hook, and opened the door. "Rachel, *stop!*"

I halted on the stoop, the spring breeze lifting my hair and the birds chirping, my bag and Ivy's sword hanging from my shoulder, my vanity case in one hand and my coat over an arm. At the curb, Jenks was fiddling with the van's sliding door, opening and closing it like a new toy. The sun glistened in his hair, and his kids flitted about his head. Heart pounding, I turned.

Framed in the open door, Ivy looked haunted, her usually placid face severe, with panic in her dilated eyes. "I bought a laptop for you," she said, her eyes dropping as she extended it.

Oh God, she had given me a piece of her security. "Thank you," I whispered, unable to breathe as I accepted it. It was in a leather case, and probably weighed all of three pounds.

"It's registered to you," she said, looking at it as I slung it over my free shoulder. "And I already added you onto my system, so all you have to do is plug in and click. I wrote down a list of local numbers for the cities you're going to be passing through to dial up with."

"Thank you," I whispered. *She had given me a piece of what made her life sane.* "Ivy, I'll be back." It was what Nick had said to me. But I'd come back. It wasn't a lie for me.

Impulsively I set my case on the stoop and leaned forward to give her a hug. She froze, and then hugged me back. The dusky scent of her filled my senses, and I stepped away.

Kisten waited quietly behind her. Only now, seeing Ivy standing there with one arm hanging down and the other clasped around her middle, did I understand what he'd been trying to tell me. She wasn't afraid for me, she was afraid for herself, that she might slip into old patterns without me there to remind her who she wanted to be. *Just how bad had it been?*

Ire flashed through me. Damn it, this wasn't fair. Yeah, I was her friend, but she could take care of herself! "Ivy," I said, "I don't want to go, but I have to."

"Then go!" she exploded, her perfect face creasing in anger and her eyes flashing to black. "I never asked you to stay!"

Motions stiff, she spun with a vamp quickness and yanked open the door to the church. It boomed shut behind her, and left me blinking. I looked at it, thinking that this wasn't good. No, she hadn't asked me, but Kisten had.

Kisten picked up my case, and together we went down the stairs, my laces flapping. Nearing the van, I awkwardly dug in my shoulder bag for the keys, then hesitated by the driver's side door when I remembered Kisten hadn't yet given them to me. They jingled as he held them out. From inside the van came the excited shrieks of pixies. "You'll keep an eye on her?" I asked him.

"Scout's honor." His blue eyes were pinched from more than the sun. "I'm taking some time off."

Jenks came from around the front of the van, silently taking my coat, vanity bag, and the sword—the last bringing a growl of anticipation from him. I waited until I heard the sliding door shut, then slumped at the sound of Jenks's passenger-side door closing.

"Kisten," I said, feeling a twinge of guilt. "She's a grown woman. Why are we treating her like an invalid?"

He reached out and took my shoulders. "Because she is. Because Piscary can drop into her mind and force her to do just about anything, and it kills a piece of her every time he does. Because he has filled her with his own blood lust, making her do things she doesn't want to do. Because she is trying to run his illegal businesses out of a sense of duty and maintain her share of your runner firm out of a sense of love."

"Yeah. That's what I thought." My lips pressed together and I straightened. "I never said I would stay in the church, much less Cincinnati. Keeping her together is not my job!"

"You're right," he said calmly, "but it happened."

"But it shouldn't have. Damn it, Kisten, all I wanted to do was help her!"

"You have," he said, kissing my forehead. "She'll be fine. But Ivy making you her lodestone wouldn't have evolved if you hadn't let it, and you know it."

My shoulders slumped. Swell, just what I needed: guilt. The breeze shifted his bangs, and I hesitated, looking at the oak door between Ivy and me. "How bad was it?" I whispered.

Kisten's face lost all emotion. "Piscary . . ." He exhaled. "Piscary worked her over so well those first few years that her parents sent her away for her last two years of high school, hoping he would lose interest. She came back even more confused, thanks to Skimmer." His eyes narrowed in an old anger, still potent. "That woman could have saved Ivy with her love, but she was so driven by the urge for better blood, hotter sex, that she sent Ivy deeper."

I felt cold, the breeze shifting my curls. I'd known this, but there was obviously more.

Seeing my unease, Kisten frowned. "When she returned, Piscary played on her new vulnerabilities, lapping up her misery when he rewarded her for behavior that went contrary to what she wanted to believe. Eventually she abandoned everything to keep from going insane, turning herself off and letting Piscary make her into whatever he wanted. She started hurting people she loved when they were at their most vulnerable, and when they abandoned her, she started enticing innocents."

Dropping his eyes, Kisten looked to his bare feet. I knew he was one of the people she had hurt, and I could tell he felt guilty for leaving her. "You couldn't do anything," I said, and his head jerked up, anger in his eyes.

"It was bad, Rachel," he said. "I should have done something. Instead, I turned my back on her and walked away. She won't tell me, but I think she killed people to satisfy her blood lust. God, I hope it was by accident."

I swallowed hard, but he wasn't done yet. "For years she ran rampant," he said, staring at the van but his eyes unfocused, as if looking into the past. "She was a living vampire functioning as an undead, walking under the sun as beautiful and seductive as death. Piscary made her that way, and her crimes were given amnesty. *The favored child.*"

He said the last with bitterness, and his gaze dropped to me. "I don't know what happened, but one day I found her on my kitchen floor, covered in blood and crying. I hadn't seen her in years, but I took her in. Piscary gave her some peace, and after a while she got better. I think it was so she wouldn't kill herself too soon for his liking. All I know is she found a way to deal with the blood lust, chaining it somehow by mixing it with love. And then she met you and found the strength to say no to it all."

Kisten looked at me, his hand touching my hair. "She likes herself now. You're right that she isn't going to throw it all away just because you aren't here. It's just . . ." He squinted, his gaze going distant again. "It was bad, Rachel. It got better. And when she met you, she found a core of strength that Piscary hadn't been able to warp. I just don't want to see it break."

I was shaking inside, and somehow my hands found his. "I'll be back."

He nodded, looking at my fingers within his. "I know."

I felt the need to move. I didn't care that it now came from the need to run from what I had just learned. My eyes dropped to the keys. "Thanks for letting me use your van."

"No biggie," he said, forcing a smile, but his eyes were worried, so terribly worried. "Just return it with a full tank of gas." He reached forward, and I leaned against him, breathing in his scent one last time. My head tilted and our lips met, but it was an empty kiss, my worry having pushed any passion out. *This was for Jenks, not Nick. I didn't owe Nick anything.*

"I slipped something in your suitcase for you," Kisten said, and I pulled away.

"What is it?" I asked, but he didn't answer, giving me a smile before he reluctantly stepped back. His hand trailed down my arm and slipped away.

"Good-bye, Kist," I whispered. "It's only for a few days."

He nodded. " 'Bye, love. Take care of yourself."

"You too."

Bare feet soundless, he turned and went back into the church. The door creaked shut, and he was gone.

Feeling numb, I turned and yanked open my door. Jenks's kids flowed out of his open window, and I got in, slamming the door behind me. The laptop slipped under the seat with my bag, and I jammed the keys into the ignition. The big engine turned over and settled into a slow, even rumble. Only now did I look across to Jenks, surprised again at seeing him there, sitting beside me in Kisten's sweats and his shockingly yellow hair. *This was really weird.*

His seat belt was on, and his hands dropped from where he'd been fiddling with the visor. "You look small," he finally said, looking both innocent and wise.

A smile quirked the corner of my lips. Shifting into gear, I accelerated down the street.

Eight

"**F**or the love of Tink," Jenks muttered, angling another one of the Cheetos into his mouth. He meticulously chewed and swallowed, adding, "Her hair looks like a dandelion. You think someone would have told her. There's enough there to make a quilt out of."

My gaze was fixed on the car ahead of us, going an aggravating fifty-six miles an hour on the two-lane, double-yellow-lined road. The woman in question had white hair frizzed out worse than mine. He was right. "Jenks," I said, "you're getting crumbs all over Kisten's van."

The crackle of cellophane was faint over the music—happy, happy music that didn't fit my mood at all. "Sorry," he said, rolling the bag down and shoving it in the back. Licking the orange from his fingers, he started messing with Kist's CDs. *Again.* Then he'd fiddle with the glove box, or spend five minutes getting his window at ju-u-u-u-ust the right height, or fuss with his seat belt, or any of the half a dozen things he'd been doing since getting in the van, all the while making a soft commentary that I think he didn't know I could hear. It had been a long day.

I sighed, adjusting my grip on the wheel. We had been off the interstate for the last 150 miles or so, taking a two-lane road instead of the interstate up to Mackinaw. The pine forest pressed close on either side, making the sun an occasional flash. It was nearing the horizon, and the wind coming in my window was chill, carrying the scent of earth and growing things. It soothed me where the music couldn't.

The National Forestry sign caught my eye, and I smoothly braked. I had to get out from behind this woman. And if I heard that song one more time, I was going to jam Daddy's T-Bird down Jenks's throat. Not to mention "Mr. Bladder the size of a walnut" might need to use the can again, which was why we were on the back roads instead of the faster interstate. Jenks got frantic if he couldn't pee when he wanted to.

He looked up from rifling through the glove box as I slowed to bump over the wooden bridge spanning a drainage ditch. He'd been through it three times, but who knows? Maybe something had changed since the last time he had arranged the old napkins, registration, insurance, and the broken pencil. I had to remind myself that he was a pixy, not a human, despite what he looked like, and therefore had a pixy's curiosity.

"A rest stop?" he questioned, his green eyes innocently wide. "What for?"

I didn't look at him, pulling in between two faded white lines and shifting into park. Lake Huron lay before us, but I was too tired to enjoy it. "To rest." The music cut off with the engine. Reaching under the seat, my healing knuckles grazed my new laptop when I shifted the seat rearward. Closing my eyes, I took a slow breath and leaned back, my hands still on the wheel. *Please get out and take a walk, Jenks.*

Jenks was silent. There was the crackle of cellophane as he gathered up the trash. The man never stopped eating. I was going to introduce him to a mighty burger tonight. Maybe three-quarters of a pound of meat would slow him down.

"You want me to drive?" he asked, and I cracked an eyelid, looking askance at him.

Oh, there's a good idea. If we were stopped, it'd be me getting the points, not him. "Nah," I said, my hands falling from the wheel and into my lap. "We're almost there, I just need to move around a little."

With a wisdom far beyond his apparent age, Jenks ran his eyes over me. His shoulders slumped, and I wondered if he knew he was getting on my nerves. Maybe there was a reason pixies were only four inches tall. "Me too," he said meekly, opening his door to let in a gust of sunset-cooled wind smelling of pine and water. "Do you have any change for the machine?"

Relieved, I tugged my bag onto my lap and handed him a fiver. I'd have given him more, but he had nowhere to put it. He needed a wallet. And a pair of pants to put it in. I had hustled him out of the church so fast that all he had was his phone, clipped proudly to his elastic waistband, which had since been depressingly silent. We'd been hoping Jax would call again, but no such luck.

"Thanks," he said, getting out and tripping on the flip-flops I'd bought him at the first gas station we stopped at. The van shifted when he shut the door, and he made his way to a rusted trash can set about fifty feet from the parking lot, chained to a tree. His balance was markedly better, with only the usual trouble most people had walking with slabs of orange plastic attached to their feet.

He dumped the trash and headed for a tree, an alarming intentness to his pace. I took a breath to call out, and he jerked to a stop. Slumped, he scanned the park, making his way to a clapboard restroom instead. Such were the trials in a day of the life of a six-foot-four pixy.

I sighed, watching him slow at the bed of straggly daylilies to talk to the pixies. They buzzed about him in a swirl of gold and silver sparkles, coming from all over the park like fireflies on a mission. Within moments a cloud of glowing dust hovered over him in the darkening air.

I turned at the hush of a car pulling in a few slots down. Three boys like stair steps exploded out, arguing about who switched whose dead batteries in their handheld games. Mom said nothing, wearily popping the trunk and settling it all with a twelve-pack of double A's. Money was offered by Dad, and the three ran to the vending machines under a rustic shelter, shoving each other to get there first. Jenks caught the smallest before he fell into the flowers. I had a feeling

Jenks was more worried about the plants than the boy. I smiled when the couple leaned against the car and watched them, exhaling loudly. I knew the feeling.

My smile slowly faded into melancholy. I had always planned on children, but with a hundred years of fertility facing me, I was in no hurry. My thoughts drifted to Kisten, and I pulled my eyes from the boys at the vending machines.

Witches married outside their species all the time, especially before the Turn. There were perfectly acceptable options: adoption, artificial insemination, borrowing your best friend's boyfriend for a night. Issues of what was morally right and wrong tended not to matter when you found yourself in love with a man you couldn't tell you weren't human. It sort of went with the whole hiding-among-humans-for-the-last-five-thousand-years thing. We weren't hiding now, but why limit oneself simply because there wasn't a safety issue anymore? It was way too soon for me to think about kids, but with Kisten, any children would have to be engendered by someone else.

Frustrated, I got out of the van, my body aching from my first day without a pain amulet since my beating. The couple drifted away, talking between themselves. *There wouldn't be any children with Nick either,* I reminded myself, *so it isn't like this is anything new.*

Painfully stretching to touch my toes, I froze, realizing I had put him in present tense. Damn. This was not a choice between them. *Oh God,* I thought. *Tell me I'm only doing this to help Jenks. That nothing is left in me to rekindle.* But the wedge of doubt wiggled itself between me and my logic, settling in to make me feel stupid.

Angry with myself, I did a few more stretches, and then, wondering if the black on my aura had soaked in, I tapped a line and set a circle. My lips curled in revulsion. The shimmering sheet of energy rose black and ugly, the reddish light of sunset coming in from around the trees adding an ominous cast to the black sheen. The gold tint of my aura was entirely lost. Disgusted, I dropped the line, and the circle vanished, leaving me depressed. Even better, Mom and Dad Cleaver called to their kids and, with an unusual hushed haste at their loud questions, jammed everyone into the car to drive away with a little squeak of tire on pavement.

"Yeah," I muttered, watching their brake lights flash red as they settled into traffic. "Run from the black witch." I felt like a leper, and leaned against the warm van and crossed my arms over my chest, remembering why my folks always took us to big cities or places like Disney World on vacation. Small towns generally didn't have much of an Inderland population, and those who did live in them usually played their differences down. Way down.

The *snick-slap-snick* of Jenks's flip-flops grew louder as he returned down the cracked sidewalk, the swirl of pixies dropping back one by one until he was alone. Behind him were the outlines of two islands, both so big they looked like the opposite shore. Far off to the left was the bridge that had clued me in that this was where Jax was. It was starting to glitter in the dimming light as night fell. The bridge was huge, even from this distance.

"They haven't seen Jax," Jenks said, handing me a candy bar. "But they promise to take him in if they do."

My eyes widened. "Really?" Pixies were very territorial, even among themselves, so the offer was somewhat of a shock.

He nodded, the half smile glimmering under his mop of hair turning him guileless. "I think I impressed them."

"Jenks, king of the pixies," I said, and he laughed. The wonderful sound struck through me, lifting my spirits. It slowly died to leave an unhappy silence. "We'll find him, Jenks," I said, touching his shoulder. He jumped, then flashed me a nervous smile. My hand fell away, and I remembered his anger at me for having lied to him. No wonder he didn't want me to touch him. "I'm sure they're in Mackinaw," I added, miserable.

His back to the water and his face empty of emotion, Jenks watched the sporadic traffic.

"Where else could they be?" I tore open my candy bar

and took a bite of caramel and chocolate, more for something to do than hunger. The van was radiating heat, and it felt good to lean against the side of the engine. "Jax said they were in Michigan," I said, chewing. "Big green bridge held up by cables. Lots of fresh water. Fudge. Putt-putt golf. We'll find him."

Pain, hard and deep, crossed Jenks's face. "Jax was the first child Mattie and I were able to keep alive through the winter," he whispered, and the sweetness left the wad of sugar and nuts in my mouth. "He was so small, I held him in my hands to keep him warm for four months while I slept. I've got to find him, Rache."

Oh God, I thought as I swallowed, wondering if I had ever loved anyone that deeply. "We'll find him," I said. Feeling totally inadequate, I reached to touch him, pulling away at the last moment. He realized it, and the silence grew uncomfortable.

"Ready to go?" I said, folding the wrapper over the rest of the candy and reaching for the door handle. "We're almost there. We'll get a room, grab something to eat, and then I'm taking you shopping."

"Shopping?" His thin eyebrows rose, and he walked to the front of the van.

Our doors shut simultaneously, and I buckled myself in, refreshed, and my resolve strengthened. "You don't think I'm going to be seen with a six-foot piece of dessert dressed in a nasty pair of sweats, do you?"

Jenks brushed the hair from his eyes, his angular face showing a surprising amount of sly amusement. "Some underwear would be nice."

Snorting, I started the van and put it into reverse, snapping off the CD player before it started up again. "Sorry about that. I had to get out of there."

"Me too," he said, surprising me. "And I wasn't about to wear any of Kisten's. The guy is nice and all, but he stinks." He hesitated, plucking at his collar. "Hey, uh, thanks for what you said back there."

My brow furrowed. Checking both ways, I pulled onto the road. "At the rest stop?"

Sheepish, he shifted his shoulders in embarrassment. "No, in the kitchen about me being the only backup you ever needed."

"Oh." I warmed, keeping my eyes on the car ahead of us, a black, salt-rusted Corvette that reminded me of Kisten's other vehicle. "I meant it, Jenks. I missed you the past five months. And if you don't come back to the firm, I swear I'm going to leave you like this."

His panicked expression eased when he saw I was joking. "For the love of Tink, don't you dare," he muttered. "I can't even pix anyone. I sweat now instead of dusting, did you know that? I've got water coming off me instead of dust. What the hell can I do with sweat? Rub up against someone and make them puke in disgust? I've seen you sweat, and it's not pretty. I don't even want to think about sex, two sweaty bodies pressed against each other like that? Disgusting. Talk about birth control—it's no wonder you only have a handful of kids."

He shuddered and I smiled. *Same old Jenks.*

I couldn't keep myself from stiffening when he began rummaging in the music, and apparently sensing it, he stopped, putting his hands in his lap to stare out the front window at the darkening sky. We had come out of the woods and were starting to see homes and businesses strung out along the road in a thin strip. Behind them was the flat blue of the lake, gray in the fading light.

"Rachel," he said, his voice soft with regret. "I don't know if I can come back."

Alarmed, I looked at him, then the road, then at him again. "What do you mean you don't know. If it's about Trent—"

He held up a hand, his brow pinched. "It's not Trent. I figured out he's an elf after helping Ceri last night."

I jerked and the van crossed the yellow line. A horn blew, and I yanked the wheel back. "You figured it out?" I stammered, feeling my heart pound. "Jenks, I wanted to tell you. Really. But I was afraid you would blab, and—"

"I'm not going to tell anyone," he said, and I could see it was killing him. It would have brought him a huge amount of prestige in the pixy world. "If I do, then it means you were right in not telling me, and you weren't."

His voice was hard, and I felt a stab of guilt. "Then why?" I asked, wishing he had brought this up when we were parked, not when I was trying to navigate the outskirts of an unfamiliar town, bright with neon lights.

For a moment he was silent, his young face pensive as he put his thoughts in order. "I'm eighteen," he finally said. "Do you know how old that is for a pixy? I'm slowing down. You nicked me last fall. Ivy can snag me whenever she wants."

"Ivy's got Piscary's undead reactions," I said, scared. "And I was lucky. Jenks, you look great. You aren't old."

"Rachel . . ." he said around a sigh. "My kids are moving out to make their own lives. The garden is starting to go empty. I'm not complaining," he rushed on. "The wish for sterility I got from you is a blessing, since the last three years of children in a pixy's life have a very low life expectancy and it would kill Matalina knowing she was having children that wouldn't live a week past her. Little Josephina . . . she's flying now. She's going to make it."

His voice cut off, cracking, and my throat tightened.

"Between that wish and the garden," he continued, staring out the front window, "I'm not worried about any of my children surviving past Matalina and me, and I thank you for that."

"Jenks—" I started, wanting him to stop.

"Shut up," he said hotly, his smooth cheeks reddening. "I don't want your pity." Clearly angry, he put a hand on the open windowsill. "It's my own fault. It never bothered me until I got to know you and Ivy. I'm old. I don't care what I look like, and I'm mad as all hell that you two are going to have your damn runner business from now until forever and I'm not going to be a part of it. That's why I didn't come back. Not because you didn't tell me what Trent was."

I didn't say anything, gritting my jaw and miserable. I hadn't known he was that old. Signaling, I made a right turn to follow the strip along the water's edge. Ahead of us was the huge bridge connecting the upper peninsula of Michigan with the lower, all lit up and sparkling.

"You can't let that stop you from coming back," I said hesitantly. "I do demon magic and Ivy is Piscary's scion." Turning the wheel, I pulled into a two-story motel, an outside pool snuggled up in the el the rooms made. I stopped under the faded red and white striped canopy, watching the kids in swimsuits and plastic arm-cuffs run in front of the van, confident I wouldn't hit them. The mother trailing behind them gave me a grateful wave. I thought they must be either insane or Weres since it was only sixty out. "Any of us could die tomorrow," I finished.

He looked at me, the lines of anger smoothing out. "You won't die tomorrow," he said.

Putting the van into park, I turned to him. "How do you figure that?"

Jenks undid his belt and gave me a sideways smile that rivaled Kisten's for mischief. "Because I'm with you."

A groan slipped from me. I had walked right into that one.

Smiling, he got out, glancing up at the first stars, almost unseen behind the town's lights. Stiff from the long ride, I followed him into the tiny office. It was empty but for an astounding display of knickknacks and pamphlets. Hands out, Jenks headed for the shelves of miniatures like a starving man, his pixy curiosity and need to touch making the display irresistible. The door shut behind us, and seeing him lost in the throes of pixy bliss, I punched him in the arm.

"Ow!" he exclaimed, holding it and giving me an injured look. "What was that for?"

"You know why," I said dryly, finding a smile as I turned to the casually dressed woman who came in from a back room through an open archway. I could hear a TV in the background, and smell someone's lunch. Or dinner, rather, seeing as she was human.

She blinked as she took us in. "Can I help you?" she asked, becoming hesitant when she realized we were Inderlanders. Mackinaw was a tourist town, and probably not big enough to draw a huge resident Inderland crowd.

"Yes, a room for two, please," I said, reaching for the registration card and pen. A frown came over me at the form. *Well, we could go under my name,* I thought, writing Ms. Rachel Morgan in my big loopy script. The clicks of the ceramic and pewter figurines being picked up and set down were audible, and the woman behind the counter winced, watching him over my shoulder. "Jenks, could you get the plate number for me?" I asked, and he slipped out, the seashell door chime clunking roughly.

"That will be two twenty," she said stiffly.

Great, I thought. *Cheap, cheap, cheap. You gotta love small towns in the off-season.* "We're only staying the night, not the week," I said, putting down the church's address.

"That *is* the nightly rate," she said, her voice tartly smug.

My head came up. "Two hundred twenty dollars? It's the off-season," I said, and she shrugged. Shocked, I thought for a moment. "Can I get a discount for Were Insurance?"

Her eyes were mocking. "We only offer discounts for AAA."

My lips pressed together and I went warm. Slowly I curled my hand up and brought it below the level of the high partition, hiding my bandaged knuckles. *Crap, crap, crap. You gotta love those small-town mentalities.* She had upped the rates for us, hoping we'd go somewhere else.

"Cash," she added smugly. "We don't take plastic or personal checks."

The chipped sign behind her said they did, but I wasn't going to walk out of there. I had my pride, and money was nothing compared to that. "Do you have one with a kitchen?" I asked, shaking inside. *Two hundred and twenty dollars would really take a chunk out of my cash.*

"That will be thirty extra," she said.

"Of course it will," I muttered. Angry, I jerked my bag

open and pulled out two hundreds and a fifty as Jenks came in. His eyes went from the money in my hand to the woman's satisfaction, and finally to my anger, figuring it out immediately. Hell, he had probably heard the entire conversation with his pixy hearing.

His gaze rose to the fake camera in the corner, then out the glass door to the parking lot. "Rache, I think we hit prime-time gold," he said, taking the pen chained to the desk and writing the plate number on the form. "Someone just peed *into* the pool, and I can smell shower mold from here. If we hurry, we can get a shot of the bridge at sunset for the opening credits."

The woman set a key on the counter, her motions suddenly hesitant.

Jenks flipped open his phone. "Do you still have the number for the county's health department from our last stop?"

I steeled my face into a bored countenance. "It's on my clipboard. But let's wait on the opening shot. We can do a sunrise frame. Tom had a cow the last time we burned film before he had a chance to canvas the local hot spots for the worst offenders."

The woman went ashen. I dropped the bills on the counter and took the worn key on its little plastic tag. My eyebrows rose; number thirteen, how apropos. "Thanks," I said.

Jenks jerked to get in front of me as I turned to leave. "Allow me, Ms. Morgan," he said, opening it gracefully, and I strode out the door, pride intact.

Somehow I managed to keep a straight face until the door clanked shut. Jenks snickered, and I lost it. "Thanks," I said between snorts. "God, I was ready to smack her a good one."

"No problem," Jenks said, scanning the rooms, his gaze settling on the last one tucked at the short end of the el. "Can I drive the van over there?"

I thought he more than deserved it, and I left him to work it out as I walked across the dark lot throwing up heat to the sounds of the kids splashing in the pool. The underwater lights had come on, and they reflected up against the open umbrellas to look inviting. If it hadn't been so cold, I'd have asked Jenks if pixies could swim. Finding out if my mental image of Jenks in a Speedo matched reality would be worth a few goose bumps.

The key stuck for a moment, but with a little wiggling it engaged and the door swung open. Out flowed the scent of citrus and clean linen.

Jenks pulled the van around to the empty spot before the door. The headlights fell into the room to show an ugly brown carpet and a yellow bedspread. Flicking on the light, I went in, heading for the pretend kitchen and the second door at the back. I set my bag on the bed, concerned when I realized the door led to the bathroom, not a second room.

Muttering about caves, Jenks came in with my suitcase, his eyes roving the low ceiling. He dropped my bag by the door, tossed me the keys to the van, and headed out, flicking the light switch several times because he could.

"Ah, Jenks," I called, fingers smarting from the keys. "We need a different room."

Jenks came in with my laptop and Ivy's sword, setting them on the round table under the front window. "How come? I was kidding about the shower mold." He took a deep breath, nose wrinkling. "That smells like . . . Well, it's not shower mold."

I didn't want to know what he was smelling, but when I silently pointed to the single bed, all he did was shrug, his lusciously green eyes innocent. Gesturing helplessly, I said, "One bed?"

"So?" Then he flushed, his eyes darting to the box of tissues on the bedside table. "Oh. Yeah. I won't fit in the Kleenex box anymore, will I?"

Not looking forward to talking to that lady, I headed for the door, snagging my shoulder bag in passing. "I'll get a new room. Do me a favor and don't use the bathroom. She'll probably charge us a cleaning fee."

"I'm coming with you," he said, falling into step with me.

The kids from the pool were making a quick, wet-footed

dash to their room, shivering under skimpy white towels when we crossed the parking lot. Jenks opened the office door for me, and the sound of seashells clunking mixed with the sound of a tearful argument when we entered. "You charged them the Fourth of July weekend rate?" I heard a man say, and her blubbering answer. I looked at Jenks in a mute question, and he cleared his throat loudly. Silence.

After a hushed conversation, a short, follicle-challenged man in a plaid shirt emerged, brushing his balding plate. "Yes?" he said with an artificially interested look. "What can I get for you? Extra towels for the pool?" From somewhere out of sight the woman made a hiccup of a sob, and he reddened.

"Actually," I said, putting the room key on the chest-high partition between us, "I'd like to see about getting a different room. We need two beds, not one. My fault for not making that clear." I smiled as if I hadn't heard anything.

The man's gaze went to Jenks, and he flushed deeper. "Ah, yes. Number thirteen, right?" he said, snatching it and giving me a new one.

Jenks headed for the knickknacks, but at my heavy sigh, he went to the pamphlets instead. Setting my bag on the counter, I smugly asked, "What's the price difference for that?"

"None," was his quick reply. "Same rate. Anything else I can do for you? Make reservations for you and the rest of your party, maybe?" He blinked, looking ill. "Will they be staying with us as well?"

Jenks turned to look out the glassed door, his hand to his smooth chin while he tried not to laugh. "No," I said lightly. "They called to tell us they found a place on the other side of town that filled up their pool with lake water. That wins out over moldy bathrooms any day."

The man's mouth worked but nothing came out.

Jenks jerked into motion, and I glanced behind me to see him hunched and gripping one of the pamphlets close to his face. "Thank you," I said, holding up the key and smiling.

"We may be staying a second night. Do you have any two-day specials?"

"Yes, ma'am," he said, eyes going relieved. "Second night is half price during the off-season. I'll put you down for it if you like." He glanced at his unseen wife through the archway.

"That sounds great," I said. "And a late checkout for Tuesday?"

"Late checkout on Tuesday," he said, scribbling something in his registration book. "No problem. We appreciate your business."

I nodded and smiled, touching Jenks's arm and pulling him out the door since he wasn't moving, fixed to the pamphlet in his grip. "Thanks," I called cheerfully. "Have a good night."

The door chimes thunked dully, and I exhaled into the cooler night air. The parking lot was silent but for the nearby traffic. Satisfied, I glanced at the key in the dim light under the canopy. Room eleven this time.

"Rache." Jenks shoved the pamphlet at me. "Here. He's here. I know it! Get in the van. They close in ten minutes!"

"Jenks!" I exclaimed when he grabbed my arm and pulled me stumbling across the lot. "Jenks, wait up! Jax? He's where?"

"There," he said, shaking the pamphlet in front of my face. "That's where I would go."

Bewildered, I peered at the colorful trifolded paper in the dim light of the streetlamp. My lips parted and I reached to dig my keys out while Jenks threw our stuff back into the van and slammed the motel door shut, shaking in impatience.

The Butterfly Shack. Of course.

Nine

Humming nervously, Jenks put the jar of honey in the basket with my bandages and the rest of his groceries. He fidgeted, and my eyebrows rose. "Honey, Jenks?" I questioned.

"It's medicinal," he said, reddening and turning to stand before the array of baking supplies, feet spread wide in his Peter Pan pose. Reaching to a top shelf, he dropped a jar of yeast in with the rest. "Bee pollen," he grumbled under his breath. "Where in Tink's bordello do they keep the vitamin supplements? Can't find a bloody thing in this store. Who laid it out? Gilligan?" His head rose and he scanned the signs hanging over the aisles.

"The vitamins would be with the medicines," I said, and he jerked.

Clearly shocked, he stammered, "You heard that?" and I shrugged. "Damn," he muttered, walking away. "I didn't know you could hear that well. You never heard me before."

I trailed behind him, arms empty. Jenks insisted on carrying everything, insisted on opening every door for me, hell, he'd flush my toilet if I let him. It wasn't a macho thing, it was because he could. Automatic doors were his favorites, and though he hadn't played with one yet by getting on and off the sensor pad, I knew he wanted to.

His pace was quick, his steps silent in the new boots I had bought him all of an hour ago. He wasn't happy about me insisting we go shopping before seeing if Jax was at The

Butterfly Shack, a butterfly exhibit and wildlife store, but he agreed that if Jax was there, he was hiding or he would have had the owner call us to come get him. We didn't know the situation, and if we knocked on the door and told the proprietor he had been harboring a pixy, one possibly wanted in connection with a theft, we might start a few tongues wagging.

So Jenks and I used the interim while the proprietor closed up shop and counted his money to do a little pre-break-in outfitting/shopping. I had been pleasantly surprised to find some upscale stores right beside the tourist-crap traps in an obviously new slab of light commercial buildings that had gone up in the last five years or so. The trees only had been in the ground that long. I was a witch; I could tell.

Since it was just before the tourist season, the selections were high and the prices were almost reasonable. That would change next week when school let out and the town tripled its population when the "fudgies"—tourists named after the candy Mackinaw was known for—descended on them.

Turns out, Jenks was a power shopper, which probably stemmed from his garden gathering background. In a very short time we had hit three clothes stores, a dance outlet, and a shoe mart. So now instead of a hunky young man in sweats and flip-flops, I was with a six-foot-four, athletic, angsty young man dressed in casual linen pants and matching fawn-colored shirt. Under it was a skintight two-piece suit of silk and spandex that had set us back a couple hundred dollars, but after seeing him in it, my head bobbed and my card came out. My treat.

I couldn't help but let my eyes ramble over him as he crouched before a display of vitamins and took off the shades I had bought him, not wanting a repeat of him grumbling over the sun all the way up there. Clearly bothered, he ran a hand under his cap in worry. The red leather should have clashed with what he had on, but on him? Yum.

Jenks looked really good, and I was wishing I had brought nicer clothes. And a camera. He was a hard man to keep up with once you got him out of sweats and flip-flops.

"Bee pollen," he said as he jiggled the sleeve of his new aviator jacket down and reached forward, blowing the dust from the lid of the glass jar. "This stuff tastes like it's already been through the bee," he said, rising to place it with the rest, "but seeing as the only flowers they have here are stale daisies and dehydrated roses, it will do."

His voice carried a hard derision, and I silently looked at the price. No wonder pixies spent more time in the garden than working a nine-to-five to buy their food like most people. The two bottles of maple syrup he wanted cost a whopping nine dollars. Each. And when I tried to substitute the fake stuff, he had added a third. "Let me carry something," I offered, feeling useless.

He shook his head, pace intent as he headed to the front. "If we don't go now, it will be too cold to find any pixies who might help. Besides, the owner has to be home and watching TV. It's almost nine."

I glanced at his phone clipped to his belt. "It's twenty past," I said. "Let's go."

"Past?" Jenks snickered, shifting the basket. "The sun's been down only an hour."

He skittered sideways when I snatched the phone from his belt and held it for him to see. "Nine-twenty," I said, not knowing if I should be smug or worried that his unerring time sense was off. I hoped Ceri hadn't ruined it.

For an instant Jenks looked horrified, then his mouth quirked. "We shifted latitude," he said. "I'm going to be . . ." He took the phone from me and peered at the clock. ". . . twenty minutes slow at sunset and twenty minutes fast at sunrise." Jenks chuckled. "Never thought I'd need a watch, but it would be easier than trying to switch over and then have to switch back."

I shrugged. I'd never felt the need for a watch unless I was working with Ivy and had to "synchronize" to keep her from having a fit, and then I just used Jenks. Feeling short next to his height, I steered him from the self-service line, or we would have been there all night. Jenks took charge of the basket, unloading it and leaving me to smile neutrally at the woman.

Her plucked eyebrows rose upon taking in the bee pollen, yeast, honey, maple syrup, beer, Band-Aids, and the ailing plant Jenks had rescued from the half-price rack in the tiny floral department. "Doing a little cooking?" she asked slyly, her grin thick with an amused conclusion as to what two people might be doing with a shopping list like ours. Her name tag said TERRI, and she was a comfortable twenty pounds overweight, with swollen fingers and too many rings.

Jenks's green eyes were innocently wide. "Jane, honey," he said to me. "Be a dear and run back for the instant pudding." His voice dropped, taking on a sultry depth. "Let's try butterscotch this time. I'm bored with chocolate."

Feeling wicked, I leaned against him, reaching to play with the curls about his ears. "You know Alexia is allergic to butterscotch," I said. "Besides, Tom will do *a-a-a-a-anything* for pistachio. And I have some of that in the fridge. Right beside the caramel drizzle and the whipped cream." I giggled, tossing my red hair. "God, I love caramel! It takes forever to lick off."

Jenks broke into a devilish grin, eyeing the woman from under his hat as he took a handful of toothbrushes from the grab rack and set them on the conveyer belt. "That's what I love so much about my Janie," he said, giving me a sideways hug that pulled me off balance and into him. "Always thinking of others. Isn't she the kindest soul you've ever met?"

The woman's face was red. Flustered, she kept trying to ring up the marked-down plant, finally giving up and putting it into a plastic bag. "Sixty-three twenty-seven," she stammered, not meeting Jenks's eyes.

Smug, Jenks pulled out the wallet he had bought all of fifteen minutes ago, shuffling to find the Vampiric Charms credit card. He carefully ran it through the machine, clearly enjoying himself as he punched the right buttons. Ivy had arranged for it ages ago, and Jenks's signature was on file as a matter of course. This was the first time he'd been able to use it, but he looked like he knew what he was doing.

The woman stared at the name of our firm when it popped up on her screen, her jaw falling to make a double chin.

Jenks signed the pad with a careful seriousness, smiling at the cashier as she extended the receipt and a strip of coupons. "Cheerio," he said, the plastic a soft rustle when he took all the bags and looped his arm through them. I glanced back when the glass doors swung apart and the night air, cold off the straits, set a few strands of hair to tickle my face. She was already gossiping with the manager, putting a hand to her mouth when she saw me look at her.

"Jeez, Jenks," I said, taking one of the bags so I could look at the receipt. *Over sixty dollars for two bags of groceries?* "Maybe we could have done something really disgusting, like lick her microphone." *And why had he bought so many toothbrushes?*

"You enjoyed it, and you know it, witch," he said, then snatched the ticker tape from me when I tried to throw it and the coupons away. "I want that," he said, tucking them in a pocket. "I might use them later."

"No one uses those," I said, head bowed while I dug in my bag for the keys. The lights flashed and the locks disengaged. Jiggling the bag on his arm, Jenks opened my door for me before going to the other side of the van and dropping his groceries beside his bags of slacks, shirts, silk boxers, socks, and a silk robe I would have protested over except that he was eventually going to get small again and I was going to claim it. The man couldn't have anything cheap, and I would've questioned his claim that oil-based fabrics would make him break out if I hadn't seen it for myself.

His door opened and he settled himself, carefully buckling in as if it was a religion. "Ready?" I said, feeling the ease of shopping start to shift into the anticipation of a run. An illegal run. Yes, we were rescuing Jenks's son, not robbing the place, but they would still throw our butts in jail if we were caught.

Jenks's head went up and down, and he zipped and un-zipped the small waist pack he had put his few tools in. Taking a steadying breath, I started the van and headed to the shops and the theater. Bridge traffic was congested, and had been for the better part of the month, according to the disgruntled clerk in the shoe outlet. Apparently it was down to one lane either way while they scrambled to make maintenance repairs round-the-clock to finish before Memorial Day. Fortunately we didn't have to cross the huge suspension bridge, just weave past the confusion.

The van was blowing cold air even though I had the heater on, and I thanked the stars that Jenks was big. Tonight would have been iffy for him if he were four inches tall. I only hoped Jax had found somewhere warm. A butterfly exhibit would have enough food, but why heat it to a comfortable seventy-five degrees when fifty will do?

The theater was in a mazelike cluster of new shops catering to tourists on foot—sort of a mini-open-aired mall plopped beside the original downtown—but they had a special lot for the cinema, and I parked between a white truck and a rusting Toyota with a bumper sticker that said FOLLOW ME TO THE U.P., EH?

The engine cut out, and I looked across the van at Jenks in the new silence. The sound of slow crickets came in from the nearby empty field. He seemed nervous, his fingers quick as they fussed with the zipper on his pack. "You going to be okay?" I said, realizing this was the first time he had been on a run where he couldn't just fly out of danger.

He nodded, the deep concern on his face appearing out of place on someone so young. Rustling in a bag, he pulled a bottle of maple syrup out from behind the seat. His green eyes met mine in the uncertain light, looking black. "Hey, um, when we get out, will you pretend to fix your shoe or something? I want to take care of the cameras on the back of the building, and a distraction might help."

My gaze went to the bottle in his hand, then rose to his wary expression, not sure how a bottle of syrup was going to fix the cameras but willing to go along with it. "Sure."

Relieved, he got out. I followed suit, leaning against the van to take off my shoe and shake a nonexistent pebble out. I watched Jenks with half my attention, understanding when he let out a trill of a whistle, anxiously touching his red hat as a curious, aggressive pixy zipped up to him in the cooling dusk.

I missed what was said, but Jenks returned looking satisfied, the bottle of maple syrup gone. "What?" I said as he waited for me to fall into step with him.

"They'll put the cameras on loop for us when we leave the building," he said, not taking my arm as Kisten or Nick might, but walking beside me with an odd closeness. The shops lining the thoroughfare were closed, but the theater had a small crowd of what were clearly locals, to judge by the amount of noisy banter. The movie showing had been out for three weeks in Cincy, but there must not be a lot to do up here.

We neared the ticket booth and my pulse quickened. "They'll loop the cameras for a bottle of maple syrup?" I asked, voice hushed.

Jenks shrugged, glancing at the marquee. "Sure. That stuff is liquid gold."

I dug in my bag for a twenty as I took that in. Maybe I could make more pimping maple syrup to pixies than running? We bought two tickets to the SF film, and after getting Jenks a bag of popcorn, we headed into the theater, immediately going out the emergency exit.

My eyes went to the cameras atop the building, catching the faintest glint of streetlight on pixy wings. Maybe it was a little overkill, but being placed at the theater if The Butterfly Shack's alarms went off might be the difference between keeping my feet on the street and cooling them on a jail cot.

Together we made our way from the service entrances in back to the front, Jenks shedding clothes and handing them to me to stuff in my bag every few yards. It was terribly distracting, but I managed to avoid running into the Dumpsters and recycling bins. Upon reaching the shuttered tourist area, he was in his soft-soled boots and his skintight outfit. We had come out a few blocks from the theater, and it was creepy being on the street at night with everything closed, reminding me how far from home and out of my element I was. The Butterfly Shack was tucked into the end of a cul-de-sac, and we headed for it, feet silent on the cement.

"Watch my back," Jenks whispered, leaving me in a shadow while he twirled the long tool in his fingers into a blur, crouching to put his eyes even with the lock.

I gave him long glance, then turned to watch the empty foot street. *No prob, Jenks,* I thought. Sure, he was married, but I could look. "People," I breathed, but he had heard and was already behind the scrawny bushes beside the door. They were butterfly bushes, if I guessed right, and scraggly. Any other business would have torn them out.

Shrinking into my shadow, I held my breath until the couple passed, the woman's heels fast and the man griping they were going to miss the previews. Five seconds later Jenks was back at the door. A moment of tinkering, and he stood to carefully try the latch. It clicked open, a nice cheery green light blinking a welcome from the lock pad.

He grinned, jerking his head for me to join him. I slipped inside and moved to get out of his way. If there was more security, Jenks could tell better than I.

The door shut, leaving the wash of streetlight coming in the large windows. As smoothly as if on wings, Jenks glided past me. "Camera behind the mirror in the corner," he said. "Can't do anything about that one if I'm six feet tall. Let's get him, get out, and hope for the best."

My gut tightened. This was more loosey-goosey than even I liked. "The back?" I whispered, cataloging the silent shelves and displays of Amazon rain forest stuffed animals and expensive books on how to design a garden for wildlife. It smelled wonderful, rich with subtle perfumes of exotic flowers and vines filtering out from behind an obvious pair of glass doors. But it was cold. The tourist season wouldn't officially begin till next week, and I was sure they kept the temp low at night to extend the life of the insects.

Jenks slipped to the back, making me feel clumsy behind him. I wondered if he would even show up on the camera, he moved so stealthily. The soft sucking sound of the outer glass door of the casual airlock was loud, and Jenks held it for me, his eyes wide to take in what little light there was. Nervous, I ducked under his arm, breathing deeply of the scent of moist dirt. Jenks opened the second door, and the sound of running water joined it. My shoulders eased despite my tension, and I hastened to keep up as he entered the walk-through exhibit.

It was a two-story-tall room, glass-walled from ten feet up. The night was a black ceiling festooned with vines and hanging planters of musky smelling petunias and jewel-like begonias. Maybe forty feet long and fifteen feet wide, the room made a narrow slice of another continent. And it was cold. I clasped my shoulders and looked at Jenks, worried.

"Jax?" Jenks called, the hope in his voice heartrending. "Are you here? It's me, Dad."

Dad, I thought in envy. What I would have given to have heard that directed at me when I needed it. I shoved the ugly feeling aside, happy that Jax had a dad who was able to rescue his ass. Growing up was hard enough without having to pull yourself out of whatever mess you got yourself into when your decisions were faster than your brain. Or your feet.

There was a chirp from the incubators tucked out of the way. My brows rose, and Jenks stiffened. "There," I said breathlessly, pointing. "Under that cupboard, where the heat lamp is."

"Jax!" Jenks whispered, padding down the slate slabs edged with moss. "Are you okay?"

A grin heavy with relief came over me when, with a sprinkling of glowing dust, a pixy darted out from under the cupboard. It was Jax, and he zipped around us, wings clattering. He was okay. Hell, he was more than okay. He looked great.

"Ms. Morgan!" the young pixy cried, lighting the small space with his excitement and zipping around my head like an insane firefly. "You're alive? We thought you were dead! Where's my dad?" He rose to the ceiling, then dropped. "Dad?"

Jenks stared, transfixed at his son darting over the exhibit. He opened his mouth, then closed it, clearly struggling to find a way to touch his son without hurting him. "Jax . . ." he whispered, his eyes both young and old—pained and filled with joy.

Jax let out a startled chirp, slamming back a good two feet before he caught himself. "Dad!" he shouted, pixy dust slipping from him. "What happened? You're big!"

Jenks's hand shook as his son landed on it. "I got big to find you. It's too cold to be out without somewhere to go. And it's not safe for Ms. Morgan to be out of Cincinnati unescorted."

I made a face, chafing at the truth, though we hadn't even seen a vampire, much less a hungry one. They didn't like small towns. "Jax," I said impatiently, "where's Nick?"

The small pixy's eyes widened and the dust slipping from him turned thin. "They took him. I can show you were he is. Holy crap, he'll be glad to see you! We didn't know you were alive, Ms. Morgan. We thought you were dead!"

That was the second time he had said it, and I blinked in understanding. *Oh God*. Nick had called the night Al snapped the familiar bond between us. Al answered my phone and told Nick I belonged to him. Then the media thought I'd died on the boat Kisten blew up. Nick thought I was dead. That's why he had never called. That's why he didn't tell me he was back on the solstice. That's why he cleared out his apartment and left. He thought I was dead.

"God help me," I whispered, reaching out for the filthy incubator full of butterfly pupa. The budded rose left on my doorstep in the jelly jar with the pentagram of protection on it had been from him. *Nick hadn't left me. He thought I had died*.

"Rache?"

I straightened when Jenks tentatively touched my arm. "I'm okay," I whispered, though I was far from it. I'd deal with it later. "We have to go," I said, turning away.

"Wait," Jax exclaimed, dropping down to the floor and peering under the cupboard. "Here kitty, kitty, kitty . . ."

"Jax!" Jenks shouted in horror, scooping his son up.

"Dad!" Jax protested, easily slipping the loose prison of his father's fingers. "Let go!"

My eyes widened at the ball of orange fluff squeezing out from under the counter, blinking and stretching. I looked again, not believing. "It's a cat," I said, winning the Pulitzer prize for incredible intellect. Well, actually it was a kitten, so points off for that.

Jenks's mouth was moving but nothing came out. He backed up with what looked like terror in his wide eyes.

"It's a cat!" I said again. Then added a frantic, "Jax! No!" when the pixy dropped down. I reached for him, drawing away when the fluffy orange kitten arched its back and spit at me.

"Her name is Rex," Jax said proudly, his wings still as he stood on the dirty floor beside the incubator and scratched vigorously under her chin. The kitten relaxed, forgetting me and stretching its neck so Jax could get just the right spot.

I took a slow breath. *As in Tyrannosaurus rex? Great. Just freaking great.*

"I want to keep her," Jax said, and the kitten sank down and began to purr, tiny sharp claws kneading in and out and eyes closed.

It's a cat. Boy, you couldn't slip anything past me tonight. "Jax," I said persuasively, and the small pixy bristled.

"I'm not leaving her!" he said. "I would have frozen my first night if it wasn't for her. She's been keeping me warm, and if I leave, that mean old witch who owns the place will find her again and call the pound. I heard her say so!"

I glanced from the kitten to Jenks. He looked like he was hyperventilating, and I took his arm in case he was going to pass out. "Jax, you can't keep her."

"She's mine!" Jax protested. "I've been feeding her butterfly pupa, and she's been keeping me warm. She won't hurt me. Look!"

Jenks almost had a coronary when his son flitted back and forth before the kitten, enticing her to take a shot at him. The kitten's white tip of a tail twitched and her hindquarters quivered.

"Jax!" Jenks shouted, scooping him up out of danger as Rex's paw came out.

My heart jumped into my throat, and it was all I could do to not reach for him too.

"Dad, let me go!" Jax exclaimed, and he was free, flitting over our heads, the kitten watching with a nerve-racking intensity.

Jenks visably swallowed. "The cat saved my son's life," he said, shaking. "We aren't leaving it here to starve or die at the pound."

"Jenks . . ." I protested, watching Rex pace under Jax's flitting path, her head up and her steps light. "Someone will take her in. Look how sweet she is." I clasped my hands so I wouldn't pick her up. "Sure," I said, my resolve weakening when Rex fell over to look cute and harmless, her little white belly in the air. "She's all soft and sweet now, but she's going to get bigger. And then there will be yelling. And screaming. And soft kitty fur in my garden."

Jenks frowned. "I'm not going to keep her. I'll find a home for her. But she saved my son's life, and I won't let her starve here."

I shook my head, and while Jax cheered, his father gingerly scooped the kitten up. Rex gave a token wiggle before settling into the crook of his arm. Jenks had her both safe and secure—as if she was a child.

"Let me take her," I said, holding out my hands.

"I've got her okay." Jenks's angular face was pale, making him look as if he was going to pass out. "Jax, it's cold out. Get in Ms. Morgan's purse until we get to the motel."

"Hell no!" Jax said, shocking me as he lit on my shoulder. "I'm not going to ride in no purse. I'll be fine with Rex. Tink's diaphragm, Dad. Where do you think I've been sleeping for the last four days?"

"Tink's diaph—" Jenks sputtered. "Watch your mouth, young man."

This was not happening.

Jax dropped down to snuggle in the hollow of Rex's tummy, almost disappearing in the soft kitten fur. Jenks took several breaths, his shoulders so tense you could crack eggs on them.

"We have to go," I whispered. "We can talk about this later."

Jenks nodded, and with the wobbling pace of a drunk made his way to the front of the exhibit, Jenks holding the kitten and me opening doors. The scent of books and carpet made the air smell dead as we crept into the gift shop. I fearfully looked for flashing red and blue lights outside, relieved at finding only a comforting darkness and a quiet cobble street.

I said nothing when Jenks awkwardly got his wallet out from his back pocket with one hand and left every last dollar of cash I had given him on the counter. He nodded respectfully to the camera behind the mirror, and we left as we had come in.

We didn't see anyone on the way back to the parking lot, but I didn't take one good breath until the van door slammed shut behind me. Fingers shaking, I started the engine, carefully backing up and finding my way to the strip.

"Rache," Jenks said, eyes on the kitten in his arms as he broke his conspicuous silence. "Can we stop at that grocery store and pick up some cat food? I've got a coupon."

And so it begins, I thought, mentally adding a litter pan and litter. And a can opener. And a little saucer for water. And maybe a fuzzy mouse or ten.

I glanced at Jenks out of the corner of my eye, his smooth, long fingers gentling the fur between Rex's ears as the kitten purred loud enough to be heard over the van. Jax was cuddled between her paws, sleeping the sleep of the exhausted. A misty smile came over me and I felt myself relax. We'd get rid of her as soon as we found a good home.

Ri-i-i-i-ight.

Ten

"**H**e's fine," I said into my cell phone, stomach tight as Rex stalked Jax across the bed. The pixy was sitting dejectedly on the lamp shade, his feet swinging while his dad lectured him.

"How did you find him so quick?" Kisten asked, his voice thin and tiny from too many towers between us.

I took a breath to tell Jenks about the cat, but he bent without slowing his harangue to scoop up the orange ball of warrior-in-training and hold her close, soothing her into forgetting what she was doing. My held breath escaped and I paused to remember what I had been saying.

"He was at a butterfly exhibit." I twisted in my seat by the curtained window, aiming the battered remote at the TV to click off the local ten o'clock news. There'd been no late-breaking story about intruders at the store, so it looked as if we'd be okay. I'd have been willing to bet that no one would even look at the camera records, despite the cash Jenks had left.

"He made friends with a kitten," I added, leaning for the last slice of pizza. The bracelet of black gold I had found in my suitcase glittered in the light, and I smiled at his gift, not caring right now that he probably gave the bit of finery to all his lovers as a not-so-subtle show of his conquests to those in the know. Ivy had one. So did Candice, the vamp who had tried to kill me last solstice. I especially liked the little skull charm he had on it, but maybe this wasn't such a good club after all.

"A kitten?" Kisten said. "No shit!"

Jingling the metallic skull and heart together, I chuckled. "Yeah." I took a bite of my pizza. "Fed her butterfly pupa in return for her keeping him warm," I added around my full mouth.

"Her?" he asked, the disbelief clear in his voice.

"Her name is Rex," I said brightly, shaking my new charm bracelet down. *What else would a nine-year-old pixy name a predator a hundred times his size?* Eyeing Jenks holding the somnolent kitten, my eyebrows rose. "You want a cat?"

He laughed, the miles between us vanishing. "I'm living on my boat, Rachel."

"Cats can live on boats," I said, glad he had moved out of Piscary's quarters when Skimmer moved in. That he docked his two-story yacht at the restaurant's quay was close enough. "Hey, uh, how is Ivy?" I asked softly, shifting to drape the back of my knees over the arm of the green chair.

Kisten's sigh was worrisome. "Skimmer's been at the church since you left."

Tension stiffened my shoulders. He was fishing to find out if I was jealous; I could hear it. "Really," I said lightly, but my face went cold when I studied my feelings, wondering if the faint annoyance was from jealousy or the idea that someone was in my church, eating at my table, using my ceramic spelling spoons for making brownies. I threw the half-eaten slice of pizza back into the box.

"She's falling into old patterns," he said, making me feel even better. "I can see it. She knows it's happening, but she can't stop it. Rachel, Ivy needs you here so she doesn't forget what she wants."

My jaw stiffened when my thoughts swung to our conversation beside his van. After living with Ivy for almost a year, I had seen the marks Piscary's manipulations had left on her thoughts and reactions, though not knowing how they had gotten there. Hearing how bad it had been twisted my stomach. I couldn't believe she'd ever return to it voluntarily, even if Skimmer opened the door and tried to shove her through it. Kisten was overreacting. "Ivy is not going to fall apart because I'm not there. God, Kisten. Give the woman some credit."

"She's vulnerable."

Frowning, I swung my feet to kick repeatedly at the curtains. Jenks had put his ailing plant on the table, and it was looking better already. "She's the most powerful living vampire in Cincinnati," I said.

"Which is why she's vulnerable."

I said nothing, knowing he was right. "It's only a few days," I said, wishing I didn't have to do this over the stinking phone. "We're heading back as soon as we get Nick."

Jenks made a harsh grunt of sound, and I pulled my eyes from his plant. "Since when were we going to get Nick?" he said, his youthful face holding anger. "We came for Jax. We got him. Tomorrow we leave."

Surprised, my eyes widened. "Ah, Kist, can I call you back?"

He sighed, clearly having heard Jenks. "Sure," he said, sounding resigned that I wasn't coming home until Nick was safe. "Talk to you later. Love you."

My heart gave a pound, and I heard the words again in my thoughts. *Love you*. He did. I knew it to the core of my being.

"I love you too," I said softly. I could have breathed it and he would have heard.

The connection broke and I turned the phone off. It needed recharging, and as I gathered my thoughts for the coming argument with Jenks, I dug my adapter out of my bag and plugged it in. I turned, finding Jenks standing in his Peter Pan pose, hands on his hips and his feet spread wide. It had lost its effectiveness now that he was six-feet-four. But seeing as he was still in those black tights, he could stand anyway he wanted.

Rex was on the floor, blinking sleepily up at him with

innocent kitten eyes. Jax took the opportunity to dart to the kitchen, alighting on one of the plastic cups in their little cellophane sleeves. Eyes wide, he watched us between bites of the nasty concoction of bee pollen and maple syrup his dad had made for him a moment after we walked in the door.

"I'm not leaving without Nick," I said, forcing my jaw to unclench. *He hadn't left me. He thought I had died. And he needed help.*

Jenks's face hardened. "He lured my son away. He taught him how to be a thief, and not even a good thief. He taught him to be a two-bit crappy thief who got caught!"

I hesitated, unsure if he was upset about the thief part or the bad thief part. Deciding it didn't matter, I took my own Peter Pan pose, pointing aggressively to the parking lot. "That van isn't turning south until we are *all* in it."

From the kitchen, Jax made an attention-getting clatter of wings. "They're going to kill him, Dad. He's all beat up. They want it, and they're going to keep beating on him until he tells them where it is or he dies."

Turning, Jenks scooped Rex up when the small predator realized where Jax was and began stalking him again. "Want what?" he said warily.

Jax froze in his reach for another cake of bee pollen and syrup. "Uh . . ." he stammered, wings moving in blurred spurts.

At that, I collapsed back into my chair and stared at the ceiling. "Look," I said, legs stretched out and tired. "Whatever happened, happened. Jenks, I'm sorry you're mad at Nick, and if you want to sit here and watch TV while I save Nick's ass, I won't think any less of you." His fingers caressing Rex froze, and I knew I'd hit a nerve. "But Nick saved my life," I said, crossing my knees as a feeling of guilt passed through me. *He saved my life, and I shack up with the first guy who shows an interest.* "I can't walk away."

Jenks shifted forward and back, his need to move obvious and odd now that he was full-sized and dressed in that far-too-distracting skintight outfit. Wishing he'd put something on over it, I pulled the map of the area I had bought in the motel office out from under the pizza box and opened it up. The crackle of map paper swung my thoughts to Ivy, and my worry tightened. *Skimmer was sleeping over?*

Skimmer was Piscary's lawyer, out from the West Coast and top of her class, eminently comfortable in using manipulation to get what she wanted. Ivy didn't want a vampiric lifestyle, but Skimmer didn't care. She just wanted Ivy, and if what Kisten had said was true, she didn't mind screwing Ivy's mental state up to get her. That alone was enough to make me hate the intelligent woman.

It hadn't surprised me to find that Skimmer was responsible for part of Ivy's problems. The two had undoubtedly run wild, gaining a reputation for savage bloodletting mixed liberally with aggressive sex. It was no wonder Ivy had twined the emotions of love and the ecstasy of bloodletting together so tightly that they were one in her mind. Back then, she was vulnerable and alone for the first time in her life, with Skimmer undoubtedly more than willing to help her explore the sophisticated vampiric bloodletting techniques Ivy had gained in the time Piscary had been at her. Piscary had probably planned it all, the bastard.

It wasn't a problem for a vampire that bloodletting was a way to show that they loved someone. But by the sounds of it, Piscary twisted that until the stronger Ivy's feelings of love were, the more savage she became. Piscary could take it—hell, he'd made her what she was—but Kisten had left her, and I wouldn't have been surprised if Ivy *had* killed someone she loved in a moment of passion. It would explain why she'd abstained from blood for three years, trying to separate her feelings of love from her blood lust. I wondered if she had, then wondered what kind of a hell Ivy lived in where the more she loved someone, the more likely she would hurt them.

Skimmer had no qualms about her deep affections toward Ivy, and though Ivy clearly loved her back, Skimmer represented everything that she was trying to escape. The more often Ivy shared blood with her past lover, the greater the chance that she would be lured into old patterns, savage bloodletting patterns that would rebound on her with a vengeance if she tried to love someone who wasn't as strong as she.

And I had just walked out, knowing Skimmer would probably step back in. God, I shouldn't have just left like that.

Just a few days, I reassured myself, moving the pizza box to the floor and clicking on the table lamp. "Jax," I said, arranging the map and pushing Jenks's recovering plant to the outskirts. "You said they had him on an island. Which one?"

He might still love me. Do I still love him? Did I ever love him, really? Or had it just been that I loved his acceptance of me?

My bracelet hissed against the map, and Jax flitted close, landing to bring the bitter scent of maple syrup to me. "This one, Ms. Morgan," he said, his voice high. Pollen crumbs fell, and I blew them away when Jax rose to sit on the table lamp's shade. From the corner of my sight I saw Jenks fidget. I couldn't do this with a half-trained pixy. I needed Jenks.

Fingertips brushing the large island in the straits, I felt like Ivy with her maps and markers, planning a run. My motions went still and my focus blurred. It wasn't her need to be organized, I suddenly realized. It was a front to disguise her feelings of inadequacy. "Damn," I whispered. This wasn't good. Ivy was a lot more fragile than she let on. She was a vampire, molded from birth to look to someone for guidance even if she could garner the attention in a room from simply walking in, and could snap my neck with half a thought.

Telling myself that Nick needed me more right now than Ivy needed me to keep her sane, I pushed my worry aside and looked at the island Jax had said Nick was on. According to the fishing pamphlet I took from the front office, Bois Blanc Island had been publicly owned before the Turn. A rather large Were pack had bought everyone else out shortly afterward, making the big island into a hunting/spa kind of thing. Trespassing wasn't a good idea.

Tension quickened my pulse when Jenks put Rex on the bed and edged closer, an odd mix of angsty teen and worried dad. Taking a breath, I said to the map, "I need your help, Jenks. I'll do it without backup if I have to. But every time I do, my ass hits the grass. You're the best operative outside of Ivy that I know. Please? I can't leave him there."

Jenks pulled a straight-backed chair from the kitchen, bumping it over the carpet, and sat down next to me so he could see the map right side up. He glanced at Jax on the lamp, pixy dust sifting upward from the heat of the bulb. I couldn't tell if he was going to help me or not. "What did you two get caught doing, Jax?" he said.

The pixy's wings blurred, and dust drifted from him. "You'll get mad." His tiny features were frightened. It didn't matter that he was an adult in pixy terms, he still looked eight to me.

"I'm already mad," Jenks said, sounding like my dad when I took a week's grounding instead of telling him why I'd been banned from the local roller rink. "Running off with a snapped-winged thief like that. Jax, if you wanted a more exciting life than a gardener, why didn't you tell me? I could have helped, given you the tools you need."

Eyebrows high, I leaned away from the table. I knew the I.S. hadn't taught Jenks the skills that landed him his job with them, but this was unexpected.

"I was never a thief," he said, shooting me a quick look. "But I know things. I found them out the hard way, and Jax doesn't need to."

Jax fidgeted, turning defensive. "I tried," he said, his voice small. "But you wanted me to be a gardener. I didn't want to disappoint you, and it was easier to just go."

Jenks slumped. "I'm sorry," he said, making me wish I was somewhere else. "I only wanted you to be safe. It's not an easy way to live. Look at me; I'm scarred and old, and if I didn't have a garden now, I'd be worthless. I don't want that for you."

Wings blurring, Jax dropped to land before his dad. "Half

your scars are from the garden," he protested. "The ones you almost died from. The seasons make me think of death, not life, a slow circle that means nothing. And when Nick asked me to help him, I said yes. I didn't want to tend his stupid plants, I wanted to help him."

I glanced at Jenks in sympathy. He looked like he was dying inside, seeing his son want what he had and knowing how hard it was going to be.

"Dad," Jax said, rising up until Jenks put up a hand for him to land on. "I know you and Mom want me to be safe, but a garden isn't safe, it's only a more convenient place to die. I want the thrill of the run. I want every day to be different. I don't expect you to understand."

"I understand more than you know," he said, his words shifting his son's wings.

Rex skulked to the pizza box on the floor and stole a crust, running to the kitchen. She hunkered down, gnawing on it as if it was a bone and watching us with big, black, evil eyes. Seeing her, Jenks took a deep breath, and tension brought me straight. He had decided to help me. "Tell me what you two got caught doing. I'll help get Nick out under two conditions."

My pulse quickened, and I found myself tapping my pencil on the table.

"What are they?" Jax asked, a healthy tone of caution mixing with hope.

"One, that you don't take another run until I give you the skills to keep your wings untattered. Nick is dangerous, and I don't want you taken advantage of. I may have raised a runner, but I did *not* raise a thief."

Pixy dust sifted from Jax as he looked from his dad to me and back again in wide-eyed amazement. "What's the other?"

Jenks winced, his ears reddening. "That you don't tell your mother."

I stopped my snicker just in time.

Jax's wings blurred into motion. "Okay," he said, and a zing of adrenaline brought me back to the map. "Nick and I were contracted by a Were pack. These guys."

He dropped from Jenks's hand to land on the island, and my thrill turned to unease. "They wanted a statue," Jax said. "Didn't even know where it was. Nick called up a demon, Dad." Dust sifted to make him look as if he was in a sunbeam. "He called up a demon and the demon told him where it was."

Okay. Now I'm officially worried. "Did the demon show up as a dog and turn into a guy wearing green velveteen and smoked glasses?" I asked, setting my pen down and holding my arms to myself. *Why, Nick? Why are you playing with your soul?*

Jax shook his head, green eyes wide and frightened. "It showed up as you, Ms. Morgan. Nick was mad and yelled at it. We thought you were dead. It wasn't Big Al. Nick said so."

My first flush of relief turned to a deep worry. A second demon. Better and better. "Then what?" I whispered. Rex jumped into Jenks's lap, nearly giving me a heart attack since I thought she had been going for Jax. How Jenks knew she hadn't been eluded me.

The dust rose and fell from Jax. "The demon, uh, took what they agreed on and told Nick where the statue was. A vampire in Detroit had it. It's older than anything."

Why would a vampire have a Were artifact? I wondered. I glanced at Jenks, his hands keeping Rex from falling over while she inexpertly cleaned her ears.

Jenks puckered his brows, his smooth features trying to wrinkle but not managing it. "What does it do, Jax?" he said, shocking me again with how at odds his youthful face was to the tone of his voice. He looked eighteen; he sounded like he was forty with a bad mortgage.

Jax flushed. "I don't know. But we got it okay. The vampire had been staked in the 1900s, and it was just sitting there, forgotten in the slop."

"So you found it," I prompted. "What's the problem? Why are they hurting him?"

At that, Jax took to the air. Rex's eyes went black for the hunt, and Jenks soothed her, fingertips lost in her orange fur.

"Uh," the pixy said, his voice high. "Nick said it wasn't what they said it was. Another pack found out he had it and made a better offer, enough to pay back what the first pack paid him to finance the snatch, plus a whole lot more."

Jenks looked disgusted. "Greedy bastard," he muttered, his jaw clenched.

I took an unhappy breath, leaning into my chair and crossing my arms over my chest. "So he sold it to the second group and the original pack wasn't happy about it?"

Jax shook his head solemnly, slowly drifting downward until his feet hit the map. "No. He said neither of them should have it. We were going to go to the West Coast. He had this guy who could give him a new identity. He was going to get us safe, then give the first pack their money back and walk away from the entire thing."

My face scrunched into a frown. *Right.* He was going to get himself safe, then sell it to the highest bidder online. "Where is it, Jax?" I asked, starting to get angry.

"He didn't tell me. One day it was there, the next it was gone."

In a sudden motion, Rex jumped up onto the table. Adrenaline surged, but Jax rubbed his wings together in a coaxing sound and the kitten padded over.

"It's not at our cabin, though," the small pixy said, standing under the kitten's jaw and stretching to rake his fingers under her chin. "They tore it apart." Stepping out from between Rex's paws, he met my eyes, looking scared. "I don't know where it is, and Nick won't tell. He doesn't want them to have it, Ms. Morgan."

Greedy S.O.B., I thought, wondering why I cared if he loved me or not. "So where's their money?" I asked. "Maybe all they want is that, and they'll let him go."

"They took it." Jax didn't look happy. "They took it the same time they took him. They want the statue. They don't care about the money."

I put my hand on the table to entice Rex to me but all she did was sniff my nails. Jenks curled a long hand under her belly to put her on the floor, where she stared up at him. "And they're here?" Jenks asked, my attention following his to the map.

Jax's head bobbed. "Yup. I can show you exactly where."

My eyes met Jenks's and we exchanged a silent look. This was going to take longer than a simple snatch and dash. "Okay," I said, wondering if there was a phone book in the room. "We're here at least another night, probably through the week. Jax, I want to know everything."

Jax shot almost to the ceiling. "All right!" he shouted, and Jenks glared at him.

"*You* are staying here," he said, his tone thick with parental control, though he looked like a kid himself. His arms were crossed, and the determination in his eyes would have rocked a bulldog back from a bone.

"Like hell I—" Jax made a startled yelp when Jenks snatched him out of the air. My eyes widened. I didn't know what Jenks was worried about. He hadn't slowed at all.

"You will stay *here,*" he barked. "I don't care how old you are, you're still my son. It's too cold for you to be effective, and if you want me to teach you anything, it starts now." He let go of Jax, and the pixy hovered right where Jenks had left him, looking scared. "You have to learn how to read before I can even take you out with me," Jenks muttered.

"Read!" Jax exclaimed. "I get along okay."

Uncomfortable, I rose and stretched, opening drawers until I found the yellow pages. I wanted to know my resources, seeing as we were out of Cincinnati. An island, for God's sake?

"I don't have to know how to read!" Jax sputtered.

"Like hell you don't," Jenks said. "You want this life? That's your choice. I'll teach you what I know, but you're going to earn it!"

I sat at the head of the bed, where I could see them while flipping through the thin pages. It was last year's book, but nothing changed fast in small towns. I slowed when I found a large number of charm shops. I knew there must be a resident population of witches taking advantage of the heavy-duty ley lines in the area.

Jenks's anger vanished as quickly as it had come, and more softly he said, "Jax, if you could read, you could have told us were you were. You could have hitched onto the first bus to Cincy and been home by sunset. You want to know how to pick the locks? Loop the cameras? Bypass security? Show me how bad you want it by learning what will help you the most first."

Jax scowled, slowly descending until his feet settled in a glowing puddle of pixy dust.

"Here." Jenks took the pencil I had left behind and leaned over the map. "This is how you write your name." A few more silent moments. "And that is the alphabet." I frowned at the sharp snap of the pencil being broken, and Jenks held the broken nub of graphite out to Jax. "Remember the song?" he prompted. "Sing it while you practice the letters. And L-M-N-O-P is not one letter, but five. It took me forever to figure that out."

"Dad . . ." Jax whined.

Jenks stood, tilting the lamp shade to better light the map. "There are fifteen makers of locks in the U.S. You want to know which one you're picking before you blow yourself and your runner into the ever-after?"

Making a sharp noise with his wings, Jax started writing.

"Make the letters as big as your feet," Jenks said as he came to see how I was progressing with the phone book. "No one can read your writing unless you do, and that's the entire point."

Guilt in his eyes, Jenks sat beside me, and I shifted so I wouldn't slip into him. From the table by the door came the alphabet song, sounding like a death dirge. "Don't worry about it, Jenks," I said, watching Rex follow him up onto the bed to make tiny jumps over the bedspread to him. "He'll be okay."

"I know he will," he said, the worry settling into his eyes.

Rex plopped herself into his lap, and he dropped his gaze. "It's not him I'm worried about," he said softly. "It's you."

"Me?" I looked up from the turning pages.

Jenks wouldn't bring his gaze from the kitten, a puddle of orange in his lap. "I have only a year to get him up to snuff so you'll have backup when I'm gone."

Oh God. "Jenks, you aren't a carton of milk with an expiration date. You look great—"

"Don't," he said softly, eyes on his smooth fingers among Rex's fur. "I've got maybe one more tolerable year. When it goes, it goes fast. It's all right. I want to make sure you're okay, and if he's working for you, he won't be tempted to do anything stupid with Nick again."

I swallowed, forcing the lump out of my throat. I had not gotten him back just to lose him. "Damn it, Jenks," I said as Jax started the alphabet song again. "There's got to be a spell or a charm . . ."

"There isn't." Finally he met my eyes. They held a deep bitterness, touched with anger. "It's the way it is, Rache. I don't want to leave you helpless. Let me do this. He won't let you down, and I'll feel better knowing he won't be working for Nick or the likes of him."

Miserable, I sat beside him, wanting to give him a hug or cry on his shoulder, but apart from that time in front of Terri at the grocery store, he had always jumped when I touched him. "Thanks, Jenks," I said, turning to the pages before he could see my eyes swimming. There was nothing I could say that wouldn't make him and me feel worse.

His grip shifted in Rex's fur, clearly wanting to change the subject. "What do the boat rentals look like?"

Taking a breath, I focused on the time-smeared print. "Okay, but there's still the problem of noise." He looked blankly at me, and I added, "It would be stupid to think they don't watch the water, and it's not like we can just boat up to the beach and not expect to be seen. Even at night there's noise. It carries too well over water."

"We could paddle across," he suggested, and I gave him a telling look.

"Ah, Jenks? It's not a lake, it's a friggin' freshwater ocean. Did you see the size of the tanker going under the bridge when we came into town? The wake from it could tip us. I'm not canoeing it unless your name is Pocahontas. Besides, the ambient light will give us away, first-quarter moon or not. To expect fog is ridiculous."

He made a face, glancing at Jax and clearing his throat to get him to start singing again. "You want to fly it? I lost my wings."

"We're going to swim it." I flipped forward a few pages. "Underwater."

Jenks blinked. "Rache, you gotta stop using that sugar substitute. *Under* the water? Do you know how cold it is?"

"Just listen." I found the page, and after taking Rex off his lap, I dropped the book onto it. It was my turn to hold the cat. She wiggled and squirmed, settling as the warmth of my hands covered her. "Look," I said, charmed when Rex patted at my swinging bracelet. "They have scuba diving off the wrecks, charm enhanced so you don't freeze to death. The water's pretty clear here despite the current, and since they're privately owned, you can take whatever you want off the wrecks. It's a poor man's treasure-hunting excursion."

He snorted. "I've never been swimming, and unless you took a class I wasn't aware of, you don't know how to dive."

"Doesn't matter." I pointed to the half-page ad. "See? They're licensed to take you out regardless of experience. I've heard of these things. They teach you enough so that you don't kill yourself, then you go out with a guide. Once you sign that release form, they're off the hook except for gross negligence."

Eyebrows high, he looked at me. "Gross negligence? As in losing two divers? Won't someone notice when we don't get back on the boat?"

My fingers in Rex's fur moved faster, and she peered up at

me with her sweet kitten face. "Well, I wasn't going to try and slip away from them. I, uh, was going to talk to the owner. Maybe arrange something."

Jenks glanced at his son literally hovering over his work, then back to me. "You'd trust a human to keep his mouth shut?"

"God, Jenks. You want me to knock them out and steal their stuff?"

"No," he said, the quickness of his reply telling me he thought I should do just that. Sighing, he frowned. "Let's just say you talk to the owner and they go along with your little stunt. How do you plan on getting back to the mainland with Nick?"

Yeah, there was that. "Maybe they'll give us an extra tank and stuff so we can all swim back. If we can't get to the mainland, we can get to Mackinac Island. Look, you could almost walk underwater to it. From there we can take the ferry to either side of the straits to help confuse our trail." Pleased, I tucked a curl out of my way.

Jenks rose, setting the book next to me on the bed. "It has a lot of ifs."

"It's one big if," I admitted. "But we don't have time for a week's worth of recon, and if we start asking around, they're going to know we're here. It's our best way to get on the island undetected. And I'd rather be out of sight underwater making my escape than on top of the water where they can follow us. We can come up anywhere on shore and disappear."

Jenks snorted. "How very James Bond of you. What if Nick's beat up so bad he can't swim?"

I felt a flush of worry. "Then we steal a boat. It's an island; they must have boats. That's not a bad idea in itself. We could boat all the way to Toledo if we have to. If you have a better idea, I'm listening."

Head down, he shook his head. "It's your run. Just tell me where to stand."

My first wash of relief that he would go along with it was short-lived as I started to make a mental list of what we'd have to do for the prep work. "New sleepy-time potions," I murmured, my fingers soothing Rex into sleep while Jenks went to check on Jax's progress. "A real map. And we need to do the tourist thing; talk to the local fishermen over coffee and find out what the boat patterns are coming off and going to Bois Blanc. You want to do that? You like to talk."

"Tink's panties, you're starting to sound like Ivy," Jenks complained lightly, leaning over the table and pointing out a mistake to Jax. I blinked, then turned from the sight of his eighteen-year-old butt in those black tights of his. *Married pixy—my new mantra.* "And that's not necessarily a bad thing," he added as he straightened.

I looked at the hotel phone, wanting to find out if they were open yet for the season or we would have to hang around a week, but I remained where I was with Rex. It was probably a human-run establishment and would be closed for the night. "No mistakes, Jenks," I said, feeling cold but for where Rex lay. "Nick's life might depend on it."

Eleven

The wind was bitter despite the bright morning sun, and I squinted at the horizon, holding onto the side of the boat as we jostled out to the wreck site. Jenks sat beside me in the lee of the cabin, both amazed and appalled that he could see his breath and wasn't freezing to death. It hadn't seemed this cold when we were on the dock, but it was frigid out here, with the water still holding the cold of ice, even through the rubber of the wet suit. *When in hell were they going to give us our warmth amulets?*

"You okay?" Jenks asked, his voice raised against the chortling engine.

I nodded, taking in his cold-reddened hands wrapped about his lidded coffee, trying to eek out some warmth from it as we bounced on the choppy waves the wind had whipped up. He looked nervous, though I didn't know why. He'd done well at the practice pool yesterday. I patted his knee, and he jumped. Cringing, I turned to watch the other passengers—high school students on a field trip.

We had lucked out yesterday. My call to Marshal's Mackinaw Wrecks got us an afternoon of practice at the high school pool and a place on today's boat. I still hadn't managed to talk to Captain Marshal, and it was down to the wire now. The man, whose day job was as the high school's swim coach, had been very nice as he treaded water and painstakingly coaxed Jenks in past his knees, but everytime I tried to talk to him about why I wanted to go out on his boat, someone, usually his assistant, interrupted. Before I knew it class was over and Marshal was gone, without my having gotten more than a good look at him in his Speedo and a bad case of the flushing stammers as I tried to gain his attention and his help. The guy probably thought I was a flaky redhead. I knew his assistant, Debbie, did.

Today was the season's first run, traditionally taking out the high school dive team to find what the last winter's storm had unearthed before the currents could cover it again. Come Friday and the first of the fudgies, all the real stuff would be carefully cataloged, and the nails and buttons planted for the tourists would be in place. Ethical? I didn't know. It would be disappointing to spend this much money and have nothing to show for it, even if it was fake.

With his youthful physique, Jenks fit in, looking good in the rented wet suit and his red local-yokel knit hat down tight about his ears. Cheeks ruddy with cold, he sipped at his coffee, so thick with sugar it was syrupy. *God, he looked good enough to eat,* I thought, then flushed and crossed my legs at my knees despite making it harder to keep my balance.

"Want some coffee with your sugar, Jenks?" I asked, and he froze as a wave dropped us.

"You going to ask Captain Speedo before or after you get in the water?" Jenks shot back.

I gave him a soft thwack on his leg to burn off a burst of angst. He didn't jump this time and I felt better, not minding that he was quietly laughing at me.

While Jenks snickered, I turned to Marshal. The captain had been watching me from the corner of his eye since I boarded. Unlike the rest of us in wet suits, he was wearing only a black Speedo and a red windbreaker, his bare, comfortably muscled legs showing goose bumps. Clearly the man was cold but too much of a stud to admit it. Bracing myself against the bouncing waves, I opened my mouth to attract his attention, but Debbie called to him, drawing him away again.

Damn it. I slumped back down in my seat. What in hell was wrong with me?

Forcing my breathing to slow, I waited for his assistant to finish asking him whatever deathly important question she had. The sun glinted prettily on the water, and I found myself thinking this was an ungodly time to be out here, much less awake. Jenks was fine, seeing as he was usually up long before sunrise, and I could hear him muttering, "Nine forty-eight, nine forty-eight," as he tried to shift his internal clock. The thrum of the engine was lulling me into a drowsy state despite the caffeine and the nap Jenks had made me take yesterday.

Trying not to yawn, I straightened, my hand straying to my waist pack with my charms and splat gun safe in their zippy bags. A good deal of yesterday had been spent in the almost unusable kitchen. I'd purchased a disposable copper insert for spelling at a discount store, and Jenks traded maple syrup for everything else I needed to craft the sleepy-time charms and the scent disguise spells.

The paint ball gun shop had been the hardest to find, being "left where the old post office used to be, past the Baptist church that burned down in 'seventy-five, and right at the Higgan's farm turnaround. Can't miss it."

Between yesterday's predive class, grilling Jax for details, my six hours spelling, and the three hours we spent at the Mackinaw Fort doing the tourist thing, I was mentally and physically tired. But the oddest thing by far had been watching Jenks teach Jax how to read.

The little pixy was picking it up faster than I would have thought possible. While I stirred my spells, Jenks and Jax had watched *Sesame Street,* of all things, the music and puppets seemingly making a direct line to the pixy mentality. One song in particular seemed to have wedged itself into my head, the tune-worm settling firmly around my cerebral cortex like an alien from an SF movie.

Seeing my foot tapping to its catchy beat, I stilled it, wondering if I'd be stuck with the tune the rest of the day and what Elmo would find wrong with this situation. The splat gun in my fanny pack? The six-foot pixy beside me? Take your pick, Elmo, and try not to giggle.

Bois Blanc Island was taking on definition, the top of a lighthouse peeking over the trees making me glad I was going in underwater. We had already passed the no-automobile Mackinac Island, and the huge bridge was to the left and behind us, spanning the narrows between the two peninsulas. Yeah, narrows. It stretched over four freakin' miles. An ocean-going tanker was passing under the bridge, looking like a mouse under a chair.

The bridge was enormous, and according to the place mat under my burger last night, it came in only feet shorter in height than Carew Tower, the support towers being five hundred feet up and two hundred feet down to bedrock. It was the third longest suspension bridge in the world, the longest in the western hemisphere. It was a big sucker, claiming five men's lives in its construction, one never found; hitting water at that height was like hitting a cement parking lot. I'd expect to see something like it in a big city, not out in the boonies where moose and wolves crossed the ice in the winter.

I lurched when the thrum of the engine dropped in pitch and the boat slowed, rocking as our own wake rolled under us. The six guys clustered at the back of the boat jostled and pushed, showing off for Debbie, all done up in her rubber wet suit. Her chest looked like a Barbie doll's, whereas mine was more like her little sister Ellie's. I couldn't help but wonder if she was the reason most of the slobbering sacks of hormones had joined the diving club in the first place.

"God, I feel old, Jenks," I whispered, tucking a stray red curl behind an ear.

"Yeah, me too."

Damn it. I wondered if I could jam my foot any farther down my throat. The wind seemed to shift as the boat turned, and Debbie expertly hooked the buoy and tied us off. The diving flag went up the pole, the engine cut out, and the level of excitement grew.

"Divers, listen up!" Marshal said, standing to garner everyone's attention. "Look to your guides. They'll give you your warmth amulets and make sure they're working, though

I'm sure you'll sing out once you hit the water if they aren't."

"You got it, Coach," one of the kids sang out in a high falsetto, gaining laughs.

"That's Captain when we're on the water, smartass," Marshal said, flicking a glance at Jenks and me. "Debbie, you take the boys," he said, unzipping his windbreaker. "I'll take Mr. Morgan and his sister."

Not feeling at all bad for the lie on the release form, I stood and the butterflies started.

"Any time, Rache," Jenks muttered, and I thwacked him with my foot.

Two of the boys gave each other high-fives, clustering around the woman in rubber as she comfortably fended off their exuberance. She knew them by name, and it looked like this was an old game. My pulse quickened when the line of tanks got shorter as they unlatched them from the side and spun them to the back of the boat. Everyone seemed to know what to do, even the guy who drove us out there, now settling himself in the bow in the sun with a handheld game.

"Miss?"

I jerked, bringing my attention back to find myself eye-to-chest with Captain Marshal. My God, he was tall. And really, really . . . hairless. Completely. Not a hint of hair on him marred the even honey tone of his skin. No beard. No mustache. No eyebrows, which had bothered me yesterday until I realized that like a lot of professional swimmers, he probably used a potion to remove it. Earth charms aren't very specific, taking off *everything,* which might sound like a good idea, but isn't unless you don't mind being bald. Everywhere.

He was smiling, his brown eyes expectant. The man was in his late twenties by the look of his lean muscled legs, bare to the wind, and the defined abs stacked above his tiny Speedo. Bald looked good on Marshal, I decided. Well-defined legs, wide shoulders, and in between was mmmm-mmmm good. And he was a witch with his own business. *My mother would love this one,* I mused, then grimaced, remembering the last time I'd thought that.

"I'll be your guide today," he said, glancing from me to Jenks, now standing behind me. "We're going to let the dive team get out of the way, and then we'll follow."

"Sounds good," I said, hearing a forced cheerfulness in my voice, but inside I was scrambling. There were too many people. I wanted to ask him privately, but I was running out of time.

"Here's your charms," Marshal continued, handing me a plastic bag with two redwood disks in them. His gaze landed on my neck, still bruised from Karen, and fell away. "They're already invoked. You can put them on now, though you'll be toasty until you get in the water."

"Uh, thanks," I stammered, fingering them through the insulating plastic. They were stickered with his name and license number on one side. All I needed to do was put one on so it touched my skin and even the slight chill from the morning would be gone.

I handed the bag to Jenks, who immediately shook one into his palm, sighing in relief at the warmth. Satisfied they worked, I gave serious consideration to shooting everyone with a sleepy-time charm and just stealing everything. "Um, Mr. Marshal . . ."

He ducked his head, smiling at me to show even white teeth. I could smell the heady scent of redwood coming from him like spice. He made his own charms; I could tell. "Captain Marshal," he said as if it was a joke. "Marshal is my first name."

"Captain Marshal," I amended. "Look, I've got to ask you something."

Debbie called, and he put up a long finger. "Just a sec," he said, and walked away.

"Damn it!" I exclaimed under my breath. "What in hell is wrong with that woman! Can't she do anything without asking him?"

Jenks shrugged, squinting at the morning sun as he took

off his knit hat and messed with his gear. "She thinks you like him," he said, and I blinked.

"Miss?"

I jumped and spun when Marshal's hand landed on my shoulder.

He tightened his grip, and I looked into the depth of his brown eyes, surprised. "Ready to go?"

"Uh," I stammered, my gaze flicking behind him to Debbie. She was glaring, adjusting her fins with sharp motions before she fell over the back of the boat. It was just me, Marshal, Jenks, and the guy at the front of the boat hunched over his game in the sun. Yesterday's fiasco at the pool was making a whole lot more sense. "Ah, Marshal? About the dive . . ."

The witch's lips turned up into a smile. "It's okay, Ms. Morgan," he said solicitously. "We'll take it step by step. I know the straits look daunting, but you did well at the pool."

Pooal, I thought, liking his mild accent. "Uh, it's not that," I said as he selected a tank and beckoned me closer. But when I met his eyes, I was shocked to find him grinning at me, more than a hint of attraction in his dark gaze. "Captain Marshal, I'm very sorry," I said flatly. "I should have brought this up earlier. I didn't come out here to dive on the wreck."

"Sit," he said. "Right there so I can get your tank hooked up."

"Captain." He took my shoulders and sat me down, reaching to adjust my gear. "I meant to ask you before we got all the way out here . . ." I looked at Jenks for help, but he was laughing at me. "Damn it," I swore. "I'm sorry, Marshal. I'm out here on false pretenses."

"I'm flattered, Ms. Morgan," Marshal said, glancing up under his hairless eyebrows. "But you paid for a dive on my wreck, and I feel obligated to do my best to fulfill it. If you're going to be in town a few more days, maybe we can have dinner."

My jaw dropped, and I realized why he had been watching me. Oh God. Debbie wasn't the only one who thought I was interested in him. Suddenly I saw my stammering attempts at trying to talk to him in an entirely new way. Jenks snickered, and I felt myself blush.

"Captain Marshal," I said firmly. "I'm not looking for a date."

The man's face slowly lost its expression, his faint smile wrinkles easing to a smooth nothing as he straightened. "I, uh . . . You're not? I thought you two were brother and sister."

"He's my partner," I said, adding a quick, "business partner."

"You like women?" Marshal stammered, backing up a step and looking like he was going to die of embarrassment. "Shit, I hate it when I misread people. God, I'm sorry."

"No, it's not that either." I said, wincing as I pulled the hair out of my mouth, which the wind had tugged from my braid. "You're an attractive man, and any other time I would be salivating at the idea of a private lesson at your pool . . . *pooal* . . . but I need your help."

Marshal zipped his coat up, looking uneasy. I glanced at Jenks and took a breath. "My old boyfriend is on that island, and I need to rescue him without anyone knowing about it."

Smooth features blank, he stared at me, the sun glinting off the top of his head.

"I'm an independent runner," I said, shuffling in my waist pack and handing him one of my black business cards. "A pack of Weres kidnapped my old boyfriend and they're holding him. I need to get over there undetected, and you were in the book. Uh, if I could borrow a second set of gear and tanks for him to swim out with, that would be . . . great. I'm prepared to pay for it. You, uh, have my credit card on file, right?"

Brown eyes blinking, Marshal brought his gaze up from the business card. Squinting, he peered at Jenks, moving his head this way and that like an owl. An intent look came into his eyes, almost predatorial. Jenks backed up a step, and nervous, I watched. "What are you doing?" I finally asked.

"Looking for the camera."

My jaw clenched. "You don't believe me."

"Should I?"

Disgusted, I felt my anger rise. "Look," I said as the wake from a passing ship hit us and the bobbing boat added insult to my clenched stomach. "I could have come out here and shot you all with sleepy-time potions and took what I needed, but I'm asking for your help."

"And because you decided to not break the law means I should?" he said, feet spread wide against the boat's movement. "Even if I wanted to, I couldn't let you swim off like that. Even if I *believed you,* I wouldn't let you swim off like that. Not only would I lose my license, but you'd probably kill yourself."

"I'm not asking you to break your license," I said belligerently. "I'm asking you to let me borrow a set of gear and tanks."

Marshal ran a hand over his bald head, nearly laughing in anger. "It took me three years to get my license," he said with a mixture of disbelief and frustration. "Three years. That was for the dive business. Add on another four to get my earth magic degree so I could make my own amulets and the boat could be cost effective. You're a selfish little white-bread brat if you think I'm going to jeopardize that because your boyfriend ran off and you want to catch him cheating on you. Everything was given to you, was it? You know nothing about hard work and sacrifice!"

"He did *not* run off with another girl!" I shouted, and the guy at the front of the boat sat up to look at us. Furious, I lowered my voice and stood so I could poke my finger at his chest—if I had the guts. "And don't you *dare* tell me I don't know anything about hard work and sacrifice. I worked for seven years as a peon in the I.S., busted my butt to break my contract with them, and put my life on the line every day trying to make rent! So you can shove your holier-than-thou crap right back up where it came from. My old boyfriend bit off more than he could handle and he needs my help. The Weres took him," I said, pointing to the island, "and you are my best shot at getting over there undetected!"

Seeming taken aback, he hesitated. "Why didn't you just go to the I.S.?"

My lips pressed together, thinking this could go south really fast if he called the I.S. out here with his radio. "Because they're incompetent boobs and rescuing people is what I do for a living," I said, and he eyed me suspiciously, his gaze going to my bruised neck again. "Look, I'm usually better at it then this," I added, refusing to explain the teeth marks. "I'm sort of out of my element up here. I tried to ask you earlier, but *Debbie* kept interfering."

At that, Marshal smirked and relaxed. "Okay. I'm listening."

I glanced at the bow of the boat and the man with his game. *Like he would even notice if a great white shark bit off the back of the boat?* "Thanks," I breathed, sitting down again. Marshal did the same, and Jenks dropped to sit cross-legged where he could see both of us. The sun glinted on his yellow hair, and it was obvious the warmth spell was working: his lips were red again and he was very relaxed, almost basking.

"See," I said, embarrassed, now that I seemed to have my hat in my hand. "My boyfriend, my old boyfriend," I reiterated, flushing, "turns out he's . . ." I couldn't tell him he was a thief. "He recovers things."

"He's a thief," Marshal said, and I blinked. Seeing my muddle, the man snorted. "Let me guess. He stole something from the Weres and got caught."

"No," I said, tucking a windblown strand away. "Actually, he was contracted by them to recover something, and when he found it, he decided to give them their money back and keep it. I need to get him off that island."

Marshal looked at Jenks, who shrugged.

"Fine," I said, feeling stupid. "I don't blame you if you want to take me back to the dock and tell me to get lost in a ley line. But one way or the other I'm going over the side of this boat. I'd rather it be in a wet suit with one of your charms." Eyes squinting, I peered at him. "Could I at least buy a spell from you? So he doesn't freeze on the way back?"

Marshal's smooth face scrunched up. "I'm not licensed to sell my charms, only use them in my work."

My head bobbed, and I felt a finger of relief wedge itself between my heart and the band wrapped about it. "Yeah, me too. How about a trade?"

He leaned toward me, and after meeting my eyes to ask for permission, took a deep sniff of me. I could smell a hint of chlorine on him over his redwood scent. Apparently I smelled witchy enough, since he settled back, satisfied. "What do you have?"

A exhalation of relief slipped from me. Pulling my waist pack around, I dug in it. "Ah, on me? Not much, but I can send you something once I get home. I've got some sleepy-time potions in splat balls and three scent amulets."

Jenks closed his eyes, seeming to soak in the sun. He was smiling.

"Scent amulets?" Marshal said, a hand tracing the line of muscle of his upper arm, hidden under his windbreaker. "When would I ever use one of those?"

Affronted, I froze. "I use them all the time."

"Well, I don't. I bathe every day."

Jenks snickered, and I warmed. "They aren't deodorant charms," I said, offended. "They disguise your scent so Weres can't follow you."

Marshal glanced from me to the island. "You're serious. Damn, who are you, girl?"

Sitting straighter, I stuck my pasty white hand out, thinking it must be really clammy from the cold damp on the water. "Rachel Morgan, third partner of Vampiric Charms out of Cincinnati. That's Jenks, second partner of the same."

Marshal's hand was warm, and as we shook he gave Jenks a sideways glance, a smile quirking the corner of his lips. I didn't think he believed me yet. "You're the silent partner, eh?" Marshal said, and Jenks cracked an eyelid and let it shut. "You know," he went on, releasing my hand, "I was willing to go along with the joke because you're cute and we don't get many cute witch tourists. But this?" He gestured to the distant island. "Can't we just go to dinner?"

My eyes narrowed. I leaned forward until I was too close for my comfort. "Look, Mr. Captain of the good ship *Lollypop.* I don't *care* if you believe me or not. I *need* to get to the island. I'm *going* over the side of your boat. I want to trade for an extra charm from you so my boyfriend—" I gritted my teeth. "—my *ex*-boyfriend doesn't freeze on the way back. Actually, I want to trade for three, because I don't have any warmth amulets and I think they're pretty cool. The equipment, I'd like to arrange for an extended rental. If I lose them on the way, which is a distinct probability, you can take the price of them off my card. You got it on file."

He looked at me, and I felt queasy from the adrenaline. "Is it real?"

"Yes it's real! It ran through, didn't it?"

Hairless brow furrowed, he eyed me. "How do I know your magic is good? You smell good, but that doesn't mean fish guts."

I looked at Jenks, and he nodded. "He's a pixy," I said, tossing my head to him. "I made him big so he could handle the cold temps up here while we rescued his son." Okay, technically Ceri made the curse, but I could stir rings around this guy.

Marshal seemed impressed, but what he said was, "His son is your boyfriend?"

Exasperated, I felt my hands start to shake with my desire to scream. "No. But Jenks's son was with him. And he's not my boyfriend, he's my former boyfriend."

Exhaling long and slow, Marshal eyed first Jenks, then me. I waited, breath held.

"Bob!" the man shouted to the front of the boat, and I stiffened. "Come on back here and help me get my gear on. I'm going to take Mr. and Ms. Morgan on an extended tour." He looked at me, taking in my obvious relief. "Though I don't know why," he finished softly.

Twelve

I didn't like the cold. I didn't like the feeling of so much water pressing on me. I didn't like that in some way I was connected to the ocean, with nothing between me and it but water. And I really didn't like that I had watched *Jaws* last month on the Classic Channel. Twice.

We had been swimming for some time, caught between the gray of the water surface and the gray of the unseen bottom, deep enough that a passing boat wouldn't clip us but shallow enough that the light still penetrated well. Marshal was clearly on edge about leaving the security of the diving-boat flag, but he was young enough to like breaking the rules when it suited him. I think that was why he was helping me. Life up here couldn't be that exciting.

The claustrophobic feeling of breathing underwater had eased, but I still didn't like it. Marshal had taken a heading from the boat, and all we had to do was follow it using the compass in the air gauge. Jenks had taken point, I was second, and Marshal brought up the rear. It was cold despite the amulets, and the farther we went, the more grateful I was becoming.

Marshal wasn't getting anything out of this but a good story he couldn't tell anyone. He had only asked one thing of me, and I quickly agreed, adding my own request.

He would get us to the island undetected, but he was going to take his equipment back with him. It wasn't that he was worried about losing the investment in his gear, but that Jenks and I might try to swim back through the shipping channel and get ourselves chopped to bait by a tanker. Good enough reason, but I agreed to it not because of my safety, but Marshal's.

I wanted him out of there and safe. He lived here. If I got caught and the Weres suspected he had helped us, they might go after him. I made him promise he'd go back to his boat, finish his dive, and return to the dock as if nothing had happened.

I had asked him to forget me, but I selfishly hoped he wouldn't. It had been fun talking about spells with someone who stirred them for a living. I didn't find that very often.

Slowly the water around me brightened from light reflecting off the rising bottom, and my adrenaline spiked when I realized we'd reached the island. The current had kept the dropoff sharp, and about thirty feet from the shore we stopped, my fins resting on the smooth, fist-sized rocks the bottom was made of.

Step one—check, I thought when I broke the surface, my pulse pounding from the stress of the dive. Marshal had warned us, but it still came as a surprise. Swimming with the sedate pace of a fish sounded easier than it was. My legs felt like rubber and the rest of me like lead.

The return to wind and sound was a shock, and I squinted through my fogged-up mask at the empty shore. Relieved, I edged in until I could sit neck deep in slightly warmer water. Pulling off my mask and mouthpiece, I took in crisp air that didn't taste like plastic.

Jenks was up already, and red pressure lines marked his face. He looked as tired as I felt. Different muscles, I decided. Too cold, perhaps. Marshal came up beside me in an upwelling of bubbles, and I turned to the boat, glad to find its white smear some distance away. The farther it was, the less likely the Weres would think it was a threat.

"You okay?" I asked Jenks, and he nodded, clearly miserable with cold despite the amulet Marshal had given him. Satisfied to simply sit and catch my breath, I scanned the empty shore. It looked peaceful enough, with a few gulls stomping about on the narrow beach, screaming as they weighed the possibility of a snack coming their way.

"I could've flown that in three minutes," Jenks said, wiggling out of his harness.

"Yeah," I said, following suit. "And collapsed from cold halfway to become fish food."

"Jax made it," he said sourly. "And I might collapse from the cold anyway. How do you stand it, Rache? Tink's titties, I think parts of me fell off."

I snorted, removing my gloves to fumble numbly at my belt. With Jenks's help I got out of my own gear and felt a hundred times lighter. Somewhere along the way I'd scratched the healing gashes of my knuckles back open, but my hands were too cold to bleed. I looked at the white-rimmed wounds, thinking I'd never get them healed over at this rate.

Marshal stood, sleek in his custom-designed wet suit of gold and black, his mask resting atop his forehead. "Rachel," he said, his brown eyes worried. "I changed my mind. Leaving you here isn't a good idea."

Jenks glanced at me, and I stifled a sigh, having half expected this. "I appreciate that," I said, lurching to stand and almost falling down again, "but the best way you can help me is to get yourself back out to your boat and finish your day as if you'd never heard of me. If any Weres come sniffing around, tell them you took me out on your boat and I hit you on the head and stole your gear. You didn't go to the I.S. because you were embarrassed."

From beside me, Jenks looked at Marshal's muscular physique, clearly defined under the thick rubber, and chuckled. Marshal's smile widened, the water glinting on his face. "You're really something, Rachel. Maybe—"

Fins and gear in hand, I headed for the beach to get out of my wet suit. "No maybes," I said, not looking back. As my bare feet splashed in the sparkling surf, I dropped everything but my waist pack, reaching for a ley line and not finding one. I wasn't surprised. I had a spindle of ley line energy in my head, but I couldn't make a circle unless I tapped a line. It was limiting, but not debilitating.

"I've got your business card at the boat," Marshal insisted, following me. Jenks was right behind him, his pixy strength letting him carry his gear and our tanks both.

"Burn it?" I suggested. Stumbling on the smooth, fist-sized rocks, I sat down before I fell over. I didn't feel a bit like James Bond as I pulled a rock from under me and tossed it aside.

Jenks dropped everything where I had, then came to sit beside me with a weary sigh. With his help I peeled out of the wet suit, to feel cold and exposed.

Marshal stood awkwardly between me and the water, an obvious target should anyone come out of the nearby woods. "I should have known something was wrong when you wore running tights under your wet suit," he said as the suit came off.

The rocks were cold through the wet spandex, and setting my waist pack on my lap, I unzipped it. Everything was dry inside the zippy bags, and as Jenks got out of his suit, I put my lightweight running shoes on, fingers fumbling from the cold. Marshal's eyes widened at the splat gun peeking from around the rim. Letting him get an eyeful, I handed Jenks his scent disguise amulet, then dropped mine around my neck, tucking it behind the collar of my black two-piece running outfit. Reminded, I took Marshal's warmth charm and extended it to him. Marshal took a breath to protest, and I said, "It's got your name on it."

I nudged Jenks, and he reluctantly handed his over too. While he and I prepared to move, Marshal's expression slowly turned from puzzlement to alarm. It was a lot colder without the amulets, and I felt the wind keenly through the wet spandex. Tension had me stiff when I rolled up the wet suit as best I could and handed it to him.

"This isn't good," Marshal said as he took it and I sat on the rocks and looked up at him.

"No, it isn't," I said, cold, wet, and tired. "But here I am."

Feet shifting on the rocks, his glaze drifted to the splat gun, and while he fidgeted, I handed Jenks his share of the splat balls, which he dropped into a mesh bag hanging from his waist. I had offered to get him his own gun at the shop where I picked up the paint balls to fill with the sleepy-time potions, but he'd wanted the impressive-looking slingshot instead. It fastened to his arm and looked as effective as a crossbow. I was willing to bet he was as accurate with it too.

Ready to go, Jenks stood in a clatter of sliding stones, taking a stick of driftwood and swinging it as if it was a sword. He was gracefully controlled, and Marshal watched for a moment before he extended a hand to help me up. "You're a good witch, right?"

I took it, feeling the warmth and strength behind it. "Despite how it looks? Yes," I said, then tugged the cuff back down over my demon scar. My fingers slipped from his, and he dropped a step away. *I was a white witch, damn it.* Behind me, Jenks thrust and parried, silent but for his feet in the stones. We had to get going, but Marshal stood in front of me, looking sleek in his wet suit, warmth amulets dangling from his fingers.

He looked behind him at his boat and our gear piled on the shore. Lips tight in decision, he bowed his head and peeled the sticker off an amulet. "Here," he said, handing me the charm.

I blinked, the cold vanishing as my fingers touched it again. "Marshal . . ."

But he was moving, lean muscles bunching as he gathered a handful of equipment and strode to the edge of the vegetation. "Keep them," he said as he dropped the gear in the scrub, then went back for another, second load. "I changed my mind. I thought you were joking about this rescue thing. I can't leave you here without a way off. Your boyfriend can use my gear. I'm going to tell my boys you panicked and made me radio the water taxi to get you back to land. If you have to swim for it, hug Round Island to get to Mackinac Island and take the ferry. You can leave everything in a locker at one of the docks and mail me the key. If you don't swim off, leave everything here, and I'll pick it up the next time we get a good fog."

My heart seemed to swell and my eyes warmed from gratitude. "What about your driver?"

Marshal shrugged, his rubber-clad shoulders looking good as the sun glinted on him. "He'll go along with it. We go way back." His eyes went narrow with worry. "Promise me you won't trying to cross the straits. It's too far."

I nodded, and he handed Jenks his amulet back. "Watch the ferries coming in to Mackinac Island. Especially the ones that hydroplane. They come in fast. There's a second warmth amulet in my gear for your boyfriend. I have it for emergencies." He winced, his hairless eyebrows rising. "This sounds like one."

I didn't know what to say. From beside me, Jenks peeled the sticker from his amulet and fed it to one of the gulls ringing us. It flew squawking away, three more in hot pursuit. "Marshal," I stammered. "You might lose your license." *Best-case scenario.*

"No, I won't. I trust you. You aren't a professional diver, but you're a professional something, and you need a little help. If you have any problem, just dump the gear and swim at the surface. I'd, uh, rather you didn't, though." His brown eyes seemed to flit among the trees. "Something weird has been going on over here, and I don't like it." He smiled, though he still looked worried. "I hope you get your boyfriend back okay."

Relief slipped into me. God, what a nice guy. "Thank you, Marshal," I said, leaning forward and pulling myself up to give him a kiss on the cheek. "Can you reach your boat okay?"

He nodded, discomfited. "I do a lot of free swimming. Piece of cake."

I remembered my stint of swimming in the frozen Ohio River, hoping he would be okay. "Soon as I can, I'll call you to let you know we made it okay and where your stuff is."

"Thanks," he said, head swinging back up to me. "I'd appreciate that. Someday I'm going to track you down, and you're going to tell me what this was all about."

I felt a sloppy smile come over me. "It's a date. But then I'll have to kill you."

Laughing, he turned to go, then hesitated, the sun glinting on his suit. "Burn your card?"

Brushing my wet hair back, I nodded.

"Okay." This time he didn't stop. As I watched, he waded into the surf, diving into a wave and starting for his boat with clean, smooth strokes.

"*Now* I feel like James Bond," I said, and Jenks laughed.

"Into the woods," Jenks said, and with a last backward look at Marshal, I headed for the scrub. The smooth rocks were hard to walk on, and I felt like an idiot wobbling after him. It was warmer without the wind, and after only a few steps the beach turned into a thick brush.

The first of the spring-green leaves closed over us, and as I picked my way through the vegetation, Jenks asked, "Do you like him?"

"No," I said immediately, feeling the tension of a lie. How could I not? He was risking his livelihood, and maybe his life.

"He's a witch," Jenks offered, as if that was all it took.

Toying with the idea of letting the stick I was holding fling back to slap him, I said, "Jenks, stop being my mother."

The brush thinned as we forced our way into the interior and the trees grew larger.

"I think you like him," Jenks persisted. "He's got a nice body."

My breath came quick. "Okay, I like him," I admitted. "But it takes more than a nice body, Jenks. Jeez, I do have a *little* depth. You've got a great body, and you don't see me trying to get into your Fruit of the Looms."

He reddened at that, and finally breaking through into a clearing, I stopped, trying to find my sense of direction. "Which way do you think the compound is, anyway?"

Jenks was better than a compass, and he pointed. "Want to run until we get close?"

I nodded. Jenks was wearing Marshal's warmth amulet and looked toasty, but it was too much for me. Without it I felt sluggish, and I hoped I didn't hurt myself until I warmed up. Between Jax and the old plot map in the local museum, we had a good layout of the island.

Jenks ran a finger between his heel and his shoe before taking a deep breath and breaking into a slow lope that wouldn't stress us too much and would give us time to dodge obstacles instead of running into them. Jax had said most of the buildings in use were by the island's lakes; that's where we were headed. I thought of Marshal swimming for his boat and hoped he was okay.

As usual, Jenks took point, leaping over decaying logs and dodging boulders the size of a small car, which had been dumped by the last glacier. He looked good running ahead of me, and I wondered if he would run a few laps with me at the zoo before I switched him back. I could use the morale boost of being seen with him. It was quiet, with only birds and animals disturbing the morning. A jay saw us, screaming as it followed until losing interest. A plane droned overhead, and the wind kept the tops of the trees moving. I could smell spring everywhere, and I felt as if we had slipped back in time with the clear air, the bright sun, and the spooked deer.

The island had been privately owned since forever, never developed from its original temperate-zone mix of softwood forest and meadow. Officially it was now a private hunters' retreat, patterned after Isle Royale farther north, but instead of real wolves tracking down moose, it was Weres sporting with white-tailed deer.

During a careful questioning, Jenks and I had found that the locals didn't think highly of either the year-round residents or the visitors who passed through their town on the way to the island, never taking the time for a meal or to fill up their gas tank. One man told Jenks they had to restock the deer every year since the animals could and did swim for the mainland—which made me all warm and fuzzy inside.

According to the records and what little Jax told us, a primitive road circled the island. I was breathing hard but moving well when we found it, and Jenks cut a hard right as soon as we crossed it. He slowed too, but we still ran right into the deer carcass.

Jenks jerked to a stop, and I plowed into him, pinwheeling to keep from falling into the hollowed-out body, its head flung over its back and its eyes cloudy.

"Holy crap," he swore, panting as he backed up, white-faced. "It's a deer, isn't it?"

I nodded, transfixed and breathing heavily. There was surprisingly little smell since the temperatures had been keeping the decomposition slow. But what worried me was that it had been gutted, the entrails eaten first and the rest remaining as a slow smorgasbord.

"Let's get out of here," I said, thinking that even though the Weres were on a private island, they were doing their entire species a great disservice. Remembering and honoring your heritage was one thing. Going wild was another.

We backed away, the low growl rumbling up from behind us pulling me to a heart-pounding halt. *Damn*. From the other side came a high yip. *Double damn*. Adrenaline pulsed through me, making my head hurt and my hand drop to the reassuring feel of my splat gun. Jenks turned, putting his back to mine. *Shit. Why couldn't anything be easy?*

"Where are they?" I whispered, bewildered. The clearing looked empty.

"Rache?" Jenks said. "My size recognition might be off, but I think it's a real wolf."

I followed his gaze, but I didn't see anything until it moved. My first flush of fear redoubled. A Were, I could reason with, shouting things like I.S. investigations, paperwork, and news crews, but what could you say to a wolf whose kill you ran into? And what in hell were they doing with real wolves? God, I didn't want to know.

"Get your ass up a tree," I said, fixed on the yellow orbs watching me. My gun was in my hand, arms extended and stiff.

"They're too thin," he whispered. "And I've got your back."

My gut clenched. Three more wolves came skulking out

from the brush, snarling at each other as they closed the distance. It was a clear indication that we should leave, but there was nowhere to go. "How good are you with that slingshot?" I said loudly, hoping the sound of our voices would chase them off. *Ri-i-i-ight.*

I heard a low thrum of vibrating rubber, and the closest wolf yipped, shying before it snapped at its pack mate. "It didn't break against the fur," Jenks said. "Maybe if they're closer."

I licked my lips, my grip on my gun tightening. Crap, I didn't want to waste my spells on wolves, but I didn't want to end up like that deer either. They weren't afraid of people. And what that likely meant gave me an unsettled feeling. They'd been running with Weres.

My pulse jackhammered when the nearest wolf started an unnerving pace to me. The memory of Karen pinning me to the floor and choking me into unconsciousness raced through me. Oh God, these wolves wouldn't pull their punches. I couldn't make a protective circle.

"Use 'em, Rache!" Jenks exclaimed, his back to mine. "We've got three more coming from my side!"

Adrenaline burned, tripping me into an unreal high of the calm-of-battle. I exhaled and squeezed the trigger, aiming for the nose. The nearest wolf yelped, then dropped in its tracks. The rest charged. I gasped, praying the compressed air would hold out as I continued to shoot.

"Stop!" shouted a distant masculine voice. The sound of tearing bushes spun me.

"Rachel!" Jenks cried, falling away.

A black shadow crashed into me. I screamed, clenched into a ball as I hit the ground. Leaf mold hit my cheek. The musky scent of Were filled my senses. The memory of Karen's teeth on my neck paralyzed me. "They're alive!" I shouted, covering my face. "Damn it, don't hurt me, they're alive!" This wasn't an alpha contest, but an attack in the woods, and I could be as scared as I wanted.

"Randy, stand down!" the masculine voice shouted.

I still had my gun. I still had my gun. The thought of it slid through my panic. I could plug the son of a bitch if I needed to, but putting him down might not be the best way to go about this. Now that we were found, I'd rather talk my way out of it.

The Were standing over me grabbed my shoulder in his mouth, and I almost lost it. "I submit!" I shouted, knowing it would likely trigger a different set of reactions. My hand still gripped my gun, and if things didn't change really fast, I was going to drop him.

"Get off her," Jenks said, his voice low and controlled. "Now."

All I could see was werewolf hair, long, brown, and silky. The heat from him was a moist wave of musk. I shook from the adrenaline as the Were snarled, my shoulder still in its mouth. I heard three pairs of people feet come to a thumping halt around us.

"What is he?" I heard one whisper.

"He's going to be a chew toy if he doesn't put that sling-shot down," another answered.

I took a breath, willing myself to stop trembling. "If this moldy wolf hide doesn't get off me, I'm going to *spell him!*" I shouted, hoping my voice wasn't shaking.

The Were growled, and I couldn't help but shriek, "I'll do it!" when his grip tightened.

"Randy, get your wormy ass off her!" the first voice exclaimed. "She's right. They aren't dead; they're knocked out. Stand down!"

The pressure on my shoulder increased, then vanished. Hand on my shoulder, I sat up, trying not to shake as I took in the clearing. It was full of downed wolves and Weres, all but one in their people shift.

Jenks was surrounded by three Weres in brown fatigues holding conventional weapons. I didn't know what they were, but they looked big enough to leave holes. He still hadn't lowered his arm with the slingshot on it, and it was pointed at a fourth Were standing a little apart from everyone else. *He* didn't have a drawn weapon, but it was clear he was in charge since he had a shiny little emblem on his cap instead of a patch like everyone else. He looked older too. There was a pistol in a holster on his belt, and brown face paint marked his skin. Swell, I'd fallen into a freaking survivalist group. Just peachy damn keen.

The Were that had pinned me was nosing the three downed wolves. In the nearby distance a wolf howled, and I shivered, pulling my legs straight. "Can I stand up?"

The Were with the emblem on his hat snorted. "I don't know, ma'am. Can you?"

Funny, funny man. Taking that as permission, I sullenly got to my feet, brushing the sticks and leaf mold off. He had a twang to his voice, as if having grown up in the South.

"Your weapon?" he said, eyes tracking my movements. "And the bag and any charms."

I debated for all of three seconds, then emptied the chamber and broke all the balls underfoot before tossing it. He caught it with an easy grace, an amused smile on him. His gaze lingered on my neck and the clearly Were bite marks, and I made a face of exasperation. God! Maybe I should have worn a turtleneck to storm the rebel fortress.

"Witch?" he said, and I nodded, throwing him my pack and two amulets. I could have given them to Marshal, for all the good they had done me.

"I came for Nick," I said, shivering in the new cold. "What do you want for him?"

The surrounding Weres seemed to relax. Jenks jerked when one reached for his slingshot, and I did nothing when they wrestled him to the ground and took it and his belt pack away, looking like bullies falling on a kid after school. Jaw gritted at the grunts and thumps of fists into flesh, I watched the leader instead, wanting to know whom we faced. He wasn't the alpha, I decided, while his men smacked Jenks into a temporary submission. But by his clean-shaven face and his bearing, he was high up in the pack.

Standing my height in heavy-looking military boots, he

made a good-sized Were, well-proportioned and tidy in his fatigues, with narrow shoulders and a body that looked like it was used to running. Trim, not blocky in the least. Maybe late thirties, early forties—his hair was cut too close to his skull to know if it was gray or simply blond.

Jenks shoved the three Weres off him in disgust and got to his feet, a sullen, beaten pixy. He was bleeding from a scratch on his forehead, and his face went ashen when he saw the blood on his hands. With that, he lost all his will to fight, obediently wobbling into place behind me when we were encouraged to head back to the road.

Time to go meet the boss.

Thirteen

As we jostled down the shaded road, the wind from our passage dried my sweat and made my curls into lank tangles. Jenks and I were in the back of the open-aired Hummer—whoo-hoo, a convertible—the Were with the pin on his black cap sitting opposite us along with three other guys, weapons pointed. It was kind of sad, really, as it wouldn't take much to wrestle one away and fall out of the vehicle if I wanted to risk being shot. But Jenks was bleeding from a scalp wound, shaking as he sat beside me, his hand pressing the clean bandage they gave him against it. It hadn't looked bad when I first saw it, but by his reaction, he'd be dead in five minutes. I wanted to see how bad it was before we did anything spectacular.

The Were in wolf's clothing was up front with the driver, squinting against the wind, his tongue hanging out. It would have been funny if it hadn't been for the guns.

"Do they have to drive so fast?" I muttered to Jenks. "There're deer out here."

The guy in charge met my eyes. They were brown, pretty in the flickering light coming through the skimpy tree cover and reminding me of David's boss, being both everywhere and nowhere at the same time.

"They don't move much 'cept for dusk, ma'am," he said, and I bobbed my head. *Especially if they're dead and gutted,* I thought sourly.

Not really caring, I turned away. What I'd wanted to know

had been answered; he wasn't adverse to Jenks and me talking. I didn't know if we were prisoners or guests. But there were those weapons . . .

Mr. I'm-in-charge adjusted his cap, then jiggled the driver's elbow, pointing to the radio. "Hey," he drawled into the mike after the driver passed it to him. "Somebody pick up."

After a moment a slurred, crackling "What?" came back.

The man's thin lips went thinner. "Three of Aretha's pack are down at Saturday's kill. I want a tank truck out there—now. Get a full data spread before you douse them."

"I don't have any saltwater made up," whoever it was complained. "No one told me we were collecting data this month."

"That's because we aren't," he answered, anger growing in his face, though it wasn't in his slow speech. "But they're down, and since Aretha has pups in her, I want an ultrasound. And be careful. They're riled up and likely to be unpredictable."

"An ultrasound?" came an indignant voice. "Who the hell is this?"

"This here is Brett," he drawled, shifting his cap farther back and squinting at the sun. We hit a bump, and I clutched at a support post. "Who the hell is this?"

There was no answer except static, and I snickered, glad I wasn't the only one in trouble. "So," I said when Brett gave the mike to the driver and settled back. "Are you a survivalist group or a wolf research station?"

"Both." He shifted his brown eyes between Jenks and me. The large pixy had his head bowed over his knees, ignoring everyone in his effort to keep his hand to his wound.

I pulled a strand of hair out of my mouth, wishing I had on more than my black tights. I looked like a thief, and the men surrounding me were getting their money's worth. They were in baggy camouflage, and from what I could see, each had a Celtic knot tattooed in the arch of their ears that matched the emblems on their hats. *Huh.*

Most packs had a tattoo that all members subscribed to,

but they usually put them in a more traditional place. Weres loved body decoration, standing in stark contrast to vamps, who shunned getting ink even if a parlor would give them any. It seemed that pain was part of the mystique, and since vamps could turn pain into pleasure, it was a rare artist who would work on vamps, living or dead. But Weres indulged themselves freely, and the best artists could run on four feet as well as two. I was glad David hadn't brought up the idea of a pack tattoo.

Jenks was starting to hyperventilate, and I put a hand on his shoulder. "Take it easy, Jenks," I soothed, growing anxious when the light brightened and we slowed, easing into a pleasant-looking compound. There was a lake nearby, with a mishmash of small cabins and larger homes surrounding it, well-tended dirt paths everywhere. "I'll get you something as soon as we stop."

"You will?" he said, tilting his head to meet my eyes. "You'll fix it?"

I nearly laughed at his panicked expression until I remembered it was a pixy wife's ancestral duty to keep her mate alive and no one else's—and Matalina wasn't here.

"Matalina won't mind," I said, then wondered. "Will she?"

His eighteen-year-old features scrunched into relief. "No. I didn't want to assume—"

"Good Lord, Jenks," I said, weight shifting when we stopped. "It's no big deal."

Brett's eyes were bright in speculation at the exchange, and he made us remain seated until everyone else got out. The Were in wolf's clothing was last, and as soon as Jenks and my feet hit the parking lot, Brett directed us to head to the lake. The people who saw us were curious, but the only ones stopping to watch wore either bright flamboyant clothes or casual business attire, both of which looked out of place among the predominant fatigues. Clearly they were not military, and I wondered what they were doing there. Everyone was on two feet, which wasn't surprising since it seemed there were two or possibly three packs on the island—three *big* packs—and when packs mixed, fur flew if they didn't stay people.

It was highly unusual to have Were packs mixing like this. Indeed, I could see it in the thinly veiled disdain that the Weres in fatigues showed the street Weres, and the belligerent why-should-I-care-what-you-think attitude of the colorfully dressed pack in response.

Chickadees called in the chill spring air, and the sun was dappled through the pale green leaves of the saplings. It was a nice spot, but something smelled rank. Literally. And it wasn't the breath of the Were padding on four feet to my right.

My worried gaze followed Jenks's to the lake. Logs were arranged in a circle around a large defunct bonfire, and I could faintly smell the acidic odor of hurt and pain over the scent of old ash. All of a sudden I did *not* want to go over there.

Jenks stiffened, nostrils flaring. He dug in his heels with a defiant clench to his jaw. Tension slammed into me, and every man with a weapon tightened his grip as we came to a collective halt. The Were on four feet growled, ears flat and his lip curled to show white teeth.

"Now y'all just ease down," Brett said softly, cautiously evaluating Jenks's resolve and rocking back. "We aren't going to the pit. Mr. Vincent will want to see you." He cocked his head at the driver. "Put them in the living room, get them a med kit, and back off."

My eyebrows rose, and the men surrounding us with their matching fatigues and cute caps looked among themselves, their grips on their weapons shifting. "Sir?" the driver stammered, clearly not wanting to, and Brett's eyes narrowed.

"You got a problem?" he said, his slow drawl making twice as many syllables as was warranted. "Or is security for a witch and a—whatever he is—beyond you?"

"I can't leave them alone in Mr. Vincent's living room," the driver said, clearly worried.

A Jeep with a milky-white tank and coiled hose was leaving, and Brett smiled, squinting in the sun. "Deal with it," he said. "And next time, don't start to Were 'less I tell you.

Besides, he looks smart," he added, indicating Jenks, "and right quiet. A gentleman. So I'm willing to wager he won't be doing anything rash." His amiable demeanor fell away to leave a hardened will. "Capiche?" he said to Jenks, every drop of casual country boy gone.

Jenks nodded, his face both serious and scared. I didn't care if this was their standard good cop/bad cop ploy as long as I didn't have to go to the lake. Relieved, I smiled at Brett, not having to fake my gratitude. In the brighter light at the outskirts of the parking lot, I could tell that his hair was silver with age, not sunlight, putting him closer to forty than thirty. Brett's answering smile made his face wrinkle, his eyes amused as he clearly realized I was playing the grateful captive and not as helpless as I let on.

"Randy?" he said, and the Were on four feet pricked his ears. "You're with me." Turning on a heel, he strode to the second largest building off the lot, the pony-sized Were trotting beside him. The driver watched them go, his lips moving in an unheard curse. With obvious anger he jerked his weapon, indicating we should take an alternate path. Jenks and I fell into step before they could touch us. *Time for a little bad cop?*

We were headed away from the pit, but I didn't feel much better. The walkway was made of flat slate, and Jenks's running shoes were silent beside mine. The Weres scuffed in their boots behind us. The building we were headed for looked like it had been built in the seventies, low-slung and made out of a salmon-colored stone, with high small windows that overlooked the lake. The middle section was taller, and I imagined it had vaulted ceilings since it wasn't quite high enough for a full second story. I slowed as I approached the entryway, thinking the massive wood and steel door looked like it belonged to a vault.

"You want me to just walk in?" I asked, hesitating.

He sneered, clearly not happy about his boss reprimanding him by giving him an awkward task that, if we ran, he would be punished for. Not to mention Brett had taken with him the only member of his team that might have a chance of catching us.

Taking that as a yes, Jenks reached in front of me to pull the door open, leaving his blood behind on it. It would be a good marker of where we were for someone looking if they forgot to clean it off. I don't think anyone even noticed, and we slipped inside.

"Down the hall and to the left," the driver said, gesturing with the butt of his weapon.

I was tired of his attitude; it wasn't my fault Brett was mad at him. I took Jenks's elbow—apparently the sight of his blood was making him woozy again—and led the way past sterile walls to a bright spot at the end of the hall. It was clearly a living room, and I evaluated it for possibilities while the driver had a hushed conversation with the armed sentry in the archway. More weapons, but no face paint or insignia on them this time apart from the tattoo.

The low ceilings of the hallway gave rise to that story and a half I had noticed from outside. To my right a bank of windows opened onto an enclosed courtyard landscaped with shrubs and a formal fountain. To my left was the exterior wall facing the lake, a catwalk tucked under the high windows. Defense was written all over the sunken room, and my mind pinged on my first idea—that this was a survivalist's group. I was willing to bet that when they left us alone, someone would still be watching, so it was no surprise when Jenks muttered, "There are six cameras in here. I can't place them all, but I can hear their different frequencies."

"No kidding," I said, eyes roving but seeing nothing in the plush sunken living room with two opposing couches, a coffee table, two chairs by the windows, and what I thought was a modest entertainment center until I realized it held two huge flat screen TV's, three satellite boxes, and a computer that would have made Ivy salivate.

I followed Jenks down the shallow step to sit at the couch, farthest in, barking out a derisive, "Hurry up with that first-aid kit," when the driver hustled everyone out.

He hefted his rifle in a show of aggression, and I gave him a simpering smile. "Right," I said, flopping on the couch and stretching my arms out along the top of it. "You're going to plug me in your boss's living room and get blood all over his carpet because I was snippy. Do you know how hard it is to get blood out of carpet? Be a good little pup and do what you're told."

Jenks fidgeted, and the man flashed red, his jaw muscles clenching. "You keep backing into your corner," he said as he lowered his weapon. "When it comes to it, I'll be there."

"Whatever." I looked at the ceiling, baring my already bruised throat to him though my gut twisted. With Weres, your rank determined how you were treated, and I wanted to be treated well. So I was going to be a bitch in more than one definition of the word.

I never heard him leave, but I let out my held breath when Jenks relaxed. "He's gone?" I whispered, and he made an exasperated face.

"Tink's panties, Rache," he said, sitting on the edge of the couch beside me and putting his elbow on his knee. "That was rash even for you."

I brought my head back down to look at him. Surrounded by carpet and walls, I could smell the lake on me, and I ran a hand through my tangled damp curls, getting my fingers stuck. I thought about pushing his elbow off his knee, but didn't since he was still bleeding. Instead I sat up and reached for the bandage pressed against his head.

"Don't," he said, sounding frantic as he drew back.

Lips pursed, I glared about the room at the unseen cameras. "Where's my damn first-aid kit!" I shouted. "Someone better bring me my kit, or I'm going to get pissed!"

"Rache," Jenks protested. "I don't want to see the pit. It smelled awful."

Seeing his worry, I tried to smile. "Believe me, I'm trying to stay out of it. But if we act like prey, they'll treat us like a wounded antelope. You've watched Animal Planet, right?"

We both looked up when a small girl dressed in jeans and

a sweater came in from the room's only door. She had a tackle box in her hand, and she silently set it on the table before Jenks and me. Not meeting our eyes, she backed three steps away before turning around.

"Thank you," I said. Never stopping, she looked over her shoulder, clearly surprised.

"You're welcome," she said, stumbling on the step up out of the sunken area. Her ears went red, and I guessed she was no more than thirteen. Life was good in a traditional Were pack if you were on top, crap if you were on the bottom, and I wondered where she fit in.

Jenks made a rude sound, and I opened it up to find the usual stuff—minus anything sharp and pointy. "So why were you nice to her?" he asked.

I dug until I found a good-sized bandage and a packet of antiseptic wipes. "Because she was nice to me." Pushing the tackle box aside to make room on the table, I sat sideways. "Now, are you going to be nice to me, or am I going to have to get bitchy?"

He took a deep breath, astonishing me when he went solemn and worried. "Okay," he said, slowly peeling the bandage away. Eyes fixed to the blood on it, he started to breathe fast. I almost smiled, seeing that it was little more than a scratch. Maybe if he was four inches tall and had a thimbleful of blood it might be a problem, but this was nothing. It was still bleeding, though, and I tore open the antiseptic wipes.

"Hold still," I said, pulling away when he fidgeted. "Darn it, Jenks. Hold still. It's not going to hurt that bad. It's just a scrape. The way you're acting, you'd think it was a knife wound that was going to need stitches."

His jerked his gaze from the bloodstained bandage to mine. The light coming in from the courtyard made his eyes very green. "It's not that," he said, reminding me that we were being watched. "No one but Matalina has ever tended me before. Except my mother."

I set my hands on my lap, remembering hearing somewhere that pixies bonded for life. A trickle of blood headed for his eyes, and I reached for it. "You miss Matalina?" I said softly.

Jenks nodded, his gaze going to the rag as I dabbed at his forehead, gently brushing aside his yellow curls. His hair was dry, like straw. "I've never been away from her this long before," he said. "Ten years, and we've never been apart for more than a day."

I couldn't help my twinge of envy. Here I was, tending an eighteen-year-old ready to die and missing his wife. "You're lucky, Jenks," I said softly. "I'd be ecstatic if I could manage a year with the same guy."

"It's hormonal," he said, and I drew away, affronted.

"I think I saw some alcohol in here," I muttered, flipping the tackle box back open.

"I meant between Matalina and me," he said, the rims of his ears reddening. "I feel bad for you, stumbling about searching for love. With Matalina, I just knew."

Making a sour face, I teased out another antiseptic wipe and carefully dabbed his scrape to pick out a leaf chip. "Yeah? Well witches aren't that lucky."

I threw the bloodied pad on the table, and Jenks slumped, going soft and misty-eyed. "I remember the first time I saw her," he said, and I made a *mmmm* of encouragement, seeing that he'd finally quit fidgeting. "I had just left home. I was a country boy. Did you know that?"

"Really?" The bandage I had pulled out was too big, and I rummaged for something smaller. Spotting a Handi Wipe, I gave it to him to clean his fingers with.

"Too much rain and not enough sun," he said as he set his rag aside and opened the package as if it held gossamer. Carefully, he unfolded the cloth. "The garden was bad. I could either fend for myself or take the food out of my sibling's mouth. So I left. Hitched a ride on a produce truck and ended in Cincinnati's farmers' market. I got beat up the first time I trespassed in the streets. I didn't know crap."

"Sorry," I said, deciding that Jenks might take offense at the Barbie Band-Aid and shuffled through until I found a

He-Man one. *Just who were they giving first aid to? Kindergarteners?*

"It was just plain luck Matalina found me sleeping under that bluebell plant and not one of her brothers. Luckily she found me, woke me, and tried to kill me in that order. I was even luckier when she let me stay the night, breaking her family's first rule."

I looked up, my tension easing at the love in his eyes. It was shocking to see it there, honest and raw in so young a face.

He gave me a weak smile. "I left before sunup, but when I heard a new housing development was going in near Eden Park, I went to look over the plans. They were putting in lots of landscaping. I asked Matalina to help me, and when the trucks came, we were there. One person can't hold anything, but two can have the world, Rache."

I had a feeling he was trying to tell me more than his words were saying, but I didn't want to listen. "Hold still," I said, pushing his hair out of the way and putting the bandage on. I leaned back, and his bloodied hair fell to hide it. Turning to the table, I gathered my mess into a pile, not knowing what to do with it.

"Thank you," Jenks said softly, and I flicked a glance at him.

"No prob. Matalina stitched me up right nice, so I'm glad to return the favor."

There was a scuffing at the open archway and we turned. A small man in slacks and a red polo shirt had come in, his pace quick and confident—busy, was the impression I got. Two men in fatigues were right behind him. They had pistols in leg holsters, and I stood. Jenks was quick to follow, tossing his stained curls out of his way.

The man's hair was cut close to his head, military style, with a whiteness that stood out in sharp contrast to his deep tan and wind-roughened features. There was no beard or mustache, which didn't surprise me. Presence flowed from him like cologne as he stepped down into the living room, but it wasn't Trent Kalamack's confidence based on manipulation. No, it was a confidence born from knowing he could pin you to the floor and hurt you. He was in his early fifties, I guessed, and I'd dare call him squat and compact. None of it was flab.

"Boss man, I presume?" I whispered, and he came to a jerky halt four feet away, the table between us. His intelligence was obvious as he looked Jenks and me over, fingers fumbling at his shirt pocket for a pair of glasses while we stood there in our thief-black outfits.

The man took a breath and let it out. "Hell," he said to Jenks, his voice rough, as if he smoked a lot. "I've been watching you the last five minutes, and I don't know what you are."

Jenks looked at me and I shrugged, surprised to find him that open and honest. "I'm a pixy," Jenks said, tucking his hand behind his back so the man wouldn't try to shake it.

"By God, a pixy?" he blurted, brown eyes wide. Glancing at me, he put his glasses on, took a breath, and added, "Your work?"

"Yup," I said, reaching out to shake his hand.

My breath hissed and I jerked back when the two men that had come in with him cocked their weapons. I hadn't even seen them pull them.

"*Stand* down!" the man bellowed, and Jenks jumped. It was shockingly loud and deep, carrying the crack of a whip. I watched, heart pounding until the two men lowered their sights. They didn't put the guns away, though. I was starting to hate those little hats of theirs.

"Walter Vincent," the man said, hitting the *t*'s sharp and crisp.

I glanced at the men behind him, then extended my hand again. "Rachel Morgan," I said more confidently than I felt. "And this is Jenks, my partner." This was weird, civilized. *Yes, I've come to rob you, sir. / How delightful; won't you have some tea before you do?*

The Were before me pursed his lips, his white eyebrows going high. I could see his thoughts jumping and I found myself thinking he had a rugged attractiveness despite his age, and that he was likely going to have someone hurt me. I was a sucker for a smart man, especially when the brains came packaged in a body that was carefully maintained.

"Rachel Morgan," he said, his voice rising and falling in amazement. "I've heard of you, if you can believe it. Though Mr. Sparagmos is of the belief that you're dead."

My heart gave one hard beat. *Nick was here. He was alive.* I licked my lips, suddenly nervous. "It was only a bad hair day, but try telling that to the media." I exhaled, never looking away, knowing I was challenging him but feeling I had to. "I'm not leaving without him."

Head bobbing, Walter backed up two quick steps. The men behind him had a better shot at me, and my heart found a faster pace. Jenks didn't move, but I heard his breathing quicken.

"Truer words may never have been spoken," Walter said. It was a threat, and I didn't like the complete unconcern in his voice. Jenks moved to stand beside me, and the tension rose.

A small man in fatigues silently came in with a sheet of paper, distracting him. Walter's eyes slowly slid from me, and my pent-up shudder broke free. My lips pressed together in annoyance that he had gotten to me. Walter stood by the wide window, light spilling in over him and his paper as he squinted at it. While reading, he pointed to the first-aid kit, and silently the man collected it all and left.

"Rachel Morgan, independent runner and equal third holder in Vampiric Charms," Walter said. "Broke from the I.S. last June and survived?" His attention came back to me. Curiosity high in his rugged, tanned face, he sat in an overstuffed chair and let the paper fall to the floor. No one picked it up. I glanced at it, seeing a blurry shot of me with my hair all over the place and my lips parted like I was on Brimstone. I frowned, not remembering it being taken.

Walter put an ankle on one knee, and I pulled my gaze up, waiting.

"Only someone very smart or very wealthy survives an I.S. death threat," he said, thick powerful fingers steepled. "You aren't smart, seeing as we caught you, and you clearly work for your bread and butter. Being from Cincinnati, you're logically one of Kalamack's more attractive sacrificial sheep."

I took an angry breath, and Jenks caught my elbow, jerking me back. "I don't work for Trent," I said, feeling myself warm. "I broke my I.S. contract on my own. He had nothing to do with it, except that I paid for my freedom by almost nailing his ass for trafficking in biodrugs."

Walter smiled to show me small white teeth. "Says here you had breakfast with him last December after a night on the town."

My flush of anger turned to one of embarrassment. "I was suffering from hypothermia and he didn't want to drop me at the hospital or my office." One would have gotten the law involved, the other my roommate, both to be avoided if one's name was Kalamack.

"Exactly." Walter leaned forward, his eyes fixed on mine. "You saved his life."

Rubbing my fingers into my forehead, I said, "It was a one shot deal. Maybe if I had been thinking I would've let him drown, but then I would've had to give the ten thousand back."

Walter was smug as he leaned into his chair by the window, the sun glinting on his white hair. "The question you will answer is how did Kalamack find out about the artifact's existence, much less that someone knew where it was and where that person is?"

Slowly I sat on the edge of the couch, feeling sick. Jenks moved to the other side of the coffee table, sitting to watch my back, Walter, and the door all at the same time. Male Weres were known to cut females of any species a lot of slack since their hormones guided their thoughts, but eventually logic would kick in and things were going to get nasty. I glanced at the two men by the door, then the plate-glass window. Neither one was a good option. I had nowhere to go.

"I've nothing against you," Walter said, bringing my attention from the possibility of throwing one of them into the glass to break it, thus solving two problems at once. "And I'm willing to let you and your partner go."

Astonished, I stupidly did nothing when the small man pushed up from his chair in a smooth, very fast motion. The two men by the door were already moving. My breath caught and I stifled a gasp when the compact Were was suddenly on me.

"Rache!" Jenks shouted, and I heard the click of safeties. There was a scuffle that ended with his grunt of pain, but I couldn't see him. Walter's face was in the way, calm and calculating, his fingers lightly around my neck, just under my chin. Adrenaline pulsed to make my head hurt. Almost too fast to realize, the older Were had pinned me to the couch.

Heart pounding, I jerked back my first instinct to struggle, though it was hard, really hard. I met his placid brown eyes, and fear struck me. He was so calm, so sure of his dominance. I could smell his aftershave and the rising scent of musk under it as he hung over me, his small but powerful hand under my chin the only place we touched. His pulse was fast and his breathing quick. But his eyes were calm.

I didn't move, knowing it would trigger an entirely new set of ugliness. Jenks would suffer and then me. As long as I didn't do anything, neither would Walter. It was a Were mind game, and though it went against all my instincts, I could play it. My fingers, though, were stiff and my arm was tense, ready to jab his solar plexus even if it did get me shot.

"I'm willing to let you go," he repeated softly, his breath smelling of cinnamon toothpaste and his thick lips hardly moving. "You will return to Kalamack and tell him that it's mine. He won't have it. It belongs to me. Damn elf thinks he can rule the world," he whispered so only I could hear. "It's our turn. They had their chance."

My heart pounded and I felt my pulse lift against his fingers. "Looks to me like it belongs to Nick," I said boldly. *And how had he known Trent was an elf?*

I took a quick breath of air, jerking when he pushed himself away and was suddenly eight feet back. My gaze shot to Jenks. He had been dragged to the middle of the room, and he now held himself to favor his right leg. He gave me an apologetic look he didn't owe me, and the two men holding him let go at a small gesture from Walter. The dry blood in Jenks's his hair was turning a tacky-looking brown, and I forced my eyes from him and back to Walter.

Ruffled, I refused to touch my neck, instead draping my arms over the top of the couch. Inside I was shaking. I didn't like Weres. Either hit me or back off, but this posturing and threats was useless to me.

Exuding confidence and satisfaction, Walter sat, taking the couch opposite me and mirroring me almost exactly. Clearly the Were wasn't going to break the silence, so I would. It would cost me points in this inane game, but I wanted to see the end of it before the sun went nova. "I don't give a damn about your artifact," I said, voice soft so it wouldn't shake like my hands were threatening to. "And as far as I know, Trent doesn't either. I don't work for him. *Intentionally.* I'm here for Nick. Now . . ." I took a slow breath. ". . . are you going to give him to me, or am I going to have to hurt a few people and take him?"

Instead of laughing, Walter's brow furrowed and he sucked on his teeth. "Kalamack doesn't know," he said flatly, making it a statement, not a question. "Why are you here? Why do you care what happens to Sparagmos?"

I pulled my arms from the couch, putting one hand on my hip and the other gesturing in exasperation. "You know, I asked myself that same question just this morning."

A smile came over the Were, and he glanced to a decorative mirror, presumably two-way. "A rescue of the heart?" he said, and I warmed at the mockery in his voice. "You love him, and he thinks you're dead. Oh, that's classic. But it's stupid enough to be the truth."

I said nothing, gritting my teeth. Jenks shifted closer, and the sentries adjusted the grip on their weapons.

"Pam?" Walter called, and I wasn't surprised when a

diminutive woman entered, arms swinging confidently, an amulet dangling from her fingers. She was dressed in lightweight cotton capri pants and a matching blouse, her long black hair coming to her mid-back. Defined eyebrows, thick pouty lips, and a delicate facial bone structure gave me the impression of a china doll. *A very athletic china doll,* I amended when she pointedly dropped the amulet on the coffee table in accusation.

Truth charm, I guessed by the notches on the rim, and I pulled my gaze away from the clatter of it hitting the table. Weres used witch magic more than vamps, and I wondered if it was because they needed the boost of power more than the vamps, or if it was that vamps were so sure of their superiority they felt they didn't need witch magic to compete with the rest of Inderland.

"She's not lying," the woman said, giving me a quick smile that was neither warm nor welcoming. "About anything."

Walter sighed as if it was bad news. "I'm sorry to hear that," he said softly.

Damn. I looked at Jenks. His eyes were wide and he looked anxious. He had heard it too. Something had shifted. *Double damn.*

Six more men came in and Walter stood, curving his arm familiarly about Pam's waist and tugging her closer. "Pit them," he said, sounding regretful, and Jenks stiffened. "I want to know if anyone is coming after her." He smiled at Pam. "Try not to do anything that can't be undone? We may have to give them back to whoever backed her in this. She many not belong to Kalamack, but she belongs to someone."

"Whoa! Wait up," I said, standing. "You'd let me walk out of here if I worked for Trent and was after your stinking statue, but you're going to put me away if all I came for was Nick?"

Jenks groaned, and I froze when Walter and Pam looked to the truth amulet on the table. It shone a nice, friendly green. "And you knew it was a statue, how?" Walter said softly.

Crap on toast. Stupid, *stupid* witch. Now they wouldn't

stop until they found out about Jax. I knew Jenks's thoughts were on a similar path when he jiggled on his feet, anxious.

"Find out what they know," Walter said, and a wild look came over Jenks.

I fought to not move as someone put his hands on me, exerting a steadily growing pressure to fall into motion. Brett's stocky figure eased into the archway, his expression clearly saying he thought they were making a mistake. "I'm not going to talk," I said, shaking inside. "There isn't a spell stirred that can make me saying anything, much less the truth."

Walter favored me with a smile that showed his small teeth. "I wasn't planning on using spells to make you talk. We have drugs for that," he said, and I went cold. "Sparagmos has quite a resistance to them and we've since turned to older methods. He's resisting those too, but maybe we can move him by hurting you. All he does is weep when we ask him where the statue is. Pam, will you supervise her interrogation? My ulcer acts up when I hurt a woman."

He started for Brett and the archway, leaving Jenks and me with a room full of weapons. Frantic, I looked from Jenks to Walter standing by the door, giving a quiet set of instructions to Brett. I scanned the room as if for options, finding none.

"If she knows, someone else does too. Find out who," Walter finished.

"Rache?" Jenks whispered, clearly tensed to move but waiting for me to give the word.

"I claim ascension," I said, frightened. *Oh God. Not again. Not on purpose.*

Walter jerked, but it was Pam who spun, her dark hair furling with the motion and her lips parted, a surprised doll with red cheeks.

"I claim the right for pack ascension," I said louder. I wasn't about to fight her, but I could stall for time. Kisten would know something was wrong if I didn't call him in three days. At that point I didn't care if I had to be rescued or not. "I want three days to prepare. You can't touch me," I added for good measure.

Anger pulled Walter's white eyebrows tight, and furrows lined his brow. "You can't," he said. "You aren't a Were, and even if you were, you'd be nothing but a two-bite whore."

Jenks didn't relax, but he was listening, as was everyone in the room. Poised. Waiting.

"I can," I said, shrugging out of the grip of whoever held me. "I do. My pack number is O-C(H) 93AF. And as an alpha, I can claim ascension over whomever in hell I want to. Look me up. I'm in the catalog." Shaking, I gave Pam a shrug I hope she understood meant it was nothing personal. She looked at the bruises on my neck, her eyebrows rising but her thoughts unknown.

"I don't want to front your lousy tick-infested pack," I said, making sure everyone knew where I was coming from. "But I want Nick. If I best your alpha, then I claim him and leave." I took a slow breath. "We all leave. Intact and unharassed."

"No!" Walter barked, and everyone but Pam and I jumped.

Jenks looked worried, his green eyes pinched. "Rache," he said, apparently not caring everyone could hear him. "Remember what happened the last time?"

I shot him a poisonous look. "I won last time," I said hotly.

"By a point of law," he said, jerking to a standstill when he tried to take a step and the men surrounding him threatened violence.

"Jenks," I said patiently, ignoring the pointed weapons. "We can try to fight our way out of some crazy survivalist's group, swim for shore, and hopefully elude them, or I can fight one stinking Were. One way, we end up hurt and with nothing. The other way, I'm the only one who gets hurt, and maybe we walk away from this with Nick. That's all I want."

Jenks's face fell into an unusual expression of hatred that looked wrong on him. "Why?" he whispered. "I don't know why you even care."

I dropped my eyes to the carpet, wondering that myself.

"This isn't a game," Walter said, his round face going red. "Get the medic up here with the drugs. I want to know who sent them and what they know."

The man grabbed me and I tensed.

"Ah, Walter, dear?" Pam said, and everyone in the room froze at the ice in her voice. "What, by Cerberus's balls, are you doing?"

In the silence, Walter turned. "She isn't a Were. I thought—"

His words cut off at Pam's low noise. Her eyes were squinting and her hands were on her hips. "I've been challenged." Her voice got louder. "How am I supposed to walk out of this room and not have every last whining dog think I'm a coward? I don't care if she's a leprechaun and has green tits, she just pissed in my food dish!"

Jenks snickered, making Walter's ears redden. "Sweetie . . ." he coaxed, but he was hunched and submissive. I cocked an eyebrow at Jenks. Maybe I'd been going about Weres all wrong. It was the women who held the balls of the alpha males that really had the power.

"Sugar Pup," he tried again when she pushed his hand off her. "She's stalling for time. I want to know who's coming to bail her out before they get here. She's not a Were, and I don't want to jeopardize gaining the artifact by adhering to old traditions that don't belong anymore."

"It's those traditions that put you where you are now," she said scathingly. "We don't have to give her three days." Pam turned to me, simpering. "We do it now. Think of it as me softening her up. It will be fun. And if she cheats with her magic, the pack can rip her to shreds."

My hope did the proverbial swirl down the crapper. Walter apparently didn't know what to do either as he stood in blank surprise while Pam kissed his cheek, smiling. "Give me twenty minutes to change," she said, then sashayed out.

I looked at Jenks. *Shit.* This was not what I had planned.

Fourteen

L ittle sun made it past the fragile spring leaves, and I shivered. *It is the cold,* I thought, not the rank smell of ash and emptied bowels or the people joining the noisy throng in twos and threes. And it wasn't that Jenks had his hands cuffed before him. And it couldn't be from the air of a festival growing as everyone gathered to see me get mauled. No, it had to be from the chill May afternoon.

"Yeah, right," I whispered, forcing my hands from my elbows and rocking to my toes to loosen my muscles. The scent of old smoke was strong from the nearby fire pit, almost hiding the rising odor of musk. I had a feeling they would've lit the bonfire to add to the travesty if it had been later. As it was, the people in fatigues and little caps were arranging themselves in small knots in one corner. Across the clearing, the street Weres in their baggy, colorful clothes were more cool as they portrayed an indifference that was fake but effective nonetheless. Between them was the third group, wearing slacks and dresses. They were quietly laughing at the guys in fatigues, but were clearly wary of the rougher, wild cannons the street Weres made with their show of jewelry and loud voices. The excited chatter was getting on my nerves.

Under it was the sensation of gathering power. It tickled through me, and my expression blanked as I slowly recognized the unfamiliar feeling. With thoughts of the fiasco at Mrs. Bryant's running through me, I opened my mind's eye to see the surrounding Weres' auras. My gut twisted as they swam into view.

Crap on toast, I thought, glancing worriedly at Jenks. All three packs had the same sheen of brown rimming their auras. Most Weres had an outermost haze reflecting the predominant color of their male alphas, and the chance that all three alpha males on the island had brown auras was slim. They were bound into a round under one Were. Damn it, this wasn't fair!

And the bond was strong too, I realized as I scanned the compound for a way out of this. Strong enough to sense, as it hadn't been at David's intervention, which didn't bode well for the upcoming alpha contest. Listening to the jeers and chatter around me, I couldn't help but feel as if the extra strength came from the subordinate members joining it.

Walter wasn't an especially powerful alpha, and I wasn't vain enough to think that they had done this just to see me get torn apart. I was getting the sensation that they had been bound to a common goal for weeks, maybe. Days, at the least.

Disconcerted, I dropped my second sight and stretched where I stood, legs spread wide and bending at the waist to place the flat of my arms against the hard-packed dirt. I had to find a way to break the round or today would be a repeat of Karen without the happy ending.

My butt was in the air, with only my black tights between me and their imaginations, and at a rude laugh, I came up in a slow exhale. I turned to Jenks. They had let him wash the blood off his hair, and his blond mop was in loose ringlets, throwing his green eyes in stark relief. Youthful features pinched, he stood absolutely still for once, and I didn't think it was because of the armed guard. Actually, I was surprised they had him here, but he *was* providing a lot of entertainment and was a curiosity in himself. I could understand their confidence. Even if we got away, how could we escape survivalists, street-racer gangs, and Weres with credit cards?

About the only thing going for me was that my rudimentary ley line skills hadn't made it to Walter's report. I was a strict earth witch, according to it, and seeing as I hadn't made a circle or hit the wolves with anything other than an earth charm, they had no idea I could work the lines too. Just as well. They would have put one of those nasty black ratchet-wristbands on me for fear I'd tap a line through my familiar and make them all toads. That I didn't have a familiar was a mute point. The band would have still made me helpless, robbing me of the energy I had in my chi and spindled in my head. And I wanted to use it.

I looked at my feet and stifled a shiver of nervousness. I'd wanted to turn Jenks his proper size before this got started. Jax waited at the hotel, and as long as it was warm, Jenks could fly back and they could get out of here. This wasn't a rescue anymore; we were down to salvage.

Excitement rose through the surrounding Weres—sending the feeling of sandpaper over the skin of my aura now that I was aware of it—and I followed everyone's attention as Pam made her sedate way to us. Her red robe fluttered about her bare feet, and with her hair flowing about her, she looked exotic, walking under the trees as if belonging to the earth. My muscles tensed, and avoiding her eyes, I went to Jenks for a last word.

"Stop!" one of his guards barked before I had gone three feet, and I froze, hip cocked.

"Give me a break," I said loudly, as if I wasn't shaking inside. "What, by the Turn, do you think I'm going to do?"

Pam's voice rose high, carrying a derision I wasn't sure was aimed at me or the guys with guns. "Let her talk to him," she said. "It may be the last time she has her wits about her."

That's nice, I mused, the threat of their doctor with his needles keeping me quiet.

Pam swayed to a halt before two women. They didn't look enough alike to be friends. The tallest was wearing a well-worn leather halter and classically torn jeans, and the other had on an inappropriate dress suit and heels. Visiting alphas, I guessed.

The four men around Jenks had lowered their weapons a

smidge, and I sidled past. I was finding it easier to ignore the barrels pointed at me, though stress had me wound tighter than Ivy's last blind date. "Jenks," I said. "I want to turn you small."

His worry melted into disbelief. "What the hell for?"

I grimaced, wishing the guards weren't hearing this. "You can fly back to the mainland while it's warm, get on a bus, go home, and forget I ever asked you to help me with this. I don't know if I have enough ever-after spindled to invoke both spells, and I can't let you risk being stuck like this if I—" I grimaced. "—if I get hurt," I finished. "I don't think Ceri can reverse the curse herself, so she'd have to twist a new one, and for that she'd need demon blood. . . ." I wanted him to tell me I was being an ass and that he was with me to the end, but I had to offer.

His brow furrowed. "Are you done?" he said softly. I said nothing, and he leaned forward, putting his lips beside my ear. "You're a dumbass witch," he whispered, his words soft but intent, and I smiled. "If I could, I'd pix you for a week for even suggesting I up and leave you here. You're going to unwind that ever-after in your head to Were. Then you're going to pin that woman. And then we will get the hell off this island with Nick.

"I'm your backup," he said, taking a flushed step backward. "Not a come-easy friend who flies away at the first sign of a problem. You need me, witch. You need me to carry Nick if he's unconscious, hotwire the jeep to drive back to the beach, and steal a boat if he can't swim. And Jax is fine," he added. "He's a grown pixy and can take care of himself. I made sure before we left that he knew the number to the church and could read Cincinnati off the bus schedule."

The lines in his face eased, and a crafty glint replaced the hard anger in his eyes. "I don't need to be small to get out of these cuffs." He sent one eyebrow up, turning into a scallywag. "Five seconds, easy."

The wash of relief flowing through me was distressingly short-lived. "But I'm not going to let her pin me," I said.

"I'm going to fight until I can't anymore. If I die, you're stuck like this."

His smile widened. "Aw, you aren't going to die," he said mischievously.

"Why? Because you're with me?"

"Ooooh, she can be taught." Hiding his hands from the guards, he bent his thumb, moving it in a stomach-turning disjointedness so the cuffs could slide right off. "Now get out there and get a mouthful of bitch ass," he finished, jiggling his wrists so the metal links fell back in place.

I snorted. "Thanks, Coach," I said, feeling the first fingers of possibility ease my slight headache, but as I looked over the noisy throng, I grew depressed. I did *not* want to do this. It was a demon curse, for God's sake. *And the easiest way to get out of this,* I thought. Ceri had said the payment wouldn't be that bad. The smut would be worth escaping being drugged. I'd seen her make the curse. Nothing had died to make it. *I* was paying the price, not some poor animal or sacrificial person. Was it possible for a curse to be technically black but morally white? Did that make using it right, or was I just a chicken-ass taking the easy way out and rationalizing myself out of a lot of pain?

You can't do anything if you're dead, I told myself, deciding to worry about it later.

Nauseated, I looked over the heads of the growing conglomeration of Weres. The energy coming off them seemed to swirl around me like a fog, making my skin tingle. Okay . . . I was going to be a wolf. I wouldn't be helpless like before. Pam might not feel any pain, but if I got ahold of her neck, she was going down in a modified sleeper.

A quick glace at Pam, and I shook my hands to loosen them. As challenger, it was my place to assume the field first. Breath held, I took five steps into the clearing. The noise increased, and a swift memory of being a contestant in Cincy's illegal rat fights flitted through me and was gone. What was it with me and organized beatings, anyway?

Pam turned. Head high, she smiled at the women with her and touched the shoulder of the one with the most polish in parting. Light on her bare feet, she came forward, the crowd's noise turning softer, more intent. It was easy to see the predator in her despite her diminutive size, and she reminded me of Ivy, though the only similarity was their grace.

"Rache?" Jenks said loudly, the alarm in his voice bringing me around. He pointed with his chin to Walter approaching on the same path his wife had used. There were two men with him: one in a suit, and the youngest in head-to-toe red silk, his walk a jewelry-jangling swagger.

Walter halted at the edge of the circle, and on impulse I opened my second sight. Walter's aura wasn't rimmed in that hazy brown sheen—it was permeated with it. The entire three packs had begun to accept his dominance.

I quickly scanned the other two alpha males' auras. Theirs were clear of Walter's influence, as were their wives', but the visiting alphas had to know it was happening. That they were voluntarily letting him do this to their packs scared the crap out of me. Whatever Nick had stolen must be big for them to bind themselves for so long that Walter was starting to claim them all. It went against all Were tradition and instinct. It just wasn't done.

Walter looked utterly satisfied. He glanced at me, his eyebrows rising as if knowing I could visually see the mental connection he was fixing over another alpha's pack. Smirking, he looked to Pam and gestured.

Pam reached for the tie to her robe. "Wait!" I called, and a ripple of laugher went through them. They thought I was frightened. "I have a spell to Were with, and I don't want to get shot using it."

There was a collective hesitation, and most of the conversations were stilled, the street gang muttering the loudest. I shifted from foot to foot, waiting. Pam recovered smoothly, coming to a halt a good ten feet from me. "You can Were?"

she said, a mocking smile on her. "Walter, honey, I didn't think earth witches could do that."

"They can't," he said. "She's lying so she can put a black spell on us."

"I can Were," I said, letting my second sight fade. "It's a ley line, ah, charm, and if I had wanted to put a spell on you, I would have done it already. I'm a white witch." My stomach hurt and I had to go to the bathroom. Oh God. I was a white witch, but it was a black curse. I had sworn I wouldn't, and here I was, jumping head first into the hole. It didn't matter that the black was negligible. It was going to be on my soul. What in *hell* was I doing here?

Walter looked at the crowd when a few called to get on with it. "Pam?" he asked, and the slight woman beamed, playing up to them.

"Challenger's choice," she said, and the assembled Weres cheered.

Walter nodded. "Your choice," he said to me. "Do you want to start on two feet, making part of the contest how fast you can Were, or do you want to Were and then begin?"

"I know what challenger's choice is," I said snottily. "I *have* done this before. And this isn't legal. My alpha isn't here, and there aren't six other alphas to adjudicate in his absence."

Walter's face showed shock for an instant, then he hid it. "We have six alphas," he said.

"*She* doesn't *count*!" I said, pointing, but all they did was laugh at me. *Like I really thought they would do this by the book?*

"We start from four legs," I said softly, knowing she was going to Were fast anyway, so I might as well have a chance to catch my breath before we got on with it.

The crowd liked that, and Pam nonchalantly undid the tie to her robe, letting it slip from her to pool at her feet and leave her stark naked. She looked like a goddess with her perfect tan, standing with one foot slightly before the other. Even her stretch marks added to her image of proud survivor. The noise of the crowd never changed or acknowledged her new, ah, look.

I flushed, dropping my gaze. God help me, I wasn't going to do the same. Jenks's clothes had vanished with even his scars when he turned. I expected it would be the same for me, and I wouldn't show up as a wolf in black tights and a lacy pair of underwear—as amusing as that would be. No way was I going to show them I was a nasty pasty color with freckles.

A shiver of adrenaline went through me. That, the crowd responded to, and I watched a visiting alpha bring her a sheaf of pungent wolf's bane. A murmur of approval rose when she curtly refused. No one offered me any. *Bitches.* Not that it would have helped.

Pam closed her eyes, and my lips parted as she started to change. I'd only seen Hollywood's version, and by God, they had it right. Her features molded, elongating in the face and thinning in the arms and legs in a gross caricature of human and wolf. I had no idea where she was getting the power to shift since Weres couldn't, and didn't, use ley lines to Were like werefoxes did, which was why they could control their size, a talent werewolves envied.

Pam collapsed to her—I guess they were almost haunches now—and propped herself up with her emancipated arms. Her entire skin flashed to black and silky fur appeared. A whine came from her, and her eyes flashed open, still human and grotesque. Her face was ugly, with a long muzzle still holding human teeth. She was neither wolf nor human, caught in the middle and completely helpless. *And damn, it was fast!*

"Rache!" Jenks shouted. "Do something!"

I looked across the cheering Weres to him as Pam fell over into a stiff-legged posture, shaking as her insides rearranged. *Oh yeah.* Heart pounding, I shut my eyes. Immediately the smell of rising musk and the stink of my own sweat struck me. Over it was the smell of maggot-infested flesh from the as yet unseen pit. I didn't think there was anyone still alive in it, but I couldn't tell for sure. The sound of the crowd beat on me, the waves of force coming off them distracting. I put my hands together over my chi and hoped it wasn't going to hurt too badly.

"*Lupus,*" I breathed, my eyelashes fluttering.

I took a breath, eyes flashing open when the ever-after unrolled from my thoughts. Like a scab peeling away, it had a delicious painfulness, a feeling of returning to an earlier state. A sheet of black-stained ever-after filmed me, and I couldn't see clearly. My hearing was gone, wrapped in a muzzy blanket.

My balance shifted and my knees and hands hit the earth, almost seeming to sink. I threw my head back and gasped at the feeling of electricity stacking me differently. But it didn't hurt as the earth charm had when I turned into a mink. This wasn't a cobbling together of parts and pieces, but a pulse of growth from atoms to memories, natural and painless as breathing. I was alive, as if every nerve was feeling for the first time, as if the blood moved for the first time. I was alive. I was here. It was exhilarating.

Head up, I laughed, letting it spill from me, a chortling chuckle, that expanded into a howl. The black ever-after dropped from me and my hearing exploded into existence, filling my ears with the sound of me. I was alive, damn it, not just existing, and everyone would know.

My exuberant howl rose, silencing everyone. In the distance there was an answer. I recognized it. It was Aretha, the wolf we'd met when we first came on the island. She met my voice with her own, telling me she was alive too.

And then the price for me breaking the laws of nature hit me. My voice cut off in a strangled gurgle. Unable to breathe, I fell, clawing at my new muzzle with dull nails. Panicking, I felt the crushing weight of black soak in. I shuddered, and my eye stung as I forgot to close them and I rubbed my face into the earth. Tighter, the band of blackness clenched around my soul.

No! I thought, seeing the gray of unconsciousness tingle at the edge of my sight. I would survive. I wouldn't let it kill me. I could take this. Ceri had, and a thousand times worse. I could do this. But it hurt. It hurt like shame and despair made real.

My will rose, accepting what I had done. Panting, I forced my tongue into my mouth. There was dirt on it, and my teeth were gritty. Shaken, I lay and did nothing, content to feel my lungs work. Everything was in black and white except for the last few feet. I could see color if it was close enough. And as my eyes took in the world while I figured out how to get up, my mind started inventing colors until it seemed natural. The sounds, too, were alien. Piecing them together was beyond me, and what I couldn't decipher retreated into a background hiss.

"Rache!" Jenks shouted, and I winced when my ears flicked backward. Appalled, I felt my tail thump. *This is pathetic.* I held my breath to get up when I found I wasn't coordinated enough to do both at the same time, yet. Frustrated, I staggered to my feet, feeling the new way my muscles worked and nearly falling again.

Pam was still sprawled on the earth, panting as she finished changing. She had to be close; Karen had Wered in about thirty seconds. It was about that now. The scent of ash and decayed flesh was choking. Under it I could smell the packs about me like fingerprints, the scent of gunpowder on some, the stink of grease on others, mild, expensive fragrance on the rest. Pam was a weird mix, her alienness of being part human and part wolf like the taste of rotten eggs in my nose and on my tongue.

I sneezed, just about going over. The crowd gasped, and I suddenly realized they were silent, watching me in a mix of shock and awe. So I had Wered? So what? I had said I could.

"She's red!" someone whispered.

Surprised, I looked at what I could see of myself. *Holy crap, I was!* I was a freaking red wolf, with softly waving red fur that turned black about my feet. *Hey, I was pretty!*

On all fours, I swung my head up to Jenks. His eyes flicked to mine, then out again, telling me to pay attention to what was going on. "She's a red wolf," someone in baggy pants said, shaking his neighbor's arm. "She Wered perfectly." His voice grew in awe. "Look at her! She's a fucking red wolf!"

The murmur was lifted up and repeated, and if a wolf could flush, I did. What did it matter what color I was? All I had to do was pin Pam.

As if hearing my thoughts, Pam surged to her feet in a splurge of motion. She was huge, having retained all her human mass. Lips curling from her long muzzle, she let a soft growl slip from her, her brown eyes fixed on me. My pulse surged and my hind foot slipped back. The crowd cheered at that, hurting my ears. Pam's growl continued, promising me pain. Walter would probably try to stop her from killing me until I gave them the information they wanted, but I doubted he was going to be successful.

"Take your best shot," I barked, and she lunged, the packed dirt spurting out behind her.

Pam's rumble turned aggressive as she halved the distance between us. My thoughts lit on Karen, her jaws around my neck and my crippling fear. But then I saw the pride in her eyes, and something snapped. Under the fur and lean muscle, she was intelligent, and with that comes a knowledge of pain—even if she wouldn't feel it.

I forced my muscles to bunch and darted forward, silent and low to the ground.

We met in a confusion of snapping teeth and stumbling paws. She hadn't expected this, and her reach for my throat landed on my hindquarters. She twisted for my neck, forefeet almost on me. Belly on the ground, I ducked under her and found something to bite. It was a narrow leg of fur and bone. I bit down hard. *I would not die here because of another woman's pride.*

The ugly rasp of bone scraped my teeth like nails on a chalkboard. A yelp of pain burst from her, giving me a surge of hope. *She had felt it?*

Pam fell on me as I took her support away. She rolled and

I backed up on all fours. I was covered in dirt, and by the dull throb, I think she had bit my hip.

The Weres surrounding us screamed their approval, the well-dressed businessmen somehow looking uglier than the men in fatigues brandishing their weapons in salute of their alpha. Jenks looked ready to fly to my side, held back by increasingly lax soldiers. I wondered why they hadn't taken her pain other than when she Wered, then realized that's what they were after. David's boss had wanted a quick resolution to an office problem. But these Weres?

I scanned their faces as they cheered. They were savage, cocky, and looking for blood. This was not normal Were behavior, even if we were in the woods away from even the pretense of I.S. law. It wasn't just the military and street Weres either. The ones in business suits and dress shoes were in on it. And as Pam and I circled to access the damage, I had a sickening feeling the difference was from all of them binding together in a round. They *all* had the ego of an alpha flowing through them, but lacked the sophistication to deal with it. They were wallowing in the natural high, aggressive as an alpha but without the control.

I'd have been really worried about it if I didn't have Pam to deal with.

Across the clearing, Pam held a foot off the ground, her eyes determined. Crouched low, I snarled. I knew it was a submissive posture, but I wasn't a wolf inside.

"Rache!" Jenks shrilled an instant before Pam attacked. I backpedaled, but she found me. I went limp when her larger jaws gripped my neck and shook me. Pain flamed and my air was cut off. I all but panicked, sending my forefeet to find her eyes. They wouldn't reach.

She shook me again, her strength terrifying. My spine felt like it was on fire. Pain clouded my thoughts. The screams of the watchers beat at me, telling me to submit. Still in her grip, I swung my hind feet up, curling into a ball. I dug at her face, desperate. She yelped when I found her eyes, flinging me spinning to the feet of the watchers.

"Rachel!" Jenks cried, and I got to my feet, shaking.

"Get Nick!" I barked, hackles raised as I limped forward before I got kicked. I didn't know how this was going to end anymore. I wasn't going to submit. We didn't all have to die.

Pam was panting, the skin around one eye torn. Blood seeped from it, and she tracked my movement, accessing.

"Get Nick!" I shouted again, knowing he wouldn't understand. "I'll catch you up!"

I didn't know if it was the truth or a wish.

"This is hard, Rache," he said softly, but I could hear him. So could Pam. "I'll come back for you after I find him."

Pam's ears pricked as she realized we were still going to make a play for Nick. Head tilted to protect her eye, she sprang forward with a savage sound. She was headed for Jenks.

"Run!" I howled, leaping to intercept her. She skidded to a halt, with me between her and Jenks. I had bitten her twice, and she was learning that small meant faster. I couldn't look to see if he left, but by Pam's eyes tracking something behind me, I had to believe he had. No one was paying attention to him now. Determination swelled in me. He was my vanguard, and this time I had his back. I wouldn't let this she-wolf past me.

Pam shifted her feet in frustration. In what was probably an attempt to warn them, she lifted her muzzle to the sky and howled. The Weres surrounding us joined her, thinking she was trying to cow me. Their human voices almost matched hers.

"You won't get past me!" I barked, then in a bold show, I lifted my own head and howled, trying to drown out her voice. *I am alive. And I will stay that way!*

Pam's howl cut off in surprise, and my voice rose against the rest, its higher pitch sounding more authentic, ringing with defiance. From nearby came another howl. Aretha.

The surrounding Weres went absolutely silent, their faces wondering, fear in some of them. For a moment my voice twined with Aretha's alone, and then they died together.

Pam looked shocked that the wolf had answered me. She stood with her tail drooping, blood dripping from one eye and her rear foot held off the ground. I hurt everywhere: my back, my hip. And the smell of blood came from my pulsing ear. *When had she done that?*

But Jenks was waiting for me. Snarling, I gathered myself and lunged.

Pam fell back, jaws snapping at my neck as I tried for her front leg. I jerked out from under her, a sharp stab in my ear telling me she had scored again. I rolled, and she followed. Flipping to my feet, I met her yap with my own toothy, aggressive grin.

She came at me without pause, and I skittered away. The watchers were silent now. Breathless. Someone was going to die, and Jenks wasn't with me anymore.

I found her neck. My grip slipped when my teeth closed and she jerked back. She had my leg in her mouth, and a rush of adrenaline pulsed. I had half a second before she'd crush it.

I fell to the earth and pulled. Teeth closed on my footpad. I yipped, scrambling up and away. Panting, we hesitated. Behind us the circle of Weres had turned into knots of tense people. No one had noticed Jenks was gone. Pam gathered herself, and I felt a burn of anger.

I didn't have time for this.

But she hesitated, freezing as her attention went to the lake's edge behind me. My fur rose and my skin prickled. I didn't turn. I didn't need to, and alarm showed in Pam's eyes when she saw me track the second wolf skirting the edges of the parking lot behind her, visible past the knots of people. A frightened whisper rose, fingers pointing and hands going to mouths as they realized Aretha had braved the compound, desensitized to the smell of Weres and pulled by the sound of my fight with Pam. Aretha had come, and she didn't look happy.

Ears pricked, the wolf confidently padded across the lot and came under the shade of the surrounding trees. The first roundness of her belly gave witness to the pups she carried, and I felt afraid. Pam and I were fighting for dominance on her island. Her pack had surrounded us as we fought, blind to everything else. *Shit.*

Don't run, Pam, I thought when she went frightened. For all her Wereness, she was also human. She was hurt and surrounded by a wild alpha's pack. And she stank like Were, not wolf. "Pam!" I barked, seeing her start to turn. "Don't!"

But she did. Spinning, she ran, betting they would fall on me as she went for the safety of the buildings. As the joke goes, you don't have to be faster than the wolf chasing you, just faster than everyone else running away.

I jerked, digging my feet into the ground to keep from following when three gray shadows streaked past me after her. The crowd panicked, falling into chaos and scattering. Women screamed and men shouted. Someone shot their weapon off, and I skittered sideways, nails gouging the packed dirt. My pulse hammered.

But my eyes were riveted to the four wolves dodging trees and picnic tables. Terrified, Pam streaked past the security of walls and into the trees. In seconds they were gone. A yip of pain rose sharp over the noise of frightened people. Walter shouted for silence, and in the new stillness there were unseen savage snarls and barks. Then a terrifying silence.

White-faced, Walter gestured, and a cluster of men with unslung weapons raced into the trees after them. I felt sick. This wasn't my fault.

A feminine gasp pulled me spinning around. My heart pounded and I felt my knees go wobbly. Aretha had silently entered the clearing as if the surrounding people didn't exist. Ear flicking, she stopped a good fifteen feet from me, her fur the color of silver bark. I looked at her with my wolf eyes, seeing the grace and beauty—and her utter alienness. I might look like a wolf, but I wasn't one, and we both knew it.

I started, freezing again when she lifted her muzzle. An eerie, soft howl rose from her, picked up by three more voices along the ridge. She was checking to see who had won.

Adrenaline scoured through me. Aretha lowered her head, her yellow eyes fixing on me a last time before she turned and padded across the lot, satisfied.

The wind in the trees slipped down to ruffle the fur about my sore and battered body. *What in* hell *had just happened?*

A twig snapped, and I skittered like a shying horse, heart pounding when I came to an ungraceful halt. It was the street Weres' alpha, pale but determined with his pack around him. "It's not my fault!" I barked, knowing he wouldn't understand.

The Were's Brimstone-weathered face was one of awe as he flicked his eyes from me to where Aretha had vanished. His tattoos from multiple packs made him look rough and uncouth, but his face was as clean-shaven as Jenks's. Bending, he plucked a tuft of red hair that Pam had pulled from me, looking at it as if it meant something. "The she-wolf," he said to Walter, as his roving eyes told me he meant Aretha, "she chose Morgan to live and your alpha to die."

The surrounding Weres started to talk, their voices growing in anger as their shock wore off. I panted, my bruised paw held up off the ground while I waited, feeling the seconds slip away. A shudder rippled over me, making my fur rise. Something was happening.

The street Were tucked the red tuft behind his jacket as if he'd made a decision. "The oldest stories say the statue belonged to a red Were before it was lost," he said, and his wife joined him. "Morgan held her ground when your alpha ran," he said, gesturing. "She won. Give Sparagmos to her. Love will loosen that thief's memory when pain and humiliation won't. I don't care who holds the statue as long as I can have a part of it."

"You gave your allegiance to me!" Walter exclaimed.

"I said I'd follow you when you said you had it!" the young Were said, his hands making fists and his jewelry chiming. His wife was a head taller than he was, but it didn't make him look any less threatening. "You don't. Sparagmos does, and she's claimed him. Dissolve my blood oath. I'll follow a red wolf as soon as a white one. Either way, I'm not following you."

"You lowlife cur!" Walter snarled, red-faced, his white hair standing out starkly. "I have Sparagmos, and I'll have the statue, and I'll have your head as an ashtray!"

The crowd was splitting. I could see it. I could smell it. Old patterns were emerging, both comfortable and familiar. The hair on the back of my neck pricked, and with a small effort I pulled my second sight into focus. My heart quickened. A pearly white now rimmed the street Weres, and an earthy red covered the ones in suits. It had broken that fast.

The entire clearing had shifted. The street Weres were dropping back into the woods. I could smell the whiff of Brimstone. If they went wolf, nothing would contain them.

"Sir," a grief-stricken Were in fatigues interrupted, and I turned to the six men carrying Pam, their slow steps saying it was too late.

"Pam!" Walter exclaimed, grief raw in his voice. The Weres set her gently down, and the man fell to kneel beside her, savagely driving them away before his hands dove into her fur, pulling her up into him. "No," he said in disbelief, his wife's body close to him.

Aretha's pack had torn open Pam's throat, and her blood clotted her black fur and stained his chest. His head going back and forth, the powerful man struggled to find the pieces of his world, scattered like the dead leaves shifting between us.

"No!" Walter shouted, his head coming up and his eyes finding me. "I will *not* accept this. That witch wolf is *not my alpha,* and I will not give Sparagmos to her. Kill her!"

Gun safeties clicked off. *Holy shit!* Panicking, I leapt for the slice of parking lot I could see. An instant and I was through. A screamed curse spurred me on. Nails digging, I reached the woods. My feet slipped on leaves and weak-stemmed plants and I almost went down.

Struggling for balance, I kept driving forward. I listened for the sound of shots, but I was away—for the time being. They had Hummers and cell phones. Against that I had a six-foot pixy and a three-minute head start, tops. *Pam was dead.* This wasn't my fault!

Behind me came the distinctive calls of a mob organizing. They were all people right now, but that was going to change. I had known the peace wouldn't last. Weres were Weres. They never bonded together. They couldn't. It went against everything they were made of.

Thank God for that, I thought as I tracked the scent of snapped twigs, following Jenks. The pixy could find Nick by smell if nothing else. We could still get off this damned island. Maybe the breakup of the round would buy us a few minutes more.

Nick, I thought, my heart racing from more than my escape. So it wasn't the way we planned it. So sue me.

Fifteen

My pace wasn't smooth in any sense of the word, loping through the warming forest, stumbling every time my front foot came down too hard. There were booms in the distance that my wolf hearing couldn't identify, but nothing close. My back hurt in time with my steps, and my front paw was throbbing. The wind cut a sharp pain across my ear where it was laid open. I went as fast as I could, my nose a good four inches above the ground as I tracked the sapling-snapped scent of Jenks.

I was on borrowed time. The island was big, but not that big, and grief would likely make their feet faster, not slower. Eventually someone would catch up to me. If nothing else, Jenks would run into resistance when he found Nick. They had radios.

Faster, I thought, promptly tripping. Pain iced through me and I lunged to catch myself before my face plowed into the ground. My bruised foot gave way, and cursing myself, I held my head high and took the fall, biting my tongue as I came to a sliding halt in the dirt. I was tired of being a wolf. Nothing looked right, and if I couldn't run, there was little joy. But I couldn't say my trigger word and switch back until I reached the mainland and tapped a line.

Besides, I thought, getting up and shaking myself, *I'd be naked.*

I sneezed the dirt and leaf mold out of my nose, whining when my entire body spasmed in pain. The sharp crack of clean wood on metal rang out. My head came up and my breath heaved. A man shouted, "Just shoot him!" and there were three pops in quick succession.

Jenks! Forgetting my hurts, I jerked into a run.

The light brightened around me as the forest thinned. Shockingly fast, I came out into what looked like an old state park with logs bolted into the ground to show parking spots. A Jeep was parked in the shade of a cement-block building painted brown, and near the entrance I saw Jenks attacking two men with a length of wood still sporting leaves.

I bolted forward. Like a dancer, Jenks swung the stick in a wide arc, the wood hitting one man on the ear. Not watching him fall away in pain, Jenks spun, jamming the splintered butt into the solar plexus of the second man. With a silent ferocity, he spun to the first, bringing the stick down with both hands against the back of his neck. The man fell without protest.

Jenks shouted, an exuberant cry of success, as he spun the stick above his head in a wild spiral, slamming it first against the back of a knee, then the skull of the second man. I came to a four-posted halt, shocked. He had downed both of them in six seconds.

"Rache!" he cried cheerfully, tossing his blond curls out of his eyes to show his He-Man bandage. His cheeks were red and his eyes were glinting. "I take it we're going to plan B? He's inside. I can smell crap for brains from here."

Heart pounding, I vaulted over the downed Were in fatigues blocking the door, my nose taking in the stale coffee in the tiny kitchen, the forty-year-old mold in the bathroom, and the pine air freshener fighting the stale musk in the tiny living room festooned with weapons and a two-way radio frantically demanding that someone pick up. My muscles tensed at the scent of blood under the masking odor of chlorine. Nails clacking on white tile, I padded through the narrow hallway, searching.

There was a closed door at the end of a dark hallway, and I waited impatiently for Jenks. He reached over me, pushing it open with a squeak. It was dark, the dim light coming from a dust-caked high window of wire-embedded glass. The air stank of urine. There was a rickety table cluttered with metal and pans of liquid. Nick was gone, and my hope crashed to nothing.

"Oh my God," Jenks breathed, his breath catching.

I followed his eyes to a dark corner. "Nick," I whispered. It came out in a whine.

He had moved at the sound of Jenks's voice, his head lolling up, his eyes open but unseeing from under his long bangs. They had tied him against the wall in a crucifix position in a cruel mockery of suffering and grace. His clothes had burned patches, singed hair and red skin showing past them. Black crusts of blood marked him. His cracked and bleeding lips moved, but nothing came out. "I will not . . ." he whispered. "You can't . . . I will . . . keep it."

Jenks pushed past me, cautiously touching a knife to judge the silver content before picking it up. I was stuck in the threshold, not believing it. They had tortured him. They had hurt him for that damned statue. What in hell was it? Why didn't he just give it to them? It couldn't be money. Nick was a thief, but he loved life more. I think.

"You can't do anything here, Rache," Jenks said, his voice catching as he started to saw at Nick's bonds. "Go keep an eye on the front. I'll get him down."

I jerked when Nick began shouting, clearly thinking they were at him again, calling my name over and over.

"Knock it off, crap for brains!" Jenks yelled. "I'm trying to help you!"

"My fault," Nick moaned, collapsing to lean forward against his bonds. "He took her. He should have taken me. I killed her. Ray-ray, I'm sorry. I'm sorry . . ."

Shaken, I backed out of the room. They hadn't told him I was alive. Sickened, I turned tail and bolted, nails sliding on the tile. I tripped on the man at the door, rolling into the yard. The sun struck me, jolting my horror into the beginnings of anger. Nothing was worth this.

The blue jays were screaming in the distance, and the sound of an engine grew closer.

"Jenks!" I yipped.

"I hear them!" he shouted back at me.

Pulse racing, I looked at the men sprawled in the packed dirt. Grabbing the shoulder of the nearest, I dragged him into the building, not caring if I broke the skin or not. He might have been dead for all I cared. I jerked him halfway down the hallway in short splurges of motion, left him and went back for the second. Jenks was coming out the door as I got him past the sill and inside. I dropped him, my back hurting and my jaws aching.

"Good idea," Jenks said, Nick's arm draped over his neck and shoulder.

Nick hung against Jenks, clearly unable to support his own weight. His head was down and his feet moved sluggishly. His breath came in pained gasps. There were red pressure marks about his wrists, and it didn't look like he could move his legs yet. When he brought his head up, his eyes were cloudy with a smear of gel. Arm moving slowly, he tried to wipe them, blinking profusely. A dry cough shook him. Clenching his arm about his lower chest, he held his breath to try to stop.

"Go," Jenks prompted, and I tore my eyes from Nick. I felt sick again, and as my paws hit the dirt outside, I wondered just where Jenks expected us to "go." There was only one road out of there, and someone was coming up it. And stumbling about with a sick man in the woods was a sure way to be caught.

"Just . . . go behind the building!" Jenks said, and I trotted an uneasy path beside him, feeling small. Nick tried to help as his muscles started to regain their movement. Jenks eased him to the ground, propping him up against the painted brick. It was chill back there, out of the sun, and he held his legs and groaned. I thought of Marshal's warmth amulets. We had only one left—if they hadn't found our gear. Maybe

Nick and Jenks could share it somehow. My fur could keep me warm. *Could I swim that far as a wolf?*

"Stay here," Jenks said to me, standing to look tall. His brow was furrowed. "Keep him quiet. I can take care of them, and then we'll drive out of here."

I put a foot on his shoe for his attention, looking up at him pleadingly. I hadn't liked running apart. I didn't want to do it again. We did better together than alone.

"I'll be careful," Jenks said, turning toward the sound of an approaching vehicle. "If there're too many, I'll hoot like an owl." I raised my doggie eyebrows, and he chuckled. "I'll just shout for you."

At my head bob, he crept away, silent in his black tights and running shoes. I looked at Nick. He didn't have any shoes, and his pale feet looked ugly. *Nick,* I thought, nudging him.

He stirred, wiping the goo from his eyes and squinting. "You're too small for a Were. I thought you were a Were. Good dog. Good dog . . ." he murmured, sinking his fingers into my wavy red fur. He didn't know who I was. I didn't think he recognized even Jenks. "Good dog," he said. "What's your name, sweetheart? How did you get on this hellhole of an island?"

I took a heaving breath, hating this. He looked awful in the brighter light. Nick had never been a heavy man, but in the week Jaxs said he had been on the island, he had gone from trim to emaciated. His long hands were thin and his face was sallow. A beard hid his cheekbones, making him appear like a homeless man. He stank of sweat, filth, and a deep-seated infection.

Looking at him, one would never have guessed at his wickedly quick mind. Or know how easily he could make me laugh, or the love I felt for his complete acceptance of who I was without any need to apologize; a man whose danger was in calling demons and his willingness to risk everything to be smarter than everyone else.

Until I had accidentally made him my familiar and he

seized when I pulled a line of ever-after through him. My eyes closed in a long blink as I recalled the three months of heartache when he avoided me, not wanting to admit that every time I pulled on a line, he relived the entire terrifying moment in his mind, until he couldn't even be in the same city.

I'm sorry, Nick, I thought, putting my muzzle on his shoulder and wishing I could give him a hug. The familiar bond was broken now. Maybe we could return to the way we were. But a wiser voice in me asked, *Do you want to?*

My head came up and my ears pricked at the sound of someone downshifting. I padded to the edge of the building, peeking around to see an open Jeep rocking to a stop. Nick moved to follow, and I growled at him. "Good girl," he said, thinking I was growling at them. "Stay."

My lip curled and I felt my annoyance rise. *Good girl? Stay?*

Two of the four men with weapons got out, calling out for Nick's captors. My pulse quickened as they entered the building. Jenks and I were running without even a sketch of a plan except for, "Stay here, I'll take care of them." What lame-ass kind of a plan was that?

Shifting my front feet, I was debating whether I should do something when Jenks fell out of the tree and into the Jeep. Two savagely powerful blows with his stick and the men in the vehicle silently slumped. Jenks jerked the cap off the last one's head even as he collapsed. Wedging it onto his head, he grinned and gestured for us to stay.

A shout came from inside the building, and Nick and I shrank back.

Heart pounding, I watched Jenks yank one of the men up. There were three quick pops from the building as the two men came out, and blood leaked out of the Were in front of Jenks, shot.

Jenks dropped the Were and jumped into the tree like a monkey. Branches shook and leaves drifted down. The two

Weres with guns shouted at each other, stupidly running over and aiming into the canopy. And I say stupid because they completely forgot there might be someone else here.

"Sweetheart!" Nick shouted as I bolted out to help Jenks.

Thanks a hell of a lot, Nick, I thought as both Weres turned. I barreled into the first, my only goal being to knock him down. The man's eyes were wide. Snarling, I barked and yapped, trying to stay on top of him in the hopes that his buddy wouldn't shoot me lest he hit him instead.

There was the pop of a gun and the crack of wood. In my instant of distraction the Were shoved me off. "Crazy wolf!" he shouted, turning the barrel of his weapon at me. Behind him, Jenks stood frozen in panic. The first man was slumped at his feet, but Jenks was too far away to help me.

A boom of thunder echoed, and the man pointing his weapon at me jumped. My heart pounded and I frantically waited for the pain.

But the Were spun, leaving me to stare in surprise at the hole in his back. My attention flicked behind him to Nick, propped up against the building with a shotgun.

"Nick, no!" I barked, but he took aim again, and with his face white and his hands shaking, he shot him a second time. The Were's gun went off as the slug hit him, but it was a death pull. Nick's second shot had gone straight into his neck. I sprang away and the Were fell, choking as his lungs filled, drowning him in his own blood. He clawed at his throat, gasping.

God help me. Nick had killed him.

"You sons of bitches!" Nick cried from the dirt, having fallen from the recoil this time. "I'll kill you all, you fucking dog-face bastards! I'll kill you—" He took a shuddering breath. "I'll kill you all. . . ." He sobbed, crying now.

Frightened, I looked at Jenks. The pixy stood under the tree, white-faced and scared.

"I'll kill you. . . ." Nick said, hunched on all fours.

I slowly skulked over to him. I was a wolf, not a Were. He wouldn't shoot me. Right?

"Good girl," he said when I nudged him. He wiped his face and patted my head, a broken man. He even let me pull the shotgun from him, and my tongue worked at the bitter taste of gunpowder. "Good girl," he murmured, standing up and wobbling forward.

Though clearly not wanting to touch him, Jenks helped him into the back of the Jeep, where Nick collapsed. Jenks unceremoniously dumped the unconscious men in the front out of the vehicle, and I scrambled into the passenger side, trying to ignore that the man Nick shot had finally stopped making noises. Jenks started the Jeep, and after a few jerks while he learned the practical aspect of how to drive a stick, we started down the road. I touched the radio with my nose, and he turned it up so we could hear.

Jenks looked at me, the wind brushing his bangs back. "He can't swim," he whispered. "And we only have one warmth amulet."

"I can swim." Nick had his head in his hands, his elbows on his knees against the jostling of the rough road.

"They must have a dock somewhere," Jenks continued, not paying him any mind but for a nervous glance. "They probably already have people waiting for us, though."

"I'll kill myself before I let them take me back there," Nick said, thinking Jenks was talking to him. "Thank you. Thank you for getting me out of that hell."

Jenks's lips pressed together and his grip clenched the wheel as he shifted to a lower gear and took a tight turn. "I can smell an oil and gas mix to the south, almost exactly where we came in. It's probably the marina."

Nick pulled his head up, the wind shifting his lank hair from his eyes. "You're talking to the dog?"

Sparing him a glance from under his new cap, Jenks turned away. "She's a wolf. Get it right, crap for brains. Tink's knickers, you have got to be the stupidest lunker I've ever lit on."

Nick's eyes went wide and he clutched the side of the Jeep. "Jenks!" he stammered, going whiter. "What happened to you?"

Jenks's jaw clenched but he stayed silent.

Nick looked at me. "You're a person," he said, looking gaunt. "Jenks, who is she?"

I trembled, unable to say a thing. Jenks gripped the wheel tighter, and the engine nearly stalled when he slowed to go around a turn and didn't downshift. "No one cares little green turds about you," he said. "Who do you think she is?"

Nick took a gasping breath, leaning forward to slip to the floor of the Jeep. "Rachel?" he said, and I watched his pupils dilate just before he passed out and his head hit the seat.

Jenks took a quick look over his shoulder. "Great. Just freaking great. Now I'm going to have to carry him."

Sixteen

I had scrambled back to sit with Nick, worried at the stink of infection and that he hadn't regained consciousness yet. The wind from our passage as Jenks jostled us down the road to the supposed marina lifted the hair about my ears, giving me a fuzzy "view" of the sounds around me but an expanded picture of the smells. The chatter from the radio was loud and heavy, bringing Jenks up to speed on Pam's death and the breakup of the round. That we might have stolen a Jeep and were listening apparently hadn't crossed anyone's mind. The survivalists had divided their forces to maintain dominance of the island as well as search for us. It could only help.

Jenks adjusted his new Were cap, slowing when Brett's twang filtered out. I swiveled my ears forward, glad for the easier pace. "All teams keep a three-to-one ratio of fur to feet," the man was saying. "The cell is empty. They're armed, two dead, so watch your tail. No sign of their boat, so they're probably headed for the dock. I want a five-to-one-ratio there."

Jenks slowed to pull off into the short grass eking out a living by the packed dirt. I lifted my head in question, meeting his worried eyes with mine. *Why was he stopping?*

"They know we're coming," he said, awkwardly twisting to make a three-point turn and head back the way we'd come. "I can't fight that many Weres. We're going to have to swim."

My heart pounded and a whine slipped from me. Angular face tight, Jenks accelerated. "I won't let you drown," he said. "Or maybe we can find somewhere to hide until things settle," he added, knowing as well as I that the longer we remained, the more likely it was that we'd be caught. But Nick was unconscious, and the idea of me dog-paddling all the way was daunting even if I would have a break traversing Round Island in between. I couldn't swim it as a person. What would being a wolf do for me? The entire situation was crap, but we had to get off the island.

"Shut up! Everyone shut up!" came a frantic voice through the radio, and I leaned over Nick, my ears swiveling. "This is the lighthouse. We have a problem. Unknown incoming force! Six boats from the Mackinac ferry dock. Mixed Weres!" the high-pitched, young voice said. "Uniformed. They know she's in trouble, and they're coming for her!"

Really? Somehow I didn't think it was an unexpected rescue, but a second Were faction taking advantage of the chaos. *Damn it, that would make Mackinac Island tricky!*

Brett's voice crackled out, chilling me. "Radio silence. Search leaders check in by cell phone. The rest of you, find them! Fire on them if you have to, but they can't have Sparagmos!"

The radio turned to a grating hiss.

Jenks pulled the Jeep to the side of the road. "Wake him up," he said tightly, undoing his belt and getting out. "This is where we came in."

My nose wrinkled when I scented the faint taste of decay on the breeze as the heat of the sun hit that deer carcass. Muscles tense, I hesitated, then licked the side of Nick's nose, not knowing what else to do. Hell, it worked in the movies.

Feet spread wide, Jenks looked up and down the road, squinting from under his borrowed cap. My tongue had made a long wet mark on Nick, but otherwise there was no change. Leaning into the Jeep, Jenks jerked Nick's head up by the hair and slapped him.

Nick exploded into motion. Screaming obscenities, he

lashed out, arms flung blindly. Frightened, I jumped from the Jeep. My nails dug into the dirt and I stared at him.

Wild-eyed, Nick took a shuddering breath upon realizing where he was. His haunted look turned into a glare, and he stared at Jenks standing belligerently with his hands on his hips and that pack hat on his head. The jays yelled back at him, and I wished they would shut up.

"We walk from here, crap for brains," Jenks said darkly. "Let's go. Ever scuba dive?"

Nick eased himself out of the Jeep, stumbling when his bare feet hit the hard-packed road. "Once or twice," he rasped, hunched into himself and holding his ribs.

My ears pricked and I wondered if he was serious. If I wasn't so worried about Nick, I might be able to concentrate on keeping my own head above water. Jenks, too, seemed surprised, saying nothing more as he led the way into the scrub.

One foot raised, I hesitated. Jenks was going the wrong way, toward the interior, not the beach. A questioning whine brought him around, and he gestured for me to join him, kneeling just inside the scrub off the road. Nick wobbled into the brush, and I trotted to Jenks, worried.

The pixy peered into my eyes, and I was thankful he didn't try to pet me. "Nick stinks," he said, and Nick cleared his throat in protest. "They've got my scent, and yours," he added, "but they aren't as obvious as Nick's. If you still had your scent amulets, we might be able to slip their lines, but not the way we are. I'm betting both the island Weres and the ones coming from Mackinac will start their search from the beaches and move in."

So they catch us inland instead of on the beach, I thought, but Jenks shifted his weight, regaining my attention. "I want you to take crap for brains to that carcass and sit tight. Hide yourself in its stink. I'll drive the Jeep down the road to confuse the trail, then come back."

He wanted to separate? Again? My black paws fidgeted, and Jenks smiled.

"It'll be okay, Rache," he said. "I'll go tree to tree like a squirrel. They won't trail me to you. Once they pass us, we'll slip out clear and easy."

It wasn't him leading them back to us I was worried about, and I whined.

"You can do this," he said softly. "I know it goes against your nature to sit and hide, and if it was just us, I'd say charge ahead and kick anyone's ass between us and the water. . . ."

I made a doggie huff. Nick couldn't do it. We had to adapt to his condition. Agreeing, I sent my tail thumping. Yeah, it was degrading, but everyone knew dog-speak, and no one knew Rachel/wolf-speak but me.

Jenks smiled, standing to look tall above me. His pleased expression shifted to one of annoyance and he looked at Nick. "Got all that?" he asked, and Nick nodded, not looking up. "There's a deer carcass thirty feet from here. Go make nice with it."

With a numb weariness, Nick picked his way there, old leaves crunching under his bare feet.

"Stay down until I get back," Jenks said, carefully manipulating the keys so they wouldn't jingle.

I watched him retrace his steps, glancing both ways before breaking the camouflage of the surrounding brush and vaulting into the Jeep. Almost stalling it, he eased onto the road and drove away with the enthusiasm of an eighteen-year-old playing cops and robbers.

Not liking this at all, I turned and followed Nick. "A dead deer?" he said, squinting down at me as he lurched forward. "Is that what I smell?"

What could I say? Silent, I nudged my shoulder into him to force him to the right, trying to smell if Aretha was nearby. I didn't think so. It had gotten noisy, and though she wasn't afraid of Weres, it was likely she'd taken her pack to the thicker parts of the island.

Nick grimaced when we found the deer. I sat, wondering how we could make this work better. The clearing was covered with evidence of our earlier tussle. The smell of wolves, Jenks, me, and Weres were faint under the stench of decaying tissue and saltwater, but we couldn't just sit next to it and hope everyone avoided it because it stank.

Blue eyes pinched, Nick looked over the situation. "There," he said, his swollen hand shaking as he pointed to a deadfall where a downed tree had left a hole where its roots had been. "If I can get the deer over there . . ."

I watched him shake his sleeve down to use as insulation and grab the carcass by a hoof. Struggling, he started dragging it the necessary twenty feet. Nick went ashen when he unearthed a maggot farm under it, and gagging, I kicked leaves to cover them.

Nick, though, had a belly full of fear, which was apparently stronger than revulsion. Jenks was gone, and with that, I could almost see him starting to think again. With renewed strength he dragged the deer to the tree, its roots in the air. Getting the carcass before the hollow under the roots, he let the legs drop. He looked at me, and I bobbed my head. Though gross, if he wedged himself between the deer and the fallen snag, and maybe covered himself with leaves, he would be hidden from sight and smell.

Face twisted in disgust, Nick slowly found the ground between the deer and the exposed roots of the toppled tree, jerking when sticks hit his bare skin past the burn holes. Carefully raking the debris collected in the lee of the hollow, he covered himself, meticulously placing the dry leaves on top as he worked from his feet upward. "Good?" he asked when he finished, his head lightly covered. I nodded, and he closed his eyes, exhausted. His filth melted into the surrounding forest like camouflage; the scent of infection was hidden by the reek of decay.

Nervous, I eased closer, trying not to breathe as I crawled into the space behind him, settling myself so my head was on his shoulder, my ears brushing the top of the miniature cavelike shelter. It was a stretch, but I curled my tail over my nose as a filter. All that was left was waiting for Jenks. The sheltering roots made a roof against the open sky, and the scent of dirt was a pleasant alternative. It was all I could do to not jam my nose into it. A blue-eyed fly crawled over the deer, laying eggs I couldn't see. If it landed on me, I was outta there.

While the jays called and the wind brushed the treetops, I studied Nick's haggard face, so close beside mine. The warmth of our bodies touching was guiltily pleasant. His breathing was slow, and I realized he was asleep when his eyes jerked in REM sleep. I had no idea what he had endured, but I couldn't imagine whatever they wanted could be worth it.

The screaming of the jays grew closer, and with a wash of fear I realized their calls had meaning. Something small raced through the underbrush and was gone, fleeing. My ears pricked and I scanned what I could of the disturbed clearing. Softer, then growing louder, I heard a whisper of wind. I could hear leaves moving, then nothing. The scent of oil, gas, and nylon touched my nose, and a surge of adrenaline made me cold. They were around us. God save us, we had gone to ground none too soon.

Heart pounding, I looked into the silent green, afraid to shift my head. A leaf fluttered down, and I prayed Nick didn't wake. I couldn't see anyone, but I could hear them. It was as if ghosts were passing before me, silent and invisible but for their scent.

My eyes flicked to where the sun glinted on smooth skin. A trembling took my feet, and I forced myself to not move. There were two of them, one on two feet, one on four. I didn't think they were the island Weres, but rather, off the boats from Mackinac Island—their uniforms looked like government issue and their gear was more aggressive.

The taller Were grimaced at the stink, and I slitted my eyes to nothing when the one on four feet nudged his leg and silently pointed with his nose. With a whisper, the Were checked in using the radio clipped to his lapel. There was the pop of a channel opening thirty feet away, and I saw a distant shadow of brown and green come to a halt, waiting to see what they had found.

Shit. There was a line of them. If we were found, it wouldn't be two Weres I'd be fighting, but a platoon.

I caught the word Jeep, but there was no jubilation, so I figured Jenks was still at large. Only now did the two Weres enter the clearing, the one in fur finding the broken splat balls and the three damp spots where Aretha and her pack had been doused with saltwater to break the sleepy-time charm. The other touched the ground where the deer had lain. His head came up, his eyes going right to the deer. I panicked, thinking he had seen us, but with a click, he got the attention of the Were on four feet. Together they looked over the clearing where we had been attacked, discussing with body signals what might have happened. The deer, they avoided.

The screaming jays grew closer, calling from right overhead for an instant until they continued, following the unseen line. The Were in fur snapped his teeth, and the other rose. Taking a red flag from a pocket, he jammed it into the ground, marking the clearing. Silently they headed farther inland. There was the soft scritch of cloth rubbing, then nothing.

My blood pounded. To lay there and wait for them to pass us had been one of the most frightening things I'd ever done. The jays' noise went soft, and I exhaled, started to pant.

Waiting for Jenks, my thoughts returned to the soft sureness the invading Weres had shown. Their sly hesitancy made the stark brutality of the three packs I had just escaped stand out all the more. Weres weren't savage—they just weren't—and I felt a spike of worry remembering the ugly ferocity of them ringing me. It had been more than them wanting to see a fight. They had been like a different species, younger and more dangerous, lacking the control that the alphas gave them. The trouble a cocky Were pack in Cincy could get into was enough to give me the shivers. The only reason Inderlanders and humans could coexist was because everyone knew their place in the social order.

I was so intent on my thoughts that I all but barked in surprise when Jenks dropped out of the tree above me.

"Holy crap," he whispered, eyes dancing. "I was sure that one saw you. Damn, that deer stinks worse than a fairy's ass-wipe. Let's get out of here."

I couldn't agree more, and leaving my disturbing thoughts about the strength Weres found in packing up, I crawled from my shelter, leaping over Nick in my haste. His eyes flashed open and he came up on an elbow after seeing Jenks, leaves falling to hide the deer's glassy eye. "I fell asleep," he said, sounding ashamed. "Sorry."

"We're behind their line." Jenks didn't offer to help him stand, and I waited while Nick slowly gained his feet using the snag as support. His hands were swollen and there was a soft sheen of moisture on some of the burns as they oozed, bits of leaf chips stuck to them. I whined at Jenks to be nicer, but he wouldn't look at me, moving to play vanguard to the road.

I tried to find evidence of the invading Weres' passage as we went, seeing nothing. Nick stumbled behind me, stinking of dead deer, and I tried to pick a way that would be easy for him. His breathing grew labored as the forest thinned and we came out onto the road. A quick dart across and the forest closed in again.

Jenks was nearly silent to my wolf hearing, and I was pretty quiet myself. Nick tried, but every misplaced step brought a stumbling snapping of twigs and leaves. Being barefoot didn't help, and I was wondering why we hadn't taken someone's boots. After a few moments I trotted to Jenks, giving the pixy a look I tried to make meaningful before I loped away to make sure no one was nearby. Sound didn't travel as well as one might think in the woods, and as long as no one was close, Nick could make all the noise he wanted.

"Rache," Jenks hissed as I trotted off. "You playing scout?" he guessed, and I bobbed my head in an unwolflike manner. Nick came even with him, panting. He leaned against a dead tree, which promptly snapped with the sound of a gunshot.

While Jenks cursed him in thinly veiled disgust, I slunk through the brush, starting a sweep to the left when I couldn't hear Nick stumbling about anymore. Somewhere ahead of us was our scuba gear. Maybe we could hide out on Round Island. Unless by some miracle Marshal was still there. I prayed he wasn't, not wanting to have to make that choice.

Jenks and Nick's forward progress was maybe a third of mine, and it wasn't long before I had made a complete circuit and found nothing. I started a back-and-forth pattern before them, one ear on their progress, one on the forest ahead. Sooner than expected the green light filtering through the leaves brightened and I heard the sound of what seemed surf. But my heart almost stopped. I realized that the hiss of what I had thought surf was radio static.

"Their radio silence is continued," a voice said, and I froze, one paw lifted as I slowly crouched, all of my muscles protesting. In the background were sporadic thumps echoing against water. I was sure this was where we came in and not the marina. And Brett had said they hadn't found our boat, which meant they hadn't found the scuba gear either. It must be the six boats we had heard about. *Great. Just great. Out of the frying pan and into government control.*

"They haven't regained him," a higher, masculine voice said through a radio. "The third air tank and gear says she's probably headed right for you. Move the boats behind the curve of the shore and keep watch. With any luck, they'll walk right in on you. If you retrieve him, don't wait. Move out and radio from the water."

"Aye, sir," the Were said, and the radio retreated to a hiss. *Damn it,* I thought. They had seen the tanks from the water and landed right where we had to leave. They knew everything the island Weres did, having listened in to their efforts to regain us. Someone else wanted Nick too. *Just what the devil was this thing?*

I tried not to pant, my head weaving as I attempted to spot them. I caught a glimpse of a green outback hat and a clean-shaven face. The noise behind them became loud with decisions being made, and I got scared. Slowly I backed away, carefully putting my feet down until I couldn't hear voices anymore. Turning tail, I made a beeline to Jenks.

I found them together, Jenks looking marginally more accommodating as he held Nick's elbow and helped him over downed sticks. Nick moved like an eighty-year-old man, head down and struggling for balance. Jenks heard me and brought them to a stop. "Trouble?" he mouthed.

I nodded, and Nick groaned, looking desperate behind his beard.

"Shut up," Jenks whispered, and I shifted my sore front paw nervously.

"Show me," Jenks said, and leaving Nick to fend for himself, I led him to my spot. Jenks's motions grew slower, almost seductive, as the brush grew thicker at the edge of the island, until he eased into a crouch beside a tree at the edge of the brush.

I settled in beside the large pixy, panting as I relished the cooler air coming off the water. "Marshal is gone," Jenks said, his viewpoint higher than mine. "Good man. There're four Weres with semiautomatics. . . . That might be a Were in fur in the shadow of that tree. In any case, our gear is gone. Probably on one of the boats." His eyes squinted. "Tink's panties, if I was myself, I could just flit over and see, or get them to shoot themselves, or stab them in the eye with a thorn. How do you do this, Rache, being the same size as everyone?"

My teeth parted and I gave him a canine grin.

Jenks adjusted his weight, eyes fixed on the peaceful beach littered with boats drawn up onto the rocky shore. Two men were standing guard while two more prepared to move the first boat out. "I have an idea," he whispered. "You go over to that pile of break-wall rock, and when they're looking at you, I'll circle to come up behind them and whack them a good one."

His eyes were glinting, and while I wasn't keen on the looseness of the plan, I did like his confidence in it. And since we didn't have much of a choice, I flicked my ears.

"Good," Jenks whispered. "Get wet before they see you so you look black, not red."

Giving me a smile that made him look like he was plotting

to steal the teacher's apple, not a boat from four Weres with semiautomatics, Jenks dropped back to tell Nick the plan. I headed out, skirting the brush line. My pulse quickened. I didn't like being a decoy, but since I could probably cross the beach in four seconds, coming to Jenks's aid wouldn't be hard.

My knees went wobbly at the expanse of stony beach between me and the surf line. The sun was sparkling on the water, and the waves looked formidable past the slight protection of the inlet. Two Weres with weapons were facing the forest, while two more readied to move the first boat, confident they would hear anyone coming from the water long before they were close enough to be a threat. They were right.

A last slow breath, and I trotted out, walking right into the cold water and rolling. Immediately I lost my need to pant, the water freezing without Marshal's amulet. My first feeling that having this second faction of Weres seeing our gear was bad luck shifted to possibly good luck. Nick couldn't survive water this cold, and now Jenks and I would only have to take out five people, not whatever they had at the marina waiting for us.

There was an attention-getting yap, and I swung my head up, going still as a startled wolf might. But I would have frozen anyway. Five people were watching me, four with weapons and one with teeth. I think it was this last one that scared me the most. Damn, he was big.

My pulse jackhammered. I had nowhere to go but the woods, and if I was recognized as being more than a wolf, they would be on me in seconds. Fortunately, their expressions were curious, not suspicious.

A small movement behind them evolved into Jenks, and I fought with my instincts to watch him, instead pricking my ears and staring at them as if wondering if they were going to throw me the meat from their picnic lunch.

The men were talking softly, their hands loose on their weapons. Two wanted to lure me closer with food, and they told the one in fur to back off before he scared me.

Idiots, I thought, sparing them no pity when Jenks fell on them from behind. Screaming wildly, he swung his leaf-born stick and bludgeoned the first into unconsciousness before the rest even knew they were under attack. I sprang into movement, feeling like I was in molasses until I was free of the water. Jenks was a blur as he fought, but it was the Were in fur that I was worried about, and I ran across the rocky beach, flinging myself at his hindquarters.

Even now they didn't get it, and he turned with a yelp, surprised to find me on him.

Snarling, I fell away, hackles raised. Giving a short bark of realization, he sprang forward, ears back. Holy shit, he was huge, almost four times my current weight. Spine protesting, I skittered back, my only goal to remain out from between his teeth.

Immediately I knew I was in trouble. I couldn't put any distance between us. Pam had fought like a choreographed dancer. This guy was military, and I was way outclassed. Fear slipped into me, and I shifted directions erratically, zigzagging across the rocky beach, my bruised foot slipping on the smooth stones. A great paw hit me and I went sprawling.

Adrenaline pulsed, and I yipped as he fell on me. On my back, I clawed at his face, struggling to wiggle out. His breath was hot and his tongue was tattooed with a clover.

"Enough!" Jenks shouted, but neither of us paid any attention until a short burst of gunfire sent him jerking off me.

Panting, I flipped to my feet. Three men were unconscious, bleeding about their heads. A fourth looked sullen but beaten soundly. Jenks stood alone. The sun shone on his black tights and blond curls, and the semiautomatic in his hands gave his Peter Pan pose some threat.

"Nick!" he yelled, hefting the weapon. "Get out here. I need you to watch them for a sec. Think you can do that, crap for brains?"

The two Weres tensed when Nick wobbled out, but at Jenks's threat, they remained still. They shifted again when Jenks handed Nick his weapon, glancing among themselves as Nick held it with markedly less proficiency. Faces ugly, they settled back, clearly waiting.

With that gunfire, we had only minutes until all hell broke loose, and while Nick held them at a muscle-fatigued, shaking standstill, Jenks took the spark plugs from all but one boat, throwing them into the water with all the weapons he could find.

"Rache?" he said, gesturing from the boat he had chosen, and I willingly jumped onto it, nails skittering on the fiberglass deck. Slipping, I fell into the cockpit and the fake grass carpet. Our gear and wet suits were a pleasant surprise. I hadn't been looking forward to finding out what their loss would have done to my credit card balance. Marshal would be pleased.

Nick was next, wading out to the side and handing Jenks the weapon before lurching over the side. Cracked lip between his teeth, he cranked the engine as the requests for information coming from the radio on the beach grew intense.

Still in the water, Jenks pushed the boat out with one hand, keeping the weapon trained on them with the other. My mouth dropped when he flung himself up into a blackflip to land on the bow of the boat. The semiautomatic never lost its aim. The two Weres blinked but didn't move. "What, by Cerberus, are you?" one asked, clearly shocked.

"I'm Jenks!" he called back, clearly in an expansive mood, catching his balance when Nick revved the engine. Jenks turned the near fall into a graceful motion, slipping into the cockpit to stand beside me, weapon still pointed. Nick idled us around, then jammed the lever full throttle. Staggering, I caught my balance. Jenks doffed his hat to the watching Weres and laughed, throwing his weapon into our wake.

We sped away as the first of the returning Weres came boiling out of the forest, all snapping teeth and barking voices. Someone was already in the water looking for the spark plugs. We had done it—for the moment. All that was left was to make it across the straits without swamping ourselves in the heavy waves and get lost in the general populace. Then there was the matter of how to get Nick safe. And me, seeing that my cover was blown and every Were east of the Mississippi knew I had Nick—who knew where the statue was, whatever the statue was.

I squinted into the wind, my breath escaping in a doggy huff when I realized Nick's rescue was only starting. What could he have possibly stolen that was worth all this?

Jenks reach across and tunked the gas lever to slow us down. "How did you know how to use that weapon?" Nick asked him, his voice rough and his hands shaking on the wheel. He was squinting in the bright light as if he hadn't seen it for days. He probably hadn't.

Jenks grinned as we jostled over the waves, hitting every one wrong. His bandage was falling off, but his mood was both exhilarated and triumphant. "Ah-nold," he said, hitting an Austrian accent hard, and I barked in laughter.

I watched the island retreat behind us, relieved no one was following—yet. It would only take minutes to lose ourselves in the light boat traffic, maybe fifteen to reach the mainland. We would ditch the boat, keeping the gear to return to Marshal when we could. I didn't care if we had to take it to Cincy with us, he was going to get his stuff back.

Jenks tunked the speed down some more, and Nick tunked it back up. I couldn't blame him, but the waves were bouncing us around like a piece of popcorn. Jenks handled the jostling better than me despite my four feet against his two, and he started rummaging, opening every panel and lifting every seat. It was his pixy curiosity, and feeling ill, I wobbled to Nick, put my head into his lap and gave him the sad-puppy-dog-eyes look, hoping he'd slow our pace. Burn my britches if it didn't work, and smiling for the first time since I'd found him, he dropped a thin hand to my head before he decreased the speed.

"Sorry, Ray-ray," he murmured over the noise of the engine. "I can't . . . I can't go back." He swallowed hard and his breath quickened. "But you did it. Thank you. I owe you one. I owe you my life." Hands trembling, he met my eyes, his grip on the plastic-coated wheel clenching and releasing. "I thought you were dead. You have to believe me."

I did. He wouldn't have left that rose in the jelly-jar vase if he hadn't.

Jenks made a call of discovery. "Anyone hungry?" he shouted over the wind and engine. "I found their food stores."

Nick jerked. "I'm starved," he said, all but panicked as he looked over his shoulder.

Jenks's first ugly face emptied when he saw Nick's eyes. "Yeah," he said softly, gesturing for Nick to move. "I guess you are. You eat. I'll drive."

I jumped up onto the copilot's chair to get out of the way, and Nick stood unsteadily, gripping the boat and shaking with the thumping of the waves. He wobbled to the back bench, taking a moment to arrange the wool blanket Jenks had found about his shoulders before settling himself and ripping open energy bars with his teeth since his nails were torn to the quick.

Jenks took his place behind the wheel. He turned the boat slightly to the bridge, and the ride smoothed out. I watched the play of emotions over his smooth face. I knew he was as mad as a jilted troll at the altar that Nick had led his son astray, but seeing Nick beaten, abused, and so weak he could hardly open that stupid wrapper, it was hard not to feel sorry for him.

Just wanting Jenks to lighten up a little, I put my head in his lap and peered up at him.

"Don't look at me like that, Rache," Jenks said, his eyes scanning the approaching shoreline for the run-down marina we had planned out earlier as a possible landfall. "I saw you pull it on Nick, and it doesn't work on me. I have fifty-four kids, and it won't work."

Sighing heavily, I arched my wolf eyebrows. Sure enough, he glanced down.

"Tink's panties," he muttered. "Okay. I'll be nicer. But as soon as he's better, I'm going to punch him."

Pleased, I pulled my head up and gave him a lick on his cheek.

"Don't do that," he muttered, wiping the moisture away. But his embarrassment was tinged with understanding.

I'd be content with that, but before I could teeter back and see if Nick would open one of those government-issue energy bars for me, Jenks stood, one hand on the wheel, the other holding his cap to his head. "Ah, Rache?" he said over the roar of the engine and the brush of wind. "Your eyes might be better than mine. Is that Ivy on the dock?"

Seventeen

Squinting into the wind, I sat on the copilot's chair watching the decades-old rusted gas pumps on the dock become clearer. Ivy was standing with the sun glinting on her short black hair, leaning casually against a piling. She was in jeans and a long sweater, but with the boots and shades, she managed to look svelte as well as ticked. A frumpy older man was next to her, and worry went through me at what had gone so wrong in Cincinnati that she had to come and get me. *Unless she's here because she thinks I can't handle this.*

The man beside her looked both nervous and excited in his faded overalls, holding himself a careful five feet away as the breeze shifted his plaid coat open to the wind. They probably didn't get many living vamps up here, and he was clearly more curious than wary.

Jenks decreased our speed, and I could hear the sounds from the shore. My emotions were swinging from one extreme to the other. If Ivy had come because she didn't think I could do this, I was going to be pissed—even if it wasn't going that well. If she was up here because there was a problem back home, I was going to be worried. I'd thought she couldn't even leave Cincinnati, so whatever it was, it must be bad.

My weight shifted as the boat slowed, and I fidgeted with worry. Jenks cut the gas to idle and we drifted closer. "Can we tie up here?" he shouted to the man, who was probably manager of the marina.

"You bet!" he called back, voice high and excited. "Take her right down to slip fifty-three. Your friend already paid for it." He pointed where he wanted us to go, looking flustered. "That's a big dog you got there. We have a leash law this side of the straits."

I watched Ivy for her reaction to seeing me as a wolf, but her expression behind the sunglasses was amused, as if it was all a big joke.

"Come on down when you get settled," the man said, hesitating when he saw Nick hunched under his blanket. "I need to register you."

Swell. Proof we were here.

Ivy was already walking down the empty dock to the slip the man had indicated. Behind me, Nick shuffled around, finding the docking ropes and flinging bumpers over the sides. "You ever dock a boat before?" he asked Jenks.

"No, but I'm doing okay so far."

I stayed where I was while the two men figured it out, easing our way into the slip in sudden bursts of engine and calls to go forward or reverse. Ivy stood on the dock and watched, as did a few people readying their boats for the water. Nervous, I slunk to the lowest part of the boat to hide. The island Weres and the Weres we stole the boat from would track us down, and a big red dog was memorable. We had to start putting distance between us and our borrowed boat.

Jenks cut the engine and levered himself out, landing lightly on the wooden dock to tie off the back end. Ivy rose from her crouch where she had tied the bow. "What in Tink's contractual hell are you doing here?" Jenks said, then glanced at the people nearby sanding the bottom of their boat. "Didn't think we could handle it?" he added, softer.

Ivy frowned. "Nice Band-Aid, Jenks," she said sarcastically, and he reached to touch it. "You're big enough to bite now, mosquito, so shut up."

"You'd have to catch me first," he said, flushing. "Give us some credit. It was only a snag and drag."

I would have told him to lighten up but my thoughts were spiraling around the same question. Clearly angry, Ivy nudged the rope over the edge so no one would trip on it. "Hello, Nick," she said, running her gaze over his blanket-draped, barefoot, hunched form. "Someone rocking your boat?"

Under her disapproving eye, Nick tried to pull to his full height, cutting the motion short with a grunt. He looked awful. His beard was nasty, his hair greasy, and his smell was pungent now that the wind wasn't pulling it away. "Hi, Ivy," he rasped. "Piscary send you out for some fudge?"

Stiffening, she turned. My pulse quickened at the reminder of the undead vamp. She shouldn't have been here. There was going to be a price to pay, which made me think it had to be more than her checking on Jenks and me. She could have called if that was all it was.

I made a little woof to get Jenks's attention, but it was obvious by his sudden concern that he'd come to the same conclusion. Hands on his hips, he took a breath as if to ask, glanced at Nick, then let it out. "Hey, uh, Ivy," he said, a whole lot nicer. "We need to get out of here."

Ivy followed his gaze to the smear the island made on the horizon. "Are you hot?" she asked, and when he nodded, she added, "Then let's get him in the van."

Finally, we were moving.

"You brought the van?" Jenks hopped back into the boat, the fiberglass under my feet barely trembling. "How did you know we were here?"

"I drove around until I found your motel," she said, eyes on me. "The town's not that big. I've got Kist's Corvette parked at the restaurant across the street from your room."

At least they were being nice to each other. I wanted some clothes and a moment to change, and if Ivy brought the van—which we'd packed in case we needed to bug out in a hurry—then all the better. Head weaving to gauge the distance, I jumped to the dock, my nails skittering. There was an *Ooooh* of appreciation from the people across the inlet sanding the bottom of their boat, and I flicked my ears back and then forward.

"I've got to go register," Jenks said, as if proud of it, then hesitated, his earlier annoyance gone. "I'm glad you're here," he said, surprising me. "*She* can't drive anymore, and I'm not getting in a car with crap for brains behind the wheel."

"That's enough!" I snapped, having it come out as aggressive barks. The entire marina took notice. Drooping, I sank to the damp planks like a good dog. It was Tuesday, but being the last Tuesday before Memorial Day, there were a few retirees working on their boats.

Jenks snickered. With a jaunty step, he headed to the bird-spotted dockmaster's office. I still didn't know why Ivy was there, and probably wouldn't as long as Nick was listening.

On the dock, Ivy dropped to one knee, peering at my eyes to make me uncomfortable. There was a new sparkle of gold in her earlobes. *When had she started wearing earrings?*

"Are you okay?" she asked, as if trying to see if it was really me. I shifted to snap at her, and she grabbed the ruff around my neck, holding me. "You're wet," she said, the warmth of her fingers finding my damp skin under the fur. That a mouthful of nasty teeth had just missed her arm seemed to have made no impression. "There's a blanket in the van. You want to change?"

Flustered, I pulled back gently, and this time she let go. I bobbed my head, turning to look at Nick. Seeing my attention on him, he drew the blanket tighter to hide his burned clothing, shivering. I wanted to talk to Ivy, but I wasn't about to turn witch where everyone could see. Having the surrounding locals watch her talk to a big dog was bad enough.

"Let's get out of here," she said, standing up and stepping into the boat. "Let me help you with your . . . scuba gear?" she finished after pulling off the tarp. Her eyes went to mine. "You can dive?" she asked, and I shrugged, in as much as a wolf could shrug.

With a rough motion, Ivy drew the cover back before the curious people still sanding that same three-foot section of boat could see. She eyed me, then the shack where Jenks was, wanting to talk to me alone. "Hey, Nick," she said, a ribbon of threat in her voice. "It's going to take some time to get this packed. They have facilities for people who have their boats here. You want to shower while we load the van?"

Nick's long face went longer as his lips parted. "Why do you care if I'm comfortable?"

True to form, Ivy sneered. "I don't. You reek, and I don't want you stinking up the van."

Brow furrowed, she looked to the shack on the dock. "Hey, old man!" she shouted, her voice echoing on the flat water in the harbor, and Jenks poked his head out of the dock office. "Buy him a shower, will you? We've got time."

We didn't, but Jenks nodded, vanishing back inside. My wolfen brow furrowed, and Nick didn't seem happy either, probably guessing we were getting rid of him for a moment. Lifting a cushion, he brought out a pair of gray flannel government-looking sweats and size-eleven sneakers that had been tucked away for a returning Were to slip into. They'd likely be too small, but it was better than what he was wearing. Hunched under his blanket, he tottered to the edge of the boat, halting before Ivy, since she was blocking his path.

"You're one lucky bastard," she said, hand on a hip. "I would have let you rot."

Hand clenching his blanket closed, he edged past her. "Ask me if I care."

Ivy gathered herself to come back with a remark, but then he reached for a piling to pull himself out and the blanket slipped to show the burn marks. Horrified, she met my gaze.

Unaware that she had seen, Nick clutched his things close and made his meticulous way to a nearby cinder-block building, following the blue-lettered sign that promised showers. The dockmaster ambled out of his office, plastic token in his hand. While the man gave Nick a bar of soap and a sympathetic touch on his shoulder, Jenks made his slow way to us.

Nick's gaunt, battered silhouette vanished around the corner, bare feet popping against the cement. Turning, I found Ivy beside the captain's chair. "My God, what did they do to him?" she whispered.

Like I could talk?

Jenks came to an awkward, scuffling halt on the dock above us, squinting as he looked at the island. "We don't have time for him to shower," he said, adjusting his clan cap, his Band-Aid gone. He had turned the cap inside out so the emblem was hidden, and it looked good on him. Probably start a new trend.

"He is not getting into Kisten's van smelling like that." Ivy's gaze went to the tarp hiding the gear. "What do you want to do with these?"

Jenks looked at me for direction, and I huffed. "Bring 'em," he said. "Marshal will want them back. Though I suggest we keep them until we're clear."

"Marshal?" Ivy questioned.

Grinning, Jenks resettled the tarp in the limited floor space and started moving the equipment onto it. "A local witch Rachel sweet-talked into letting us rent his equipment. Nice guy. He and Rachel have a date when this is over."

I whined, and Jenks laughed. Ivy wasn't amused, and she pushed off from the captain's chair, saying nothing and avoiding my gaze as she helped stack the gear into the sling of the tarp. Between her vampire strength and Jenks's pixy stamina, they lifted the tarp with all the equipment onto the dock, the watching people none the wiser for what was in it.

While I sat on the dock and watched, Jenks and Ivy wiped the boat free of fingerprints under the pretense of cleaning it. Snapping the weather tarps into place as they went, they worked their way from the bow to the stern, eliminating every shred of easily traced evidence that we had been in it. Jenks was the last to leave, vaulting to the dock to land beside me in a show of athletic grace that made Ivy's eyes widen in appreciation.

"Got your people legs, I see," she murmured, then grabbed one end of the tarp. Jenks grinned, and looking as if the rolled up tarp weighed no more than a cooler, the two of them headed for the van. I trailed behind, sullen and bad tempered. I had been up nearly twenty-four hours, and I was tired and hungry. If one of them tried to put a leash on me, I was going to take that someone down.

Jenks quickened his pace after they reached the gravel parking lot, in a good mood despite having missed his afternoon nap. "How did you know we might show up here?" he said as he dropped his end of the bundle and slid the side door to the van open with a harsh scraping sound.

"Dad!" Jax shrilled, exploding out to make circles about us. "How did it go? Where's Nick? Did you see him? Is he dead? Oh wow! Ms. Morgan is a wolf!"

"Ah," Jenks said, "we got him. He's in the shower. He stinks."

I went to jump into the van, stopping when Rex took one look at me, swelled into an orange puffball, and vanished in a streak of common sense under the front seat. *Poor kitty. Thinks I'm going to eat her.*

"Hey, Ms. Morgan!" the little pixy said, landing on my head until I flicked my ears at him. "Nick is going to be mad. Wait until you see what Ivy brought."

Jenks frowned. "That's Ms. Tamwood, son," he said, unloading the tarp into the van.

Jax flitted into the van, darting among the belongings we'd shoved in pell-mell earlier. The small pixy flitted to the floor and in a high voice tried to coax Rex out, using himself as bait. I sat in the sun and watched, mildly concerned that no one was stopping him. I wanted a pair of shorts and a shirt so I could change too, but I was in a hurry and figured I could change in the van behind the curtain. Jax had turned his efforts to get Rex out to obnoxious clicks and whistles, and it hurt my head.

Ivy yanked open the driver's side door and got in, leaving it ajar to let the cool afternoon breeze shift the tips of her hair. "You want to take Nick to Canada before you head home, or are you going to just cut him loose?"

I made a sick face, but seeing as I was a wolf, it probably looked like I was going to hawk up a bird. It wasn't that simple anymore, but I had to change before I could explain. The van smelled like witch, pixy, and Ivy, and I didn't want to get in until I had to. I could see my suitcase, but opening it was a different matter.

Jenks stepped into the van, lurching for Jax and missing. Mumbling almost aloud, he began arranging things so we'd all fit, all the while keeping a tight watch on his son.

"What is it, Rachel?" Ivy asked warily, watching me through the rearview mirror. "You don't look happy for someone who just finished a run, even if it was pro bono."

Jenks dropped my suitcase onto a box and opened it up. "It went great," he said, his youthful face eager as he sifted through my things. "By the seat of our pants, the way Rache works best."

"I hate it when you work like that," Ivy said, but I felt better that Jenks, at least, was thinking about me not having hands.

"They caught us, but Rachel worked out a deal to fight their alpha for Nick." Jenks held up a pair of my panties so everyone could see. "I've never seen a Were go wolf that fast. It was incredible, Ivy. Almost as fast as Rachel's magic."

I felt a spike of worry, remembering their savagery when they were bound under a common cause and one Were. It still had me on edge. Ivy went still, then turned in her seat to look at him. My tail swished in an apology, and a faint wrinkle showed in her brow. "Deal?"

Jenks nodded, hesitating between the long-sleeve T-shirt and the skimpier tank top. "If she pinned their alpha, we got Nick. I didn't see it all 'cause I was looking for crap for brains, but the sound of the fight brought in a real wolf pack. The alpha Rachel was fighting ran away. I say that means Rachel won." I breathed easier when he put the tank top back. "Wasn't her fault their alpha got chewed by real wolves."

Ivy took a breath in thought, holding it. I met her eyes,

knowing she had figured out the real problem, and I winced. A quick shot of adrenaline shivered through me. "They know who you are?" Ivy said, her gaze following mine to the island behind us.

Hearing the concern in her voice, Jenks straightened until his head brushed the ceiling. "Aw, hell," he said. "We can't go home. They'll follow us, even if we don't have Nick. Damn it all to Disneyland! Where's crap for brains? Jax! What did you two steal, anyway? How are we going to convince four Were packs that we don't have it or that Nick told us where it is?"

Jax was gone. I'd seen him zip out of the van three pixy heartbeats after his dad had started using Disney's name in vain. Angry, Jenks jumped into the parking lot and headed for the showers, arms moving and face red. "Hey! Crap for brains!" he shouted.

I rose, stretching, before I loped after Jenks. He skidded to a halt when I stopped in front of him and leaned into his legs to try to tell him it was okay, that we'd find a way around this latest problem. Jenks peered down at me, his shoulders stiff. "I'll be nice," he said, his jaw tight. "But we're leaving, and we're leaving now. We've got to get under the leaves and hope spiders spin webs above us before they start looking."

I wasn't sure how spiders fitted into his equation, but I padded back to the van while he pounded on the shower door. Ivy got the engine going, and when I jumped into the front passenger seat, she leaned over to crack the window for me. The dusky scent of incense slipped over me, familiar and rich with undertones only my subconscious had been aware of before. Comforting.

The thump of a metal door closing pulled my attention to the lot. Jenks slipped into the van, clearly upset. Fifteen feet behind him I saw Nick, beard gone and hair dripping, spotting his gray sweats. He was moving better, head up and looking around. I had been right that the shoes were too small; he was still barefoot, the sneakers dangling from two fingers.

"You're too good to him, Rachel," Ivy said softly. "You should be spitting mad, and you aren't. He's a liar and a thief. And he hurt you. Please," she whispered. "Think about what you're doing?"

Don't worry about it, I thought, enduring the indignity of thumping my tail in an effort to convey I wasn't going to let Nick back into my life. But when the memory of his battered body and his will to remain silent against drugs and pain returned to me, I had a hard time staying angry with him.

Eighteen

"**G**ood God," I whispered, sitting on the van's cot and looking at my legs, horrified. They were hairy—not wolf hairy, but an I-couldn't-find-my-razor-the-last-six-months hairy. Utterly grossed out, I took a peek at my armpit, jerking away. *Oh, that's just . . . nasty.*

"You okay, Rachel?" came Ivy's voice from the front of the moving van, and I snatched up my long-sleeve black shirt and covered myself, though a heavy curtain was between me and the rest of the world passing at an awkward start-and-stop thirty-five miles an hour.

"Fine," I said, hurriedly slipping into it and wondering why my nails were the right length, though they'd lost their polish. My red frizz was longer though, bumping about past my shoulders, where it had been before Al cut a chunk out of it last winter. I had a feeling my extra-hairy condition might be laid at the feet of Ceri. She had twisted the curse to switch me back, and apparently they hadn't shaved in the Dark Ages.

I was thankful as all hell that Jenks, Jax, and Rex were in Kisten's Corvette behind us. Getting dressed in the back of a van was bad enough. Doing it with pixies watching would have been intolerable. I'd done that before. I didn't want to do it again.

Shuddering at the long red hair on my legs, I shook out a pair of socks, wishing I had footies. My face scrunched up as I put them on. This was going to change as soon as I found ten minutes to myself in the bathroom with a bottle of Nair. Why Jenks had shown up smooth as a baby's butt was beyond me. Maybe pixies didn't have hair except atop their heads.

I jerked my jeans on, flustered when the distinctive sound of my zipper going up filled the silence. Grimacing, I drew the curtain aside and fluffed my hair. Before me rose the bridge, taking up much of the skyline. The traffic was still stop-and-go, even more so now that it was down to one lane in either direction due to construction. But Nick had his truck across the straits in St. Ignace, so that's where we were headed.

"Hi, guys," I said, finding a place to kneel where I could see out the front. "I'm back."

Ivy glanced at me through the rearview mirror, her gaze lingering on my frizzing red curls. Nick looked up from rummaging in the console for change for the bridge toll, smiling though a faint tremor showed in his pianist-long hands as he shuffled about. Finding the right amount, he sat back and pushed his damp hair from his forehead.

The shower had done him good. After a week of deprivation, his narrow physique was positively gaunt, making his clean-shaven cheeks hollow and his Adam's apple more prominent. Where his lean frame had made him look scholarly before, it now only left him skinny. The gray sweats hung loose on him, and I wondered when his last hot meal had been.

His blue eyes, though, had regained the sheen of intelligence as the shower, energy bars, and distance all helped him deal with what he'd endured. He was safe—for the moment.

My mind pinged back to him leaning against the brown cinder-block building, a broken man weeping as he pulled the trigger on the shotgun.

Ivy cleared her throat, and I met her gaze through the oblong glass, returning her accusing stare with a shrug. She knew what I was thinking.

"Watch the car!" I exclaimed, and she jerked her attention

back to the road. I was already reaching for a handhold when she hit the brakes, narrowly missing the bumper of the Toyota before us. Swinging forward from the momentum, I glared at her.

Nick had braced himself against the dash, and though his look was full of disgust, he said nothing. Ivy smiled at the irate driver we had almost hit, showing her pointy canines so the guy would back off and be glad we weren't stopping to make sure everyone was okay.

As we waited for the light, I stretched for my bag and charms. Nick was hurting, and there was no need for it. Yeah, I was mad at him, but him being in pain wouldn't help anyone.

The smoothness of two pain amulets filled my hand, and I slowly dropped one. I didn't hurt at all since turning back into a person, my sore back and nipped hand completely pain free. Wondering, I dug deeper for a finger stick. The prick of the blade was easily dismissed, and I massaged the three drops out. The clean scent of redwood rose, and the blood soaked in.

"Ah, Rachel?" Ivy called intently, and I stuck my finger in my mouth.

"What?"

There was a short silence, then, "Never mind."

She cracked the window, and with the cool air off the water shifting my hair, I decided to hang back here for a while. Getting her home ASAP was an excellent idea. Vamps were homebodies—high-maintenance, party-till-you-die, don't-look-at-me-funny-or-I'll-kill-you homebodies, but homebodies nevertheless. And for obvious reasons. I still didn't know why she was here. How she was going to handle her hunger without the net of people she had left in Cincinnati worried me. Maybe it'd be easier out of Piscary's influence. God, I hoped so.

The van eased into motion, and I rifled through my bag for a complexion charm. It was too bumpy to put on makeup, but I could at least look rested and relaxed. *And it would get rid of the bags under my eyes,* I thought morosely, flipping open my little compact mirror. Squinting in the dim light, I looked closer.

"Hey, Ivy?" I bolted forward, hunched as I lurched up to the front. "Are my freckles gone?" Eyes wide, I leaned out between Ivy and Nick, tilting my head so they both could see.

Ivy glanced from the road to me, then back again. A slow smile spread across her face, telling me my answer before she said a word. "Open your mouth," she said.

Bewildered, I did, and she looked, making me nervous when she smoothly halted without watching the car that had stopped before us.

From my right came Nick's soft, "Are they gone?" and Ivy nodded.

"What's gone?" Shoving the pain amulet at Nick, I opened my mouth and tried to see what they were looking at. "My fillings are gone!" I exclaimed, shocked. Pulse hammering, I looked at my wrist. "That's still there," I said, looking at Al's demon mark and wanting to check the underside of my foot for Newt's, which I didn't because of all that hair. I looked at my elbow instead. "But the scar from when I fell off my bike isn't," I added.

Twisting, I tried to see the back of my shoulder where I'd cut myself falling into the lawn mower doing cartwheels. Ah, I had been doing the cartwheels, not the lawn mower.

"Your neck is unmarked," Ivy said softly, and I froze, meeting her eyes in the mirror. There was the faintest swelling of black. "Do you want me to see if it's really gone?" she asked.

I leaned back, suddenly aware of her. Nick cleared his throat in a subtle show against it, which halted my first impulse to say no. If it was gone, it would be worth all the blackness I had put on my soul. Despite my better judgment, I nodded.

Ivy exhaled long and slow, the sound setting my blood to thrum. Her eyes dilated to a full black, and I stiffened, fixed to them through the rearview mirror. Though her fingers were still on the wheel, I felt as if she was touching my neck with a shocking intimacy, pressing with a light but demanding insistence.

I inhaled, and like a sudden flame from a match, it sparked a tingling assault. Heat poured through me, following the line from my neck to my chi. A small sound escaped me, and if I'd been able to think, I would have been embarrassed.

Ivy broke our eye contact through the mirror, holding her breath as she struggled to pull her hunger back. "It's still there," she said, her voice both rough and smooth. Wavering where I sat, her eyes met mine and darted away. "Sorry," she added, fingers clenching the wheel.

Blood pounding, I retreated to the cot. To ask her to do that had been stupid. Slowly the tingling vanished. My scar wasn't puckering my skin, but obviously the vampire virus was still fixed there. I was terribly glad I was a witch and couldn't be Turned. Ever. I had a feeling that was one of the reasons Ivy put up with so much of my crap.

The van was uncomfortably silent, windy now that Ivy had rolled the window completely down. It was cold, but I wasn't going to say anything. My perfume, which blocked my scent from mixing with Ivy's, was in here somewhere. Maybe I ought to find it.

The tension slowly eased as we moved to the bridge. I looked at my hands in the dusk of the van, seeing them smooth and perfect, every flaw that marked my passage through time gone. It seemed like the curse had reset everything: no freckles, no childhood scars, no fillings . . .

Panic slid through me. Frightened, I lurched to the front, kneeling between them. "Nick," I whispered. "What if I lost what Trent's dad—"

Nick smiled, smelling like hotel soap as he took my hand. "You're fine, Ray-ray. If the vamp virus is still fixed in your cells, then whatever Trent's father changed will be there too."

I felt unreal as I pulled my hand from his. "Are you sure?"

"Your freckles are gone but you still have your sensitivity to vampires. That would suggest the charm resets your form by your DNA. And if your DNA was changed, by a virus or . . ." His eyes flicked to Ivy staring out the window, her grip deceptively loose on the wheel. ". . . something else, the change is carried over." Smiling, he leaned closer. I froze, then jerked back when I realized he was going to kiss me.

Face emptying of emotion, Nick settled in his seat. Flushing, I moved away. I didn't want him to kiss me. *What in hell is wrong with him?*

"It wasn't a charm, it was a demon curse," Ivy said darkly, jerking the car into motion. Though the traffic was stop-and-go, the roughness had been on purpose. "She put a hell of a lot of black on her soul while saving your ass, crap for brains."

Nick's eyes widened and he turned in his seat. His expression grew haunted. "A demon curse? Ray-ray, please tell me you didn't buy a demon curse to help me."

"I'm a white witch, Nick," I said tartly, my words harsher at the reminder of what I'd done to myself. "I didn't make a deal with anyone. I twisted the curse myself." Well, Ceri twisted it, actually, but pointing *that* out didn't seem prudent.

"But you can't!" he protested. "It's demon magic."

Ivy tunked the brakes, and I caught my balance when the van stopped quick at a new yellow light. Behind us, Jenks blew the car's horn, which Ivy ignored. "Are you calling her a liar?" she said, turning in her seat to look at Nick squarely.

His long face reddened, his newly shaved cheeks a shade paler. "I'm not calling her anything, but the only place you can get a working demon charm is from a demon."

Ivy laughed. It was ugly, and I didn't like it. "You don't know shit, Nick."

"Stop it, both of you!" I exclaimed. "God, you're like two kids fighting over a frog."

Angry, I retreated to sit on the cot, leaving two silent, sullen people in the front. The soft clinks of the toll money slipping through Nick's fingers were loud. As we crept forward in the slow line, I forced myself to be calm. Most likely Nick was right that I wouldn't suddenly find myself dying from a childhood disease again, but it was still a worry.

"Look there," he said suddenly, his voice thick with warning. "Ray-ray, stay down."

Immediately I crowded to the front to earn Ivy's huff of impatience. Before us spread the bridge, its glory marred by construction crews. We were nearly on it, and the guy holding the Slow sign was watching everyone far too intently. I could tell from three cars away that he was a Were, a Celtic knot tattoo encompassing his entire right shoulder.

"Damn it," Ivy muttered, her jaw clenching. "I see him. Rachel, hold on."

I braced myself when Ivy flicked the turn signal and pulled a right to get out of the bridge traffic at the last moment. Peering out the dirty square of a window in the back, I saw Jenks following. Jax and Rex were scampering about on the dash, and I don't know how Jenks managed to keep the car on the road.

The van rocked as it found its new momentum, and I felt ill. "Now what?" I said, finding Jenks's old flip-flops and putting them on.

Ivy sighed. Her grip on the wheel tightened and relaxed. Glancing into the rearview mirror, her eyes met mine. Nick's truck would have to wait. I listened to the traffic and Nick's frightened breathing. I could almost hear his heart, see it pulse in his neck as he fought the fear of his entire week of torture.

"I'm hungry," Ivy abruptly said. "Anyone want a pizza?"

Nineteen

Eyes on the rearview mirror, Ivy eased the van to a halt in the restaurant lot in the shade between two semis. The sound of traffic was loud through her window, and I couldn't help but be impressed at being so well hidden this close to the main road. Shifting the gearshift into park, she undid her seat belt and turned. "Rachel, there's a box under the floorboard. Will you get it for me?"

"Sure." While Ivy got out, I scuffed back the throw rug and pried up the metal plate to find, instead of a spare tire, a dusty cardboard box. Trying to keep it from touching me, I set it on the driver's seat. Ivy looked out from between the two trucks when Jenks parked across the lot. She whistled, and Jax darted up before his dad could even get out of the car.

"What's up, Ms. Tamwood?" the small pixy said, stopping before her. "Why did we stop? Are we in trouble? Do you need gas? My dad has to pee. Can you wait for him?"

I was pleased to see that Jax was wearing a scrap of red tucked into his belt. It was a symbol of good intentions and a quick departure should he stray into another pixy's territory. Seeing him learning the ropes made me feel good, even if the reason behind it was depressing.

"The Weres have the bridge," Ivy said, gesturing for Jenks to stay where he was beside Kisten's car. He was fumbling with his inside-out cap, and with the jeans he now had on over his running tights and his aviator jacket, he looked good. "Tell your dad to get a table if it looks okay," Ivy added, squinting from behind her sunglasses. "I'll be there in a sec."

"Sure thing, Ms. Tamwood."

He was gone in a clattering of wings. A light breeze shifted Ivy's hair, and standing beside the open door, she pried the dusty flaps up to pull out a roll of heavy ribbon. A faint smile quirked the corner of her mouth, and Nick and I waited for an explanation.

"I haven't done this in years," she said, looking to the narrow slice of visible parking lot. "I don't think they saw us," she said, "but by tonight they will have tracked you and Jenks to your motel, and that lady will tell them you were driving a white van. If we're going to be in town longer than that, we need to change a few things."

I recognized the thick tape in her hands as magnetic striping, and my eyebrows went up. *Cool. A vehicle disguise.*

"There's a license plate somewhere in there," she said, and I nodded, going back for it. "And the screwdriver?"

Nick cleared his throat, sounding impressed. "What is that? Magnetic pinstripe?"

Ivy didn't look at him. "Kisten has black lightning and flaming crosses too," she said.

And illegal flash paint, I mentally added when she shook a can of specially designed spray paint.

She moved the box to the running board of the nearby semi. The door thumped shut, sealing Nick and me inside. "By the time I get done with her, she could win the goth division in a car show," she said.

Smirking, I handed her the Ohio plate and screwdriver through the window. Even the tags were up to date.

"Sit tight," she said, taking them. "Nobody moves until I get Jenks's take on the restaurant."

"I'm sure it's fine," I said, moving to the front seat. "I'm so hungry, I could eat a seat cushion."

Ivy's brown eyes met mine from over her sunglasses, and her motion of shaking the spray can slowed. "It's not the food I'm worried about. I want to be sure it's mostly human." Her face went worried. "If there are any Weres, we're leaving."

Oh, yeah. Worried, I slumped behind the wheel, but Ivy looked unconcerned, taking a rag from the box and starting to wipe the road dust off the van. I was glad she was there. Sure, I was a classically trained runner, and while subterfuge was a part of that, hiding from large numbers of people out to get you wasn't. This stuff was what she had cut her teeth on. I guessed.

Nick undid his belt when Ivy edged out of sight. I could hear her work, the sporadic hisses of paint followed by squeaks as she wiped down the bumpers before the illegal paint took. The smell of fixative tickled my nose. I glanced at Nick, and he opened his mouth.

"Hey, a disguise sounds like a good idea," I blurted, twisting to reach my bag. "I've got a good half dozen in here. They're for smell, not looks, since Weres track by smell and will find us that way long before they see us. They took the ones I had on the island, but I made extra."

I was babbling, and Nick knew it. He puffed his breath out and settled back while I rummaged for them. "A disguise sounds good," he said. "Thanks."

"No prob," I answered, bringing out a new finger stick along with a handful of amulets. I broke the safety seal and arranged four amulets on my knees. I didn't know how to treat Nick anymore. We had done well together until it fell apart, but it had been a long, lonely three months until he finally left. I was mad at him, but it was hard to stay that way. I knew it was my need to help the downtrodden, but there it was.

The silence was uncomfortable, and I pricked my finger anew. I invoked them all to make the scent of redwood blossom, then handed him the first. "Thank you," he said as he took it, lacing it over his head, where it fell to clink against his pain amulet. "For everything, Ray-ray. I really owe you. What you did . . . I can never repay you for that."

It was the first time we'd been alone since pulling him out of that back room, and I wasn't surprised at his words. I flashed him a blank smile then looked away, draping my amulet over my head and tucking it behind my shirt to touch my skin. "It's okay," I said, not wanting to talk about it. "You saved my life; I saved yours."

"So we're even, huh?" he said lightly.

"That's not . . . what I meant." I watched Ivy spray an elaborate symbol on the hood, her hidden artistic talents making something both beautiful and surprising as she blurred the gray paint into the white of the van to look very professional. Glancing at me in question, she tossed the can to the box and went to the back to change the plate.

Nick was silent, then, "You can Were, now?" he asked, stress wrinkles crinkling the corners of his eyes. The blue of them seemed faded somehow. "You make a beautiful wolf."

"Thank you." I couldn't leave it at that, and I turned to see him miserable and alone. *Damn it, why did I always fall for the underdog?* "It was a one-shot deal. I have to twist a new curse if I want to do it again. It's . . . not going to happen again." I had so much black on my soul, I'd never be rid of it. I wanted to blame Nick, but *I* was the one who took the curse. I could have submitted to the drugs and stuck it out until someone came to rescue my ass. But no-o-o-o. I took the easy way by using a demon curse, and I was going to pay for it dearly.

His head went up and down, not knowing my thoughts but clearly glad I was talking. "So it isn't like you're a Were now in addition to being a witch."

I shook my head, startled when my longer hair brushed my shoulders. He knew the only way to become a Were was to be born one; he was trying to keep the conversation going.

Ivy came to the door, smelling of the fixative and wiping the gray from her fingers with a rag. "Here," she said, handing the old plate through. "If you look in the console, there should be an altered registration taped to the top. Can you switch them out?"

"You bet." *Swell. Let's add falsifying legal documents to the list*, I thought, but I took the Kentucky plate and screwdriver, giving her two amulets in their place. "These are for you and Jenks. Make sure he puts it on. I don't care what he says it makes him smell like."

Ivy's long fingers curved around them, shifting so they dangled from the cord and wouldn't effect her. "Scent disguise? Good thinking—for you." Showing the faintest blush of nervousness, she handed one of them back. "I'm not wearing one."

"Ivy," I protested, having no clue why she'd never accept any of my spells or charms.

"They don't know what I smell like, and I'm not wearing it!" she said, and I put up a hand in surrender. Immediately her brow smoothed, and she dug in a pocket for the keys to the van, handing them to me through the window. "I'll be right back," she said. "If I'm not out in four minutes, go." I took a breath to protest, and she added, "I mean it. Come rescue me by all means, but plan it out, don't burst in with your hair flying and in flip-flops."

A half smile came over me. "Four minutes," I said, and she walked away. I watched her in the side mirror. Her shoulders were hunched and her head was down—and then she was gone.

"I've got a bad feeling about this," I said.

"What?" Nick said softly. "That she's walking into a trap?"

I turned to him. "No. That she's not going to leave until it's over."

Worry filled his eyes; he was going to say something I didn't want to hear. "Rachel—"

"By the Turn, I'm hungry. I hope she hurries up," I babbled.

"Rachel, please. Just listen?"

I closed the console and eased into the seat. This conversation would happen whether I wanted it to or not. Breath slipping from me, I looked at him, to find his haggard face determined.

"I didn't know you were alive," he said, panic in his eyes. "Al said he had you."

"He did."

"And you never answered your phone. I called. God knows I did."

"It's at the bottom of the Ohio River," I said flatly, thinking he was a wimp for not calling the church. Then I wondered if he had and Ivy simply hung up on him.

"The paper said you died in a boat explosion saving Kalamack's life."

"I almost did," I said, remembering waking up in Trent's limo, having passed out after I pulled the man's freaking elf-ass out of the freezing water.

Nick stretched a swollen hand across the consol between us, and I jerked out of his reach. Making a frustrated sound, he put an elbow on his closed window and looked at the nearby semi. "Damn it, Ray-ray, I thought you were dead. I couldn't stay in Cincinnati. And now that I find you're alive, you won't even let me touch you. Do you have any idea how I mourned?"

I swallowed, the memory of the budded red rose in the jelly jar vase with the pentagram of protection on it lifting through me. My throat tightened. *Why did it have to be so confusing?*

"I missed you," he said, brown eyes thick with pain. "This isn't what I had planned."

"Me neither," I said, miserable. "But you left me long before you left Cincinnati. It took me a long time to get over you lying to me about where you had been, and I'm not going back to the way things were. I don't care that it wasn't about another woman. Maybe that I could understand, but it was money. You're a thief, and you let me believe you were something else."

Nick slumped into a defeated stillness. "I've changed."

I didn't want to hear this. They never changed, they simply hid it better. "I'm seeing someone," I said, my voice low so it wouldn't shake. "He's there when I need him, and I'm there for him. He makes me feel good. I don't want to return to how things were, so don't ask me to. You were gone, and he—" I wiped a hand under my eye, embarrassed that they were wet. "He was there," I said. *He helped me forget you, you bastard.*

"You love him?"

"Whether I love him or not isn't relevant," I said, hands in my lap.

"He's a vampire?" Nick asked, not moving one inch, and I nodded.

"You can't trust that," he protested, long hands gesturing weakly. "He's just trying to bind you to him. You know that. God, you can't be that naive! Didn't you just see what happened with your scar? With Ivy?"

I stared at him, my feelings of betrayal rising anew, both angry and frightened. "You told me once that if I wanted to be Ivy's scion, that you would drive me back to the church and walk away. That you loved me enough to leave if it meant I would be happy." My heart was pounding and I forced my clenched hands apart. "Well, what's the difference, Nick?"

He bowed his head. When he looked up, his face was tight with emotion. "I hadn't lost you then. I didn't know what you meant to me. I do now. Ray-ray, please. It's not you making decisions anymore, but vampire pheromones. You've got to get out before you make a mistake you can't walk away from!"

A movement in the mirror caught my eye. *Ivy. Thank God.* I reached for the door handle. "Don't talk to me about making mistakes," I said, grabbing my bag and getting out.

I slammed the door, glad to see Ivy for the distraction if nothing else. The van was now gray at the bottom, shading to white at the top and plastered with professional-looking decals. The cloying scent of fixative was a fading hint. Ivy was watching the nearby road as she approached, her subtle finger motions telling me to stay between the shelter of the dirty trucks.

Rocking to a halt, I crossed my arms and waited by the back bumper, lips pressed while Nick shut his door and shuffled forward. "All clear inside?" I said brightly when Ivy joined us. "Good. I'm starved."

"Just a minute, I want my stuff." Slipping past me, she

yanked the driver's side door open and retrieved a rolled-down paper bag from under the front seat. She shut the door hard before pushing past Nick and pulling me into her wake. A pause at the head of the shelter the two semis made, and we started for the restaurant, my flip-flops noisy next to her vamp-soft steps. Behind us, I could hear Nick. By all rights, as the most vulnerable member of the group, he should have been between us, but I didn't feel like protecting him, and the danger was minimal.

"Your hair is longer," Ivy said as we crossed the paved lot to the low wood-slatted building snuggled in among the pines. *Squirrel's End? How . . . redneck.*

"You aren't kidding," I said, wincing at the memory of my legs. "You didn't happen to bring a razor with you, did you?"

Her eyes widened. "A razor?"

"Never mind." *Like I was going to tell her I looked like an orangutan?*

"Are you okay?" she asked again, her voice heavy with concern.

I didn't look at her. I didn't need to. She could read my emotions on the wind easier than I could read a billboard at sixty miles an hour. "Yeah," I said, knowing she wasn't asking about the run, but about Nick.

"What did he do?" she said, her arms moving stiffly. "Did he make a pass at you?"

I glanced askance at her, then back to the nearing door. "Not yet."

She snorted, sounding angry. "He will. And then I'll kill him."

Annoyance sifted through me, the jolts from my steps going all the way up my spine. "I can take care of myself," I said, not caring that Nick was listening.

"I can take care of myself too," she said. "But if I'm making an ass out of myself, I'd hope you'd stop me."

"I am *handling* this," I said, forcing my voice to be pleasant. "How about you?" I asked, turning the tables. "I didn't think you could leave Cincinnati."

Her expression went guarded. "It's only for a day. Piscary will get over it." I was silent, and she added, "What, like the city will fall apart because I'm not there? Get real, Rachel."

My head nodded, but I was still worried. I needed her help planning how to get out of my latest fix, but she could do it by e-mail or phone if she had to.

"We should be safe enough here for a while," she said, her eyes canvassing the building as we slowed at the door and Nick came even with us. "It's all humans."

"Good," I replied faintly, feeling out of place and vulnerable. Paper sack crinkling, Ivy opened the door for me with her free hand, leaving Nick to handle the swinging, blurred-glass door by himself. I had shifted back to witch with absolutely nothing in my stomach at all, and starved, I breathed deeply of the smell of grilled meat. It was nice in there: not too bright, not too dim, no smoky smell to ruin it. There were animal parts on the walls and few people, seeing as it was Tuesday afternoon. Maybe a tad too cold, but not bad.

The menu was on the wall, and it looked like basic bar food. There were no windows but for the door, and everyone seemed willing to mind their own business after their first long look. The short bar had three fat men and one skinny one, each sitting on green vinyl stools torn to show the white padding. They were shoving food in their mouths as they watched a recap of last week's game, talking to a matronly woman with big hair behind the bar.

It was only three in the afternoon—according to the clock above the dance floor whose hands were fishing poles and numbers were fly lures. A dark jukebox filled a distant corner, and a long light with colored glass hung over a red-felted pool table.

The bar had Northern Redneck all over it, which made me all warm and fuzzy. I didn't like being the only Inderlanders in the place, but it was unlikely anyone would turn ugly. Someone might get stupid after midnight with seven shots of Jäger and a room of humans to back him, but not at three in the afternoon and only five people in the place counting the cook.

Jenks and Jax were at a table in the rear, a bank of empty booths between them and the wall. The large pixy waved for us to join them, and I felt a moment of worry that he had his shirt open to show his scent amulet. I was guessing he was proud he was big enough to have one and wanted to show it off, but I didn't like flaunting my Inderland status. They had an MPL—a Mixed Public License—posted, but it was obvious that this was a local human hangout.

"I'm going to the restroom," Nick muttered.

He made a beeline for the archway beside the bar, and I watched him, the idea flitting through me that he might not come back. I looked at Jenks, and after I nodded, the big pixy sent Jax to follow him. Yeah, I was stupid when it came to matters of the heart, but I wasn't *stupid*.

Ivy's presence hung a shade too close for comfort as we wove through the empty tables, past the pool table and the gray-tiled dance floor. Jenks had his coat off and his back to the wall, and Ivy took the chair beside his before I could. Peeved, I put my fingers on the worn wood of the chair across from her, twisting it sideways so I could see the door. The guys at the bar were watching us, and one moved down a stool to talk to his neighbor.

Seeing that, Ivy frowned. "Stand up, pixy," she said, her low voice carrying an obvious threat. "I don't want Rachel sitting next to crap for brains."

In a heartbeat Jenks's amusement turned to defiance. "No," he said, crossing his arms. "I don't want to, and you can't make me. I'm bigger than you."

Ivy's pupils swelled. "I would have thought you'd be the last person equating greater size with greater threat."

His foot under the table jiggled, squeaking. "Right." With an abrupt motion he pushed his chair out, snatching up his coat and edging from behind the table to take the seat next to mine. "I don't like sitting with my back to the door either," he grumbled.

Ivy remained silent, the brown returning to her eyes quickly. I knew she was carrying herself carefully, very aware that the clientele wasn't used to vampires and voluntarily putting herself on her best behavior. That Jenks had moved to suit her hadn't gone unnoticed, and I fixed a cheerful smile to my face when the woman approached, setting down four glasses of water with moisture beading up on them. No one said anything, and she fell away a full four feet, pulling a pad of paper from her waistband. What she wanted was obvious. Why she hadn't said anything in greeting was obvious too; we had her on edge.

Ivy smiled, then toned it down when Becky, by her name tag, paled. Putting the flat of my arms on the table, I leaned forward to look brainless. "Hi," I said. "What's the special?"

The woman darted a glance at Ivy, then back to me. "Ah, no special—ma'am," she said, reaching nervously to touch her white hair, which had been dyed blond. "But Mike in the back makes a damn, uh, he makes a good hamburger. And we've got pie today."

Nick silently joined us, with Jax on his shoulder, looking uncomfortable as he took the last seat next to Ivy and across from Jenks. The woman relaxed a notch, apparently realizing he was human and deciding the rest of us were probably half tamed. I didn't know how they did it since they couldn't smell Inderlander on us, as we could on ourselves. Must be some secret human finger motion or something.

"Hamburger sounds good," Ivy said, her eyes down to look meek, but with her stiff posture it only made her look pissed.

"Four hamburgers all around," I said, wanting to be done with it and eating. "And a pitcher of Coke."

Nick scooted his chair closer to the table, Jax leaving him for the warmer light hanging over the table. "I'd like two hamburgers, please," the gaunt man said, a hint of defiance in his voice, as if he expected someone to protest.

"Me too," Jenks chimed up, bright eyes wickedly innocent. "I'm starved."

Nick leaned to see the menu on the wall. "Does that come with fries?"

"Fries!" Jenks exclaimed, and Jax sneezed from the lamp hanging over the table. Pixy dust sifted down along with the mundane type. "Tink-knocks-your-knickers, I want fries too."

The woman wrote it down, her plucked and penciled-in eyebrows rising. "Two half-pound burgers with fries for each of the gentleman. Anything else?"

Nick nodded. "A milk shake. Cherry if you have it."

She blew out her breath, taking in his gaunt frame. "How about you, hon?"

Becky was looking at Jenks, but he was eyeing the juke-box. "Coke is fine. Does that thing work?"

The woman turned, following his gaze to the machine. "It's busted, but for five bucks you can use the karaoke ma-chine all you want."

Jenks's eyes widened. "Most excellent," he said in a surfer-boy accent. From above us came Jax's exuberant shout that all the bugs in the lamp shade had been dried out by the heat and he was going to eat their wings like chips if she didn't mind.

Oh God. And it had been going so well.

Ivy cleared her throat, clearly appalled when Jax flitted from lamp to lamp, growing more excited by the amount of pixy dust he was letting slip. "Ah, I think that will do it," I said, and the woman turned away, bumping into a table as she watched Jax on her way to the kitchen. The hair on the back of my neck had pricked; everyone in the bar was look-ing at us. Even the cook.

Jenks followed my gaze, his blond eyebrows high. "Let me take care of this," he said, standing up. "Rache, do you have any money? I spent mine at The Butterfly Shack."

Ivy's eyes darkened. "I can handle this."

A small noise came from Jenks. "Like at the FIB?" he scoffed. "Sit down, weenie vamp. I'm too big to get shoved into a water cooler."

Feeling the tension rise, I shuffled in my bag and handed Jenks my wallet. I didn't know what he had in mind, but it was probably a lot less scary than what Ivy had planned, and it wouldn't land us in the local jail either. "Leave some in there, okay?"

He gave me a lopsided, charming smile, his perfect teeth catching the light. "Hey, it's me." Making a click to tell Jax to join him, he ambled to the bar, his pace more provocative than it ought to have been. The man couldn't have any idea how good he looked.

"No honey toddies!" I shot after him, and he raised a backward hand. Ivy wasn't happy when I met her gaze. "What?" I protested. "You've seen him on honey."

Nick snickered and set his glass of water down. Jax flew a glittering path to the karaoke machine ahead of his dad, Jenks's pace intent as he followed. Becky had her eyes glued to the small pixy as she talked on the phone, and I had a feeling he was intentionally dusting heavy. I wondered how this would get everyone's eyes off us. A distraction, maybe?

The father and son clustered at the screen, a reading lesson ensuing while they looked at the song menu. Ivy glanced at them, then Nick. "Go help them," she muttered.

Nick pulled his gaunt face up to hers. "Why?"

Ivy's jaw clenched. "Because I want to talk to Rachel."

Frowning, Nick rose, his chair scraping on the wooden floor. Our drinks arrived, and the woman set his cherry shake, three glasses of Coke, and a condensation-wet pitcher on the table. Milk shake in hand, Nick shuffled to Jenks and Jax, looking tired in his gray sweats.

I sipped my Coke, feeling the bubbles burn all the way down. My stomach was empty and the smell of the cooking meat was giving me a headache. Setting the glass aside so I didn't slam it, I slumped, relying on Ivy to keep an eye on my back. I watched her relax muscle by muscle until she was calm.

"I'm glad you're here," I said. "I really made a crap pit of everything. He was in the middle of a survivalist group, for

God's sake. I never expected that." *I should have done more recon,* I thought, but I didn't need to say it. It was obvious.

Ivy shrugged, glancing at Nick, Jenks, and Jax. "You got him out. I wasn't planning on staying," she added, "but since I'm here, I'll stick around."

I blew my breath out, relieved. "Thanks. But is that . . . prudent?" I hesitated, then ventured, "Piscary's going to be royally ticked if you aren't there by sundown."

Her gaze tracked Jax flitting madly from Nick to Jenks. "So what?" she said, fingers fidgeting with her new earrings. "He knows I'll be back. It's only a six-hour drive."

"Yes, but you're out of his influence, and he doesn't—" My words cut off when she rolled her fingertips across the table in a soft threat. "He doesn't like that," I boldly finished, pulse quickening. Here, surrounded by humans, was probably the only place I'd dare push her like this. She was on her best behavior, and I was going to use it for all it was worth.

Ivy bowed her head, the black sheet of her shorter hair not hiding her face. The dusky scent of incense became obvious, and a soft tickle shivered through me. "It will be okay," she said, but I wasn't convinced. She lifted her head, and a faint blush of worry, or perhaps fear, colored her. "Kisten is there," she said. "If I leave, no one cares but the higher-ups—who aren't going to do anything anyway. Kisten is the one who can't leave. If he does, it will be noticed, talked about, and acted upon by idiots who haven't had their fangs for a month. We're fine."

This really wasn't what I had been worried about. Part of me wanted to take her explanation at face value and drop it, but the other part, the wiser, stupider half of me, wanted her to be honest so there would be no surprises. I turned when the front door opened and a woman came in, talking loudly to Becky as she shrugged out of her coat and headed for the back.

"Ivy," I said softly, "what about your hunger? You don't have your usual . . ." I stopped, not sure what to call the people she tapped for blood. *Donors? Special friends? Significant others?* I settled on, "Support net?"

Ivy froze, sending a jolt of adrenaline through me. *Crap. Maybe I should keep my mouth shut.* "Sorry," I said, meaning it. "It's not my business."

"Your timing sucks," she said, and the tension eased. I hadn't overstepped the friendship boundaries.

"Well . . ." I said, wincing. "I don't know what you do."

"I can't go out and knock up a streetwalker," she said bitterly. Her eyes were hard, and I could tell she wasn't responding to me but to a deeper guilt. "If I let it be a savage act that I can satisfy with anyone, I'll be a monster. What kind of a person do you think I am?"

"That's not what I said," I protested. "Cut me some slack, will you? I don't know how you take care of yourself, and I was too afraid to ask until now. All I know is you go out anxious and jittery and come home calm and hating yourself."

My admission of fear seemed to penetrate, and the creases in her forehead smoothed. She uncrossed her legs, then crossed them under the table. "Sorry. It surprised me you asked. I should be good for a few days more, but the stress—" Ivy cut her thought short and took a breath. "I have a few people. We help each other and go our separate ways. I don't ask anything from them, and they don't ask anything from me. They're vamps, in case you're interested. I don't make ties with anyone else . . . anymore."

Single, bi vamp looking for same for blood tryst, not relationship, I thought, hearing her unspoken desire in her last sentence, but I wasn't ready to deal with it.

"I don't like living like this," Ivy said, her words unaccusing and her eyes a deep, honest brown. "But it's where I am right now. Don't worry about it. I'll be okay. And as far as Piscary is concerned, he can burn in hell—if his soul hadn't already evaporated."

Her face was expressionless again, but I knew it was a front. "So you're going to stay?" I asked, both embarrassed and proud that I had learned I could ask for help when I needed it, and boy did I need it.

She nodded, and I exhaled, reaching for my drink. "Thank you," I said softly.

The idea of leaving everything to play dead the rest of my life scared the crap out of me the way a death threat couldn't. I liked my life, and I didn't want to have to leave it and start over. It had taken me too long to find friends who would stick with me when I did something stupid. Like turning a simple snag and drag into an interspecies power struggle.

Shifting one shoulder up and down in a half shrug, Ivy reached under her chair for that paper bag. "Do you want your mail," she asked, "seeing as I brought it all this way?"

She was changing the subject, but that was fine by me. "I thought you were kidding," I said as Ivy set the sack on the table and I dragged it closer. Jenks and Jax were excited about something they had found on the list, and people had given up watching them in glances and were blatantly staring. At least they weren't looking at us.

"It's the package I'm curious about," Ivy said, glancing at Nick and Jenks while they pointed at the screen.

I dumped everything out, putting the obvious thank-you-for-saving-my-ass note from a previous run back in the bag along with the insurance bill from David's company and a late season seed catalog. What was left was a paper-wrapped parcel the size of my two fists. I looked closer at the handwriting, my eyes jerking to Nick in the corner. "It's from Nick," I said, reaching for a table knife. "What is he sending me when he thinks I'm dead?"

Ivy's face held a silent distain clearly directed at Nick. "I'd be willing to bet it's whatever the Weres are after. I thought it was his handwriting, but I wasn't sure."

Very conscious of Nick slurping his shake and reading track titles over Jenks's shoulder, I pulled the package off the table and put it in my lap. My pulse quickened and I made short work of the outer wrapping. Fingers cold, I opened the box and pulled out the heavy drawstring bag. "It's got lead in it," I said, feeling the supple weight of the fabric. "It's wrapped in lead, Ivy. I don't like this."

She casually leaned forward to block Nick's view. "Well, what is it?"

Licking my lips, I tugged the opening wider and peered down, deciding it was a figurine. I gingerly touched it, finding it cold. More confident, I drew it out and set it on the table between us. Staring at it, I wiped my hands off on my jeans.

"That is . . . really ugly," Ivy said. "I think it's ugly." Her brown eyes flicked to me. "Is it ugly, or just weird?"

Goose bumps rose, and I stifled a shiver. "I don't know."

The statue was a yellowish color with stained striations running through it. Bone, I guessed. Very old bone; it had left the cold feeling on my hands that bone does. It stood about four inches high and was about as deep. And it felt alive, like a tree or a plate of moldy cheese.

I furrowed my brow as I tried to figure out what it was a statue of. Touching only the base, I turned it with two fingers. A noise of disgust slipped from me; the other side had a long muzzle twisted as if in pain. "Is it a head?" I guessed.

Ivy put her elbow on the table. "I think so. But the teeth . . . Those are teeth, right?"

I shivered, feeling like someone had walked over my grave. "Oh," I whispered, realizing what it reminded me of. "It looks like Pam when she was in the middle of Wereing."

Ivy flicked her eyes to mine and back to the statue. As I watched, her face went paler and her eyes went frightened. "Damn," she muttered. "I think I know what it is. Cover it up. We are in deep shit."

Twenty

I jerked when Nick suddenly appeared at the table. His long face was flushed, angry and frightened all at the same time—a dangerous mix. "What are you doing?" he hissed at Ivy, snatching the statue up and holding it close. "You brought it here? I sent it to her so no one would find it. I thought she was dead. They couldn't make me tell who had it if I sent it to a dead woman, and you brought it here? You damned fool vampire!"

"Sit," Ivy said, her jaw clenched and her eyes shifting to black. "Give it to me."

"No." Nick's grip tensed to a white-knuckled strength. "Save the aura shit for someone it works on. I'm not afraid of you."

He was, and Ivy's hand trembled. "Nicholas. I'm hungry. I'm tired. I don't give a crap about your stupid ass. My partner is in deep shit because of you. *Give it to me.*"

Adrenaline pulsed, hurting my head. Nick was near panic. The karaoke machine started up with something sad and melancholy. Jenks was watching us, but the rest of the bar hadn't a clue that Ivy was about ready to lose it, pushed to the edge from stress and being far from home.

"Nick," I soothed. "It'll be okay. Give it to me. I'll put it away."

Nick shifted and Ivy jerked, almost reaching for him. Licking his cracked lips, Nick said, "You'll hold it for me?"

"I'll keep it," I assured him, fumbling for the lead-lined bag and extending it. "Here."

Hollow-cheeked face frightened, he carefully placed it into the pouch. His swollen fingers started curving around it, and I pulled it to me, tightening the drawstrings. It wasn't any magical hold it had on him; it was greed.

Hand shaking, Ivy grabbed her drink and downed it to ice. I kept an eye on her while I put the statue in my bag, then put the bag on my lap. It felt heavy, like a dead thing. From the corner came Jenks singing "Ballad of the Edmund Fitzgerald." The skinny guy at the bar was watching him, having turned completely from the game recap. *Jenks could sing?*

"Sit," Ivy breathed, and this time Nick did, taking Jenks's spot beside me and putting Jenks's coat on the chair beside Ivy. "Where did you find that?" she muttered.

"It's mine."

I shifted in my chair, smelling our food coming. The woman didn't look at anyone as she placed the food down and left. The tension was so thick, even she could sense it. I stared at my plate. There was my fabulous burger, oozing juice, with lettuce, onions, mushrooms, cheese, and, oh God, there was bacon on it too. And I couldn't eat it because we had to argue about Nick's ugly statue first. *Well, to hell with that,* I thought, removing the top bun and picking the onions off.

Ivy refilled her glass from the pitcher, a growing rim of brown around her pupils. "I didn't say whose is it. I said, where did you find it?"

Nick pulled his plate closer, clearly wanting to ignore her but making the healthy decision not to. "I can't believe you brought it here," he said again, motions jerky as he rearranged his pickles. "I sent it to Rachel so it would be safe."

Ivy glared at him. "If you use smart people in your takes without telling them, don't complain when they do the unexpected and ruin your plans."

"I thought she was dead," Nick protested. "I never expected anyone to come *help* me."

I ate one of Jenks's fries. There wasn't any ketchup on the

table, but asking for some would get us thrown out. Humans blamed the Turn on tomatoes, but they were the ones who had done the genetic tinkering. "And why are they willing to pack up to get ahold of it?" I asked.

Nick looked ill. "I don't have to tell you anything."

My lips parted in disbelief, and I turned to Ivy. "He's still running his scam."

"I'm not." His eyes were wide in an innocence that couldn't reach me anymore. "But the Weres can't have it. Don't you know what it is?"

His last words were a hushed whisper, and Ivy glanced past me to the door as three underdressed, giggling women pranced in. Immediately Becky started in with a high-pitched chatter, her eyes tracking to Jenks. I think she had called them about fresh meat.

"I know what it is," Ivy said, dismissing the women. "*Where did you find it?*"

One of the guys at the bar was humming. While we sat hunched over our food and argued, Jenks had some guy at the bar singing about a tanker that had sunk forty-some years ago. Shaking my head in wonder, I returned my attention to Nick. "We're waiting," I said, then wrangled my burger to my mouth. My eyes closed as I bit into it. Sweet bliss, it was good.

His eyes stressed, Nick picked up one of his burgers, leaning his elbows on the table. "Rachel, you saw how there were three packs on that island, didn't you? All working together?"

I scrambled for a napkin. "It was freaking weird," I said around my full mouth. "You should have seen how fast their alpha Wered. And they were nasty too. Like alphas without the restraint. Cocky little bastards . . ." My words trailed off as I took another bite.

"That's what it does," Nick said, and Ivy swore under her breath. "I found it in Detroit."

"Then it's the focus?" she whispered, and I waved a hand for their attention, fry weaving between the two of them, but they weren't listening to me. "That thing can't be the focus,"

Ivy added. "It was destroyed five millennia ago. We don't even know if it even really existed. And if it did, it sure as hell wouldn't be in Detroit."

"That's where I found it," Nick said, then took a bite. A small moan came from him. "You can't destroy something that powerful," he mumbled. "Not with rocks and sticks. And not with magic." He swallowed. "Maybe with a car crusher, but they didn't have them back then."

"What is it?" I insisted, only marginally aware of the flirting going on across the room between the stanzas of men dying on the waves. *Get a clue, Jenks.*

Ivy pushed her untouched plate with her burger away. "It's trouble," she said. "I was going to make him give it to the Weres, but now—"

"Damn it!" I shouted, and the three women ogling Jenks giggled and jiggled—in that order. I lowered my voice. "Someone tell me what I have sitting on my lap before I explode."

"You're the professor," Ivy said bitingly to Nick, taking a fry from Jenks's plate. "You tell her."

Nick washed a bite of his first burger down and hesitated. "Vamps can either be born or bitten, but the only way to become a Were is to be born one."

"Duh," I said. "Witches are like that too, along with most of Inderland."

"Well . . ." Nick paused, his eyes flicking everywhere. ". . . the Were holding that thing can make a Were by a bite."

I chewed and swallowed. "And they want to kill you for that?"

Ivy brought her head up. "Think about it, Rachel," she cajoled. "Right now, vampires are at the top of the food chain."

I made a telling face at her as I took another bite, wrangling a piece of bacon.

"What I mean is we have more political power than any other Inderlander species," she amended. "Because of how we're structured, everyone looks to someone else, the top vampires owing so many favors that they're as effective as a political house member. It's a tight web, but we generally get what we want. Humans would get itchy with their trigger finger except that our numbers are held static by only the undead being able to infect a human with enough virus to make it even possible to Turn them."

I stole another of Jenks's fries, wishing I had ketchup.

"Weres, though," Nick said, "don't have political power as a group because they won't look to any but their pack leader. And their numbers can't increase any faster than their birthrate." Leaning forward, Nick tapped the table with a swollen finger, his entire mien changing as he became the instructor.

"The focus makes it possible for the number of Weres to increase very quickly. And the multiple packing you saw on the island is nothing to what will happen when it gets out that the focus is intact. Everyone will want a part of it, merging their pack into the one that holds it. You saw what they were like. Can you imagine what would happen if a vampire ran into a pack of Weres acting like that?"

Jenks's half-eaten fry dangled from my fingers, forgotten. Slowly it was starting to sink in, and it didn't look good. The problem wasn't that the focus would allow Weres to pack up. The problem was that the focus would *keep* them packed up. Worried, I glanced at Ivy. Seeing me understand, she nodded.

The island Weres had been together for days, maybe weeks, and that had been with only the promise of the focus. If they had it, the round would be permanent. I thought back to the ring of Weres surrounding me on the island, the three packs united under one Were holding the strength of six alphas. Their cocky, savage attitude had been shocking. Walter had not only drawn his dominance from them, but also channeled it back into every member without the tempering calm and moral strength that all alphas had. That wasn't even bringing up how fast they could Were if they muted each other's pain. Add to that their new aggressiveness and a resistance to pain?

I set Jenks's fry down, no longer hungry. Weres were fairly submissive in Inderland society, the alphas the only ones having enough personal power to challenge the vampires' political structure. Remove that submissive posture, and the two species were going to start clashing. A lot. That's probably why the vamps had hidden the focus in the first place.

Crap, if the vampires knew about it, they would be after me too. "This isn't good," I said, feeling ill.

Making a puff, Ivy leaned back. "You think?"

From across the bar, Jenks finished his song, immediately falling into a sleazy version of "American Woman," gyrating his hips and making the three women and one of the truck drivers cheer and whistle. Jax was above him, making sparkles. I wondered if anyone had any inkling the world was changing, starting right here in this little bar.

Wiping my fingers clean, I reached for the bag on my lap. "It can shift the balance of Inderland power," I said, and Ivy nodded, the tips of her hair swinging.

"With the explosive destruction of dropping a tiger into a dog show," she said dryly. "It's believed that Weres used to have a political structure very similar to that of the vampires. Better, since Weres never betrayed another as vampires are known to do for blood. Their hierarchy revolved around who held the focus, and eliminating it shattered the Weres' social structure, politically castrating them and leaving them squabbling in small packs."

Nick started on his second burger. "They were going to forcibly convert humanity, according to the demon texts," he said, taking off the top bun to eat it like an open-faced sandwich. "Those who wouldn't voluntarily become a Were were killed. Entire families whelped or murdered in the name of Were conquest over vampires. They would have had a good chance of succeeding but the witches crossed from the ever-after about that time and sided with the humans and vampires. Using witch magic, we beat them back."

Nervous, I slipped my flip-flop off and on to make a popping sound. I wondered what he had given a demon for learning this. I'd never heard it before, but Ivy had, so maybe I just hadn't taken the right class. I couldn't help thinking that perhaps witches were really at the top of the food chain, our independent ways and lack of political structure aside. Every earth spell on the market, whether used by human, vampire, or Were, was made by a witch. Without us, their little political wars would be fought with sticks, stones, and nasty words.

"The focus was destroyed," Ivy said, her voice low and her eyes thick with worry.

Nick shook his head. Gulping down a swig of soda, he said, "It's demon made, and only a demon can destroy it. It has been passed from vampire to ranking vampire for generations."

"Until you sold a piece of your soul for it," I whispered, and Nick went white. *Stupid-ass human,* I thought, then hid my own wrist.

Jenks finished his song amid cheers and friendly shouts. He bowed and blew kisses, stepping off the stage and making his light-footed way to us. A camera flashed, and I wished I had remembered mine. Jax flitted over the ladies at the bar, charming them thoroughly and helping his dad avoid them. The mood of the bar had shifted dramatically thanks to Jenks; now even the looks our way from the truckers had a touch of daring voyeurism.

"Food's here?" Jenks said, handing me my wallet before dropping down and grappling with the first of his burgers with the enthusiasm of a starving adolescent. Jax stayed with the women, distracting everyone and staying safely out of the adult conversation. "What'd I miss?" Jenks added, taking a bite.

I sucked at my teeth and gave Ivy a wry look. "Nick swiped a Were artifact that can tip the balance of Inderland power and start a vampire-Were war," I said, putting my wallet away next to the Were statue. *I needed to call David and get his take on this. On second thought, maybe I shouldn't.*

Jenks froze, his cheeks bulging with food. He met everyone's eyes to figure out if we were joking, but it wasn't until

Nick nodded that he remembered to swallow. "Holy crap," he said.

"That's about it." I sighed. "What are we going to do with it? We can't give it to them."

Nick picked at his fries. "I'm the one who started this. I'll take it and disappear."

In a smooth motion of grace, Ivy reclined in her chair. She looked calm and possessed, but I could tell by her fingers searching for her missing crucifix that she wasn't. "It's not that simple now, professor. They know who Rachel is. Jenks they might give up on, but by saving your ass, Rachel put her own on the line. She can't go back to Cincinnati as if it never happened. They will follow her through hell for that thing." Putting the flat of one arm on the table, she leaned forward, her face threatening. "They will hurt her just like they hurt you to get it, and I'm not going to let that happen, you dumb little shit."

"Stop it," I said as Nick reddened. "We can't give it back. What else do we have?"

Ivy picked a sesame seed off her burger, looking sullen. Nick, too, had a chip the size of Montana on his shoulder. Jenks was the only one whose face was creased in thought, not anger. "Can you make everyone forget about it?" he asked as he chewed. "Or at least forget about us?"

I pushed my plate away. "Too many people. I'd miss someone. Not to mention it would be a black earth charm. I'm not doing it." *But I'd twist demon curses?* No accounting for tastes, I guess. But Ceri's curse hadn't involved hurting people other than me.

Jenks chewed slowly. "How about putting it into hiding again?"

"I'm not putting it back," Nick protested. "I spent a year's income getting it."

Ignoring him, I frowned. *Was he still running his take?*

"They'd still come after Rachel," Ivy said. "If you can't make everyone forget," she said to me, "I can only think of one thing to get your life back after crap for brains screwed it up."

Nick took an angry breath. "You call me that again and I'm going to—"

Ivy moved. I jumped, managing to keep my reaction to a small hop when she sent her arm forward and grabbed Nick under his chin. Nick's eyes widened but he didn't move. He had grown up in the Hollows and knew that moving would only make things worse.

Ivy's eyes were almost entirely black. "You'll what, crap for brains?"

"Ivy . . ." I said tiredly. "Stop it."

Jenks looked from me to Ivy, his eyes bright and his face worried. "Lighten up, Ivy," he said softly. "You know she always sides with the underdog."

Jenks's words penetrated where mine hadn't, and in a flash of brown Ivy's pupils returned to normal. Smiling beatifically, she let go, catching Nick by the collar of his sweatshirt before he could rock back, pretending to adjust it for him. "Sorry, Nickie," she said, her pale fingers patting his hollow cheek a smidgen too hard.

As I tried to purge the adrenaline from me, Nick scooted his chair away, cautiously rubbing his throat. Moving a shade too fast, Ivy refilled her glass from the pitcher. "There's only one solution," she said, bending her straw exactly upright. "Professor here has to die."

"Whoa, whoa, whoa!" I exclaimed, and Nick stiffened, his face red in anger. "Ivy, that's enough."

Jenks pulled his plate of fries closer. "Hey, I'm right there with you," he said, his eyes roving the bar, probably for the nonexistent ketchup. "It would solve everything." He hesitated, wiping his fingers on a napkin. "You grab him, and I'll get your sword from the van."

"Hey!" I shouted, angry. I knew they weren't serious, but they were starting to tick me off. I lowered my voice when the giggling women at the bar looked at us. "Nick, relax. They aren't going to kill you."

Snickering, Jenks started on his fries, and Ivy took on a confident, almost seductive stance, slouching in her chair and smiling with one side of her mouth. "All right," she said. "If you're going to get bent out of shape about it, we won't kill him. We'll stage his spectacular, public death along with the destruction of that thing."

Nick stared at Ivy's confident figure. "I will *not* let you destroy it," he said vehemently.

She arched her eyebrows. "You can't stop me. It's the only option we have to get those Weres off Rachel's tail, so unless you have a suggestion, I suggest you shut up."

Nick went still. I eyed his brow furrowed in thought, then slid my gaze to Jenks. Jenks was watching him too, his mouth full but his jaws not moving. We exchanged a knowing look. Someone who endured a week of torture wouldn't give up that easy. Ivy didn't seem to notice, but Ivy didn't know Nick like I was starting to know Nick. *God, why was I even trying to help him?* I thought, jiggling my foot to make my flip-flops pop. Depressed, I reached for my soda.

"So you stage my death and the destruction of the focus," the apparently subdued human said, and Jenks returned to eating, pretending ignorance. "I think they're going to notice when the ambulance takes me to the hospital instead of the morgue."

Ivy's eyes tracked someone headed our way. Glass in hand, I turned to find Becky with three drinks holding umbrellas and cherries on sticks. My eyes went to the flirting women, and I cringed. Oh . . . how nice. They were trying to pick him up.

"I can get us a body," Ivy said into the silence.

I choked on my drink, coughing at the string of thoughts that remark engendered, but Becky had come forward and I couldn't say a word—even if I could catch my breath.

"Here you go, hon," she said, smiling as she set the drinks squarely before Jenks. "From the ladies at the bar."

"Oh, wow," Jenks said, apparently forgetting what accepting drinks from strangers meant when one was over four inches tall. "Look, pixy swords!"

He reached for the cherry picks, eyes glinting, and I interrupted with a quick, "Jenks!"

Ivy exhaled, sounding tired, and Jenks glanced from one of us to the other. "What?" he said, then reddened. Wincing, he looked up at Becky. "Hey, um, I'm married," he said, and I heard someone swear from the bar. It wasn't the trucker, thank God. "Maybe," he said, pushing them reluctantly to her, "you should return them to the ladies with my, uh, regrets."

"Well, shoot," Becky said, smiling. "You just keep them. I told them a hunk like you would be already hooked, landed, filleted, and cooked." Her smile widened. "And eaten."

Ivy exhaled, and Nick didn't seem to know whether to be proud or embarrassed for his species. Jenks shook his head, probably thinking of Matalina as he pushed them away.

"Did you say you had pie?" Ivy asked.

"Yes, ma'am." Becky smoothly took up the drinks, pixy swords and all. "I have butterscotch or apple. I'll bring out a wedge of apple, seeing as you're allergic to butterscotch."

Ivy blinked but her smile never faltered. "Thank you." She pushed her untouched hamburger at her, and the woman obligingly took both it and my plate. "Put a scoop of ice cream on it?" she asked. "And coffee. Everyone want coffee?" She looked inquiringly at us, smiling in a way that made me decidedly nervous, especially after that "I can get us a body" remark, and I nodded. *Coffee? Why not?*

"Sugar and cream," Jenks added faintly, and Becky sashayed away, loudly proclaiming to the three women at the bar that she had known it all along.

Ivy watched her go, then looked at me with a questioning scrutiny. I suddenly realized Becky must have talked to Terri from the grocery store. Feeling another one of my stellar, embarrassing moments coming on, I hunched forward and took another sip, hiding behind the glass. No wonder the entire bar was being nice to us. They thought I was a nympho who liked doing it with three people and pudding.

"Why am I allergic to butterscotch?" Ivy asked slowly.

My face flamed, and Jenks stammered, "Ah, Rachel and I are lovers with a thing for foursomes and pudding. Apparently she thinks you and Nick are Alexia and Tom. You're allergic to butterscotch, and crap for brains likes pistachio."

"Stop calling me that," Nick muttered.

Ivy let her breath out. Her eyebrows were arched, and she looked bemused. "Okay . . ."

I set my drink down. "Can we get back to how we're going to kill Nick? And what's this about a dead body? You'd better start talking quick, Ivy, 'cause I'm not going to play hide-and-seek with a dead guy in my trunk. I did that in college, and I'm not going to do it again."

A smile quirked Ivy's mouth. "Really?" she asked, and I flushed.

"Well, he wasn't dead," I muttered. "But they told me he was. Scared the crap out of me when he kissed my ear when I tried to lug him into—" I stopped when I felt Becky at my elbow, a tray of coffee and pie in her hand.

Smirking, Becky gave everyone their coffee and set a piece of pie à la mode in front of Ivy. Humming "American Woman," she took Jenks's and Nick's empty plates and left.

I eyed the ice cream and then my fork. "You going to eat all that?" I asked, knowing from experience Ivy rarely finished anything.

Glancing at me for permission, Ivy took my coffee cup off its saucer and put the ice cream in its place. I pulled it closer, feeling the tension start to ease. I didn't have a spoon, but my fork worked, and I wasn't going to ask Becky for one.

Ivy carefully cut the point from her pie and pushed it away to eat last. "I propose we pull a Kevorkian," she said, and I went cold from more than the ice cream.

"That's illegal," Jenks said quickly.

"Only if you get caught," Ivy said, eyes on her pie. "I have a friend of a friend—"

"No." I set my fork down. "I'm not going to help a vampire cross over. I won't. Ivy, you're asking me to kill someone!"

My voice had risen, and Ivy tossed her hair from her eyes. "He's twenty, and he's in so much pain he can't use the can without someone helping him."

"No!" I said louder, not caring people were starting to look. "Absolutely not." I turned to Jenks and Nick for support, appalled to see their acceptance of this. "You guys are sick!" I said. "I'm not going to do that!"

"Rachel," Ivy said persuasively, brown eyes showing an unusual amount of emotion. "People do it all the time."

"This people right here doesn't." Flustered, I pushed the ice cream away, wondering if it had been part of her plan to get me to accept. She knew I was a sucker for ice cream. I scowled at the laughter from the bar, turning to see Becky gossiping to the truck drivers, bent over with her rear in the air. It occurred to me they probably thought I had just been propositioned for something even a redheaded nympho would say no to. Crossing my arms in front of me, I glared at Ivy.

"He'd do it himself," Ivy said softly. "God knows he has enough courage. But he needs his life insurance check to set himself up, and if he kills himself, he loses it. He's been waiting a long time."

"No."

Ivy's lips pressed together. Then her brow smoothed. "I'll call him," she said softly. "You talk to him, and if you still feel the same way, we'll call it off. It will be up to you."

My head hurt. If I didn't say yes now, I would look meaner than Satan's baby-sitter. "Alexia," I said loud enough for the bar to hear. "You are one sick bitch."

Her smile widened. "That's my girl." Clearly pleased, she picked up her fork and ate another bite of pie. "Can you make a charm to make someone look like little professor here?"

Nick stiffened, and Jenks chuckled, "Little professor . . ." as he dumped a fourth packet of sugar into his coffee. I felt like I was in my high school lunchroom, plotting a prank.

"Yeah, I can do that," I said. Sullen, I pushed the melting ice cream around on my plate. Doppelganger charms were illegal, but not black. Why not? I was going to freaking kill someone.

"Good." Ivy speared the last of her pie, going still in thought before she ate the point, and I knew she was making a wish. *And people thought I was superstitious?* "Now all we have to do is find a way to destroy that thing," she finished.

At that, Nick stirred. "You're not going to destroy it. It's over five thousand years old."

I sent my flip-flops popping. "I agree," I said, and Nick shot me a grateful glance. "If we can substitute a fake Nick, then we can substitute a fake statue."

Ivy leaned back in her chair with her coffee. "I don't care," she said. "But you . . ." She pointed a finger at Nick. ". . . aren't going to get it. Rachel is going to put it into hiding, and you—get—nothing."

Nick looked sullen, and I exchanged that same knowing look with Jenks. This was going to be a problem. Jenks stirred his coffee. "So . . ." he said, "how are we going to knack Nick?"

I thought his verbiage left something to be desired, but I let it pass, ignoring my melting bribe. "I don't know. I'm usually on the saving-your-butt end of things."

Blowing across his mug, Jenks shrugged. "I'm partial to crushing their chest until their ribs crack and their blood splatters like Jell-O in a blender without a top." He took a sip, wincing. "That's what I do to fairies."

I frowned, appalled when he added two more packets of sugar.

"We could push him off a roof," Ivy suggested. "Drown him, maybe? We've got lots of water around here."

Jenks leaned conspiratorially toward Ivy, his green eyes darting merrily between mine and hers. "I'd suggest jamming a stick of dynamite up his ass and running away, but that might really hurt whoever is taking his place."

Ivy laughed, and I frowned at both of them. The karaoke

machine had started up again, and I felt ill when "Love Shack" began bouncing out. *Oh my God.* The skinny trucker was up on the stage with the three bimbos as backup.

I looked, then looked again. Finally I tore my eyes away. "Hey," I said, feeling the weight of the last twenty-four hours fall on me. "I've been up since yesterday noon. Can we just find somewhere to crash for the day?"

Immediately Ivy grabbed her purse from under her chair. "Yeah, let's go. I have to call Peter. It will take him, his scion, and his mentor a day to get up here. You sleep, Jenks and I will come up with a few plans, and you can pick the one that your magic will work the best with." She glanced at Jenks, and he nodded. Both of them turned to me. "Sound okay?"

"Sure," I said, taking a slow breath to steady myself. Inside I was shaking. I wasn't too keen on picking *any* plan that involved killing someone. But the Weres wouldn't give up on Nick unless he was dead; and unless there was a body, they would know it was a scam.

And I wanted to go home. I wanted to go home to my church and my life. They would hound me to the ends of the earth if they knew the focus was found and in my possession.

I stood, feeling as if I was slipping into places that I had once vowed I would never go. If we were caught, we would be tried for murder.

But what choice did I have?

Twenty-one

The scent of cinnamon and cloves was thick in the motel room, making it smell like the solstice. Nick was making ginger drops, and the warmth of the tiny efficiency oven was pleasant at my back. It wasn't unusual for him to bake, but I thought it more likely he was trying to bribe me into talking to him than a desire for homemade cookies. And since Jenks had the TV on a kids' show for Jax, and Ivy wouldn't let Nick plan his own demise, the human had little to do.

The Weres knew Jenks, so Ivy had gone shopping while I slept, laden down with a grocery list and my shoe size. All of us going out for food three times a day—or in Jenks's case, six—didn't seem prudent. We had found a suite five minutes from the bar, and after giving the low-ceilinged rooms done in brown and gold the once-over, I stated clearly that *I* had the van. Ivy took the bed in the tiny room off the main room, Nick got the bed in the main room, and Jenks wanted the sofa sleeper, happily opening it up and putting it away twice before Ivy and I finished unloading the van; she didn't want Nick touching anything. The van was tight and cold, but it was quiet, and with the circle I'd put up while I slept, safer than the motel.

I had woken cranky and stiff that morning at an ungodly nine o'clock, unable to go back to sleep after my twelve-hour nap. And since Jenks and Jax were both up, and Nick, of course, was awake, I thought I'd take the opportunity to get a jump on the magic prep. *Yeah. Right.*

"Want to lick the spoon, Ray-ray?" Nick said, his gaunt face looking more relaxed than I'd seen it since . . . last fall.

I smiled, trying to keep it noncommittal. "No thanks." I bent my attention back to the laptop screen. With Kisten's help, Ceri had e-mailed me the earth charm I needed to make the disguise amulets, with her additions to turn it into an illegal doppelganger spell. It was still white, but I wasn't familiar enough with the additional ingredients to sensitize it to mimic a particular person.

Stretching, I pulled my scratch pad closer and added pumpkin seeds to my list. The bulb over the oven glinted on my no-spell charm bracelet, and I jiggled the black gold, making an audible show of my break with Nick. Ignoring it, he continued to wedge blobs of cookie dough onto a nasty-looking pan. Then he hesitated, clearly wanting to say something but deciding against it. The first batch of cookies had come out of the oven not long ago, and the smell was heaven.

I was avoiding the cookies on some vague principle, but Jenks had a plateful as he leaned over Jax's work on the table by the curtained window. Though the TV was on, neither was paying attention to it, absorbed in their practice. Rex sat in the warmth of Jenks's lap, her pretty white paws tucked sweetly under her as she stared at me from across the room. That Jax was strutting atop the table didn't seem to be important to her right now.

Ever the vigilant father, Jenks had a gentling hand about her fur in case she remembered Jax and took a swipe at him. But the kitten was fixed on me, giving me a mild case of the creeps. I think she knew I had been that wolf, and was waiting for me to turn back.

Her ears swiveled to the back room, and a sudden thump sent her skittering. Jenks yelped when her claws dug into him, but she was already under the bed. Jax was after her in a sprinkling of gold pixy dust, coaxing in a high-pitched voice that grated on my eyeballs. From Ivy's room came a torrent of muffled curses. *Great. Now what?*

The door to Ivy's room was flung open. She wore her

usual silk nightie, and her short black hair was tousled from her pillow. Lean and sleek, she stomped across the nasty carpet, looking intent on mayhem.

The Electric Company theme song bounced as she strode into the kitchen. Eyes wide, I turned to keep her in view. Nick stood in the corner, satisfaction gleaming in his eyes, the bowl of dough in his long hands. Lips pressed tight, Ivy grabbed an oven mitt, pulled open the oven, and yanked out the tin of baking cookies. It made a muffled clatter when she dropped it onto the tin with its blobs of uncooked dough waiting to go in the oven.

Her brown eyes fixed on Nick's for an instant, then she grabbed the two tins with the oven mitt and strode to the door. Still silent, she opened it, dropping everything on the walk outside. Her speed was edging into a vamp quickness when she returned, jerking the bowl out of Nick's unresisting grip and swiping the cookies cooling on the counter into it.

"Ivy?" I questioned.

"'Morning, Rachel," she said tightly. Ignoring Jenks, she opened the door and dropped the metal mixing bowl onto the walk with the rest. Plucking the cookie out of Jenks's hand, she flicked it over the threshold, slammed the door, and vanished into her room.

Bewildered, I glanced at Jenks. The pixy shrugged, then turned the volume down on the TV. I followed his gaze to Nick. His expression was positively vindictive. My eyes narrowed and I leaned back, crossing my arms. "What was that all about?" I asked.

"Ooooh, I forgot," he said, lightly snapping his healing fingers. "Vampires are sensitive to the scent of cloves. Golly, the smell must have woken her up."

My jaw tightened. I hadn't known that. Apparently neither had Jenks, since he was the one who had gone shopping. Nick turned to the sink a little too slowly to hide his smile.

I took a breath, deciding he was lucky Ivy hadn't smacked him hard enough to knock him out. In the shape he was in, it wouldn't take much. My eyes fell on the pain amulet he was wearing, thinking the entire situation was stupid. Jenks told me earlier that Ivy had been on the Internet all last night as Nick tried to sleep. Payback?

My fingers tapped the laminated table. Standing, I closed the lid on my laptop, then slid my demon curse book off the table and into my arms. "I'll be in the van," I said blandly.

"Rachel—" Nick started, but I snatched up my list and pencil and walked out of the kitchen, the heavy book making me awkward and unbalanced. It kind of went with my mood.

"Whatever, Nick . . ." I said tiredly, not turning around.

Jenks was a mix of wary alertness. The paper on the table before him was strewn with Jax's work. He was getting better.

"I'll be in the van, if you need me," I said in passing.

"Sure." His eyes went from me to Jax trying to coax Rex out from under the bed. The sight of a pixy holding up a bed-spread calling "Kitty, kitty, kitty" looked risky even to me.

"Rachel," Nick protested when I opened the door, but I didn't turn. Reversing my steps, I snatched up my bag with the focus in it. No need to leave *that* sitting around.

"You stupid lunker," Jenks said as I left. "Don't you know she always sides with—"

The door clicked closed, cutting off his words. "The un-derdog," I finished. Depressed, I leaned against the door, the focus tucked between me and my demon book, my head bowed. Not this time. I wouldn't side with Nick, and despite the cookie incident, Nick was the underdog.

Birdsong and the chill of morning pulled my head up. It was quiet and damp, the rush-hour traffic nonexistent. The sun was trying to break through the light fog, giving every-thing a golden sheen. The nearby straits were probably beautiful, not that I could see them from where I stood.

Gathering my resolve, I shifted the weight of the demon book and dug in my pocket for the van's keys. We'd parked in the shade of a huge white pine between the road and the motel so I could set a circle without people running into it. The new hundred-dollar running shoes that Ivy had bought me were silent on the pavement, and it felt odd being up this early. Creepy. Habit made me shift through the keys so they didn't clink, and only the muffled thunk of the van unlocking broke the stillness until I lugged the side door open in a sound of sliding metal and rolling rubber. Still peeved, I stepped up and in, and slammed the door shut in frustration.

I dropped the demon book on the cot and sat next to it. Elbows on my knees, I kicked my bag under me. I didn't want to be there, but I wanted to be in the motel room less. The silence grew, and I reluctantly slid the curse book onto my lap. I was here, I might as well do something. Wedging off my shoes, I sat cross-legged with my back to the drape drawn between me and the front seat. It was dim, and I tugged the little side curtain open to let in the light.

My lightning charm rasped on the yellowing pages as I leafed through the tome looking for anything familiar. There wasn't a table of contents, making it difficult to satisfy my curiosity. Big Al used demon magic to look like people he had never seen, plucking their description and voice from memories like I picked flowers from my garden. I wasn't going to twist a demon curse for a disguise when I could use an illegal, white earth charm, but comparing the two might give me insight into how the three branches of magic pulled on each other's strengths.

The Latin word for copy caught my attention, and I leaned closer, feeling my legs protest. I needed to get out and run; I was stiffening. Slowly I pieced it out, deciding the word actually translated into transpose. There was a difference. The curse didn't make someone look like someone else, it moved the abilities of one person into another. My lips parted. That's how Al not only turned himself into Ivy, but took the abilities of a vampire as well.

My eyebrows rose, and I wondered whom Al got his vampiric abilities from. Piscary, in return for a favor? A lesser vampire he had in the ever-after? Ceri would know.

Gaze dropping to my bag, my pulse quickened at the thoughts sliding through me. I couldn't duplicate the focus without commissioning an artist—who would take forever and then have to be charmed into forgetfulness—but maybe if I moved its power to a new thing . . .

"Demon curse, Rachel," I whispered. "You're a bad girl to even think it."

The sound of a motel door opening and closing pulled a thread of caution through me. I didn't hear footsteps. Berating myself for not having done it sooner, I tapped a line. *"Rhombus,"* I whispered, instigating a series of hard-practiced lessons that flicked a five-minute setup and invocation of a circle into a heartbeat. The zing of ever-after tingled through me, making it feel as if my body was humming. It was fascinating that the line here "tasted" different, more electrical almost. I think it was all the ground water.

"Yikes," came Jenks's soft voice. "When she wants to be alone, she doesn't leave any bones about it, does she?"

There was a high-pitched answer, and I pushed the book off my lap and lurched past the curtain and into the front. "Jenks," I called, tapping the glass before I stuck the key in the ignition and rolled the window down. "What's up?"

The tall pixy turned from unlocking Kisten's Corvette. Smiling, he squinted in the haze and crossed the parking lot, two amulets about his neck and a red baseball cap on his head. One was for scent, the other, an over-the-counter charm, turned his hair black. It wasn't much, but it would do. His feet edged the black haze of ever-after between us, and I dropped the circle, my pulse temporally quickening at the surge of power before I disconnected from the line.

"I need some more toothbrushes," he said, coming closer. "And maybe some fudge."

Kneeling on the seat, I put my crossed arms on the windowsill. Toothbrushes? He had six open on the bathroom counter. "You know, you can reuse those," I said, and he shuddered.

"No thanks. Besides, I want to take Jax on a lesson on low-temperature runs so Ivy can smack crap for brains a good one if he wants to keep antagonizing her."

"Hi, Ms. Morgan," Jax chimed out, Jenks's hat lifting to show Jax peeping from under it.

A smile curved over me. "Hi, Jax. Keep your dad's back, okay?"

"You bet."

Pride crinkled Jenks's eyes. "Jax, do a quick reconnaissance of the area. Watch your temps. And be careful. I heard blue jays earlier."

"Okay." Jax wiggled out from under his dad's hat and zipped off in a clatter of wings.

I exhaled, a mix of melancholy and pride over Jax learning a new skill. "Will you stop calling Nick crap for brains?" I asked, tired of playing referee. "You used to like him."

Jenks made a face. "He turned my son into a thief and broke my partner's heart. Why should I give him a draft of consideration?"

Surprised, my eyebrows rose. I hadn't known my falling out with Nick bothered him.

"Don't get all girly on me," Jenks said gruffly. "I may only be eighteen, but I've been married for ten years. You turned into a slobbering blob, and I don't want to see it again. It's pathetic, and it makes me want to pix you." His face grew worried. "I've seen how you get around dangerous men, and you always fall for the underdog. Nick is both. I mean, he's dangerous and he's been hurt, and hurt bad," Jenks rushed on, mistaking my sick look for fear. *Crap, was I that transparent?* "He's going to hurt you again if you let him—even if he doesn't mean to."

Disconcerted, I brushed the dampness of fog from my arm. "Don't worry about it. Why would I go back? I love Kisten."

Jenks smiled, but his brow was furrowed. "Then why did we come out here?"

I fixed my gaze on the curtained windows of the motel. "He saved my life. I might have loved him. And I can't pretend my past didn't happen. Can you?"

There wasn't much Jenks could say to that. "You need

anything while I'm out?" he said, clearly changing the subject.

My lips curved upward. "Yeah. Can you get one of those disposable cameras?"

Jenks blinked, then smiled. "Sure. I'd love a shot of you and me together in front of the bridge." Still smiling, he whistled for Jenks and turned away.

The reminder of why we were there intruded, and my stomach clenched. "Uh, Jenks. I could use something else too." His eyes went expectant, and I licked my lips nervously. *You're a bad girl, Rachel.* "I need something made from bone," I said.

Jenks's eyebrows rose. "Bone?"

I nodded. "About fist-sized? Don't spend a lot of money on it. I'm thinking I might be able to move the curse from the statue to something else. It needs to have been alive at some point, and I don't think wood is animate enough."

Feet scuffing, Jenks nodded. "You got it," he said, turning to the dry, desperate-sounding clatter of pixy wings. It was Jax, and the exhausted pixy almost fell into his dad's hand.

"Tink's dia—uh, diapers," Jax exclaimed, changing his oath mid-phrase. "It's cold out here. My wings don't even work. Jeez, Dad, are you sure it's okay for me to be out here?"

"You're fine." Taking off his hat, Jenks raised his hand and Jax made the jump to his head. Jenks carefully replaced his cap. "It takes practice to know how long your wings will work in low temps and get yourself to a heat source in time. That's what we're doing this for."

"Yeah, but it's cold!" Jax complained, his voice muffled.

Jenks was smiling when he met my gaze. "This is fun," he said, sounding surprised. "Maybe I should go into business training pixy backups."

I chuckled, then turned solemn. It would make his last months more enjoyable if he could teach what he could no longer do. I knew Jenks's thoughts were near mine when the emotion left his face. "Jenks's school for pixy pirates," I quipped, and he smiled, but it faded fast.

"Thanks, Jenks," I said as he made motions to return to the car. "I really appreciate this."

"No prob, Rache." He touched his hat. "Finding stuff is what pixies do fourth best."

I snorted, pulling myself in and already knowing what Jenks thought pixies did first best. And it wasn't saving my ass like he told everyone.

Rolling up the window against the chill, I returned to my cot, wondering if Kisten had a second blanket in there somewhere. The rumble of the Corvette rose, fading to the ambient sound of passing traffic when Jenks drove off. "Bone," I mumbled, writing the word beside the Latin. My breath caught, then slipped from me in chagrin when the pencil faded. *That's right.* Ceri had used a charm to fix the print to the page. Next time I talked to her, I'd ask.

"Why?" I mumbled, feeling my mood sour. It wasn't as if I was going to make a practice of using these curses. Right? Eyes closing, I let a sound slip from me as I pushed my fingers into my forehead. *I am a white witch. This is a one-shot deal.* Too much ability leads to confusion over what's right and wrong, and obviously I was confused enough already. Was I a coward or a fool? God help me, I was going to give myself a headache.

The squeak of the motel door opening brought my head up. There wasn't an accompanying sound of a car starting, and my face blanked when a tap came on the back door of the van. A shadow moved past the dirt-smeared window. "Ray-ray?"

I should have reset my circle, I thought sourly, forcing my shoulders down and trying to decide what to do for an entire five seconds: an eternity for me.

"Rachel, I'm sorry. I brought you some hot chocolate."

His voice was apologetic, and I exhaled. Closing my "big book of demon curses," I went to the back door, thinking I was making a mistake when I opened it.

Nick stood there in his borrowed gray sweats, looking like he was ready for a run in the park: tall, lean, and battered. A survivor. He had a foam cup of instant hot chocolate in his hands and a pleading expression in his eyes. His hair was swept back and his cheeks were clean-shaven. I could smell the shampoo from his shower, and I lowered my eyes at the memory of how silky his hair was when it was toweled dry and still damp, a whisper over my fingertips.

Jenks's warning resounded in me, and I stifled my first feeling of sympathy. *Yes, he had been hurt. Yes, he had the potential to be dangerous. But damn it, I didn't have to let it get to me.*

"Can I come in?" he asked after I'd silently stared at him for a good while. "I don't want to sit alone in that motel room knowing a vamp is sleeping behind a flimsy door."

My pulse quickened. "You're the one who woke her up," I said, hand on my hip.

He smiled, to turn himself charmingly helpless. He wasn't. He knew I knew he wasn't. "I got tired of being called crap for brains. I didn't know everyone would leave."

"So you pushed her buttons, relying on Jenks and me to buffer the retaliation?" I asked.

"I did say I was sorry. And I never claimed it was smart." He raised the hot chocolate. "Do you want this or should I go?"

Logic railed against emotion. I thought of Ivy, knowing I wouldn't want to be alone in the same motel room with an angry vampire either. And there wasn't much sense in saving someone if you were going to let your partner take him apart the first chance she got.

"Come on in," I said, sounding like it was a concession.

"Thanks." It was a grateful whisper, his relief obvious. He handed me the hot chocolate and, using the side of the van to steady himself, stepped up and in. His pain amulet swung, and he tucked it behind his shirt as he straightened in the low height. I could tell by his stiff motions and his grimace that the amulet wasn't working to cover all the pain. I had only the one pain amulet left until I made more, and he'd have to ask for it.

Clearly cold, Nick shut the door, sealing us in the same darkness that I had been in before, but now it was uncomfortable. My hands on the hot chocolate, I sat dead center on the cot, forcing him to sit on the pile of boxes across from me. There was more room than before, because Ivy had dumped off Marshal's stuff at the high school pool, but it was still too close. Gingerly settling himself, Nick tugged his sleeves down to hide his shackle marks and set his clasped hands in his lap. For a moment the silence was broken only by the hush of traffic.

"I don't want to bother you," he said, watching me from under his fallen bangs.

Too late. "It's okay," I lied, crossing my legs at my knees, very conscious of the demon text beside me on the bed. I took a sip of hot chocolate, then set it on the floor. It was too early for me to be hungry. The silence stretched. "How is the amulet holding up?"

A relieved smile came over him. "Great, good," he rushed to say. "Some of the hair on my arms is starting to grow back. By this time next month I might look . . . normal."

"That's good. Great." *If we managed to evade the Weres and live that long.*

His eyes were worried as he glanced at the book beside me, taking up the space so he wouldn't. "Do you need any help with the Latin? I don't mind interpreting it for you." His long face scrunched up. "I'd like to do something."

"Maybe later," I said guardedly. My shoulders eased at his admission of uselessness. Ivy and Jenks were making a point to keep him out of everything, and it would have bothered me too. "I think I have a curse I can use. I want to talk to Ceri about it first."

"Rachel . . ."

Oh God. I've heard that tone before, usually coming out of me. He wants to talk about us. "If she says the imbalance won't be too bad," I rushed to say, "I'm going to move the magic from the focus to something else, so we can destroy the old statue. It shouldn't be too hard."

"Rachel, I—"

Pulse quickening, I tugged the demon book closer. "Hey, why don't I show you the curse. You could—" He moved, and my eyes jerked up. He didn't look dangerous, he didn't look helpless, he looked frustrated, as if he was screwing his courage up.

"I don't want to talk about the plan," he said, leaning over the space between us. "I don't want to talk about Latin or magic. I want to talk about you and me."

"Nick," I said, my heart pounding. "Stop." He reached for my shoulder, and I jumped, lashing out to block his hand before he could touch me.

Startled, he jerked away. "Damn it, Rachel!" he exclaimed. "I thought you were dead! Will you just . . . Will you just let me give you a hug? You're back from the dead, and you won't let me even touch you! I'm not asking to move in with you. All I want is to touch you—to prove to me you're alive!"

I let out my held breath, then caught it again. My head hurt. I did nothing as he shifted to sit beside me, moving the book out of the way. Our body weight slid us closer, and I shifted to face him, my knees forcing us apart.

"I missed you," he said softly, his eyes scrunched with old pain, and this time I did nothing as his arms went around me. The scent of cinnamon and flour filled my senses, instead of musty books and the snap of ozone. His hands were light, almost not there. I felt his body relax, and he exhaled as if he'd found a piece of himself. *Don't,* I thought, tensing. *Please don't say it.*

"Things would have been different if I had known you were alive," he whispered, his breath shifting the hair about my face. "I never would have left. I never would have asked Jax to help me. I never would have started this fool snatch. God, Rachel, I missed you. You're the only woman I've met who understands me, who I never needed to explain why. Hell, you didn't even leave when you found out I called up demons. I . . . I really missed you."

His hands clenched for an instant and his voice cracked. He had missed me. He wasn't lying. And I knew what it was like to be alone and the rarity of finding a kindred soul, even if he was screwed up. "Nick," I said, my heart pounding.

My eyes closed as his hands moved, pulling through my hair. I reached up, stilling them, bringing them back down to my lap. The memory of him tracing the lines of my face filled me. I remembered the touch of his sensitive fingers, following my jawline, running down my neck to follow the curves of my body. I remembered his warmth, his laughter, and his eyes sparkling when I twisted a phrase to mean something entirely new and naughty. I remembered the way he made me feel needed, appreciated for *who and what I was,* never having to apologize for it, and the contentment I found in sharing ourselves. We'd been happy together. It had been great.

And I made a good decision.

"Nick." I pulled away, my eyes opening when his hand brushed my cheek. "You left. I got myself together. I won't go back to where we were."

His eyes went wide in the low light. "I never left you. Not really. Not in my heart."

I took a breath and let it go. "You weren't there when I needed you," I said. "You were somewhere else. Stealing something." His expression went empty, and a flash of anger pressed my lips together, daring him to deny it. "You lied to me about where you were going and what you were doing. And you took Jenks's son with you. You turned him into a thief with your promises of wealth and excitement. How could you do that to Jenks?"

Nick's eyes were emotionless. "I told him it was a dangerous job and it didn't pay well."

"To a pixy, you live like a king," I snapped, feeling my heartbeat quicken.

"The familiar bond is broken. We can start over—"

"No." I shifted from him, feeling the betrayal again. *Damn him.* "You can't be part of my life anymore. You're a thief and a liar, and I can't love you."

"I can change," he said, and I groaned with disbelief. "I *have* changed," he said, so earnestly that I thought he might believe he had. "When this is over, I'll go back to Cincinnati. I'll get a noon to midnight job. I'll buy a dog. Get cable TV. I'll stop it all for you, Rachel."

His hands went out and took mine, and I looked at my fingers cradled between his long pianist hands, damaged and raw, but sensitive, enfolding mine as his arms had once protected me, kept me alive when I was bleeding my life out.

"I love you that much," he whispered. My head pounded, and he brought my fingers to his lips and kissed them. "Let me try. Don't throw this second chance away."

I couldn't seem to get enough air. "No," I said, voice low so it wouldn't tremble. "I can't do this. You won't change. You might believe you can, and maybe you will, but in a month, a year, you'll find something, and then it will be, 'Just one more, Ray-ray. Then I'll stop forever.' I can't live like that." My throat was tight and I couldn't swallow.

I pulled my eyes to his, reading in his shocked expression that he had been about to say that right now, that he still wanted to walk away from this with money in his pocket. That he may have meant everything he'd said, but also wanted to convince me to put my, Ivy's, and Jenks's life on the line for money. He was still running his damn snatch, even while knowing that if the statue wasn't destroyed, it would put my life in jeopardy.

Betrayal bubbled up, making my stomach clench. "I have a good life," I said, feeling his grip on my fingers loosen. "It doesn't include you anymore."

Nick's jaw clenched and he drew back. "But it includes Ivy," he said bitterly. "She's hunting you. She's going to make you her toy. It's always the thrill of the hunt for vampires. That's all. And once she gets you, she'll drop you and move on to someone new."

"That's enough," I said, my voice harsh. It was my greatest fear, and he knew it.

He smiled bitterly. "She's a vampire. She can't be trusted. I know she's killed people. She uses them and abandons them. *That's what they do!*"

I was shaking in anger. Kisten's bracelet hung heavy on me like a sign of ownership. "She only takes blood from people who freely give it. And she *doesn't* abandon them!" I shouted, unable to keep my voice down. "She *never* left me!"

Nick's face went hard at the accusation. "I may be a thief," he insisted, "but I never hurt anyone who didn't deserve it. Even by accident."

My breath was fast and I stood. He looked up at me, his face rigid with frustration. "You hurt me," I said.

A hopeless look flashed across him. He reached for my hands, and I stepped back. "So she's a vampire," I said loudly. "I'm *a witch!* What makes you any safer? What about you, Nick? You call up demons! What did you give that demon for the location of that . . . thing!"

Shock flashed over him for my having turned this on him. Clearly uncomfortable, he glanced at my bag on the floor and eased away. "Nothing important."

He wouldn't look at me, and my predatory instincts stirred. "What did you give the demon?" I prompted. "Jax said you gave him something."

Nick took a quick breath. His eyes met mine. "Rachel, I thought you were dead."

A cold feeling of worry slid through me. Jax had said the demon showed up as me. Had the demon known about me, or just plucked my image out of Nick's head? "What demon was it?" I asked, thinking of Newt, the insane demon who shoved me back into reality last solstice. "Was it Al?" I said softly, seething inside.

"No, it was someone else," he said, looking sullen. "Al didn't know where it was."

Someone else? Okay, Nick knew more than one demon.

"What did you give it for the location of the focus?" I asked, trying to at least look calm.

Nick's eyes lit up and he scooted forward on the cot. "That's just it, Rachel. Al always wanted useless stuff like what your favorite color was, or if you used lip gloss, but all this one wanted was a kiss."

The air slipped out of me, and I couldn't seem to make my lungs move to pull more in. *Nick gave Al information about me in return for favors?* "All it wanted was a kiss?" I managed, still trying to grasp what Nick had done. I'd feel betrayed later. Right now I only felt sick. Hand on my stomach, I turned sideways. Had the demon looked like me when Nick kissed it? *Oh God. I didn't want to know.*

"What . . ." Somehow I took a breath. "What demon was it?" I asked, knowing he wouldn't be able to tell me without risking his soul.

Sure enough, Nick stood up, his hands spread placatingly. "I don't know. I went through Al for that one. He took his own cut for brokering my question. But it was worth it."

I turned, and Nick blinked at the fury creasing my brow. "You son of a bitch," I whispered. "You've been selling me out to demons? You've been buying demon favors with information about me? What did you tell them!"

Eyes wide, Nick backed up. "Rachel . . ."

My breath hissed out. In a quick motion, I leapt at him, pinning him against the door with my arm under his neck. "What did you tell Al about me!"

"It's not that big of a deal!" His eyes were bright, and what looked like a laugh was quirking his lips. *He thought it was funny?* He thought I was overreacting, and it was all I could do to not crush his windpipe right there and then.

"Just stupid stuff," he was saying, his voice high but light. "Your favorite ice cream, what color your eyes are after a shower, how old you were when you lost your virginity. God, Rachel. I didn't tell him anything that could hurt you."

Outraged, I pushed into his neck, then rebounded to stand

two steps away. "How could you do that to me?" I whispered.

Nick rubbed his throat and moved from the door, trying to hide that I'd hurt him. "I don't know why you're so upset," he said sullenly. "You wouldn't believe the information I got in return. I didn't tell him anything important until I thought you were dead."

My eyes widened and I reached for the wall before I fell over. "You were doing this before we broke up?"

His hand still on his throat, Nick looked at me, his own anger growing. "I'm not stupid. I didn't tell him anything important. Ever. What is the big deal?"

With an effort, I unclenched my teeth. "Tell me this, Nick," I said. "Did the demon look like me when you kissed it? Was that part of the deal? That you pretended it was me?"

He said nothing.

My finger trembled as I pointed to the door. "Get out. The only reason I'm not handing you back to the Weres is because they have to see you die, and right now I'm thinking of taking the pretend part out. If you *ever* tell another demon anything about me, I'll . . . I'll do something bad to you, Nick. So help me God, I'll do something very bad."

Furious, I yanked the heavy side door open. The sound of the metal scraping shocked through me. God! He had been buying demon magic and favors with information about me. For months. *Even while we were together.*

"Rachel—"

"Get. Out."

My voice was low in threat, and I didn't like the sound of it. At the scuff of his feet hitting the pavement, I shoved the door shut. Breath held, I clasped my arms about myself and just stood there. My head hurt and the tears welled up, but I wasn't going to cry.

Damn him. Damn him to hell.

Twenty-two

Miserable, I wouldn't leave the van, afraid if I saw Ivy or Jenks I would blurt out what Nick had done. Some of my reticence was because I needed him to finish this run, and if they leaned on him hard, he might leave. Some of it was shame for having trusted him. Hell, most of it was. Nick had betrayed me on so many levels, and he didn't even get why I was upset. I hadn't been prepared for this. God! What an ass.

"I ought to give him back to the Weres," I whispered, but they had to see him die with the focus. There was no guarantee that he'd stop telling Al where I was ticklish, or that I sometimes hid the remote from Ivy just to get a rise out of her, or any of the hundreds of things I had shared with him when I thought I loved him. I shouldn't have trusted him. But I wanted to trust. Damn it, I *deserved* to be able to trust someone.

"Bastard," I muttered, wiping my eyes. "You son of a bitch bastard."

The chatter of the maids and the thumps of their cart as they wheeled it down the cracked sidewalk were soothing. It was past noon, and the motel was empty but for us. Being Wednesday, it would likely stay that way.

I lay curled up on the cot, my head on the clean smell of the borrowed hotel pillow, and my shoulders covered by the thin car blanket. I wasn't crying. I was *not* crying. Tears were leaking out as I waited for the ugly feelings to fade, but I wasn't crying, damn it!

Sniffing loudly, I reassured myself that I wasn't. My head hurt and my chest hurt, and I knew if I cared to unclench my hands from the blanket clutched under my chin that they would be trembling. So I lay there and wallowed, falling into a light doze as the heat of the day warmed the van. I barely heard the sound of Jenks and Jax returning to the room. But the shout filtering through the open door jerked me awake.

"I thought he was with you!" Ivy shouted. "Where is he?"

Jenks's response was unheard, and I jumped at the hammering on the van door. Sitting up, I put my sock feet on the floor, drained of emotion.

"Nick!" Ivy shouted. "Get your ass out here!"

Numb, I stood, grabbed the sliding door, and pulled it back with a crunch of metal to look at Ivy with bleary, empty eyes.

Ivy's anger froze, her eyes almost black as she scanned the van and saw me hunched under my blanket. The fog had lifted, and a cold breeze shifted the tips of her sin-black hair, shimmering in the light. Behind her, Jenks lingered in the doorway to the motel room, Jax on his shoulder, six bags with colorful logos in his grip and a question high in his eyes. "He's not here," I said, keeping my voice low so it wouldn't rasp.

"Oh God," Ivy whispered. "You've been crying. Where is he? What did he do to you?"

The protective tone in her voice hit me hard. Miserable, I turned away, my arms about my middle. She followed me in, the van unmoving when her weight hit it. "I'm fine," I said, feeling stupid. "He . . ." I took a deep breath and looked at my hands, perfect and unmarked. My soul was black, but my body was perfect. "He's been telling Al stuff about me in return for favors."

"He what!"

Jenks was suddenly beside her. "Jax, did you know about this?" he said tightly, the depth of his anger looking wrong on his youthful features.

"No, Dad," the small pixy said. "I only watched the one time."

Ivy's face was pale. "I'll kill him. Where is he? I'm killing him right now."

I took a breath, more grateful than I probably should have been that they would defend me like this. Maybe I was just trusting the wrong people. "No you aren't," I said, and Jenks jiggled on his feet, clearly wanting to protest. "He didn't tell Al anything too bad—"

"Rache!" Jenks yelped. "You can't defend him! He sold you out!"

My head jerked up. "I'm not defending him!" I exclaimed. "But we need him alive and cooperative. The Weres have to see him die along with that . . . thing," I said, nudging my bag with a foot. "I'll think about beating him to a pulp later." I looked up at Ivy's blank expression. "I'm going to use him, then cut him lose. And if he ever does anything like that to me again . . ."

I didn't need to finish the thought. Jenks shifted from foot to foot, clearly wanting to take things into his own hands. "Where is he?" the pixy asked, grim-faced.

My breath came and went. "I don't know. I told him to go away."

"Go!" Ivy exclaimed, and I made a wry face.

"Out of the van. He'll be back. I still have the statue." Depressed, I stared at the floor.

Jenks hopped out of the van, and the light coming in brightened. "I'll find him. Bring his punk-ass back here. It's been a while since we . . . talked."

My head came up. "Jenks . . ." I warned, and he held up a hand.

"I'll behave," he said, gaze darting over the parking lot and to the nearby bar, his face frighteningly hard. "I won't even let him know you told us what he did to you. I'll pick out a movie from the front office on the way back, and we can watch it, all nice and friendly like."

"Thanks," I whispered.

My head was down and I didn't hear him leave, but

I looked up when Jax's wings clattered and found them gone. Ivy was watching me, and when I shrugged she shut the door to seal out the cold air. The sound of the metal on metal struck through me, and I gathered myself into some semblance of order. Ivy hesitated, looking torn between wanting to comfort me and afraid I'd take it the wrong way. And there was the blood thing too. It had only been a day since she had sated it, but it had been a very stressful day. Today wasn't looking any easier.

I looked at the matted throw rug, wondering what kind of person I was, afraid to hug my friends, and sleeping with people who used me. "I'll be okay," I said to the floor.

"Rachel, I'm sorry."

My throat hurt. I put my elbows on my knees, set my head into my cupped hand and closed my eyes. "I don't know. Maybe it was my fault for trusting him. I never dreamed he would do something like this." I sniffed loudly. "What's *wrong* with me, Ivy?"

I was disgusted with myself, the emotion edging into self-pity, and I met her gaze in surprise when Ivy whispered, "There's nothing wrong with you."

"Yeah?" I shot back, and she went to the van's tiny sink and plugged in the electric kettle. "Let's take a look at my track record. I live in a church with a vampire who is the scion of a master vampire who would just as soon see me dead."

Saying nothing, Ivy got out an envelope of cocoa so old it was stiff with moisture.

"I date her old boyfriend," I continued bitterly, "who used to be said master vampire's scion, and *my* ex-boyfriend is a professional thief who calls demons and trades information about me for tips to steal artifacts that can start an Inderland power struggle. There's something *wrong* when you trust people who can hurt you so badly."

"It's not that bad." Ivy turned with the chipped mug in her hand, head down as she broke chunks of cocoa against the side of the mug with an old spoon.

"Not that bad?" I said with a bark of laughter. "It's been hidden for five thousand years. Piscary is going to be majorly pissed, along with every master vampire in every city on the entire freaking planet! If we don't do this right, they're all going to be rapping on my door."

"I wasn't talking about that. I meant about you trusting people who can hurt you."

I flushed, suddenly wary of her, standing over there at the end of the van in the dark. "Oh."

The water from the kettle started to steam, blurring her features as it rose. "You need the thrill, Rachel."

Oh God. I stiffened, glancing at the closed door.

Ivy's posture shifted irritably, and she flowed into motion. "Get off it," she said, setting the mug on the tiny counter space and unplugging the kettle. "There's nothing wrong with that. I've watched you ever since we partnered in the I.S. Every guy who tried to date you, you drove away when you found out the danger was only in your imagination."

"What has that got to do with Nick selling me out to a demon?" I said, my voice a shade too loud for prudence.

"You trusted him when you shouldn't have so you could find a sense of danger," she said, her expression angry. "And yes, it hurts that he betrayed that trust, but that's not going to stop you from looking for it again. You'd better start picking where you find your thrills a little better, or it's going to get you killed."

Flustered, I put my back to the wall of the van. "What in hell are you talking about?"

Ivy turned to face me. "*Being* alive isn't enough for you," she said. "You need to *feel* alive, and you use the thrill of danger to get it. You knew Nick dealt in demons. Yes, he overstepped his bounds when he traded information about you to them, but you were willing to risk it because the danger turned you on. And once you get over the pain, you're going to trust the wrong person again—just so you can find a jolt in that it might all go bad."

I was afraid to speak. The scent of cocoa rose as she poured hot water into the mug. Afraid she might be right, I considered it, looking over my past. It would explain a lot. All the way back to high school. *No. No freaking way.* "I do not need a feeling of danger to get turned on," I protested hotly.

"I'm not saying that's bad," she said neutrally. "You're a threat, and you need the same. I know, because I live it. All vampires do. That's why we keep to our own but for cheap thrills and one-night stands. Anyone less a risk than ourselves isn't enough to keep up, keep around, keep alive, or understand. Only those born to it are capable of understanding. And you."

I didn't like this. I didn't like it at all. "I have to go," I said, shifting my weight to stand.

The palm of her hand flashed out, hitting the side of the van to bar my way and stop me cold. "Face it, Rachel," she said when I looked up, frightened. "You've never been the safe, nice girl next door, despite everything you do to be that person. That's why you joined the I.S., and even there you didn't fit in, because, knowing it or not, you were a possible threat to everyone around you. People sense it on some level. I see it all the time. The dangerous are attracted by the lure of an equal, and the weak are afraid. Then they avoid you, or go out of their way to make your life miserable so you'll leave and they can continue deluding themselves that they're safe. You trusted Nick knowing he might betray you. You got off on the risk."

I swallowed a surge of denial, remembering the misery of high school and my history with bad boyfriends. Not to mention my idiotic decision to join the I.S., and then my even more idiotic attempt to quit when Denon started giving me crap runs and the thrill was taken away. I knew I liked dangerous men, but saying it was because I was equally dangerous was ludicrous . . . or would have been if I hadn't just spent yesterday as a wolf/witch hybrid courtesy of a demon curse that *my* blood kindled, and I now sat in a brand-new Rachel skin with no freckles or wrinkles.

"So you're a threat," Ivy said, the scent of cocoa rising

between us as she sat on the boxes across from me. "So you need the rush of possible death to keep your soul awake and turn you on. That's not bad. It just says you're one powerful bitch, whether you know it or not." Tilting forward, she handed me the chipped mug. "Dangerous doesn't always equal untrustworthy. Drink your cocoa and get over it. Then find someone to trust who's worth trusting you back."

Jaw clenched, I looked at the mug in my grip. *It was for me?* I had made her cocoa the night Piscary had raped her: mind, body, and soul. I pulled my eyes up her tight jeans and her long shapeless black sweater that hung mid-thigh.

"That's why I wait," she whispered when our eyes met.

I took a hasty breath when I realized the unseen scar beneath my new skin was tingling.

Ivy must have sensed it, for she stood. "I'm sorry," she said, reaching for the door.

"Ivy, wait." What she'd told me scared me, and I didn't want to be alone. I had to figure this out. Maybe she was right. *Oh God, was I really that screwed up?*

Her long fingers gripped the handle, ready to pull the door open. "The van stinks of us both," she said, not looking at me. "I should be good for a few days more, but the stress . . . I've got to get out of here. I'm sorry—damn it." She took a deep breath. "I'm sorry, but I can't comfort you without my blood lust getting in the way." She looked up at me, her smile faint and carrying old pain. "Not much of a friend, am I?"

Without getting up, I fumbled my fingers past the curtain of the window above me and pushed the bottom out to open it. My heart pounded, and I took in the pine-scented air and hush of the passing traffic. "You're a good friend. Does that help?" I asked in a small voice.

Ivy shook her head. "Come back to the room. Jenks will drag Nick in soon. We can all watch a movie and pretend nothing happened. It should be tremendously awkward. Tons of fun. I'll be fine as long as I don't sit next to you."

Her expression was calm, but she sounded bitter. My face scrunched up and I curved my fingers around the warmth of the cocoa. I didn't know what to think, but I was very sure I didn't want Nick to know he had made me cry. "You go. I'll come in when my eyes aren't so red."

I felt a sense of loss when Ivy stepped out of the van and then turned with her arms about her in the chill. It was obvious she knew the longer I stayed out here, the harder it was going to be for me to find the courage to come in. "Don't you have a complexion charm?" she asked.

"They don't work on bloodshot eyes," I hedged. *Damn it, what was wrong with me?*

Ivy squinted in the glare and sharp breeze, then her face brightened. "I know . . ." she said, coming back in and slamming the door shut behind her to seal out the cold. I watched her push aside the front curtain and rummage in the console. Her eyes had returned to normal, the fresh air doing as much as the shift in topics. "Kisten probably has one in here," she muttered, then turned with a tube of what looked like lipstick. "Ta-da!"

Ta-da, huh? I pulled myself straighter as she maneuvered around the clutter and sat on the cot beside me. "Lipstick?" I said, not used to having her that close.

"No. You put it under your eyes and the vapors keep the pupil constricted. It'll take the red out too. Kist uses it for hangovers—among other things."

"Oh!" I abruptly felt twice as unsure, not having known there was such a thing. I had always trusted a vampire's pupils to give away their mood.

Legs crossed at the knees, she uncapped it and twisted until a column of opaque gel rose. "Close your eyes and look up."

My lips parted. "I can put it on."

A puff of annoyance came from her. "If you put on too much or get it too close to your eye, you can damage your vision before it wears off."

I told myself I was being stupid. She looked okay; she wouldn't have come back in if she wasn't. Ivy wanted to do something for me, and if she couldn't give me a hug without her blood lust tainting it, then by God I would let her put that gunk under my eye. "Okay," I said, resettling myself and looking up. *You need the thrill of danger* flitted through my mind, and I quashed it.

Ivy shifted closer, and I felt a light touch under my right eye. "Close your eyes," she said softly, her breath stirring a curl.

My pulse quickened, but I did, and my other senses kicked in stronger. The gel smelled like clean laundry, and I stifled a shudder when a cold sensation moved under my eye. "You, ah, don't use this a lot, do you?" I asked, starting when her finger touched my nose.

"Kisten uses it when he works," she said shortly. She sounded fine—distracted and calm. "I don't. I think it's cheating."

"Oh." I seemed to be saying that a lot today. The cot shifted when she moved back and away from me. I lowered my head and blinked several times, the vapors leaving a stinging sensation that I couldn't imagine was making my eyes any less red.

"It's working," she said with a small, contented smile, answering my question before I asked it. "I thought it would on witches, but I wasn't sure." She motioned me to look at the ceiling again so she could finish, and I lifted my chin and closed my eyes.

"Thank you," I said softly, my thoughts becoming more conflicted and confused. Ivy had said vampires only bothered to get to know people as powerful as themselves. It sounded lonely. And dangerous. And it made perfect sense. She was looking for that mix of danger and trustworthiness. *Was that why she put up with my crap? She was looking to find that in me?*

A ribbon of angst pulled through me, and I held my breath so Ivy wouldn't sense it in my exhalation. That I needed danger to feel passion was ridiculous. It wasn't true. *But what if she was right?*

Ivy had once said that sharing blood was a way to show deep affection, loyalty, and friendship. I felt that way about her, but what she wanted from me was so far from what

I understood that I was afraid. She wanted to share with me something so complex and intangible that the shallow emotional vocabulary of human and witch didn't have the words or cultural background to define it. She was waiting for me to figure it out. And I lumped it all with sex because I didn't understand.

A tear slipped from under my eyelid at Ivy's loneliness, her need for emotional reassurance, and her frustrations that though I could understand what she wanted, I was afraid to find out if I had the capacity to meet her halfway, to trust her. And my breath caught when she wiped the moisture away with a careful finger, unaware that it was for her.

My heart pounded. The underside of my other eye grew cold, and she leaned away. Breath shallow with the thoughts pinging through me, I looked down, blinking profusely. There was the click of Ivy putting the top on the tube, and she gave me a guarded smile. I felt poised on the chance to make tomorrow vastly different from today, and a pulse of emotion struck through me, unexpected and heady. *Maybe I should listen to those who were my closest kin in terms of my soul,* I thought. *Maybe I should trust those willing to trust me back.*

"There you go," Ivy said, not knowing that lightning was falling through my thoughts, realigning them to make space for something new.

I looked at her beside me, her legs crossed at her knees while she lifted the front curtain to toss the tube to the front seat. In a thoughtless motion, she reached out and smeared a pinky under my eye to even it out. The scent of clean laundry wafted up. "My God," she whispered, her brown eyes on her work. "Your skin is absolutely perfect. It's really beautiful, Rachel."

Her hand dropped and my gut tightened. She gathered herself and stood, and I heard myself say, "Don't go."

Ivy jerked to a stop. She turned with an exaggerated slowness, her posture wire-tight as she stared. "I'm sorry," she said, her voice as numb as her face. "I shouldn't have said that."

I turned my lips in to moisten them, heart pounding. "I don't want to be afraid anymore."

Her eyes flashed to black. A spike of adrenaline pulled through me to set my heart racing. Ivy fumbled behind her, her face paling when she found herself on unfamiliar territory. "I need to leave," she said as if trying to convince herself.

Feeling unreal, I reached out and shut the window, drawing the curtain. "I don't want you to." I couldn't believe I was doing this, but I wanted to know. I had lived my life not knowing why I never fit in, and with her simple explanation, I had both found an answer and a cure. I was lost, and Ivy wanted to kick the rocks from my path. I couldn't read the words, but Ivy would set my fingers to trace the letters to redefine my world. If she was right, my hidden threat had made me a pariah among those I would love, but I could find understanding among my strength-crippled kin. If that meant I needed to find another way to show someone that I cared, maybe I should hide my fears until Ivy could silence them. She trusted me. Maybe it was time I trusted her.

Ivy saw my decision, her face stilling when her instincts hit her hard. "This isn't right," she said. "Don't make me be the one to say no. I can't do it."

"So don't." A thread of fear slid through me, turning into a sliver of delicious tension to settle deep in my groin and tingle my skin. *God, what was I doing?*

I felt her will battle her desires, and I watched her eyes, finding no fear in their absolute blackness. I was covered in her scent. Mine was laced about the van like silk scarves, mixing with hers, teasing, luring, promising. Piscary was too far away to interfere. The chance might never come again. "You're confused," she said, holding herself carefully, unmoving and still.

My lips tingled when I licked them. "I am confused. I'm not afraid."

"I am," she breathed, and her dark lashes drooped to rest atop her pale cheeks. "I know how this ends. I've seen it too many times. Rachel, you've been hurt and aren't thinking clearly. When it's done, you'll say it was a mistake." Her eyes opened. "I like how everything is. I've spent the better part of a year convincing myself that I'd rather have you as a friend who won't let me touch her than someone I touched only to frighten away. Please, tell me to leave."

Adrenaline coursed to settle deep. I stood, out of breath. My thoughts lit upon the dating guide she had given me and the sensations, both exquisitely alluring and darkly terrifying, that she had pulled from me before I learned what not to do. The idea flitted through me that I was manipulating her even now, knowing that she couldn't best her drives when someone was willing. I could manipulate Ivy to any end, and it sent a surge of anticipatory terror through me.

Standing before her, I shook my head.

"Tell me why. . . ." she whispered, her face creased in a deep pain, as if feeling herself starting to slip into a place she had been both fearing and wanting to go.

"Because you're my friend," I said, voice trembling. "Because you need this," I added.

Relief showed in the depths of her eyes, black in the dim light. "Not enough. I want to show you so badly that it aches," she said, her voice a gray ribbon. "But I won't do this if you can't admit it's for you as much as me. If you can't, then it's not worth having."

I stared in a near panic for what she was asking me to come to grips with. I didn't even know what to call the emotions that were making my eyes warm with unshed tears and my body long for something I didn't understand.

Seeing my frightened silence, she turned away. Her long fingers gripped the handle to open the door, and I stiffened, seeing everything dissolve to become an embarrassing incident that would forever widen the chasm between us. Panicked, I said, "Because I want to trust you. Because I do trust you. Because *I want this.*"

Her hand fell from the door. As my pulse thundered, I saw her fingers tremble, knowing she heard the truth in my voice even as I accepted it. She felt it. She smelled it in the air with her incredible senses and her even more incredible brain that could decipher it. "Why are you doing this to me?" she said to the door. "Why now?"

She turned, her haunted eyes shocking me. Breath shallow, I stepped closer, reaching out but hesitating. "I don't know what to do," I said. "I hate feeling stupid. Please do something."

She didn't move. A tear had slipped from her, and I reached to wipe it away. Ivy jerked, catching me about the wrist. Her fingers were stark next to the black gold of Kisten's bracelet, their long whiteness covering my demon mark. I stifled my instinctive jerk, going pliant when she pulled me close, leading my hand to the small of her back.

"This isn't right," she whispered, our bodies not touching but for her hair mingling with mine and my arm around her waist and her grip on my wrist.

"So make it work," I said, and the brown ring about her eye shrank.

She took the air deep into her, closing her eyes and scenting the possibilities of what I would and wouldn't do. Her eyes were black when they opened, the last sliver of brown gone. "You're afraid."

"I'm not afraid of you. I'm afraid I won't be able to forget. I'm afraid it will change me."

Ivy's lips parted. "It will," she breathed, inches away.

I shivered and closed my eyes. "Then help me not be afraid until I understand."

Her fingers lightly touched my shoulder, and I jumped, eyes flashing open. Something shifted. I took a breath, then gasped when she slid into motion. I staggered backward— her one hand gripping my shoulder, the other still holding my wrist behind her—and she followed until my back hit the wall. Eyes wide and fixed to hers, I held my breath, unwilling to object. I'd seen this before. God, I'd lived it.

Expression intent, Ivy's unchecked blood lust struck a chord and made my blood pound. Her fingers pressing into me grew firmer and her breath quickened. I told myself this was what I wanted. Believing it. Accepting it. "Don't be afraid," she breathed as she held herself poised.

"I'm not," I lied, a tremble shaking me. *Oh God, it was going to happen.*

"If you are, you'll trigger paralysis. It's not under my conscious control, and it's triggered from your fear." Her gaze broke from mine, and I felt a delicious dropping sensation plink through me when she looked at my neck. I closed my eyes as a slurry of bliss and fear rose inside me. I took in the feeling of her being so close, accepting it. *Did I need danger to remember I was alive? Was it wrong? Did it matter if no one but me cared?*

Head bowed, Ivy leaned close. "Please don't be afraid," she said, her words a tingle against my skin, to pulse deeper. "I want you to be able to touch me back . . . if you want to."

Her last words sounded lost and alone, afraid to risk the hurt again. My eyes flashed open. "Ivy," I pleaded. "I told you. This is all I can give—"

She moved, and my words froze when she put a finger to my lips. "It's enough."

Ivy's feather-light touch sent a spark of adrenaline through me. I took a clean breath when the weight of her finger fell away. I exhaled, and her free hand slipped into the narrow space between the wall of the van and the small of my back. My eyes shut as her fingers pressed into me, pulling me forward. Breath shaking, I locked my knees, wise to the sudden rush that would send me tumbling down. I felt emotion rise, knowing she was experiencing it too. "Ivy?"

I sounded frightened, and she pushed my hair aside, whispering, "How I've wanted this," her lips brushing the smooth skin under my ear. The warm dampness of her breath made me shiver at the mix of the familiar and the unknown. With a soft exhalation, she shifted her head and her lips found my collarbone, teasingly shy of my old scar. Tendrils pulsed in time with my heart, building on the ones before to an unseen height. *Oh God. Save me from myself.*

Tension pulled my eyes open when her fingers traced a

trail down my neck. Sensation blossomed, and I threw my head back and sucked in the air. Her arm slipped around my waist, catching me before I fell.

"Rachel, I . . . God you smell good," she said, and a torrent of heat flowed through me as her lips brushed against me with her words. The smoothness of her teeth across my skin sent my pulse pounding as I fought for breath. "You won't leave?" she asked. "Promise you won't."

She wasn't asking me to be her scion; she was only asking me not to leave. "I won't leave."

"You give this to me?"

Shaking inside, I whispered, "Yes."

Ivy exhaled, sounding as if she had been freed. My blood rose, mixing with my lingering fear of the unknown to drive her to a fever pitch. Her lips touched my lower neck and vertigo spun the room, burning tracings of desire to settle deep and low in me. I exhaled into the promise of more to come, calling it to me. I breathed it in like smoke, the rising passion starting a feeling of abandonment inside. I didn't care anymore if it was right or wrong. It just was.

Her grip on my shoulder tightened, and slowly there was a gentle pressure upon my skin, and her teeth slid into me without preamble.

I groaned at the rush of fear and desire. My knees gave way, and Ivy shifted her hold. Her touch was light—keeping me upright while I went flaccid, my body struck into overload—but her mouth on my neck was savage with a fierce need. And then she pulled on me.

My air came in a rush. Gasping, I stiffened, my hands springing up to clutch at her, clenching when she threatened to pull away in fear that she had hurt me. "No," I moaned, fire running through me. "Don't stop. Oh . . . God . . ."

My words hit her, and she dug her teeth into me, harder. My breath exploded. For an instant I hung, unable to think. It felt that good. My entire body was alive and aching. A sexual high flowed through me, a torrent of promise.

Somehow I took a breath, then another. They were fast,

stumbling over each other. I clutched at her, wanting her to continue but unable to say it. Her lips pulled away from me, and in a rush of sensation, the world spun back into something I could recognize.

We had moved from the wall of the van and stood against the closed door. Ivy was holding me upright against her with the fierce demand of possession. Though she had taken her lips from me, her breath came and went on my broken skin, almost an exquisite torture. There was no fear. "Ivy," I said, hearing it come from me as almost a sob.

And with that small encouragement that everything was okay, she bowed her head to me again, her mouth finding me to draw from me both my blood and my volition.

I tried to breathe, failing. I clutched her to me, tears slipping from under my closed eyes. It was as if her soul was liquid fire and I could feel her aura, swirling about mine. She wasn't just taking my blood, she was taking my aura. But I wouldn't miss what she could steal, and I wanted to give it to her, to coat her in a small part of me and protect her. Her needs made her so fragile.

The vampire pheromones rose like a drug, making her teeth into spikes of arousal. My fingers spasmed and my rough touch sparked through her. She lunged into me again, her teeth bringing me to a gasping stiffness. I couldn't think, and I held her to me, frantic she'd leave.

Through our auras mixing, I could sense her desperate need, her want for security, her desire for satisfaction, her unearthly hunger for my blood, knowing that even if I gave it freely, she would be haunted by shame and guilt.

Compassion swirled from nowhere in the high I was lost in. She needed me. She needed me to accept her for what she was. And when I realized that I had it within myself to give her at least this small part of me, the last of my fear melted away. My eyes opened, unseeing on the wall of the van. *I trusted her,* I thought, as the edges of our auras blurred into one and the last of my barriers began to fall.

And Ivy knew the instant they did.

A soft sound came from her, delight and wonder. As she held my head unmoving and her lips worried my neck, her hand slipped lower until it found my waist. Her long fingers hesitated, and while she pulled harder to make a silver spike dive through me, her cool palm slipped under my shirt to brush my middle, fingertips searching. I jerked, and she followed me.

"Ivy," I heaved, a new fear slicing through the ecstasy. "Wait . . ."

"But I thought . . ." she whispered, her voice a dark heat, and her hand went unmoving.

"You said the blood was enough," I continued, hovering near panic, trying to focus but finding it hard to open my eyes. My heart was pounding. I couldn't get enough air, and I couldn't find the desire to push her away. I blinked, wavering when I realized she was entirely supporting my weight. "I . . . can't. . . ."

"I misunderstood," she said, cradling my head against the hollow between her shoulder and her neck. The touch of her hand upon my neck grew firmer, losing its gentle feeling, to become dominating. "I'm sorry. Do you want me to stop entirely?"

A hundred thoughts dropped through me, of how stupid I was, of how vulnerable I had made myself, of the risk I was taking, of the future I was mapping for myself, of the glorious adrenaline rush she was taking me on. "No," I breathed, lost in the thought of what it would feel like to bury my face in the hollow between her ear and neck and return the favor.

A low sigh of pleasure rose soft and almost unheard, and her hand slid from my shoulder to find my back. Pressing me closer, she pulled on me again. I gasped, my hands clutching at her as I imagined the warmth of my blood filling her, knowing how it would taste, knowing how it filled the terrible hollow her future as an undead bestowed upon her.

I jerked wire-tight as teeth drove into me again. The desire to respond in kind and the need to hold back touched every part of me alight. Oh God, the twin emotions of denial and desire were going to kill me, so intense I couldn't tell if they were pain or pleasure.

Ivy's breath on my skin grew ragged, and my muscles loosened when the last of my fear slipped from me, and like the ting of a bell faded to nothing. She held me upright, her grip now devoid of any tenderness while her teeth dug deeper and the hunger pooled into her, filling old chasms, pulling on me to take the blood I willingly gave her.

I took a shuddering breath, feeling the vamp pheromones soak into me, soothing, luring, promising a high like no other. It was addictive, but I was beyond caring. I could give Ivy this. I could accept what she gave in return. And as she held me upright and filled her body with my blood and her soul with my aura, tears slipped from me. "Ivy?" I whispered breathlessly as the room spun with vertigo. "I'm sorry I took so long to listen."

She didn't answer, and I groaned when she jerked me against her, her mouth becoming deliciously savage, sending jolts through me as she searched for more, both of us lost in a haze of fulfillment. But faint in the back of my thoughts a warning stirred. Something had changed. Her touch wasn't careful. It had become . . . harsh.

My eyes opened and I stared unseeing at the dark wall of the van as my pulse went thready. It was getting hard to think around the swirl of intoxicating elation. My breath was ragged from a heavy lethargy, not passion. She was taking too much, and I moved my hand from where it was holding her shoulder to gently push her away and see her eyes.

It wasn't much of a push, but Ivy felt it.

Her grip on me tightened, turning painful even through the vamp pheromones. My thoughts pinged back to her tenderness before I reaffirmed it would only be blood we shared—and terror struck through me.

God help me. I had asked her to take the softer emotions of love away. I had asked her to divorce herself from the caring and love Kisten said she shackled her blood lust with—which only left hunger. She wasn't going to stop. She had lost herself.

Fear scoured through me. She tasted it on the air, and without a sound she jerked me off balance. Crying out, I fell. Ivy followed, and we landed together against the tiny counter.

"Ivy! Let go!" I exclaimed, then moaned when she bit deeper until it hurt.

Adrenaline surged. I fought to get free, and Ivy's grip broke. She fell away, and breathing heavily, I held my hand to my bleeding, throbbing neck and stared at her.

Her look was knowing, like that of a predator, and as ecstasy pounded through me in time with my heartbeat, my legs gave out and I slid helplessly to the floor.

Ivy stood above me, my blood red within her mouth. She looked like a goddess—above all law both of the mind and soul. Her eyes were black and she smiled without memory, knowing that I was hers to do with what she wanted with no concept of right or wrong. Ivy was gone, controlled by the hunger I forced her to feel without the buffer of love. *Oh God. I had killed myself.*

I saw her thought to finish this an instant before she moved.

"Ivy, no!" I exclaimed, putting up an arm to fend her off.

It did no good.

I shrieked when she fell on me. It was every nightmare come true. I was helpless as she pinned my shoulders to the floor of the van. I took a breath to scream, but it turned into a moan of passion when she found my neck. A feeling of silver ice cracked through me. Ecstasy brought me to a heaving, arched-back pose for an instant before I fell, gasping for air.

We settled against the floor again as one, her hair falling soft about my throat in a silken brush as she buried her teeth deep and pulled once more. Moaning, I hung in a haze of pain, fear, and elation, her teeth inside me both fire and ice. I stared at the ceiling, focus gone while the heavy lethargy of paralysis filled my veins and exquisite rapture struck me alight even as I lost the will to move.

Ivy had done as I asked. She had abandoned her feelings of love, and was out of control. And as she let go of my arms to pull my neck to her mouth, I floated in realization that had come too late. I had asked her to change for me, and I was going to die for my temerity and stupidity.

A seeping numbness filled me. My pulse went faint and my limbs went cold. I was going to die. I was going to die because I was afraid to admit I might love Ivy.

I felt the distant thump as my hand fell from Ivy to hit the dirt-caked rug. It echoed through me, coming again and again, growing in strength as if it was my failing heartbeat. Someone was shouting distantly, but it paled in importance next to the glimmers of light that rimmed the edge of my sight, mimicking the exquisite sparkles in my mind and body. I exhaled as Ivy took everything, shivering as my aura slipped from me along with my blood. Ivy was the only warm thing in the world, and I wished she would press closer so I wouldn't die cold.

The thumping of my heart seemed to hesitate at the frightening sound of metal tearing. Cold and light spilled over us, and I moaned when Ivy pulled away from me.

"Ivy!" Jenks shouted, and I realized that the thumping hadn't been my heart but Jenks pounding at the back door. "What are you doing!"

"She's *mine*!" Ivy snarled, unreal and savage.

I couldn't move. There was a thundering bump, and the van rocked. The air flashed cold, and I whimpered. I hunched into myself, pulling my knees to my chest. My fingers went warm at the blood coming from me as I found my neck, then cold. I was alone. Ivy was gone. Someone was shouting.

"You stupid, stupid vampire bitch!" he exclaimed. "You promised! You promised me!"

I clutched in upon myself, squinting in the cold, shivering violently as I looked out the back of the van. Something had happened. I was cold. It was bright. Ivy was gone.

There was the snap of dragonfly wings. "Jenks . . ." I breathed, eyes slipping shut.

"It's me, Ms. Morgan," Jax's higher voice said, and I felt the warm wash of pixy dust over my fingers clamped to my neck. "Tink's knickers, you're bleeding yourself out!"

But Ivy was crying, forcing my thoughts out of the dark van and into the sun.

"Rachel!" Ivy shouted, panic in her voice. "Oh God. Rachel!"

There was the ting of metal scraping, and a scuffle of feet.

"Get *back*!" Jenks demanded, and I heard Ivy cry out in pain. "You can't have her. I told you I'd kill you if you hurt her!"

"She's bleeding!" Ivy begged. "Let me help!"

I managed to crack my eyes. I was on the floor of the van, the scent of the matted green rug pressing into me musty and sharp. I could smell blood and cocoa. Shivering, I tried to see past the bright glare of the sun.

"Don't move, Ms. Morgan," Jax said intently, and I struggled to comprehend. My fingers were both warm and cold from my blood. There was another scrape of metal on stone, and I pulled my eyes to it, trying to focus.

The back of the van was open. Jenks was standing between Ivy and me, her long sword in his hand. Ivy was hunched and holding her bleeding arm, tears dampening her cheeks with desperate sorrow. My eyes met her panicked ones, and she lunged for me.

Jenks blurred into motion, Ivy's katana slashing. She fell away, sprawling to roll on the pavement as she scrambled to remain out of his reach. My pulse leapt in fear when he followed, the sword clanging into the pavement three times, always an instant after she moved. My God, he was fast—and I think it was only his desire to stay between her and me that kept him from following to give a killing stroke.

"Jenks! Get out of my way!" she cried as she rolled to her feet with her hands raised placatingly. "She needs me!"

"She doesn't need you," he snarled. "You almost killed her. You *stupid* vampire! You couldn't wait to get out from Piscary's influence, could you? You seduced her, and then almost killed her. *You could have killed her!*"

"It wasn't like that!" Ivy pleaded, crying now. "Let me get to her. I can help!"

"Why the hell do you care?" There was another clang of stone and metal, and I forced myself to breathe when my vision started to go black.

"Rachel!" Ivy cried, drawing my gaze to her. "I'm sorry. I didn't know this would happen! I thought I was better! I really did. I'm sorry. I'm sorry!"

Jenks made a fierce cry, lunging. Ivy sprang back, arms pinwheeling. He followed her down, and the two froze when she landed against the pavement. Blood leaked from between her fingers clenched about her upper arm, and my heart seemed to hesitate when Jenks ended his last sword swing inches from her throat. Fighting my numb daze, I dragged myself to the door. He was going to kill her. He had killed before to save my life. He was going to kill Ivy.

Jenks stood with his feet widespread and his stance terrible. "You stupid, selfish whore of a vampire," he intoned. "You said you wouldn't. You promised. Now you've ruined everything. You couldn't accept what she could give, so you took it all!"

"I didn't." Ivy sprawled in the sun with her sword at her throat, the sun glinting on it and her tears. "I told her no. I told her to stop," she wept. "She asked me to."

"She wouldn't ask for this," he spat, jerking the sword so it touched her white skin to leave a line of red. "You ruin everything you love. *Everything,* you screwed-up bitch. But I'll be damned before I let you ruin Rachel."

Ivy's eyes darted to mine, her face tear-streaked and terrified. Her mouth moved but no words came out. My gut twisted when I saw her accept his words as truth. Jenks held the sword to her throat; he was going to use it and Ivy would do nothing to stop him.

Jenks shifted his grip. He pulled the sword back. Ivy looked at me, too lost in guilt to do anything.

"No," I whispered, panicking. My grasping fingers reached the edge of the van and, feet scrabbling weakly, I pushed myself forward. Jax was in my way, shrilling something and his dragonfly wings sparkling in my darkening vision.

"Jenks, stop!" I cried out, falling out of the van. Ice hard and cold, the pavement hit my shoulder and hip, scraping my cheek. I took a breath that was more like a cry, focusing on the gray pavement as if it was my coming death. *Oh God. Ivy was going to let Jenks kill her.*

"Rachel!" There was the clatter of the sword falling, and suddenly Jenks was there, his arms picking me up and cushioning me against the hard ground. Struggling, I focused on him, shocked he was so close. He didn't like anyone touching him.

"It wasn't her fault," I breathed, focusing on his eyes. They were so green, I forgot what I wanted to say. My breath sounded harsh and my throat hurt. "It wasn't her fault."

"Shhhh," he whispered, his brow creasing when I moaned as he hoisted me into his arms and lurched to his feet. "It's going to be all right. You're going to be all right. She's going to leave. You don't have to worry about her again. I won't let any vampire hurt you. I can do this. I'll stay big, and make sure no one hurts you again. It'll be okay. I'll make sure you're safe."

The vampire saliva was wearing off fast. As he carried me, I could feel a heavy pain starting to take hold and unconsciousness gather. I was cold, and shivers shook me.

Jenks's motion stopped, and he cradled me close as he stood over Ivy. His arms filled with a hard tension. "Leave," Jenks said. "Get your things and go. I want you out of the church by the time we get back. If you stay, you're going to kill her, just like everyone else stupid enough to love you."

A sound broke from her, and he walked away, pace fast as he headed for the warm darkness of the motel room.

I couldn't find the air to speak. Ivy's heavy sobs came one after the other. I didn't want her to leave. Oh, God. I had only wanted to show I trusted her. I only wanted to understand her—and myself.

Jenks's shadow fell over me, and I trembled. Tears spilled from me as I saw everything crash down to ruin. I could hear her crying, alone and lost. She was going to leave. She was going to leave because of what I had asked her to do. And as I listened to Ivy crying, alone and guilt-strewn on the pavement, something broke inside. I couldn't lie to myself anymore. It was going to kill me.

"I asked her to bite me," I whispered. "Jenks, don't leave her there. She needs me. I asked her." A sob rose in me, hurting as it broke free. "I only wanted to know. I didn't think she'd lose control like that."

Jenks jerked to a stop under the motel overhang. "Rachel?" he said, bewildered. There was the snap of dragonfly wings, and I wondered how he could carry me if he was a pixy.

I couldn't see Ivy, but her sobs had stopped and I wondered if she had heard me. I choked on my harsh breath. Jenks's shocked eyes were inches from mine. I had promised I wouldn't leave, and I refused to let her run away in guilt. I needed them both. I needed Ivy.

"I had to know," I whispered, and Jenks's face went panicked. "Please," I breathed, my vision starting to mercifully darken. "Please get her. Don't leave her alone." My eyes closed. "I hurt her so badly. Don't let her be alone," I said, but I didn't know if it made it into words before I passed out.

Twenty-three

I was moving, and it was confusing the hell out of me. I didn't think I was unconscious, and I certainly didn't know what was going on, but someone had their arms around me and I could smell the sharp scent of chlorophyll. Piecing together if I was outside with my eyes shut or inside with my eyes open was beyond me. I was cold, but I'd been cold for forever.

I did recognize the dropping sensation followed by a bed pressing into me. I tried to speak but failed. A wide hand cradled my head, and the pillow under it was pulled away. I sank deeper into the comforter as someone propped up my knees and tucked the pillow under it.

"Stay with me, Rache," came a voice, accompanied by the smell of fudge, and I tried to remember how to open my eyes. Hands were on me, light and warm. "Don't pass out. Let me get some water in you first, then you can rest."

My head lolled, accompanied by a pulsing pain in my neck. The voice had been soft, but there was panic under it. The thought of water gave me a name to the feeling I couldn't figure out. *I'm thirsty. Yes, that's what I'm feeling.*

I felt sick, and my lids fluttered as I hung in a state too fatigued to move. I remembered this. I had done this before. "Where's Keasley?" I whispered, hearing it come from me in a soft breath of air. No one heard me over the sound of running water.

"Jax, get a straw," the intent voice said. "In the trash by the TV."

There was the sound of cellophane crackling, and someone moved my legs to wedge another pillow under them. It was as if a veil dropped away, and suddenly everything had meaning. My eyes opened and reality realigned itself. I was in the motel room. I was on the bed with my feet propped higher than my head. I was cold. Jenks had carried me in, and that winged spot of sunshine hovering by the TV was Jax.

Oh God. I had asked Ivy to bite me.

Taking a deep breath, I tried to sit up.

Jenks abruptly had his hands on me, pressing my shoulder down. *He's got big hands,* I thought, trying to focus. *And warm.*

"Not so fast," he said. "Can you swallow?"

My eyes flicked to the plastic cup in his hand. I licked my lips. I wanted it, but my neck hurt. It hurt bad. "Where's Ivy?" I slurred.

Jenks's expression closed. I focused on his green eyes while the edges of my sight grayed. Nausea tightened my gut. Kisten said she had forgotten control while under Piscary's ungentle touch, possibly killing people in the throes of blood passion. I'd thought she was better. Kisten said she was better. She looked better. Apparently by asking her to divorce her feelings of love from her hunger, I'd taken away what she had used to shackle it. In three minutes I threw her back into the pit of depravity she had struggled so long to escape. I had done it to her. Me.

"I'm sorry," I said, starting to cry, and he took both my hands in one of his to stop them from moving upward to my neck. "I only wanted to understand. I didn't mean to tip her over the edge. Jenks, don't be mad at her."

His fingertips brushed the hair from my forehead, but he wouldn't meet my gaze, not yet ready to believe. Though his smooth features looked too young for someone who had adult kids, the deep-set pain born in understanding said he had endured a lifetime of joy and sorrow.

"Let me get some water in you before you pass out," he said, turning away. "Jax!" he snapped, sounding very unlike himself. "Where's that straw? I don't want her lifting her head."

"Which one is hers, Dad?" the adolescent pixy said, his voice high in worry.

"It doesn't matter. Just get one!"

The reflected light on the ceiling darkened, and from the open door came a hesitant, "She had the Sprite. And her cup is the one with all the buttons punched in."

Jax rose three feet in a glittering column of sparkles.

How about that? Those plastic dents are of some use after all.

"Get the hell out of here," Jenks said, seething. The warmth of his fingers slipped from me as he rose to stand above me.

Guilt hit hard, and I wanted to curl up and die. *What had I done? I couldn't fix this.* All I'd wanted was to understand Ivy, and now I was lying in a motel room with holes in my neck and my two best friends fighting. My life was a pile of shit. "Jenks," I whispered, "stop."

"She wants me here," Ivy came back with immediately. I could tell she was still in the threshold, and she sounded desperate. "It was an accident. I'll never touch her again. I can help. I know what to do."

"I bet you do," he said snidely, putting his hands on his hips. Now that he was six-foot-four, it didn't look as aggressive, somehow. "We don't need you! Get out!"

I wished they would figure this out so someone would give me some water. Jax hovered above me, a red straw taller than he was in his grip. Feeling distant and unreal, I made my eyes wide so I could focus on him. "Dad?" the small pixy called, worried, but they weren't listening.

"You little twit," Ivy snapped. "It was an accident! Didn't you hear her?"

"I heard her." He left me, his feet silent on the carpet. "She'll say anything you want now, won't she? You bound her to you! Damn it, Ivy! You weak-willed, jealous sack of vampire spit. You said you could handle this! You promised me you wouldn't bite her!"

His shouting was furious, and I went even colder. What if she *had* bound me to her? Would I be able to tell?

I desperately wanted to turn my head, but Jax was standing on my nose, his bare feet warm, the scent of sugar and wax coming from the drop hanging on the end of the straw. I wanted it, then felt guilty for wanting water when my friends were going to kill each other.

"I'm not going to tell you again, Jenks. Get out of my way."

There was an intake of breath, and Jax let out a yelp and darted to the ceiling. I heard a grunt followed by a rolling thump. Adrenaline surged, and I pushed myself up, then slumped against the headboard, neck protesting.

They were grappling on the floor, moving too fast for my blood-starved brain to follow. The small end table had been knocked over, and they were a confusing tangle of legs and arms.

"You're a lying, manipulative, vamp-bitch whore!" Jenks shouted, twisting violently out of her grip. She leapt at him from a crouch, and the two crashed to the wall. Jenks moved blindingly fast, flowing out from under her, grabbing her arm and landing atop her back, pinning her to the carpet. My God, he was quick.

"Ow," Ivy said to the wall, abruptly still with Jenks atop her, her arm held at an awkward angle. His other hand held a dagger to her kidneys. *When had he gotten a dagger?* "Damn it, Jenks," she said, making a little wiggle. "Get off."

"Tell me you're going to leave and not come back," he said, breath fast and blond hair in disarray, "or I'll break your arm. And you're going to stay away from Rachel. Got it? And if I see her trying to get to you because you bound her to you, I'll find you and kill you twice. I'll do it, Ivy. Don't think I can't!"

My mouth went dry and I started to shake. I was going into shock. My hand pressed to my neck was sticky. I wanted to tell them to stop, but it was all I could do to stay upright.

Ivy wiggled, stiffening when Jenks poked her. "Listen to me, pixy man," she said, her face turned to the wall. "You're quick, you're fast, and if you stick that into me, I'm going to smack you into the ever-after. I didn't bind her to me. I tried to leave, and she asked me to stay. She wanted to know. Damn it, Jenks, she wanted to know!"

Focus blurring, I tried to pull the bedspread over me, my fingers as strong as string, accomplishing nothing. Jenks started at the movement, realizing I was upright and watching. His angular, beautifully savage face lost its emotion. "You seduced her," he said, and I dropped my eyes, shamed. All I had wanted was to understand. How could so much go wrong from wanting to understand?

Her cheek pressed against the carpet, Ivy made a helpless bark of laugher. "She seduced me," she said, and I wavered from the pain and blood loss, knowing it was the truth. "I left, but she called me back. I would have left even then, but she said she wanted this for her. Not for me, but for her. I told you if she ever admitted that, I wouldn't walk away. I didn't lie to you!"

My breathing had quickened, giving me a feeling of disjoined airiness. I was hyperventilating. Jax was flitting over me, trying to dust my bite but only making me squint to see through the sparkles. At least I think the sparkles were from him. God I hurt. I was going to either die or throw up.

Jenks pricked Ivy's sweater with his knife and she jerked. "If you're lying to me—"

Ivy's shoulders lost all their tension, and she surrendered visibly. "I thought I was better," she said, guilt slamming into me at the pain in her voice. "I worked *so hard,* Jenks. I thought I'd finally— She didn't want . . . she couldn't handle the sex, so I tried to separate it from the blood. I wanted *something* of her. And she was able to give me the blood. I—I lost control of the hunger again. Damn it, I almost killed her."

His eyes on me, Jenks let go of her arm. It hit the floor

with a thump. Ivy slowly pulled it into a more comfortable position. "You didn't separate the sex from the blood, you took the love from it," Jenks said, and I wavered, my pulse hammering. *What had I asked her to do?* "You take that away, and all that's left *is* the hunger."

My breath came in short splurges as I fought to remain upright. Did everyone know more about vampires than me? Jenks was a pixy, and he knew more about vampires than I did.

"I tried," Ivy whispered. "She doesn't want me to touch her that way." She took a shuddering breath, broken.

Jenks flicked a glance at me, seeing my cold face and realizing that she was telling the truth. Slowly he slid off her, and Ivy pulled herself upright, knees to her forehead, arms wrapped about her shins. She took a gasping breath and held it.

"Rachel didn't think it was wrong, did she?" Jenks pressed.

"She said she was sorry for waiting so long," Ivy whispered as if she didn't believe it. "But she saw the hunger, Jenks. She saw it raw, and I hurt her with it. She's not going to want anything to do with me—knowing that."

It was a very small voice, vulnerable and afraid, and Jenks watched me, not her. "Why are you trying to hide what you are?" he said softly, his words for both of us. "Do you think seeing your hunger shocked her? Do you think she's so shallow that she'd condemn you for it? That she didn't know it was in you and loved you anyway?"

Ivy shook with her head on her knees, and tears slipped from me. My head hurt and my neck throbbed, but it was nothing compared to my heartache.

"She loves you, Ivy. God knows why. She made a mistake in asking you to separate the love from the hunger, and you made a mistake thinking you could."

"I wanted what she could give me," Ivy said, curled up into herself. "Just that much would have been enough. Never again," she said. "Never, never, Jenks. She's safe. You're right. I destroy everything I touch."

I struggled to keep from passing out. She wasn't a monster. "Ivy?"

Her head jerked up. Her face was white and tracked with tears. "I thought you were unconscious," she said, scrambling to her feet and wiping her face.

Blinking, I wavered where I sat. Guilt lay thick on me, and Jenks sat cross-legged by the open door in a patch of sun, a faint, sad smile on him.

She stood in a frozen quandary. "Are you okay?" she asked, clearly wanting to rush over but afraid to. Between the blood loss and the absurdity of the question, I almost laughed.

"Uh-huh," I said, giving up on trying to have this make sense. "Can I have some water?" I whispered, then tipped over.

My neck sent a stab of pain to shock me and I couldn't breathe; my face was buried in the covers. I tried to cry out but was helpless. Damn it, even my arms wouldn't work.

"Oh God," Ivy said, her hands cold as she pulled me up. I took a grateful breath, trying to focus through the hurt. Jenks was at my feet, and he tugged them down until I was flat on my back and looking up at them with wide eyes, teetering on unconsciousness again now that the adrenaline had played itself out. The asinine relief that I had shaved my legs lifted through me and was gone.

"Here, Dad," Jax offered, that red straw in his two-fisted grip.

Jenks grabbed that absurdly small cup of water, never sloshing it as he retrieved it from the nightstand. "She's bleeding again," he said, his voice and face grim. "Dust her."

"Don't give her the water yet." Ivy was a confusing blur as I tried to focus. "I've got something to put in it."

Struggling to keep from passing out, I watched her snatch up her purse and rummage through it. My stomach clenched when she brought out a small vial. "Brimstone?" I whimpered, waiting for Jenks's protest.

But all I heard was his soft, "Not so much this time."

Ivy's oval face scrunched in anger as she unscrewed the top. "I know what I'm doing."

Jenks glared at her. "She's too weak for what you usually

give her. She can't eat enough to support that high a metabolism with all the blood you took out of her."

"And you know all about that, don't you, pixy?" she said sarcastically.

So much for playing nice. Tired, I let my eyes shut while they argued, hoping I didn't die in the interim and make the problem moot. I wasn't ever going to get my water. Ever.

"Rachel?"

It was close and direct. Startled, I opened my eyes. Jenks was kneeling beside the bed with that cup and straw in his hand. Ivy was behind him, her arms crossed over her chest, cheeks spotted with red. Anger and worry warred in her expression. I'd missed something. "No Brimstone," I slurred, my hands rising to push it away. My throat tightened as my emotions swung from one extreme to the next. They were so worried about me.

Jenks furrowed his brow, looking too severe for someone so young. "Don't be stupid, Rache," he said, catching my arms and easily forcing them down. "You either take it with Brimstone or you'll be flat on your ass for four weeks."

He was swearing. I knew I must be doing better. I could smell the water. I couldn't move my arms under his soft restraint, and I felt sick. *Why were they making me do this?*

I looked at the straw, and taking that as a yes, Jenks slipped it between my lips. Breath held, I sucked it down, thinking the rusty water tasted better than the last cold beer I'd had. Tears started leaking out, my emotions thoroughly out of control. I thought of Ivy doing the same to me, bleeding me dry with that same metallic taste of me in her mouth.

I started to cry, choking on the water. *Damn it, what in hell was wrong with me?*

"That's enough," Ivy said softly. Through my watering eyes, I saw her reach out in concern, her hand touching Jenks's shoulder. He jumped, and Ivy pulled away, her face full of an inner pain.

She thought she was a monster. She thought she couldn't

touch anyone without ruining them, and I had proved her right.

The enormity of her life's misery fell on me, and I started to shake.

"She's going into shock," Ivy said, oblivious to the real reason. I'd hurt her. I thought I had been strong enough to survive her, and by failing, I'd hurt her.

Jenks set the cup aside and rose. "I'll get a blanket."

"I've got it," she said, already gone.

My hands fluttered, and I realized I was getting sticky blood all over the bed. They were trying to help, but I didn't deserve it. I wished it had never happened. I had made a mistake, and they were both being so nice about it.

Another tremor shook me. I tried to scrunch up into myself for warmth. His green eyes pinched, Jenks pulled me upright, slipping in behind me. Curving his arms around me, he kept me from shaking apart.

Ivy wasn't pleased. "What are you doing?" she asked from across the room, her lips pressed tight as she shook out a brown motel blanket.

"I'm keeping her warm."

Jenks smelled like green things. His arms wrapped around me, and his front pressed into my back. My head was spinning and my neck was a hurting ache. I knew I shouldn't be sitting up like that, but I couldn't remember how to say "Down." I think I was still crying, since my face was wet and those noises in the background sort of sounded like me.

Ivy sighed, then came forward. "She's going to pass out if you keep her head up like that," she muttered as she draped the blanket over us.

"Pixy dust will hold her together for only so long," Jenks said softly. "And I don't want Jax to be fighting the gravity blood flow when he stitches her up."

My eyes flashed open. *Stitches? Crap, not again. I'd just gotten rid of my scars.* "Wait," I said, panic bringing me stiff at the thought of what it was going to feel like now that the vampire saliva was dormant. "No stitches. I want my pain amulet."

They didn't seem to understand me. Ivy bent close, looking at my eyes, not me. "We could take her to Emergency."

From behind me, Jenks shook his head. "The Weres would track us from there. I'm surprised they haven't found us already. I can't believe you bit her. We have four Were packs scenting for our blood, and you think *now* is a good time to change your relationship?"

"Shut the hell up, Jenks."

My stomach turned. I wanted my pain amulet. I wasn't a brave person. I'd seen the movie where they stitched up the guy with no anesthetic and bailing wire. It hurt. "Where's my amulet?" I pleaded, heart pounding. "Where's Keasley? I want Keasley."

Ivy pulled away. "She's going incoherent." Her brow furrowed, wrinkling her usually placid face. "Rachel?" she said loudly and with exaggerated slowness. "Listen to me. You should be stitched. Just four tiny stitches. I didn't rip you. It will be okay."

"No!" I exclaimed, my vision darkening. "I don't have my pain amulet!"

Ivy gripped my shoulder through the blanket. Her eyes were full of compassion. "Don't worry. With your head up like this, you're going to pass out in about three seconds."

She was right.

Twenty-four

"**J**enks, stop picking everything up before you break something," I said, then drew my hand back from one of the ceramic knickknacks neatly arranged on the store shelves. It was a pumpkin with a little cat beside it, and it reminded me of Rex.

"What?" Grinning, Jenks tossed three ceramic bells into the air and juggled them.

I pointed at the handwritten sign with YOU BREAK IT, YOU BUY IT on it. I was tired, hungry, and my new stitches hidden under my red turtleneck ached 'cause I was stupid and I deserved to hurt. Even so, the last thing I needed was to pay for broken merchandise.

Jenks watched my mood, his roguish smile fading. Tossing all three up high into the open second story, he seriously caught them one by one and set them back where they belonged. "Sorry," he said meekly.

I puffed my air out and touched his shoulder to tell him it was okay. Between the blood loss and Ivy's force-fed Brimstone, I was damn tired. Hands behind his back, Jenks continued perusing the shelves looking for a chunk of bone. He hadn't found any yesterday, and I needed it to finish this run and get the hell home.

Under the disguise amulet, Jenks looked very different with black hair and a darker complexion. He had his new aviator jacket on over the T-shirt he had bought in the previous store, making him a sexy, leggy, hunk o' pixy ass in jeans. No wonder he had fifty-four kids and Matalina smiled like Mona Lisa.

Married pixy, I told myself, forcing my eyes back to the shelf of ceramic animals. *Fifty-four kids. Beautiful wife, sweet as sugar, who would kill me in my sleep while apologizing for it.*

Jenks wasn't happy about me being out here, but when I had woken up at a late three P.M. and found Ivy and Nick had taken the bus across the straits to get his truck, I had to get out. As usual, the Brimstone had made me hungry and nauseous, filling me with a brash stupidity that I was sure came from the upper that made Brimstone so popular on the streets. Seems if you took enough medicinal grade, you still got a buzz. *Thanks a hell of a lot, Ivy.*

It was her fault I was restless; moving seemed to help. Though I knew Ivy would disagree, I thought it unlikely that the Weres would look for us here when it was more likely we had hightailed it to Cincinnati. But I wasn't going home until this was done. I wouldn't take a war back to my streets, my neighbors.

"Oh, wow," Jenks breathed. "Rachel, look at this!"

I turned, finding him standing proudly before me with a red and black striped hat on his head. The thing must have been a foot tall, like a weird top hat. "That's nice, Jenks," I said.

"I'm going to get it," he said, beaming.

I took a breath to protest, then let it out. It was on sale. Five bucks. Why not?

My fingers trembled as I sifted through a display of beads, trying to decide if they were made of bone. I'd been out here with Jenks for an hour, and though he was loaded down with fudge, T-shirts, and useless bric-a-brac only a twelve-year-old or a pixy could love, I hadn't found anything suitable yet. I knew it wasn't smart to be out there, but I was a runner, damn it, and I could take care of myself—as long as I had Jenks to back me up, anyway. That and my splat gun tucked in my shoulder bag, loaded with sleepy-time charms.

A smile quirked the corners of my mouth as I watched

Jenks ogle a rack of plastic dinosaurs. He still had that hat on, but with his physique, the man could wear anything. Feeling my attention on him, he glanced up and away. Sure, he was oohing and ahhing over the trashiest stuff, but his eyes were constantly shifting, scanning the area more closely than a candy shop owner with a store full of elementary kids.

I knew he wished Jax was with us to play scout, but the pixy had gone with Ivy and Nick. Ivy wasn't letting Nick out of her sight since Jenks had found him in Squirrel's End trying to leave his sorrow in an empty glass. If she hadn't hated him before, she did now, seeing that he had put everything in jeopardy to slam down a few in the comfort of humans.

"Rache." Jenks was suddenly at my elbow. "Come and look at what I found. It's made of bone. I think it's perfect. Let's get it and get out of here."

His brow was creased in concern, because of my increasing fatigue, and deciding I had pushed my luck far enough, I shuffled after him. I was tired, the blood loss starting to win out over Ivy's Brimstone cocktails. Hiking my bag higher, I stopped beside a case full of American Indian stuff: tomahawks, little drums, carved totem poles, strings of beads and feathers. There was some turquoise in there, and realizing by the price tags that it wasn't tourist crap but real artwork, I leaned forward. Didn't Indians carve stuff out of bone?

"Look at that necklace," Jenks said proudly, pointing through the glass. "It's got a hunk of bone for the pendant. You could get that. Put the demon curse in it, and bang! Not only do you have a new focus, but you've got yourself some kick-ass Native American bling."

Hunched over the display case, I glanced wearily up at him.

"Oh!" he exclaimed, and I followed his gaze to an ugly totem shoved into the corner of the case as if in apology. "Look at that! That would look great in my living room!"

I exhaled slowly, dubiously eyeing it. The thing stood about four inches high, and the animals portrayed were so stylized, I couldn't tell if they were beaver, deer, wolves, or bear. Blocky teeth and big eyes. It was ugly, but a right kind of ugly.

"I'm getting it for Matalina," he said proudly, and my eyes widened as I tried not to imagine what to a pixy would be akin to a six-foot totem pole in the middle of Matalina's living room. I had no idea how pixies decorated, but I couldn't imagine the woman would be pleased.

"Ma'am?" he called out, his posture upright and eager. "How much is this?"

I leaned heavily on the counter as the woman finished up at the register and hustled over. Tuning her and Jenks out as they haggled over the price, I looked at the necklace. It was out of my easy price range, but there was a statue of a wolf next to it. It was expensive too, but if it didn't work, I could bring it back.

Reaching a decision, I straightened. "Can I see that wolf statue?" I asked, interrupting Jenks trying to sweet-talk the woman into giving him a senior citizen discount. She wasn't buying that he had kids and a mortgage. I couldn't blame her. He looked like he should be in high school with that funky hat on.

Her eyebrows high and her expression cagy, the woman unlocked the case and set the statue in my hand. "It's bone, right?" I asked, turning it over to see the MADE IN CHINA sticker. *Not so authentic, then, but I wasn't going to complain.*

"Ox bone," the woman said warily. "No regulations on importing ox bone."

I nodded, setting it on the counter. It was pricey, but I wanted to go home. Or at least back to my motel room. "Would you give us a price break if we bought two pieces?" I asked, and a satisfied smile spread over the woman's face.

Delighted, Jenks took over, overseeing her wrap both pieces up and boxing them individually. My pulse slow and lethargic, I dug in my bag for my wallet.

"My treat," Jenks said, his young features looking innocent and flustered. "Go stand by the door or something."

His treat? It was all coming out of the same pot. Eyebrows high, I tried to look past him, but he got in my way, pulling off his hat and using it to hide something he had slipped onto the counter. I caught a glimpse of a bottle of Sun-Fun color-changing nail polish, then smiled and turned away. Next year's solstice gift, maybe?

"I'll be outside," I said, seeing an empty bench in the middle of the open-air mall. Jenks mumbled something, and I leaned into the glass door, glad it moved easily. The air smelled like fudge and water, and with slow steps I made a beeline for the bench before the young family with ice cream cones could reach it.

I exhaled as I settled myself on the wooden bench. The wind was light in the protected area, and the sun was warm. I breathed deeply, pulling in the scent of the marigolds behind me. It was right on the cusp of being able to plant annuals up there, but they would be sheltered from frost, being surrounded by so much stone.

Though the tourist season hadn't officially started, it was busy. People with colorful sacks drifted aimlessly in a contented pattern of idle amusement that was comforting to see, humans mostly, with the odd witch making a statement with his or her dress. It was hard to tell who was who otherwise— unless you got close enough to smell them.

The sound of unseen pixy wings was a soft, almost subliminal hum. My hands drifted up to my scent amulet, making sure it was touching my skin. I knew I shouldn't have been out there alone, but I was under two disguises. What were the chances the Weres would even be looking for me here? And if they were, they would never recognize me.

I glanced up when the shop door opened and Jenks came out, squinting in the brighter light until he put his shades on. The top of that hat poked out from the bag he carried, and I smiled. His head turned to the end of the mall where we had parked Kisten's Corvette. It was obvious he wanted to hustle me over there and get me home, but upon seeing me slumped in fatigue, he came to a silent standstill above me. Slowly I drew my head up.

"Are you—" Jenks started.

"I'm fine," I lied, wanting to pluck my turtleneck off my

stitches. Jax had used dental floss, but they still pulled on the fabric. "The couch left me tight, is all."

He grinned, sitting down cross-legged on the bench as if it was a toadstool. Jenks had slept in the van last night so neither Ivy nor I had to. Hell, I didn't even want to ride in it again—which was probably why Ivy had taken a cab across the straits to get Nick's truck.

"I was going to ask you if you were hungry and wanted a hamburger," he said, squinting, "but I like your idea better. I could go for a little scuffle. Loosen up. Get the blood flowing."

I hated feeling weak. Taking a weary breath, I straightened. "Jenks, sit like a man. That was cute when you were four inches tall, but now you look prissy."

Immediately he put his feet on the ground, knees together and a worried look on him. Puffing the hair from my eyes, I gave up and rolled my turtleneck down. So I had been bitten by a vamp. Lots of people were. "That doesn't look much better," I said.

"Well, how the hell am I supposed to sit!" he exclaimed.

Lacing my fingers over my head, I stretched carefully, feeling the stitches pull. Kisten's bracelet shifted to my elbow to make a cold spot of metal against my skin. "Have you seen Kisten slouch in the kitchen?"

With a hesitant slowness that could have been provocative, Jenks extended his legs. Lean in his tight jeans, he slumped until his neck rested atop the back of the bench. His arms went out to run along the length of the worn wood and his feet spread suggestively.

Oh—my—God. Flushing, I sat up straight. "Yeah," I said faintly. "That's better." *Fifty-four kids. Fifty-four kids. And where was that camera he was going to buy for me?*

"Give me a minute to catch my breath," I said, sneaking glances at him. "Then we can head to the car. I need a few more things to make the demon spell, but I'm too tired to do it now." It grated on me to admit it, but it was kinda obvious.

Jenks sat up with a little grunt, rummaging in a pocket of his coat to bring out a folded napkin. "Here," he said, handing it to me. "Ivy said you might be stupid enough to leave the motel, and if you did to give you this."

Irritation filled me, and I unfolded it to find one of her Brimstone cookies. "Damn it, Jenks!" I hissed, folding it up and glancing at the passing people. "You want to see me in jail?"

He smirked. "Then eat it and get rid of the evidence. Tink's a Disney whore, Rache, you're worse than my kids. You need it. It's medicinal. Just eat the damned cookie."

I felt it light in my hand, thinking it wasn't as simple as he made it out to be. The only reason I was out here was because the dose I'd taken before bed had woken me with the jitters. 'Least, I was blaming it on that. I felt like crap, though, so I opened it up and nibbled a corner.

Immediately Jenks's posture relaxed. I followed his gaze across the busy plaza to the hanging planters, finally spotting the pixies. They were chasing a hummingbird off, their ferocity surprising me. It was too early for fairies to be back from Mexico, and with a little practice, the pixies might be able to hold the plaza when they migrated up.

The silence grew as I broke off a second corner off Ivy's cookie and guiltily ate it. I hated being on Brimstone, but I hated being flat on my back more. *There had to be another way,* I thought. But it would shorten my fatigued state from three weeks to three days. It wasn't magic, but it was close. I could actually feel the drug taking hold, making my pulse quicken and the slight trembling of my fingers disappear. No wonder this stuff was illegal.

Jenks was quiet, watching the passing people with interest while he waited for my strength to return. I didn't have a dad to talk stuff over with, and my mom was too far away. Jenks was a heavy third of our firm; what he thought mattered. I took a breath, worried about what he might say after I told him what really had me out there, running from my thoughts.

I'd done some thinking that morning, hunched over the sink and squinting into the shower-fogged mirror to inspect my new stitches and scraped face. The tears were small and harmless looking, nothing like the savage rips Al had given me—but they forced me to question how long I had been pushing Ivy into biting me—'cause this hadn't come out of nowhere. So while the shower ran from hot to cold, I sat on the edge of the tub with a towel wrapped around myself, shaking and almost physically ill with the thought that Ivy had been right about at least part of it. All it had taken was a brush with death for me to admit it.

So maybe I *had* wanted her to bite me even before I moved in with her. That did mean I needed a subliminal feeling of danger to become passionate. Nobody was that screwed up.

"Thanks for helping me," I said, trying to work up to what I wanted to say. "With Ivy."

Jenks shrugged. Shifting position, he pulled himself together and watched the pixies with a professional interest. "What was I supposed to do? Walk away?"

I looked at my half-eaten cookie. Nick might have. Nick almost did the first time I had goaded Ivy into trying to bite me. Until I said no to her and she insisted. Then he stepped in to help. Looking back on the incident, it seemed obvious I had been jonesing for a bite.

"Sorry," I said, thinking of how tenuous I'd made everything. "I wasn't thinking."

Making a rude snort, he crossed his legs. "Do tell, Miss witch princess," he said. "Ivy was handling it, and you go and get curious, tipping her into all but killing you. Bloody hell! When are you going to stop being afraid of yourself?"

I ate a bite of cookie, a big one this time. "I'm scared," I said after I forced it down, dry.

"We're fine," Jenks said loudly, his eyes on the hanging flowers and clearly not knowing where my thoughts were. "We're all fine. Ivy said she isn't going to bite you again. We'll go out for pizza at Piscary's when we get home, and everything will return to normal. You're safer now than your first night spent under the same roof."

I put the last of the cookie in my mouth, nervously folding

the crumbs up into the napkin. Jenks was probably right about Ivy never again initiating a bite between us. But she hadn't initiated the first one either. The thing was, I didn't want everything to return to normal.

Jenks swiveled to face me. "Ah, you are too scared to let her bite you again, right?"

A slow breath slipped past my lips and adrenaline zinged through me, pushed by fear. It was a feeling I was beginning to understand. *I didn't need fear to feel passion. I didn't.*

"Crap on my daisies," Jenks breathed. "You aren't. Rache . . ."

Frightened, I shifted to put my elbows on my knees, wadding the napkin up and squishing it as if it was my shame. "I'm in trouble," I whispered. "She didn't bind me, but she may as well have."

"Rache . . ." It was soft and pensive, and it ticked me off.

"Just listen, will you?" I snapped, then slumped back, squinting into the sun as I looked at nothing. My throat was tight, and I shoved the napkin in a pocket. "I . . . I learned something about myself. And I'm scared it's going to kill me if I ignore it. It's just . . . God! How could I be that blind about myself?"

"It might be the vamp pheromones," Jenks coaxed. "You aren't necessarily attracted to women just because you want to sleep with Ivy."

My eyes widened and I turned to him, shocking myself that he was still wearing that disguise and only his eyes looked like him. "I don't want to sleep with Ivy!" I said, flustered. "I'm straight. I . . ." I took a deep breath, afraid to admit it aloud. "I want to try to find a blood balance with her."

"You what?" Jenks blurted, and I sent my gaze to the people around us to remind him we weren't alone. "She would have killed you!" he said, hushed now, but no less intense.

"Only because I asked her to ignore her feelings for me." Flustered, I tucked a wayward strand of hair behind an ear. "Only because I let her bite me without the buffer of emotion that she uses to control her hunger."

Jenks leaned closer, his curls flashing blond in the sun for an instant as his disguise charm bobbled. "But you're straight," he said. "You just said you were."

Blushing, I pulled the bag that had the fudge in it closer. Hunger gnawed at my middle—thanks to the Brimstone— and I dug for the little white box. "Yeah," I said, uncomfortable as I remembered her gentle touch on me growing intimate when she misunderstood. "But after yesterday, it's pretty obvious she *can* share blood without the sex." I darted a look at him, even as a shiver rose through me, unstoppable, at the reminder of how good it had felt.

"And she almost killed you trying," Jenks protested. "Rache, she is still messed up, and this is too much, even for you. She can't do it. You're not physically or mentally strong enough to keep her under control if she loses it again."

I hunched in worry, hiding my concern in trying to get the taped box open. "So we go slow," I said, wrenching the thin white cardboard to no avail. "Work up to it, maybe."

"Why?" Jenks exclaimed softly, his brow pinched in worry. "Why risk it?"

At that, I closed my eyes in a slow rueful blink. Crap. Maybe Ivy was right. Maybe this was just another way to fill my life with excitement and passion. But then I remembered our auras mixing, the desperation her soul was drowning in, and how I had eased her pain—if only for an instant.

"It felt good, Jenks," I whispered, shocked to find my vision blurring with unshed tears. "I'm not talking about the blood ecstasy. I'm talking about my being able to fill that emotional void she has. You know her as well as I do, maybe better. She aches with it. She needs to be accepted for who she is so badly. And I was able to do that. Do you know how good that felt? To be able to show someone that, yes, you are someone worth sacrificing for? That you like them for their faults and that you respect them for their ability to rise above them?"

Jenks was staring at me, and I sniffed back the tears. "Damn," I whispered, terrified all of a sudden. "Maybe it is love."

Reaching slowly, Jenks took the box of fudge from me. Twisting to a pocket, he flipped open a knife and cut the tape. Still silent, he handed me the open box and tucked the knife away. "Are you sure about this?" he asked worriedly.

I nodded, cutting a slab of fudge off with that stupid little plastic knife they put in with it. "God help me if I'm wrong, but I trust her. I trust her to find a way to make it work and not kill me in the process. I want it to work."

He fidgeted. "Have you considered this might be a knee-jerk reaction to Nick?" he said. "Are you trusting Ivy now because Nick hurt you and you simply want to trust some-body?"

I exhaled slowly. I'd already mulled that around in my head, trying it on and dismissing it. "I don't think so," I said softly.

Jenks reclined against the bench, pensive. Thoughtful my-self, I put the bite of fudge in my mouth and let it dissolve. It was butterscotch in salute to Ivy's new "allergy," but I hardly tasted it. Silent, I handed him the box of candy.

"Well," Jenks said, ignoring the knife and just breaking off a piece. "At least you aren't doing this because of your oh-so-endearing need to mix danger with passion. At least it better not be, or I'll pix you from here to the day you die for using Ivy like that."

Endearing need . . . My neck throbbed when I jerked up-right, choking as I swallowed. "I beg your pardon?"

He looked at me, eyebrows high and the sun glinting on his disguise-black hair. "You do the damnedest things in or-der to rile yourself up. Most people settle for doing it in an elevator, but not you. No, you have to make sure it's a vam-pire you're playing kissy-face with."

Heat washed through me, pulled by anger and embarrass-ment. Ivy had said the same thing. "I do not!"

"Rache," he cajoled, sitting up to match my posture. "Look at yourself. You're an adrenaline junkie. You not only need danger to make good in the bedroom, you need it to get through your normal day."

"Shut up!" I shouted, giving him a backhanded thwack on his shoulder. "I like adventure, that's all."

But he laughed at me, eyes dancing in delight as he broke off another chunk of fudge. "Adventure?" he said around his full mouth. "You keep making stupid decisions that will get you into just enough trouble that there might be the chance you can't get yourself out of. Being your safety net has been more fun than all my years at the I.S."

"I do not!" I protested again.

"Look at yourself," he said, head bowed over the fudge box again. "Look at yourself right now. You're half dead from blood loss, and you're out shopping. These disguises look great, but that's all they are: thin sheets of maybe standing between you and trouble."

"It's the Brimstone," I protested, taking the box of fudge out of his hands and closing it up. "It makes you feel indestructible. Makes you do stupid things."

He glanced from the white box to me. "Brimstone doesn't have you out here," he said. "It's your recurring lame-decision patterns that have you out here. Living in a church with a vampire, Rache? Dating a guy who summons demons? Bumping uglies with a vampire? Those caps Kisten wears won't mean crap if he loses control, and you know it. You've been flirting with being bitten for the last year, putting yourself in situation after situation where it might happen, and the first time you get Ivy out of Piscary's influence, what do you do? Manipulate her into it. You're an adrenaline addict, but at least you're making money off it."

"Hey!" I exclaimed, then lowered my voice when two passing women glanced at us. "Ivy had something to do with yesterday."

Jenks shrugged, extending his legs and clasping his hands behind his head. "Yeah. She did come up here after you. 'Course, I think part of that was her knowing you might take the opportunity after you did jumping jacks in Kisten's sweats. It didn't take much convincing on her part to bite you, did it? Nah, you were primed and ready to go, and she knew it."

Damn it, he was laughing at me. My brow furrowed, and I shoved the fudge back in a bag and out of his reach. I was not that stupid. I did *not* live my life trying to get into trouble just so I could have a good time in bed.

"I always have a good reason for the things I do," I said, peeved. "And my decisions don't hinge on what might put excitement in my life. But since I quit the I.S., I've never had the chance to make good decisions—I'm always scrambling just to stay alive. Do you think I don't want the little charm shop? The husband and two-point-two kids? A normal house with the fence and the dog that digs up my neighbor's yard and chases their cat into a tree?"

Jenks's gaze was even and calm, wise and even a bit sad. The wind ruffled his hair, and the sound of the pixies grew obvious. "No," he said. "I don't think you do." I glared, and he added, "I think it would kill you quicker than going to see Piscary wearing gothic lace. I think managing to find a blood balance with Ivy is going to be the only way you're going to survive. Besides . . ." He grinned impishly. ". . . no one but Ivy will put up with the things you need or the crap you dish out."

"Thanks a hell of a lot," I muttered, slumping with my arms crossed over my chest. Depressed, I stared at the pixies, then did a double take when I realized they'd killed the hummingbird and were gathering the feathers. *Crap, pixies were wicked when threatened.* "I am not that hard to live with."

Jenks laughed loudly, and I glanced at him, drawn by the different sound. "What about your upcoming demand to be free to sleep with whoever you damn well please while sharing blood with her, knowing she'd rather have you sleep with her?" he asked.

"Shut up," I said, embarrassed because that was one of the things I had on my list to talk to Ivy about. "She knows I'm never going to sleep with her."

The man passing us turned, then whispered something to his girlfriend, who promptly eyed me as well. I grimaced at them, glad I was wearing a disguise.

"It takes an incredibly strong person to walk away from someone they love," Jenks said, holding up two fingers as if making a list. "Especially knowing they will do something asinine, like shopping when their blood count is so low they ought to be in the hospital. You should give her credit for respecting you like that."

"Hey," I exclaimed, annoyed. "You said she wouldn't mind."

Grinning, he slid down a few feet. "Actually I said what she doesn't know won't hurt you." He put up a third finger. "You leave windows open when the heat is on."

A family of three walked past, the kids like stairsteps and noisy with life. I watched them pass, thinking they were the future I had been working for, just walking away and leaving me behind. *Was that a problem?* "I like fresh air," I protested, gathering up my things. It was time to leave.

"You're a whiner too," Jenks said. "I've never *seen* anyone so pathetic when you're sick. 'Where's my pain amulet? Where's my coffee?' God almighty, I thought I was bad."

I stood, feeling renewed from the Brimstone boost. It was a false strength, but it was there nevertheless. "Put down your fingers, Jenks, or I'm going to break them off and shove them somewhere."

Jenks stood as well, tugging his aviator jacket straight. "You bring home demon familiars. 'Oh isn't she sweet?' " he said in a high falsetto. " 'Can we keep her?' "

I hiked my shoulder bag up higher, feeling the comfortable weight of my splat gun inside. "Are you saying I should have let Al kill Ceri?" I said dryly.

Laughing, he gathered up his sundry bags, consolidating them into two. "No. I'm saying that it takes a very strong person to let *you* be *you*. I can't think of anyone better than Ivy."

My breath escaped me in a huff. "Well I'm glad we have your blessing."

Jenks snorted, his gaze going over the heads of the tourists to the archway and the parking lot where the car was. "Yeah, you got my blessing, and you've got my warning too."

I looked at him, but he wasn't paying me any attention, scanning the area now that we were ready to move again.

"If you think living with Ivy and trying to avoid getting bitten was difficult, wait until you try living with her while trying to find a blood balance. This isn't an easier road, Rache," he said, gaze distant and unaware of the worry he was starting in me. "It's a harder one. And you're going to be hurting all the way along it."

Twenty-five

The wind was whipping the decorative flags at the archway to the parking lot, and I blinked at them, fascinated. I had the remains of a burger in one hand, and a fizzy drink in the other. Jenks had insisted I get some iron-rich protein in me to chase down the Brimstone, but I suspected it had only been an excuse to get the drink, which he then spiked with even more Brimstone. Why else would I be feeling this great when my life was in the crapper? And I was feeling pretty damn good, like a weight had lifted and the sun was starting to shine.

Ivy would return soon, and though I had been all tough-girl by coming out here, it seemed prudent to get back before she found out I was gone. If Jenks and she were to be believed, I structured my life to be as horrific as possible to have fun in bed, but having Ivy mad at me might be too much for even me right now.

"What time is it?" I asked, squinting in the stiffer breeze and looking for the car. People bothered at our slow pace hustled past us, but I was enjoying the wind and the view of the straits.

Jenks snickered, clearly guessing where my thoughts were. He had slammed his twenty-ounce Dew and shook for a good thirty seconds, jittery and bright eyed, making me wonder which one of us was the better bet to drive home. Juggling his bags, he checked his wrist, beaming. "Four forty-six," he said. "Only a minute off that time."

"By the time you get acclimated, we'll be heading home," I said, then pushed into motion. "When did you get a watch?"

"Yesterday with Jax," he said, stretching to see the parking lot over the heads of the surrounding people. "I got you a camera too, and my knife. I don't like being this big."

I wasn't going to tell him it was illegal to carry a concealed knife. Besides, he was a pixy. The law didn't apply to him. I smiled at the way the sunlight glittered on his hair, even if it was black. "Big bad wolfs," I said, then sucked down another swig of pop, stumbling on the curb as we found the street. "We're going to blow their damned house down."

His motions seamless, Jenks took my drink away and dropped it into the nearest trash container. "You okay?"

"Oh yeah," I said enthusiastically. I handed him the last of my burger, which he threw away for me too. "You ought to know. You're the one who keeps spiking my food."

Giving me a wry look, Jenks gallantly took my arm. A giggle slipped from me at the show of support, appalling me. Damn it, this wasn't fair. If they got me hooked on Brimstone, I was going to be majorly pissed—if I could remember why I was mad at them, that is.

Still laughing, I pulled my head up, going cold with a pulse of fear. Leaning against Kisten's Corvette were Brett and Walter Vincent, the first one scanning the faces of the people leaving the mall, the second doing the same but with a murderous intensity. Immediately I realized what had happened, and I thanked God we weren't at the motel, trapped in a little box of a room. Jenks and I were under a disguise, and though they hadn't known about Kisten's car, it probably smelled like the pixy, seeing as he drove it yesterday. They had found us.

"Oh, fudge," I whispered, leaning heavily on Jenks's arm. Just that fast, I had gone from exuberant to panic, the Brimstone taking over my moods. "You got anything more lethal than that knife on you?" I asked.

"No. Why?" His forward momentum barely hesitated as he looked up from watching my feet. "Oh," he said softly, his fingers tightening on my arm for an instant. "Okay."

I wasn't surprised when he did an abrupt turn-about and wheeled us back into the mall. Bending close, Jenks sent the aroma of dry meadow over me. "Your disguises are working," he whispered. "Pretend we just forgot something and have to go pick it up."

I found myself nodding, scanning the contented faces around me, searching for anger in the vacationing people. My pulse was fast and my skin tingling. Pam was dead; they would be after me for that if nothing else. Weres were timid, apart from the alpha and the first few down, and since the round was broken, they would stay in the background and keep our squabble private. We'd be okay unless we got ourselves in a blind alley. And there weren't many of those in Mackinaw City.

"I'm going to call Ivy," I said, pulling my bag around and opening it.

Body tense, Jenks drew me to a stop to put my back to a brick wall and stand partially in front of me. It was a candy shop—big surprise there—and my stomach growled as I hit speed dial. "Come on, come on," I crabbed, waiting for it to go through.

The circuit clicked open and Ivy's voice filtered out. "Rachel?"

"Yeah, it's me," I said, shoulders easing in relief. "Where are you?"

"On the bridge back. Why?" She hesitated, and I could hear the distinctive sound of Nick's truck. "Why do I hear people?" she added suspiciously.

Jenks winced, and I squinted in the sun, backing up until the overhang put me in the shade. "Uh, Jenks and I went on a procurement run."

"Shopping?" she yelped. "Rachel! Damn it, can't you just sit still for a couple of hours?"

I thought of the Brimstone running rampant through me, deciding that no, I couldn't.

Jenks tossed his head, and I followed his grim gaze to a pair of elegantly dressed tourists. They had shopping bags, but they were a little too attentive. Turning his back to them, Jenks angled to block their view of me. *Damn it, this was getting dicey.* My pulse quickened and I hunched into the phone. "Look, I did some thinking, and you're right." I peeked around Jenks, then rocked back. "How long will it take for you to get to that open-air mall?"

"You did some thinking?" Ivy said softly, sounding vulnerable.

Jenks scanned the plaza. "Tick-tock, Rache."

Anxious, I turned to the phone. "Yeah. I need to start making smarter decisions. But we're at that mall and Brett and Walter are sitting on the car." The good feeling the Brimstone had instilled in me had sifted to fear, and I clamped down on my rising panic. At its heart, Brimstone was an intensifier. If you were happy, you were really happy. If you were sad, you were suicidal. Right now I was scared out of my mind. Until it wore off, I was going to be a roller coaster of emotions. *Damn it, I didn't have time for this!*

Ivy snarled something at Nick, and I heard a horn blast. "How many?" she asked tightly.

I looked past Jenks, seeing sunlit flowers and cheerful storefronts. "Four so far, but they have phones. We're wearing disguises, so they probably don't know it's us." *Calm down, Rachel,* I told myself, trying to use the drug to my advantage. *Think.*

"I knew this was going to happen. I knew it!" Ivy shouted.

"Well, I'd rather meet them here than the motel," I said, doggedly trying to pull my emotions from fear back to invincibility. It wasn't working. I was still scared.

"The bridge is still one lane either way," Ivy snarled. "I can't get around this guy. Give the phone to Jenks. I want to talk to him."

Jenks paled and shook his head.

"Jenks!" she exclaimed, "I know you can hear me. I can't believe you let her talk you into this. I told you she needed at least another course of Brimstone before she could work in the kitchen, much less go out!"

"I'm not that weak," I said indignantly, but Jenks was way ahead of me, and he took the phone, holding it so we could both hear.

"She ate that last cookie, Ivy," he said, clearly offended. "And I just gave her another dose of the stuff. She's running on full. I'm not stupid."

"I knew it!" I said, glancing past Jenks at the drifting people. "You slipped me some!"

There was a short silence, and Ivy said softly, "You picked up more Brimstone?"

Jenks met my eyes. "Yeah. And don't worry. I paid cash. It's not on the card."

"Where did you get the money, Jenks?" Ivy asked, the threat clear in her voice.

"It wasn't that expensive," he said, but I could tell he thought he'd done something wrong by his suddenly worried look.

"You ass!" Ivy said. "Get her the hell out of there! You bought street-grade, you stupid pixy! She's higher than a kite!"

Jenks's mouth worked but nothing was coming out.

"Uh, Ivy?" he squeaked. "We gotta go."

"Don't hang up!" Ivy yelled. "Give me to Rachel. Jenks, give the phone to Rachel!"

Jenks went to end the call, and I snatched the phone. I was on street-grade Brimstone? Swell. Just swell. I thought it was hitting me a little hard. I could hear Ivy telling Nick what had happened, catching the word "invincible" and "get herself killed." Jenks turned to scan the area, his posture tense and guilty looking.

"Hey, Ivy," I said, my mood having done a quick shift to anger. "The next time you and Jenks want to play doctor, just shove the Brimstone up your ass, okay? Both of you. I'm not your freaking play-doll."

"I'm on my way," Ivy said, ignoring me. "Rachel, just . . . sit somewhere. Can you do that? I'll get you out."

I leaned against the brick wall, feeling every little projection dig into me through my shirt. "Take your time," I said flippantly, ticked and nerved-up all at the same time. The adrenaline was flowing, and Brimstone had my skin tingling. "Jenks and I are going to plan B."

"Plan B?" Ivy said. "What is plan B?"

Jenks reddened. "Grab the fish and run like hell," he muttered, and I almost giggled.

"I'm going to walk out of here," I said, deciding I'd rather be invincible than scared, "and catch the trolley back to the motel. And if anyone stops me, I'm going to kick—their—ass."

"Rachel," Ivy said slowly, "it's the Brimstone. You aren't thinking. Just sit tight!"

My eyes narrowed. "I can take care of myself," I said, starting to feel really good. It wasn't the Brimstone. No, I lived for excitement! I made decisions based on what would screw my life up the most! I was a messed-up, screwed-up stupid witch who had to mix danger with her sex life in order to get turned on, and I was going to live a very short, exciting life. I went to end the call, then hesitated. "Hey, you want me to keep the phone line open?"

"Yes," she said softly. "No. Yes."

I sobered at the worry in her voice. "Okay."

My blood tingled through me, and I tucked the phone into my waistband, upside down so the mike was exposed and not muffled by my jeans. Ivy would be able to hear everything that happened. I looked at Jenks, seeing his worry and tension. "Well?" I said, pushing myself off the wall. "What do you think?"

"I think Ivy's going to kill me," he whispered. "Rachel. I'm sorry. I didn't know."

I took a breath, exhaling long and slow. It was done. If anything, I ought to thank him; I was up and walking, able to run even if I was going to pay for it later. "Don't worry about it,"

I said, touching his shoulder. "Just stop making my decisions for me, okay?"

My roving eyes fell upon the bench he and I had been sitting on. My mouth went dry and I tried to swallow. Brett was standing by it, his arms crossed and his eyes fixed on me. He was smiling. At me. "Shit," I breathed. "Jenks, they know it's us."

He nodded, his youthful face going serious. "He showed up a few minutes ago. We have six at the exit behind us and four at the bend the other way."

"And you just let me keep talking to Ivy?" I said, not believing it.

A shrug lifted his shoulders. "They're Weres. They aren't going to make a scene."

Normally I would have agreed with him. Heart pounding, I snuck a look at the six Weres at the exit. They had scads of jewelry and were in bright colors, making them from the street pack. Bringing up my second sight, I felt the last of my bravado wash out of me. Their auras were rimmed in brown again. How had Walter managed to pull them back together like that?

"Ah, Jenks?" I said, knowing Ivy was listening. "They're in a round. They aren't going to just sit there. We have to leave before the rest arrive."

Jenks looked at me, looked at the Weres, then looked at me again. His gaze went to the roof, and he was probably wishing he could fly. "There's only one layer of shops," he said suddenly. "Let's go."

Grabbing my arm, he pulled me into the fudge store. Feet stumbling, I followed him in, breathing deeply of the rich scent of chocolate. There was a small line at the counter, but Jenks plowed to the front of it amid a chorus of indignant protest. "Pardon, me. 'Scuse us," he said, flipping the barrier up between the front and the back.

"Hey!" a large woman called out, her apron tied with the smartness of a uniform. "You can't come back here!"

"Just passing through!" Jenks called cheerfully. The bags

he held rattled, and letting go of my arm for a moment, he dipped a finger into the puddle of fudge cooling on a marble table. "Needs more almond," he said, tasting it. "And you're cooking it half a degree too long."

The woman's mouth opened in surprise, and he pushed past her and into the kitchen.

"There," I said, and Jenks's eyes shot to the back door, outlined by the boxes stacked around it. The security door was open to let the hot air of the kitchen escape through a normal-looking screen door. Beyond that were the employees' cars in a nasty-looking alley, and beyond that, the main road. In the distance, the straits sparkled, looking as big as a lake.

"Ready?" Jenks asked.

I jerked my splat ball gun out of my bag. "Yup. Let's go."

"What the hell are you doing back here?" a masculine voice called.

I turned, and the man's eyes went wide at my cherry-red gun, then he got nasty. "This is my place of business!" he shouted. "Not a paint ball stadium! Get out! Get out!"

"Sorry," I mumbled, then bolted for the door when he shambled forward, hands reaching. Jenks and I dove through it, skittering into the alley in a surge of adrenaline. The bang of the heavy door slamming shut shot through me.

"Oh look, Jenks," I said, as we slowed to get our bearings. "A dead-end alley."

The wind was brisk, blowing up and against the back of the store, and with my blood humming and my steps quick, I started for the street and the cracked sidewalk beside it. It would take the Weres some time to work their way out and around to the back of the store unless they trashed the fudge shop. But I didn't think they would. Like their supposedly distant wild brethren, Weres weren't aggressive unless defending their own. But they were in a round, so who knew what they would do.

"Ivy," I said breathlessly as we jogged to the road, knowing she could hear. "We're outside between the mall and the— Shit!" I exploded, skittering to a halt when, in a sliding sound of gravel on pavement, a trio of Weres skidded around the corner.

They were wearing khaki pants and matching polo shirts to make them look like they were in uniform. Even worse, one of them dropped a duffel bag, and after unzipping it, started tossing nasty looking weapons to his buddies. I stood there, frozen. Were they nuts? This went way beyond a public show of strength. Hell, even vamps never did this! Not in broad daylight and on the street where any passing human could see, anyway.

Someone cocked their weapon, and Jenks jerked me back. My mouth was still hanging open when we landed against a salt-rusted four-door, the front full of crumpled fast food sacks.

Brett came around the corner, his pace fast and his eyes darting everywhere. Seeing me, he smiled. "We have them, sir," he said into the phone at his ear, slowing to a stop behind the three Weres with aggressive stances. "Behind the fudge shop. It's all over but the howling."

Heart pounding, I looked at the road and the sporadic traffic. The memory of finding Nick tied to the wall swam up from my subconscious. A chill purged everything from me but a fierce determination. I wasn't strong enough to survive that. I couldn't let them take me.

"You want me to make a circle and wait for Ivy, or you want to fight our way out, Jenks?" I said, my grip on my splat gun going sweaty.

In a sliding sound of metal, Jenks pulled a dull metal bar from the nearby recycling bin, swinging it a couple of times. The three Weres with guns took a more aggressive stance. "You think we need Ivy?" he asked.

"Just checking," I answered, then turned to the Weres, my arms shaking. "Right. Like you're going to shoot us?" I taunted. "If we're dead, you can't beat Nick's location out of us."

Brett's jaw clenched. From the other side, three more Weres loped into view, to make seven men. I had fourteen sleepy-time potions. I had to act, and act now.

"Subdue them," Brett said, squinting from the sun. Annoyed, he snatched the weapon from the nearest man. "Use your fists. You outnumber them, and I don't want the I.S. out here because of weapon discharges."

Adrenaline surged, making me feel weak, not strong. From beside me, Jenks shouted, then leapt forward. Half the Weres came to meet him, their speed and ferocity shocking.

Panic struck. Taking aim, I downed one with a charm. Then another. I wanted to help Jenks, but they were coming too fast. One slipped past him, and I gasped, falling to one knee.

"Not today, you son of a bitch!" I exclaimed, plugging him. He slid to within three feet of me. I leveled my gun for the next one. He got three steps closer than the first.

"Jenks! Fall back!" I shouted, retreating with my gun going *puff-puff-puff*.

Three more went down. Frantic, I tossed the hair from my face. There were a lot more then seven Weres. I had downed at least that many. Where in hell was Ivy?

"Rache!" Jenks shouted in warning. "Behind you!"

I spun. A Were in leather was running for me. Behind him, the door to the kitchen was wide-open and full of rough-looking Weres in street clothes.

I stumbled backward. They had come through the shop? Damn it! I had been afraid they would. They were not acting normal!

"Rachel!" Jenks shouted again as the Were smiled to show his beautiful, beautiful teeth and closed his grease-stained fingers about my wrist. Big mistake.

Grunting, I twisted my arm to grip his own thick wrist. My right foot came up and my sneaker smacked him in the kidneys. Wrenching around, I used his own weight to yank him down, falling to kneel so his elbow hit my upraised knee, bending it backward and snapping. He grunted as his elbow shattered.

Puffing in satisfaction, I let him go and got to my feet. *Where in hell was my splat gun?*

Spotting it alone on the pavement, I darted for it.

"Hey!" I shouted, my foot pulled out from under me. Arms flailing to get between my face and the uprushing pavement, I hit the cement. Shocked, I twisted to find the Were I had downed wasn't withering in pain and holding his broken arm, but using it!

"You bloody bastard!" I shouted, kicking at his face. "Let me go!"

But he didn't, grimly holding on. Panic slid through me as I realized they were using the full potential of the round and someone was muting his pain. He utterly ignored the broken nose I gave him with my heel, and I smacked him again. Blood gushed and he finally let go, but not before he fastened one of those damned zip-strips on my foot.

"You freaking bastard!" I shouted, scrabbling for my gun and plugging him right in the face. Furious, I turned to the two Weres following him and shot them too.

The three collapsed, and shuddering, I got to my feet, holding three more at bay, my arms shaking as I shifted the aim from one to the other.

"Jenks!" I shouted, and he was suddenly at my back. Stupid, *stupid* witch. Until I got the thing off, I wouldn't be able to make a circle. All I had were the four charms in my gun and Jenks, his back now pressing lightly against mine.

I could smell the sweat on him, reminding me of a meadow somehow. He had lost his disguise amulet at some point and his blond curls were tousled. The cut on his forehead was bleeding again, and red streaked his hands. My face went ashen when I realized it wasn't his but from the five Weres he had beaten into unconsciousness with that pipe.

Brett stood with Walter behind two military Weres, their weapons cocked and ready to gun us down if they couldn't subdue us any other way. Past them, traffic passed, and curious onlookers were being soothed by professional-looking Weres in suits and ties, probably explaining this away as being a movie shoot or something. Behind us, the street Weres waited, hanging back but ready to descend when someone gave the order.

I swallowed hard. With the strength of four alphas at his fingertips, Walter had driven them into a higher pitch of aggression, and with the lack of pain, there was nothing to stop them. Just the thought of gaining the focus had been enough to get them back together.

Incredible, I mused, grip shifting on my splat gun as I tried to figure out how four charms would be of much help. What would happen if they actually got the focus was a nightmare in waiting. Every single Were would want a piece of it. The alphas would come flocking, and soon the major cities would be fighting their own little turf wars as vampires started taking them out, having decided they didn't like aggressive Weres who felt no pain and could Were as fast as witch magic. And with the focus binding them, the round wouldn't break apart. No wonder the vampires had hidden the ugly thing.

"Jenks," I panted, knowing Ivy could hear. "They tagged me with one of those zip-strips. I can't make a circle to hold them off anymore. We can't let them get the focus. And I'm not strong enough to keep my mouth shut if they capture me."

Jenks glanced at me and away. His grip tightened on the bloody pipe. "Any ideas?"

"Nope." I panted, shifting my feet. "Unless you can hold them off long enough for me to get this damned strip off my foot."

He jiggled out his knife, handing it to me. It was smeared with blood, and I felt sick. "I'll keep them off you," he said, his face going grim.

I handed it back, knowing he was more effective with it than I was. "They're designed to be tamper resistant. It's going to take a pair of bolt cutters."

Jenks shifted his balance to his toes. "Then we fight until Ivy gets here."

"Yep," I agreed, fear settling firmly in me. This was bad. This was really bad.

My gaze darted to Brett as he scuffed his feet. Walter had joined him, the savage glint in his eyes born from his grief. From behind me came the sound of the street Weres pulling chains from around their waist and the snick of knives being opened.

Damn it all and shit on it. I did not want to die like this.

"Ma'am?" Brett drawled, drawing my attention to him. "It would save everyone a good deal of trouble if you would surrender your weapon and come with us."

"Trouble?" I shouted back, releasing some pent-up frustration. "For who?" My gaze traveled over the Weres. They kept filing in, surrounding us. There were five alphas now. The street Weres at our backs, military Weres at the front, and the credit card Weres at the outskirts, keeping everything nice and quiet and the pedestrian traffic moving.

My stomach clenched when I realized three of the street Weres behind the Dumpster weren't injured, but shifting. They were shifting in broad daylight. In a public street. With the intent to tear me to pieces. And they were doing it really fast.

"Ma'am," Brett tried again, playing the good cop or simply buying time for the turning Weres. "Put down your weapon and kick it to me."

"Go to hell, Brett," I said darkly. "I've seen how you treat your guests. I know what it is now, and you aren't getting it. And this isn't a weapon, it's a *gun!*"

Angry and frightened, I took aim and shot him.

A blur dove between us. One of his men took it instead. The Were hit the ground and skidded to a stop, out cold before his face ground into the pavement. Brett seemed shocked I'd actually shot at him, and I shrugged. At the outskirts, stupid people clapped in appreciation. I could not believe this. I was going to be hacked to shreds to the accompaniment of applause.

Brett glanced at them, then frowned. "Shoot her," he said softly. "Just shoot her in the leg."

"Good going, Rache," Jenks muttered.

Safeties clicked off. I spun. I had three charms left, and I wanted those four-legged bastards asleep before they finished putting on their wolf's clothing. Ignoring the chaos, I calmly plugged them both.

The street Weres surrounding them exploded in anger. I backpedaled as they rushed me.

"No!" Brett shouted, red-faced as he gestured. "Get out of the way!"

Jenks was a blur of motion, the thuds of the bar meeting flesh sickening. The occasional chime of metal on metal rang out as someone threw a chain into the mix. My first thought, that we were going to die, turned into an ironic relief. As long as the street Weres were surrounding us, the military faction couldn't shoot.

One of the Weres broke through Jenks's defenses, and I sprang forward. Grabbing the hairy arm someone conveniently gave me, I twisted and shoved. The Were stumbled away, howling in pain as I dislocated his shoulder. A nasty grin came over me. He had felt that. The bond was breaking. They were acting independently, and the round was falling apart!

A sharp crack shocked through me and I jumped. They were shooting anyway!

A closer burst of gunfire brought me spinning around. The Weres fell back, their aggression flaking to nothing as the packs divided. Heart in my throat, I found Jenks, weapon aimed at the sky and a savage expression on his face. The more disciplined military faction held their ground, but the street Weres panicked. In an instant they were gone, streaking past Jenks and me and dragging their downed companions, whether in fur, leather, or polyester.

"Hold together!" Walter shouted from behind a row of men, but it was too late. "Damn you!" he swore. "Hold together! He's not going to shoot you!"

Faint on the cool spring air was the sound of sirens.

"Tink's diaphragm, it's about time," Jenks swore. The

Weres who were left heard it too, and they began to exchange looks as they panted. The crowd watching started to break up, their steps fast and their faces pale as they realized that was real blood on the pavement.

"You know who I am?" Jenks shouted, bloody but unbowed. "I'm Jenks!" He took a breath, grinning. "Boo!"

Several of the well-dressed Weres jumped, and a few of the military Weres touched their tattoos as if for luck or strength.

Walter shoved himself to the front. "Hold together!" he shouted as his control over the second pack slipped away. "You swore an oath to me. You swore, damn it!"

The alpha male in a suit gave him an ugly look. Saying nothing more, he turned and walked away. His wife slipped an arm in his, seamlessly snagging a store bag and heading for the top of the wide alley. There were no more bystanders watching now, and they melted seamlessly into the tourist traffic.

Hunched and panting, I watched unbelieving as the ring of business Weres dispersed. I smiled sweetly at Walter, hefting my splat gun. It was empty, but he didn't know that. The sirens grew closer. If they had held together for five minutes more, they would have had us. It hadn't been the sirens, it had been their inability to stay together. Without the focus, they couldn't hold together when things got sticky.

Choleric, Walter gestured to Brett.

"Rache!" Jenks shouted.

At least a dozen weapons turned to us. There was only one thing to do, and I did it.

Grunting, I leapt at Brett. It surprised him, and though he was by far the better military person, I got him down, attacking not like a professional, but like a sissy girl with my arms around his knees. We hit the pavement together and I scrambled for a better hold.

My arm went around his neck and I wrenched an arm painfully. And while he would have felt no pain had they still been in a round, he certainly felt it now. "Tell them to back off!" I shouted.

Brett started to laugh, the sound choking off when I pulled.

"Ow," he said, as if I was simply bending back a finger, not ready to dislocate his shoulder. "Ms. Morgan. What the hell do you think you're doing, ma'am?"

I could hear Nick's truck. "Getting the hell out of here," I said, stumbling as Jenks helped me stand upright without losing my grip. It was as awkward as all get-out, but we managed. A ring of weapons pointed at us. Jenks took my place, his face ugly as he bent his arm and pressed a knife to Brett's throat.

"You ever see a pixy battlefield?" he whispered in the Were's ear, and Brett lost the vestiges of humor. White-faced, he went passive. Which was really scary in itself.

The flash of a blue truck sped past.

"Too far, Ivy!" Jenks shouted, and there was the squeal of brakes quickly followed by the horns and the gunning of an engine.

I looked at my waistband and the phone. An insane need to giggle rose through me. I sure hoped we weren't roaming.

Another squeal of tires, and Nick's blue truck rocked to a stop at the end of the alley.

"Mom's here to pick us up, Jenks," I quipped, limping to the curb. "I'll get the bags."

I scooped up one of our bags, seeing as it was on the way and it sort of added to the travesty. My empty splat gun never shifted from Walter, though he was behind two rows of men. Coward.

"Hi, Ivy," I said tiredly, tossing the bag into the truck bed and lurching in after it. Yeah, it was illegal to ride in the back, but seeing that we had just somehow beaten up three Were packs, I wasn't going to worry about it. "Thanks for the ride."

Nick was in the front seat, and pale. He handed a pair of bolt cutters through the window.

"Hey, thanks!" I said, then started when Brett came thumping in beside me like a sack of potatoes. The Were was unconscious, and I looked at Jenks in question when he followed him in, admittedly a hell of a lot more gracefully. "I don't want a hostage," I said. Then wondered when Jenks had knocked him out. He wasn't dead, was he?

Grim-faced, Jenks shouted, "What are you waiting for, Ivy? God to say go?"

The truck lurched, and I steadied myself against the long silver locker Nick had bolted to the truck bed. My sweat went cold in the new breeze, and thinking we had done it, I pulled the hair from my eyes and smiled at Jenks. My smile faded.

As we jostled into traffic, he was using a plastic cord to truss Brett up with a painful savagery. I thought back to seeing his kids tearing apart the fairy nest in his garden. This was a side to him I'd never truly seen before, since the difference of our sizes had insulated me from it.

From inside the truck came Nick's petrified voice, "Go faster, Ivy! They're behind us!"

Wedging myself into the corner, I held my hair out of the way and blinked. I had expected to see Jeeps or Hummers. What I found were three Weres in wolf skin, tearing down the street after us. And they were fast. Really fast. And they didn't stop for red lights either.

"Son of a Disney whore," Jenks swore. "Rache, you got any more charms in that gun?"

I shook my head, scrambling for a way out of this. My eyes darted to my ankle. "Jenks, get this thing off me."

Brett was coming around, and when he tried to get upright, Jenks lashed out, savagely connecting with his head right behind his ear. Brett's eyes rolled back and he passed out.

"Hold on!" Nick shouted. "Right turn!"

Tossing my splat gun into the front, I gripped the side of the truck. The wheels skittered and hopped, but Ivy kept it on the road. Nick yelled an obscenity, and a motor home flashed by, tires squealing. I didn't want to know how close we had come to becoming a hood ornament.

My heart pounded and my gaze shot to my foot at the feel of cold steel against my skin. Jenks's shoulder muscles bunched, and as we hit a pothole, the charmed silver band snapped.

Frantic, I sent my gaze behind us. Holy crap, they were right there!

"Ivy!" I shouted, stomach clenching. "When I say, hit the breaks."

"Are you crazy!" she shouted, glancing back at me, her short black hair framing her face and getting into her eyes.

"Just do it!" I demanded, tapping a line. Line energy filled me, warm and golden. I didn't care that it was tainted black, it was mine. I took a breath. This was going to hurt if I didn't do it right. *Big circle. Big circle.* "Now!" I shouted.

The breaks screamed. I lurched, shocked to find Jenks's arm between my head and the metal cabinet. Brett slid forward and groaned.

"Rhombus!" I shouted, the word raging from me hard enough to hurt my throat.

Heady and strong, the line energy flashed through me, expanding upward from the circle I had imagined painted on the pavement. It wasn't strong enough to hold a demon, but it would hold together long enough for what I wanted. I hoped.

I tossed my hair from my eyes even before the truck stopped rocking. Elation filled me as the pursing Weres slammed right into my circle.

"Yes!" I shouted, then spun at the sound of crunching metal and screams. It wasn't us. We were stopped! I sucked in my breath when I realized an oncoming car had smacked into the other side of my circle, amber and black in the sun. Aw, shit. I'd forgotten about the other lane.

Horns blew, and the car that had hit my circle was rear-ended.

"Oh, that was just beautiful!" Jenks said in admiration. His eyes were on the Weres making painful splurges of motion on the pavement. Apparently running into a wall hurt if you didn't have a round of alphas taking away your pain.

People were starting to get out of their cars, dazed and

excited. "Sorry!" I called out, wincing. Breaking my connection with the line, I took down the circle.

In the distance were sirens, and I could see flashing lights. Jenks tapped the window, and Ivy slowly accelerated, taking the first left she could and doubling back a street over, trying to put as much distance between us and the sirens as she could. I exhaled, falling to slump against the tool locker. I put a hand through the window, finding Ivy's shoulder. She jumped, and I whispered, "Thanks," before I pulled my hand out. We had made it. We were alive and together. And we had a hostage.

"Damn it all back to the Turn!" Jenks swore.

Nick turned to look at us, and I nudged Jenks's foot. He was messing about in his bag and he looked ticked. "What is it, Jenks?" I breathed as we jostled along, tired, so tired.

"I lost my fudge!" he swore. "That woman took my fudge!"

Twenty-six

The hamburger place was busy with kids, moms, and teenagers cutting loose after school, telling me more clearly than a page of demographics that the resident population was decidedly slanted to human. I slumped deeper into the molded plastic, my lips curling when I found the table sticky from someone's pop. Brett snickered, and I made a face at him. The defiant Were was sitting across from me, handcuffed with his own steel to the table support bolted to the floor. Pride had him hiding the fact, and no one was paying us any mind. Just two people having coffee. 'Least we would be when Jenks got back with the drinks.

The Brimstone had worn off somewhere between shaking the Weres and Ivy and Nick dropping us off here, and fatigue was seeping into me like water through mud. Ivy was sure that they knew how to track Brett's location from an active phone, and the two of them were leading the Weres on a wild goose chase until we figured out what to do with him.

That we had a hostage had really put a crimp in my already stellar day. Jenks, Ivy, and I had already gone round about it. Nick listened wide-eyed as Jenks adamantly protested that we should keep him to kill in cold blood as a warning if the Weres so much as sniffed too close to us. The scary thing was, Jenks was ready to carry it out.

This was the shocking, ruthless side to Jenks that was seldom seen and easy to miss behind his lighthearted mien—the part of him that kept his family fed and their heads underground when the snow flew. Taking Brett hostage had been as natural as breathing to him, and I truly believed he'd kill the Were with just as much thought. Though carefree and one of the best friends I'd ever had, Jenks was a cell phone, computer-savvy savage, living without law and holding to his own morals alone. I thanked God I fit in there as being important to him.

It was the first time Jenks and I had disagreed on how to handle a run. Hell, it was the first time he'd had an opinion. I think taking Brett hostage had triggered something in his pixy makeup. I was sure the argument wasn't over yet, but I did *not* want a hostage.

But I hadn't wanted Ivy to drop us off at a burger joint either, I thought sourly, hunching deeper into Jenks's aviator jacket, which he was letting me wear. I had wanted to go to Squirrel's End, where I could have a beer and quietly shake in the corner. The patrons there would have only snickered and poked each other at seeing the handcuffs. Ivy nixed it, though, pulling Nick's truck into Burger-rama saying that Squirrel's End smelled like us, and only the sanitation practices of a fast food place would hide that we'd been there and stop the trail cold.

Whatever. I was bone-tired, aching from our street brawl, and thirsty enough to down a two-liter bottle of Coke by myself. And why in hell hadn't I at least *brought* my pain amulet? It had been stupid going out like this. God help me, but if the Weres didn't kill me, I could probably do it myself.

Brett and I both jumped at the high-pitched shriek from the kid at the top of the slide behind him, and our eyes met briefly. The primary-colored play equipment was literally crawling with screaming, runny-nosed kids in open winter coats, throwing the tops that came with the mini-meals this week at each other.

My pulse slowed, and as Jenks charmed the ladies behind the counter into flustered goo, I tried to look cool and professional among the plastic toys and paper hats. It wasn't going to happen, so I tried for dangerous. I think I managed cranky when several children went wide-eyed and silent after passing my table. My hand lifted to hide the scrape on my face I got hitting the pavement, and I tried again to brush my jeans free of the dirt from the alley. Maybe I looked worse than I thought.

Brett looked great, having sat most of the scuffle out. The clean smell of woodsy aftershave came from him, and the light glinted on the silver of his short hair. Though small, he looked like he could lope from there to the state line without stopping—apart from the cuffs.

I smelled the hot meadowy scent of Jenks before I saw him, and I straightened, sliding down to make room. Jenks set the cardboard tray with two large coffees and a weenie-sized cup of steaming water that was an odd shade of pink onto the table. *Herbal tea?* I thought, claiming a coffee. Since when did Jenks like herbal tea?

I looked up from trying to pry the lid off my cup when Jenks pulled it out from my fingers. "Hey!" I said, and he put the lame cup of pink water in front of me. "I don't want tea," I said indignantly. "I want coffee."

"Diuretic." Jenks sat beside Brett. "It will do more harm than good. Drink your decaf tea."

Remembering our argument and thinking this was his way of getting back at me, my eyes narrowed. "I almost died back there," I said irately. "If I want a damn coffee, I'm going to have a damn coffee." Daring him to protest, I took my coffee with a huff.

Brett watched the exchange with interest. Eyebrows high, he reached for the second coffee, and Jenks intercepted his reach. The Were hesitated, then settled into his plastic seat with nothing. "What are you going to do with me, ma'am?" he said, the light twang in his voice obvious among the midwestern accents around us.

How in hell should I know? "Oh, I've got big plans for you," I lied, surprised at the ma'am. "Jenks wants to string you up as an object lesson. I'm halfway to letting him have his wish." I leaned back, tired. "It works great when he murders garden fairies."

Brett glanced warily at Jenks—who was nodding zealously—and I felt a weary lassitude slip over me. Crap. Why did the Brimstone pick now to wear off? A chill ran through me, tight on the heels of the idle thought that taking it to get through this week might not be a bad idea.

The Were's eyes traveled over me, hesitating at my torn turtleneck before rising to my face. From there, they never moved, but his focus kept shifting as he monitored the room by the sounds behind him. It gave me the creeps.

I sent my eyebrows up—wishing yet again that I could do the one eyebrow thing—casually tearing three packets of sugar open at once and dumping them in not because I liked it but because the coffee smelled that old. "I know where it is," I said lightly.

Just the fact that Brett didn't move said volumes. Jenks scowled, clearly not liking what I was doing, but I didn't want a hostage. I wanted to send Brett back with a message that would buy me some time and space. Now that the island Weres knew we were still in Mackinaw, they would keep looking until they found us. That we had Brett for a hostage wouldn't stop them—he had screwed up royally, and unlike the fairies that Jenks was used to dealing with, I think the Weres would just as soon see him dead—but maybe a show of goodwill and a big fat lie would buy us time enough to get my con in place.

I hoped.

"Sparagmos told you where it is," Brett said, his disbelief obvious.

"Of course he did," Jenks said, breaking his silence. "We've got it, and you don't."

Na, na, na, na-a-a-a, na. "I can put my hands on it," I amended, nudging Jenks's foot. *Shut up, Jenks.* I liked him better quiet. This was the last time we took a hostage.

Brett looked relaxed even though his one hand was cuffed under the table. Behind him, kids were fighting, hurting my ears. "Give it to me," he said. "I'll take it to Mr. Vincent and convince him to leave you alone."

Jenks jerked into motion, reaching for Brett. The Were blocked it. Someone hit a coffee and it spilled. Gasping, I stood when it threatened to run into my lap. "Damn it, Jenks!" I swore, pulling every eye to us. "What in hell are you doing?"

The restaurant was abruptly silent. A unified, "Ooooh," rose from the ball pit, and I flushed. Clear in the silence, the person coming over the loudspeaker wanted to know if he could substitute bottled water for the pop. I winced apologetically to the offended mothers speaking in hushed voices to their soccer-mom friends. "Sorry," I muttered. I sat down, and the level of noise resumed. *Crap. That had been my coffee.*

"You are in no position to be making deals or demands," Jenks said nastily as people turned away. "And if you or your mange-ridden curs touch her, you'll find everyone you care about dead one morning."

Brett's face went red.

"Just stop it," I griped, thinking this wasn't the way to arrange a cease-fire. But it told me I was right that Brett had to placate Walter with something to ease his return into the pack. Brett was in trouble; it wasn't only Jenks who wanted to kill him.

The small man's expression went sour and he settled back, clearly a lot more cautious now that he knew how fast Jenks could move. Heck, it impressed me.

"Look," I said, wedging a wad of napkins out of the dispenser and mopping up my coffee. I couldn't help but wonder if Jenks had done it intentionally. "All I want is Nick free from your reprisals. You can take Walter the stinking statue as far as I'm concerned."

Brett's dark eyes went suspicious. "You still expect me to believe you aren't working for someone and that you risked your life for . . . for him?"

My lips curled into a sour smile. "Don't call me stupid," I warned him. Jenks pushed the tea at me, and I ignored it.

"I need a day to get the statue here," I lied. "A day to get it here and tie a pretty ribbon around it for you."

The tiny clink of his cuffs made Brett's eyes twitch. "You're going to give it to me," he said flatly.

I wrapped my fingers around my foam cup to hide their trembling. "Yup. And it was your idea too."

Jenks looked at me in bewilderment, and I smiled. "I want you to back off. All of you," I added, squeezing the tea bag to make a thin rivulet of red drain into the cup. I was thirsty, and if I made for that second coffee, Jenks would probably spill it too. "I don't need to leave town to get it. I can have it here by sunset tomorrow. Watch us if you want, but one sniff I think is too close and the exchange is off and we are gone." I leaned over my tea. "Jenks and I cleaned your clocks with a pipe and some stupid sleepy-time charms. You want to risk finding out what we're really capable of when all you have to do is wait a lousy thirty-six hours?"

"An exchange?" Brett mocked, and Jenks made an odd rumble, leaving me wondering if pixies could growl. "Seems to me like it's more of a payment for getting us to leave you alone."

In a smooth, unhurried motion, Jenks reached out and slapped him. "Seems to me you should pull the brains out of your ass."

"Jenks!" I exclaimed, glancing over the fishbowl of a restaurant to see if anyone saw him.

"He's a dead wolf!" Jenks protested, gesturing sharply. "I could slice him open and leave him for the maggots, and *he* thinks he has some leverage."

My eyes narrowed. "But we aren't going to do that. Stop hitting him."

"It's what they did to Nick," he offered, starting our argument anew. "Why are you giving him any consideration beyond the chunk of meat that he turned himself into by letting us take him hostage?"

Under the table my knees were shaking. "Because that's

how we work when we're five feet tall, unless we're ignorant animals playing in the woods."

Jenks slumped back with his coffee to look sullen.

Brett's teeth were clenched at my unflattering comparison to his pack. Remembering what they had done to Nick, it was hard not to let Jenks have his way. Frustrated, I tried to hide my shaking fingers by taking a sip of my tart tea while Jenks continued to dump every last sugar packet into his coffee. I could scent his anger over the odor of french fries and bad coffee, like burnt acorns.

"I am going to give Walter the statue you couldn't retrieve through a week of torture," I said. "In return, you are going to convince Walter to give me Nick's life and not hold me responsible for Pam's death. You will leave *all* of us alone and not seek any retaliation. Ever." My eyebrows rose. "You do, and I'll come right back up here and take it back."

Brett's faint wrinkles bunched. "Why should I do that?" he asked.

"Because it was your idea," I said lightly. "And it's the only thing that's going to keep you alive. As soon as my ride gets here, I'm outta here." I took a slow breath, praying I wasn't making a mistake. "I'm going to call Walter and tell him where you are and congratulate him on having such a wonderful second in command who convinced me to give you the statue. There will be someone watching you. If Walter accepts my terms, he takes you and walks away. If not, he can leave you cuffed to the table, and you become Jenks's responsibility."

Jenks straightened and started to grin.

"The way I figure it," I said, looking through the huge plate-glass windows at nothing, "your alpha is one pissed puppy at you for having not only letting us slip through your fingers, but then being careless enough to get taken and putting him in this awkward position."

I leaned close enough that my words were a palpable sensation of my will against his face. "If you can't convince him that we're enough of a threat that he should accept my terms and back off for thirty-six hours *and* that because of your stellar negotiating skills that I will give it to *you and you alone,* he will have no reason to keep your hide attached to your soul. He's going to kill you unless you can redeem yourself. Not right away, but he'll do it. A slow slide in the hierarchy, giving everyone a shot at you on your way down. So I think a thank-you to me is in order for giving you a surefire way back into his good graces."

Brett's brown eyes were empty, again telling me he was in big trouble. "I suggest," I said, seeing Ivy and Nick pull up in the van, "that you work really hard to get Walter to see things my way. Unless you give him the focus, you'll be an ongoing reminder of *his* mistake of sending you against a superior foe without the proper understanding of what you were facing. We might look like incompetent flakes, but we've survived demons." Shaking inside, I leaned away. "I'm giving you a chance to save your skin. Take it."

The Were's eyes followed mine to the van. "Ma'am," he said slowly. "You are one hell of a negotiator."

I smiled, and Jenks and I both rose before Ivy could come in. "Thirty-six hours," I said, picking up my tea. I tried to look confident and in control, but I doubted I managed it.

Brett cocked his head. "You're not going to give it to me. You're stalling for time."

Jenks took my elbow before I fell over, and I forced myself not to show my angst. "Maybe, but he's going to kill you all the same." I arched my eyebrows and tried to look tough. "What do you owe Walter, anyway?"

The Were dropped his eyes. I turned aside, shaking; he had acknowledged me as his superior. Damn. "God help me, Jenks," I whispered as I tottered to the door. "I hope he does it."

"He will." Jenks glanced over his shoulder at Brett. "Walter will tear him apart slowly." His green eyes met mine. "That was slick. Where did you learn so much about Weres?"

"If you're beaten up by them twice in one week, you start to pick things up," I said, leaning heavily on him.

Jenks was quiet, then, "You want me to have Ivy call her vampire friend?"

Nodding, I dropped my cup in the trash on the way out. I felt as if a noose was closing even tighter, but I didn't see any other options. Already my mind was making a list: call Ceri for the recipes I wanted that I didn't already have, check the yellow pages for a spell shop that carried raw materials. Somewhere I'd have to sleep and come up with a plan.

Maybe, I thought as Jenks opened the door for me and I stepped out into the late afternoon sun, *I'd get lucky and dream of one.*

Twenty-seven

It was one of the oddest charm outlets I had ever been in, nothing like the richly scented earth magic shops I usually frequented, being brightly lit against the dark and spacious, and having a small spot up front to sit in cushy chairs and sip the marvelous coffee the owner made. The shelves were glass, and ley line paraphernalia was arranged like knickknacks. Jenks would have had an orgasm of delight.

There were only a small section of earth magic charms, and the traditional redwood scent was largely overpowered by the aroma of ginger coming from the proprietor's coffeemaker. I felt strangely out of place, thinking the banners with dragons and white-bearded wizards next to the crucibles made everything look silly. An earth witch would have sneered at most of the ritual stuff in there, but maybe that's what ley line magic used. Something was off with the merchandise, though. It didn't smell right. Literally.

Ivy was halfway across the store with my basket of goodies after I snarled at her that I was fine and to stop hovering. Now I was sorry, but she had been acting weird since picking Jenks and me up at the mall—depressed almost, avoiding me but always near—and it was getting on my nerves. It didn't help that I was feeling vulnerable, my knees shaky from blood loss again now that Jenks's street-grade Brimstone had worked itself out.

I had found the shop in the yellow pages, and after I showered and stuffed myself on an entire box of macaroni and cheese, Ivy drove me over. She'd insisted, saying the Weres would know the moment I put my toe on the street. They had, and we'd been followed by two street racers glowing blue and green neon from underneath. It was worrisome, but between the thirty-six hour truce, my magic, and Ivy's presence, they'd probably leave us alone.

As I hoped, Walter had backed off. Jax had said the trio of Weres in fatigues who picked Brett up was rough, but the lie that Brett convinced me to release the statue to him alone had kept him alive. I don't know why I cared. I really didn't.

I think Walter was using the time as I was: fortifying defenses and getting everyone in place for a last attack if I reneged on our arrangement. I was, but if I did it right, he'd never guess it had been my intent from moment one. The packs could not have the focus. The thing was demon crafted, and any power gained from it was artificial and would ultimately lead to their damnation, dragging most of Inderland along with them, probably.

My phone was to my ear while I shopped with Ceri, five hundred miles away and standing in my kitchen with Kisten. Ivy had asked him to watch the church and field the calls, and I didn't want to know what my kitchen looked like with nothing between it and pixy chaos but a vampire. Ceri was off checking some point of charm, and I could hear Kisten talking to Jenks's kids. The muted familiar sounds of home were both comforting and depressing.

I picked up a large smoked bottle of generic fixative I could use for the demon transference curse, blanching when I saw the price. *Holy crap.* Maybe I could get away with the smaller bottle. I turned the smoked bottle over in my hand and squinted at the liquid. It was supposed to have camphor in it, but all I smelled was lavender. I didn't like buying premade stuff, but I was pressed for time.

Seeing me holding the bottle, Ivy started my way to put it in the basket, halting when I returned it to the shelf and frowned. God help her, but I wasn't that weak. I could hold a stinking bottle of fixative without a Brimstone boost.

I had fixed my own lunch today, after the sandwich Ivy gave me made my fingertips tingle. I don't know how she managed to slip Brimstone into it without me realizing, but I was still mad from the two of them dosing me up without my knowledge, even if the high from Jenks's street-grade Brimstone had made the difference in where I was sleeping tonight.

Picking up the smaller bottle of fixative, I sighed, feeling my knees shake. Maybe I should just accept the Brimstone Ivy kept pushing on me and let it go. I was tired from simply walking around. Ivy wouldn't tell me how much blood she'd taken, and Jenks was no help, seeing as he thought a bleeding hangnail was reason for panic.

Shades of gray, I thought, knowing I was slipping into places I had vowed I'd never go. Damn it, I used to be able to see black and white, but things got fuzzy right about the time I found my last I.S. paycheck cursed.

My gaze drifted to the window, black with night and acting like a mirror. Seeing my reflection, I adjusted the collar of my little red jacket. It went great with the black STAFF shirt from Takata's last concert. Thanks to my last pain amulet, nothing hurt, but looking at my slumped stance, I decided I didn't look tired, I looked sick. My gut clenched when I realized I looked like a vampire's shadow, well-dressed, thin, sophisticated—and ill.

Pulse hammering, I turned away. *No more Brimstone,* I thought. *Ever. There is black. There is white. Gray is a cowardly excuse to mix our wants with our needs.* But I wasn't sure I could believe it anymore as I stood in a charm shop buying materials to twist a black curse. *Just this once,* I thought. *Just this once, and never again.*

Phone still tucked to my ear, I set the fixative down. I would have hung up and called her back later, but I was enjoying hearing the sounds of normalcy, soft and distant, five hundred miles away. It seemed farther. Relaxing, I reached for an elaborately inlaid wooden box. It was beautiful, and curiosity and a love for fine workmanship prompted me to open it to find it held magnetic chalk. It was ungodly expensive, and its presence solidified that there was a population of practicing ley line witches nearby.

I abruptly realized the proprietor was watching me over her coffee mug, and I intentionally kept fiddling with the chalk, inspecting the seals as if I was considering buying it. I hated it when they watched me as though I might steal something. Like the illegal hex above the door that would give you zits wasn't enough of a deterrent?

Technically a black spell, I mused. So why didn't I turn her in?

"Magnetic chalk?" Ivy said from my elbow, and I jumped, almost dropping the phone between my ear and my shoulder.

"I don't need it," I said, trying to cover my surprise. "Especially in a box like that. Salt works just as well, and you only have to vacuum when you're done."

Reluctantly I let my fingers slip from the beautifully crafted container. It was dovetailed, the only metal on it the hinges, latch, and reinforced corners of black gold. Once the chalk was gone, it would make an excellent place to store anything that needed extra precautions. It was the nicest thing in the shop, in my opinion.

My eyebrows rose at the package of herbs in the basket that I hadn't put there. "Is that catnip?" I asked, seeing the cellophane printed with little black footprints.

"I thought Rex might leave Jax alone if she had something else to do." Brown eyes showing embarrassment, she dropped a step away. "You okay? Do you want to sit down?"

It was the third time she'd asked since leaving the motel, and I stiffened. "I'm fine," I said. *Liar,* I thought. I was tired, weary in heart and body.

The soft clatter of the phone being picked up rustled in my ear. "Ceri," I said, before she could say anything. "Just how much fixative do I need for the transference curse?"

The sound of the pixies shrieking diminished, and I guessed Ceri had moved into the living room. "A thumb drop," she said, and I gratefully took up the smaller bottle.

"My thumb?" I complained. "What is that, about a tea-spoon? Why can't they use normal measurements?"

"It's a very old curse," Ceri snapped. "They didn't have teaspoons back then."

"Sorry," I apologized, my eyes meeting Ivy's as I placed the fixative into the basket. Ceri was one of the nicest, most giving people I knew, but she had a temper.

"Do you have a pencil?" the elf in hiding said politely, but I could hear her annoyance at my impertinence. "I want you to write this down. I know you have the inertia dampening curse in one of the books with you, but I don't want you to translate the Latin wrong."

I glanced at the proprietor—who was starting to eye Ivy skulking about—and turned my back on her. "Maybe you could give me just the ingredients right now." The clutter in my basket was odd enough already. If the proprietor was worth her salt, she'd be able to tell I was making a disguise charm. The only difference between my legal disguise charms and the illegal doppelganger spells was a point of law, a few extra steps, and a cellular sample of the person to copy. I didn't think she'd be able to tell I was also going to twist a demon curse to move the power from the statue to something else. What she would make of the ingredients for the inertia damping demon curse was anyone's guess. Ceri said it was a joke curse, but it would work.

Joke curse, I thought sourly. It was still black. If I was caught, I'd be labeled a black witch and magically castrated. I wasn't fooling myself that this was anything other than wrong. No "saving the world" crap. It was wrong.

Just this once, echoed in my thoughts, and I frowned, thinking of Nick. Telling Al about me had probably started with just one harmless piece of information.

Ceri sighed. "All you need for the joke curse is dust from inside a clock and black candles made from the fat of the un-born. The rest is incantation and ritual."

"The unborn?" I said in a horrified, hushed whisper. "Ceri, you said it wasn't that bad."

"The fat of an unborn pig," she reiterated, sounding angry. "Honestly, Rachel."

My brow furrowed. Okay, it was a fetal pig, the same thing biology students dissect, but it sounded close to the slaughtering-goats-in-your-basement kind of magic. The transference curse looked harmless apart from the black it would put on my soul, and the disguise charm was white— illegal, but white. The inertia-dampening curse was the worst of the lot—and it was the one that would keep Jenks alive—a joke curse. *Just this once.*

I was so stupid.

Stomach roiling, my thoughts flicked to Trent and his illegal labs, which saved people so he could blackmail them into seeing things his way. He, at least, didn't pretend to be anything other than what he was. Things had been a lot easier when I didn't have to think. But what was I supposed to do? Walk away and let the world fall apart? Telling the I.S. would make matters worse, and giving the statue to the FIB was a joke.

Angry and sick inside, I sidestepped Ivy to get to the candles. I'd already been there to pick out my colored candles for the transference curse. Behind the carved castles and colorful "dragon eggs" were the real goods, arranged by color and size, branded at the bottom with either what the fat had been rendered from or where they had first been lit. The woman's selection was surprisingly good, but why they were hidden behind such crap was beyond me.

"Taper or barrel?" I asked Ceri, crouching to reach one with PIG scratched on it. You can't light a candle in a pig, so it was a good bet that's where the fat had come from. I'd never been in a ley line charm shop other than the university's, and that didn't count since they only carried what the classes needed. Maybe there was a spell that used "dragon eggs," but I thought they looked lame.

"Doesn't matter," Ceri answered, and with the smallest taper in hand, I turned and rose, almost running into Ivy. She winced and backed up.

"I'm fine," I muttered, setting the candle in the basket. "Did you see any packaged dust?"

Ivy shook her head, the tips of her black hair shifting about the bottom of her ears. There was a rack of "pixy dust" by the register that was just glitter. Jenks would laugh his ass off. Maybe the real stuff was behind it, like the candles.

"You sound tired, Rachel," Ceri said, question high in her voice as I moved to the rack.

"I'm fine." Ceri said nothing, and I added, "It's stress." *Just this once.*

"I want you to talk to Kisten," she said firmly, as if she was doing me a favor.

Oh God. Kisten. What would he say if he knew Ivy had bitten me? "I told you so," or maybe "My turn"? "Ceri," I protested, but it was too late, and as Ivy fingered a display of amber bottles that were good to store oil-based potions in, Kisten's masculine voice came to me.

"Rachel . . . How's my girl?"

I blinked rapidly, the threatened tears shocking me. *Where had they come from?* "Ah, I'm fine," I said, missing him terribly. Bad things had happened, and I'd been carrying the pain since. I needed to talk to him, but not standing in a charm shop with Ivy listening.

Ivy had stiffened at the sudden emotion in my voice, and I turned my back on her, wondering if I should tell her that the glass container shaped like a full moon in her grip was generally used to store aphrodisiac potions.

"Good," he said, his voice going right through me. "Can I talk to Ivy?"

Surprised, I turned to her, but she had heard him and shook her head. "Uh . . ." I stammered, wondering if she was afraid of what he'd say to her if he knew what had happened. We were both chickenshit, but we would be chickenshit together.

"Ivy, I know you can hear me," Kisten said loudly. "You have a big problem waiting for you when you get back from your *vacation.* Everyone knows you're out of the city. You're his scion, not me. I can't go up against even the youngest undead. The only thing keeping a lid on this is that most of them are my patrons and they know if they act up, I'll ban them."

Ivy walked off, her boots loud against the hardwood floor. Her passive response surprised me. Something was really bothering her.

"She walked away," I said, feeling guilty Ivy had come up there to help me.

Kisten's sigh was heavy. "Will you tell her that there was a riot in the mall downtown last night? It was at four in the morning so it was mostly living vampires, thank God, and some Weres. The I.S. handled it, but it's going to get worse. I don't want a new master vampire in the city, and neither does anyone else."

I stood before the rack of pixy dust and rifled through the hanging vials, reading the tiny cards attached to each. If Piscary lost control of Cincinnati, Trent would have free rein. But I didn't think it was a power play by the undead vampires *or* Trent. It was more likely that the riot had been the Mackinaw Weres looking for me. No wonder Walter had agreed to a thirty-six-hour truce. He had to get his pack together.

Tired, I let the vials slip through my fingers. "I'm sorry, Kisten. We have a couple of days before we can call this done. It depends on how fast I can do the prep work."

He silently took that in, and I could hear Ceri singing with the pixies in the background. "Can I help?" he asked, and my throat tightened at the concern in his voice, even as I heard his reluctance to leave Cincinnati. But there wasn't anything he could do. It would be over one way or the other by tomorrow night.

"No," I said softly. "But if we don't call you by tomorrow midnight, we're in trouble."

"And I'll fly up there in two hours," he assured me. "Are you sure there's nothing I can do? Call someone? Anything?"

Shaking my head, I fingered a book on how to knot love charms from hair. These things were illegal. Small towns have very little in the way of policing witches, but then I saw that it was a fake, a novelty item. "We have it okay," I said. "Will you feed Mr. Fish for me?"

"Sure. Ivy told me."

"He only needs four grains," I rushed. "Any more and you'll kill him."

"Don't worry about it. I've had fish before."

"And stay out of my room," I added.

He started making a fake radio hiss, whistling and popping. "Rachel? The connection is going bad," he said, laughing. "I think I'm losing you."

A smile, the first in days, touched me. "I love you too," I said, and he stopped.

There was a suspicious hesitation. "Are you okay?" he asked.

Worry slid through me. He was starting to pay attention. "Why?" I said, realizing my hand had gone up to cover my neck. "Um, yeah," I reiterated, thinking it had sounded guilty. "I'm just stressed. Nick . . ." I hesitated. I couldn't tell him Nick had been playing kiss-and-tell. It was embarrassing to have been that stupid. "I told Nick to kiss off, and it bothered me," I said. *Not really a lie. Not really.*

He was silent, then, "Okay. Can I talk to Ivy?"

Relieved, I exhaled into the mike. "Sure."

I handed the phone to Ivy—who had come up behind me to listen, presumably—but she closed the top and handed it back. "He can handle it a few days more," she said, then turned to the counter. "Do you have everything? It's getting late."

Tension edged her voice. She was trying to hide her mood, but not doing very well. Concerned, I took the basket from her. "Everything but the dust. Maybe she has some behind the counter. God, I'm tired," I finished without thinking. Ivy didn't say anything, and I put the basket on the counter, eyeing the aphrodisiac bottle Ivy set by her catnip.

"What?" Ivy said, seeing me look at it.

"Nothing. Why don't you put your stuff in with mine?"

She shook her head. "I'm going to get something else too, but thanks."

The woman behind the counter set her coffee on her stained hot plate, her fingers reaching to take my things out of the basket. "Will that be all then, ladies?" she asked, hiding her wariness of Ivy behind her professionalism.

"You don't happen to have clock dust?" I asked, feeling it was a lost cause.

Immediately she lost her tinge of her nervousness. "From stopped clocks? Sure enough I do. How much do you need?"

"Thank the Turn," I said, leaning against the counter as my muscles started to feel the weight of standing too long. "I didn't want to have to go to Art Van and dust their floor samples. I just need a, uh, pinch."

Pinch, dash, smidgen. Yeah, real exact measurements. Ley line magic sucked.

The woman glanced at the front door. "Be but a sec," she said, then, with the fixative in her hand, she went into a back room. I stared at Ivy.

"She took my stuff," I said, bewildered.

Ivy shrugged. "Maybe she thinks you're going to run out the door with it."

It seemed like forever, but the woman came back, her loud steps warning us. "Here you go," she said, carefully setting a tiny black envelope down with the fixative. The bottle now had a string tag around it with an expiration date. I picked it up, feeling a different weight to it.

"This isn't the same bottle," I said suspiciously, and the woman smiled.

"That's the real product," she explained. "There aren't enough witches up here to support a charm shop, so I mix tourist trinkets with the real stuff. Why sell real fixative to a fudgie when they're just going to put it on a shelf and pretend they know what to do with it?"

I nodded, now realizing what had been bothering me. "It's all fake? None of it is real?"

"Most of it's real," she said, her ringed fingers punching the register with a stiff firmness. "But not the rare items." She looked at my pile. "Let me see, you're making an earth

magic disguise charm, a ley line inertia joke spell, and . . ."
She hesitated. "What on earth are you going to use the fixative for? I don't sell much of that."

"I'm fixing something," I said guardedly. Crap, what if the Weres found out? They might realize I was going to move the power of the artifact before we blew it up. If I asked her to keep quiet about it, she would likely blab it all over the place. "It's for a joke," I added.

Her eyes flicked to Ivy and she grinned. "Mum's the word," she said. "Is it for that gorgeous hunk of man with you? Saints preserve us, he's beautiful. I'd love to trick him."

She laughed, and I managed a weak smile. Did the entire city know Jenks? Ivy rocked back a step in irritation, and the woman finished wrapping my black candle in matching tissue paper and bundled everything into a paper sack. Still smiling, she totaled it up.

"It'll be $85.33 with tax," she said, clearly satisfied.

I stifled my sigh and swung my shoulder bag forward to get my wallet. This was why I had a witch's garden—and a clan of pixies to maintain it. Not only was ley line magic stupid, but it was expensive if you didn't render your own fetal pigs for making candles. *Just this once.*

Ivy pushed her two things forward, and looking the proprietor in the eye, said clearly, "Just put it on my bill. I need three ounces of Special K. Medicinal grade, please."

My lips parted and I flushed. Special K? That was Cincy slang for Brimstone, K of course said to stand for Kalamack.

But the woman hesitated only briefly. "Not from the I.S., are you?" she asked warily.

"Not anymore," Ivy muttered, and flustered, I turned my back on them. Ivy saw nothing wrong with an illegal drug that had kept vampire society healthy and intact for untold years, but buying in front of me made me feel all warm and fuzzy.

"Ivy," I protested when the woman disappeared into the back room again. "Trent's?"

Ivy gave me a sidelong glance, eyebrows high. "It's the

only brand I'll buy. And I need to restock my cache. You used it all."

"I'm not taking any more," I hissed, then straightened when the woman returned, holding a palm-sized package wrapped in masking tape.

"Medicinal?" she said, glancing at the aphrodisiac bottle. "You store it in that, lucky duck, and you'll be the one that's going to need medical attention."

Ivy's face blanked in surprise, and I dragged my bag from the counter, ready to flee. "It's an aphrodisiac bottle," I said. "Don't pick things up unless you know what they are—Alexia."

Ivy looked as guiltless as a puppy as she dropped the package into her open purse.

The woman smiled at us, and Ivy counted out thirteen hundred-dollar bills and coolly handed them over.

I blinked. Holy shit. Kalamack's medicinal stuff was five times as expensive as the street variety.

"Keep the change," Ivy said, taking my elbow and moving me to the door.

Twelve hundred dollars? I had sucked down Twelve hundred dollars of drugs in less than twenty-four hours? And that wasn't counting Jenks's contribution. "I don't feel well," I said, putting a hand to my stomach.

"You just need some air."

Ivy guided me across the store and took my bag from me. There was the jingle of the door, and a flush of cool air. It was dark and cold on the street, matching my mood. Behind us came the sliding sound of an oiled lock, and the CLOSED sign flickered on. The store's posted hours were from noon to midnight, but after a sale like that, you deserved to go home early.

Fumbling, I put a hand on the bench under a blue and white trolley-stop sign and sat down. I didn't want to chance spewing in Kisten's Corvette. It was the only thing we could drive around town in now that the truck had been seen fleeing a crash and neither Ivy nor I wanted to get in the van.

Shit. My roommates were turning me into a Brimstone addict.

Ivy gracefully folded herself to sit beside me, all the while scanning the street. "Medicinal grade is processed six times," she said, "to pull out the endorphin stimulants, hallucinogenic compounds, and most of the neuron stimulators, to leave only the metabolism upper. Technically speaking, the chemical structure is so different, it's not Brimstone."

"That's not helping," I said, putting my head between my knees. There was gum stuck to the sidewalk, and I nudged it with my toe, finding it hardened to an immovable lump from the cold. *Breathe: one, two, three. Exhale: one, two, three, four.*

"Then how about if you hadn't taken it, you'd be laying in bed needing Jenks's help to use the bathroom?"

I pulled my head up and took a breath. "That helps. But I'm still not taking any more."

She gave me a short-lived close-lipped smile, and I watched her face go as empty as the dark street. I didn't want to get up yet. I was tired, and it was the first time we had been together alone since—since the bite. Returning to the motel room with Jenks, Jax, the kitten, and Nick to make my peachy-keen illegal charms and black curses had all the appeal of eating cold lima beans.

A station wagon passed us, the muffler spewing a blue smoke that would have earned the driver a ticket in Cincinnati. I was cold, and I hunched into my coat. It was only eleven-thirty, but it looked like four in the morning. "You okay?" Ivy said, obviously having seen me shiver.

"Cold," I said, feeling like a hypochondriac.

Ivy crossed her legs at her knees. "Sorry," she whispered.

I lifted my gaze, finding her expression lost in the shadow from the streetlight behind her. "It's not your fault I didn't bring my winter coat."

"For biting you," she said, her voice low. Her attention touched upon my stitches, then dropped to the pavement.

Surprised, I scrambled to put my thoughts in order. I'd

thought I was going to be the one to bring this up. Our pattern had always been: Ivy does something to scare me, Ivy tells me what I did wrong, I promise Ivy not to do it, we never bring it up again. Now she wanted to talk?

"Well, I'm not," I finally said.

Ivy's head came up. Shock shone from her dark eyes, raw and unhidden. "You said on the phone that you'd done some thinking," she stammered. "That you were going to make smarter decisions. You're leaving the firm, aren't you? As soon as this run is over?"

Suddenly I saw her depression in an entirely new light, and I almost laughed in relief for my misunderstanding. "I'm not leaving the firm!" I said. "I meant smarter decisions on who I trusted. I don't want to leave. I want to try to find a blood balance with you."

Ivy's lips parted. Turned as she was to me, the streetlight glinted on her perfect teeth, and then she snapped her mouth shut.

"Surprise," I said weakly, my pulse fast. This was the scariest thing I'd done in a while—including standing down three Were packs.

For six heartbeats Ivy stared at me. Then she shook her head. "No," she said firmly, resettling herself to face forward and put herself in shadow. "You don't understand. I lost control. If Jenks hadn't interfered, I would have killed you. Jenks is right. I'm a danger to everyone I care about. You have no idea how hard it is to find and maintain a blood relationship. Especially if I leave you unbound." Her voice was calm but I could hear panic in it. "And I'm by *God* not going to bind you to me to make it easier. If I do, everything would be what *I* want, not what *we* want."

I thought of Jenks's warning and had a doubt, then remembered Kisten telling me of her past and felt a stab of fear. But the memory of her heavy sobs as she lay crumpled on the pavement filled me, the despair in her eyes when Jenks said she ruined everything she cared about. No, he had said she ruined everything she loved. And seeing that same despair hiding in her fierce words, determination filled me. I couldn't let her believe that.

"You said I needed to trust the right people," I said softly. Heart pounding, I hesitated. "I trust you."

Ivy threw her hands in the air in exasperation and turned to face me. "God, Rachel, I could have killed you! As in dead! You know what that means? Dead? I do!"

My own ire flared, and I sat up. "Yeah? Well . . . I can be a little more savvy," I said belligerently. "I can take some responsibility for keeping things under control, be a little more aware of what's going on and not let you lose yourself . . . like that. We'll do better next time."

"There isn't going to *be* a next time." Stoic and unmoving, Ivy sat deathly still. The streetlight glinted on her short hair, and she stared at the shadowy pavement, intermittently lit from yellow bulbs. Abruptly she turned to look at me. "You say you want to find a blood balance, but you just refused to take more Brimstone. You can't have your cake and eat it too, witch. You want the blood ecstasy? You need the Brimstone to stay alive."

She thought this was about the ecstasy? Insulted she thought me that shallow, my lips pressed together. "This isn't about you being Ms. Good Feeling and filling me with that . . . that euphoria," I said angrily. "I can get that from any vamp on the riverfront. This is about me being your friend!"

Emotion poured over her face. "You made it very clear you don't want to be that kind of a friend!" she said loudly. "And if you aren't, then there's no way I can do this! I tried to fix myself, but I can't. The only way I can keep from killing people now is if I shackle the hunger with love, damn it! And you don't want me to touch you that way!"

I'd never seen her show her feelings like this, but I wasn't going to back down—even though she was starting to scare me. "Oh, get off it, Ivy," I said, sliding a few inches from her. "It's obvious from yesterday that you can share blood without sleeping with someone." She gaped at me, and I flushed. "Okay, I admit it—it didn't turn out all that well, but God! It kind of surprised both of us. We just need to go slow. You don't have to have sex to find a feeling of closeness and understanding. Lord knows I feel that way about you. Use that to shackle your hunger." My face flushed hot in the cool night air. "Isn't that what love is?"

She continued to look at me, hiding her emotions again behind her black eyes.

"So you almost killed me," I said. "I let you do it! The point is, I saw you. For one instant you were the person you want to be, strong and comfortable with who she is and what she needs, with no guilt and at peace with herself!"

Ivy went pale in the streetlight. Terrified. Embarrassed, I looked away to give her time to cover her raw emotions.

"I liked being able to put you there," I said softly. "It's a hell of a good feeling. Better than the euphoria. I want to put you there again. I . . . liked seeing you like that."

Ivy stared at me, her hope so fragile, it hurt to see it. There was a sheen of moisture to her eyes, and she didn't say anything, just sat with a stiff, frightened posture.

"I don't know if I can do this," I admitted, talking because she wasn't. "But I don't want to pretend it didn't happen. Can we just agree that it did and play it day by day?"

Taking a breath, Ivy broke out of her stance. "It happened," she said, voice shaking. "It's not going to happen again." I leaned forward to protest, but she interrupted me with a quick, "Why didn't you use your magic to stop me?"

Surprised, I sat back. "I—I didn't want to hurt you."

She blinked fast, and I knew she was trying not to cry. "You trusted that I wouldn't kill you, even by accident?" she asked. Her perfect face was again blank of emotion, but I knew it was the only way she had to protect herself.

Remembering what Kisten had once said about living vampires craving trust nearly as much as they craved blood, I nodded. But the memory was followed by fear. He also said Piscary had warped her into something capable of mindlessly killing what she loved so he could lap up her despair when she came to him, shamed and broken. But she was not that same person. Not anymore. "I trusted you," I whispered. "I still do."

A truck was approaching, the headlights shining on her face to show a shiny track of moisture. "That's why we can't do this, Rachel," she said, and I was afraid that Piscary might own her still.

The approaching panel truck drove past too slowly. A sliver of warning brought me still, and I watched it without appearing to, taking the cold night air smelling of diesel fuel deep into me. The truck braked too long and was hesitant when it made the turn.

"Yes, I saw it," Ivy said when my shoes scraped the cement. "We should get back to the room. Peter will be here by sunup."

She was ending the conversation, but I wasn't going to let her go that easy. "Ivy," I said as I rose, gathering my bag from beside hers, wanting to try again. "I—"

She jerked to her feet, shocking me to silence. "Don't," she said, eyes black in the streetlight. "Just don't. I made a mistake. I just want everything to be the way it was."

But I didn't.

Twenty-eight

There was an unfamiliar car next to Nick's dented pickup when we pulled into the motel's lot. Ivy was driving, and I watched her eyes go everywhere before she turned the wheel and stopped in an open spot. It was a black BMW with a rental sticker. At least it appeared black; it was hard to tell in the streetlight. Engine still running, Ivy looked at it, her gaze giving nothing away. Thinking Walter had changed his mind, I went to get out.

"Wait," Ivy said, and I tensed.

From our room, a shaft of light spilled from a curtain being pulled aside. Nick's long face peered out, and upon seeing us, he let the fabric fall. Ivy cut the engine, the low rumble dying to leave only the memory of it echoing. "Okay," she said. "Now you can get out."

I would have gotten out even if it had been Water, but relieved, I yanked the door open and eased from the leather seats. Our cut-short conversation at the trolley stop had left me unsettled. I'd let her think all she had to do was say no and everything was settled, but she would be replaying the conversation in her head for days. And when the time was right, I was going to bring it up again. Maybe over a carton of red curry takeout.

I got our bags from the back, their soft rattle mixing with the aggressive rumble of the street-racer escort we had to the motel. "I hate plastic," Ivy said, taking the bags from me and rolling them so they quit rattling.

The door to our room opened and I squinted at the light. *So that's why Ivy always used canvas bags.* It wasn't because she was especially ecominded. They were quiet.

The light cut off as Nick slipped out and eased the door shut behind him. The street Weres in the lot across the road revved their cars, and I waved sarcastically to them. They didn't wave back, but I saw the flicker of a lighter when they lit up and settled in.

Nick looked more than a little concerned as he came to meet us, his eyes fixed on the Weres. His tall, gaunt stature still leaned slightly, and he favored his left foot. "Your vampire friends are here," he said, pulling his attention from the Weres to touch on the black BMW. "They flew in from Chicago on a puddle jumper soon as the sun was down."

My attention jerked to the motel room door and I stopped moving. *Great. I looked like warmed-up crap.* "What are they doing here already?" I asked no one in particular. "They aren't supposed to be here until almost dawn. I don't have any of my spells made up yet."

Ivy looked bothered too. "Apparently they wanted some time to settle in before sunrise," she said, running her hands down her leather pants and tugging her coat straight.

Rudely knocking Nick's shoulder, she pushed past him. I fell into place behind her, ignoring Nick trying to get my attention. Jenks had been running interference for me, telling Nick I was tired from too much spelling and the scuffle with the Weres. He didn't know Ivy and I had had a blood tryst, and though I didn't give a fig leaf what the bastard thought, I was guiltily glad that the collar of my jacket made it hard to see my tiny stitches.

Ivy walked in without preamble, dropping the bags just inside the door and moving to the three people at the table by the curtained window. They looked terribly out of place in the low-ceilinged room full of beds and our suitcases, and it would have been obvious who was in charge even if Ivy hadn't stopped before the oldest, gracefully executing a soft bow that was reminiscent of a martial arts student to her instructor. He smiled to show a slip of teeth and no warmth.

I took a slow breath. This might be a little hairy.

DeLavine was one of Chicago's higher master vampires, and he looked it, dressed in dark slacks and a linen shirt. He had trimmed and styled sand-colored hair, a youthful face, and a sparse frame that gave him an ageless look. It was probably a charm that kept him looking a late thirty-something. Most likely he was wrinkled and twisted. Vampires usually spent every last penny of their first life, using a yearly witch potion to look as young as they wanted.

His eyes were dark, showing only the slightest widening of pupils. A twinge came from my neck when his gaze traveled lightly over me in dismissal. His attention returned to Ivy, making me both relieved and ticked; he thought I was her shadow. How nice was that?

DeLavine sat like a king surrounded by his court, a glass of water on the scratched table beside him and his legs confidently crossed. Atop the back of an empty chair was a carefully folded, long cashmere coat; everyone else was still wearing theirs. He had the air of someone who had taken time out of his busy schedule to personally take his child to the doctor's office and was waiting to see how they were going to help his little boy get over the chicken pox.

Though concerned, he wasn't worried. He reminded me of Trent, but where Trent moved on logic, DeLavine clearly moved out of hunger or a forgotten sense of responsibility. Rex sat in the middle of the floor before him, head cocked as if trying to figure out what he was.

I'm right there with you, cat.

Standing behind DeLavine was a living vampire. The woman was nervous, an unusual emotion for a high-blood vampire. She was thin and graceful, which was a trick since she was kind of big on top and hippy. Her straight, unstyled long hair was graying, though she looked no older than me. If not for her worry, she would have been beautiful. Haunted-looking, her eyes constantly moved, landing on me more often than not. Clearly she wasn't comfortable with this. Her hands were on the shoulders of a second, seated vampire. *Peter?*

He was obviously ailing, sitting as if trying to pull himself straight but not quite able to manage it. His vivid blue eyes were surprising against his black hair and dark complexion. Pain showed in the tension his pleasant expression carried, and I could smell an herb that should have been prescription only but wasn't because humans didn't know it was a massive painkiller when mixed with baking powder.

His slacks and casual shirt were as expensive looking as his mentor's, but they and his coat hung on him as if he had lost a lot of weight. He seemed in full control of his faculties despite the painkiller, his gaze meeting mine with the look of someone seeing their savior.

I didn't like that. If things went as planned, I was going to kill him. *Shades of gray. Just this once. Gotta save the world and all that.*

Nick edged in behind me, moving furtively to the kitchen, where he leaned against the sink with his arms crossed, the bulb over the stove making him even more gaunt. I imagined he was trying to stay unnoticed, but no one wanted to acknowledge his existence anyway.

Between Nick and the vampires, Jenks sat cross-legged on the couch beside the artifact. I had put the ugly thing in his keeping, and he took the task seriously. He looked odd sitting like that, but the hard slant to his eyes balanced out his prissy-boy image. Ivy's sword across his knees helped too. The vampires were ignoring him. If I was lucky, they'd ignore me.

"DeLavine," Ivy said respectfully, dropping her coat on the bed and inclining her head. She had the air of a favored messenger that was to be treated well. The undead vampire lifted a hand in acknowledgment, and she turned to Peter. "Peter," she said more casually, gesturing for him to remain seated as she shook his hand.

"Ivy Tamwood," the ailing vampire said pleasantly, his

voice resonant for his narrow, disease-thin body. "I've heard much about your good works. Thank you for seeing me."

Good works? I thought, then remembered the missing-person runs that had populated her schedule during the first three months of our firm's existence.

"It's a pleasure to meet you," he continued, releasing her hand. "You can imagine the uproar you put my house in when you called." He smiled, but I saw a tinge of fear.

"Shhhh," the undead vampire admonished, sensing it and patting his knee. "It's a moment of pain. Nothing you haven't lived your entire life with." It was the first time he had spoken, and his voice carried an accent so faint it showed only in a soft lengthening of vowels.

Peter dropped his eyes, head bobbing. I thought I was going to be sick. This was wrong. I didn't want to do it. I hadn't wanted to from the first. We could find another way.

"DeLavine, Peter," Ivy said, motioning for me to come forward. "This is my partner, Rachel Morgan. It will be her spells that will make this work."

I couldn't help but notice that the woman behind them was being disregarded and didn't seem to have a problem with that. Feeling like a prize mule, I took off my cap and shambled forward, conscious of my hat-flattened hair, my faded jeans, and my STAFF T-shirt. At least it was clean.

"Pleasure to meet you, sir," I said, not offering my hand to DeLavine. No freaking way. "Peter," I added, shaking his.

He smiled to show me his teeth, his hand cold as it slipped into mine. There was a strength to his grip, but I could see the fear in his eyes. *I couldn't do this.*

"Rachel Morgan," the ailing vampire said, his gaze touching upon my neck and politely rising back to my eyes. "I'd like to talk to you about why I—"

"Rachel," DeLavine interrupted softly, and I started. "I want to see you. Come here."

My gaze jerked to Ivy and my pulse leapt. Her face was blank of emotion, and with that comfortable thought, I turned to him. When dealing with an unfamiliar vampire, it was always better to acknowledge their existence, then talk to their subordinates unless they showed an interest. *Oh God, I didn't want to be interesting.*

"So you will free my Peter of his mortal pain," he said, his voice going right to the bottom of my lungs and making it hard for me to breathe.

"Yes, sir." I looked him in the eye and fought the familiar rising pull of tingles.

He gazed back, more than a hint of testing seduction in his widening pupils. Behind me, I felt Ivy step forward, and from the corner of my sight, Jenks slowly uncrossed his legs to put his feet on the floor. Tension pulled through me, and though DeLavine's focus never moved from me, I knew he was becoming aware that I wasn't for casual use and discard, despite what I looked like.

The refined man stood in a soft rustle, and I retreated a step, common sense overpowering my desire to appear cavalier. Rex, too, got to her feet, stretching before going to twine about the vampire's feet. I forced myself to breathe, and Ivy's presence behind me imparted a feeling of security I knew was false. My legs felt questionable, and his pupils widened when he sensed it. *I'm not afraid,* I thought, lying to myself. Well, not any more than would help keep me alive.

"I know you," DeLavine said, and I steeled myself against the pheromones he was kicking out. He reached forward, and I stifled my jerk when he arranged a strand of wild hair. "Your youth distracted me. I almost didn't see since you're all but ignorant of yourself. You're Kalamack's witch."

"I'm not his. I don't work for him. Much," I protested, putting little weight behind it, then stiffened when he distinctly pushed Ivy out of the way and circled behind me. I heard her fall back, catching herself but not protesting. In the kitchen, Nick paled. Jenks stood, his sword gripped tightly. Peter looked distressed, and the woman tensed. DeLavine was aware of everyone, but focused entirely on me.

"You are a remarkable woman," the undead vampire said from behind my shoulder. There were no tingles, no hint of passion, but it was coming, I could feel it simmering under his silky voice. "And your skin . . . so perfect, not a mark from the sun. But, bless my soul," he said with a mocking slowness. "Someone . . . has bitten you."

He exhaled, and my eyes closed when a wash of bliss rose from my new wound, melting my fear like spun sugar. He was bespelling me. I knew it. I couldn't fight it. And God help me, I wanted to. All I could manage was a small sound in protest when his fingers moved the collar of my leather jacket aside.

"No," Ivy whispered, fear in her voice. My eyes opened, only to be caught by DeLavine's. He was before me now, a hand raised against Ivy behind me. Rex twined about my feet, purring. *This wasn't supposed to happen. This is* not *what was supposed to* happen!

Jenks's face was drawn tight. He had been told not to interfere, knew it would make matters worse. Beyond him, Nick was stiff with horror. I didn't think it stemmed from DeLavine. I think it was from the new stitches on my neck and what they meant. Ivy had bitten me, and my face warmed at his unvoiced accusation. He thought I had failed, that I had let my passions rule me and let Ivy take advantage of it.

My jaw clenched and my chin rose. It was none of Nick's business what I did with whom. And I hadn't given in because of passion; I had tried to understand her, or maybe myself.

But DeLavine took it as defiance and gently caressed the sore edges of my bite.

Adrenaline jerked through me. My weakened pulse tried to absorb it, and failed. I gasped when feeling raced from his soft brush against the healing wound, streaming through me, both familiar and alien since it came from an unfamiliar vampire. The difference struck a chord in me I hadn't known was there, and my vision darkened when my blood loss couldn't cope with the new demand.

Jenks moved. From the edge of my sight I saw Ivy crash into him. "Sorry," she grunted, making a mallet of her hands by covering her fist with another and slamming it into his head.

Mouth open, Nick stood in the kitchen, watching the pixy's eyes roll up and him drop like a stone, unconscious. The human backed up until he could back up no more. He thought Ivy had given me to DeLavine. What she had done was save Jenks's life, and probably everyone else's, since a pitched fight would set DeLavine off. This way, only I would die.

"Let me . . ." DeLavine whispered for me alone, and he circled with Rex trailing happily behind him, the vampire scenting everything, weighing, calculating.

My breath came in a heave, and I held it. My knees were locked to keep me upright. Ivy couldn't do a thing, and I could hear her frustration in her breathing as she forced herself to not interfere. She couldn't best DeLavine. Not without leaning on Piscary's strength, and she was out of his influence. DeLavine knew it. That we had invited him here to help Peter meant little.

"Bitten and unbound," the undead vampire said, and a shudder rippled through me. "Free for the taking. I sense two demon marks on you. I feel two bites, but only one reached your soul, and so carefully—so careful she was, a kiss so soft, but a whisper. And someone . . . someone has put their mark in your very . . . cells. Claimed by many, belonging to none. Who would look to me to get you back?"

"No one," I rasped, and his eyes fixed on mine, stilling my next word. I stood upright under his control and would have fallen if his will wasn't propping me up.

"Please," Ivy whispered, standing beside Jenks slumped on the floor. "I beg favor."

With a light interest, DeLavine touched the unscared side of my neck. "What?" he said.

"Leave her as mine." Ivy's pale face made her eyes look even blacker. "I ask this as a thank-you for helping Peter." She licked her lips and held her arms down. "Please."

DeLavine lifted his eyes from me, and I blinked, finding a thread of will returned to me. "This," the vampire said, lifting my chin with a finger, "should belong to a master, not you. Piscary has indulged you beyond reason. You're a spoiled child, Ivy, and you should be punished for stepping out of your master's influence. Taking her as mine will bother Kalamack and put me in good with Piscary."

Ivy's eyes flicked to me and away. I could almost feel her thoughts realign themselves, and my pulse hammered when her posture melted from tense to seductive.

God save us. She was going to give him what he wanted so he would leave me alone. I couldn't let her do this. I couldn't let her turn herself into filth for me. But as tingles raced through me to set my mind confused, I could only watch.

"Such a sweet sip," DeLavine said, his back to Ivy. A new glint was in his eyes, making me unsure if he was talking about Ivy or me. "A wolf in sheep's clothing, stinking of Brimstone, but still very weak," he said. "I might kill you by mistake, witch. But you'd enjoy it." He inhaled, taking my volition. Exhaling, his breath under my ear sent a jolt of desire right to my core. "Do you want this?" he breathed.

"No," I whispered. It was easy. Ivy had given me the fear to find the strength to say it.

But DeLavine was delighted. "No!" he exclaimed, his pupils wide and dilated, his lust-reddened lips curling upward. "Curiouser and curiouser." His fingers traced the line along my shoulder that I knew he wanted to send his nails, digging to cause pain and a delicious path of blood to my neck that his mouth could follow.

Eyes on mine, he smiled to show his long canines. The thought of them sinking into me pulled a shiver from the depths of my soul. I knew how it would feel, and the fear of my blood being raped from me mixed with the memory of how good it could be. I closed my eyes, starting to hyperventilate, fighting him, losing to him. DeLavine eased closer, almost touching. I could sense his need to crush my will rise higher. He didn't care about Peter. Not anymore. I was too damn interesting.

"So strong a will," he said. "I could flake your consciousness from your soul like stone."

He moved, and behind him I saw Ivy gather her resolve.

No, I pleaded silently, but her fear for me was stronger than her fear for herself. Guilt, shame, and relief kept me silent when, shifting forward with a sigh to tell him where she was, she touched DeLavine's shoulder.

I watched in horror and fascination as Ivy's long leg slipped between his from behind. She curved a sinuous arm around his chest so that her fingertips played with the base of his neck. Tilting her head, she sent her lips to mouth his ear. And while DeLavine looked at me with Ivy bringing his hunger fully awake, she whispered, "Please?"

My blood pounded as she put her teeth on his ear and tugged. "I'm fond of her. . . ." she added. "I want to keep her the way she is."

DeLavine took his eyes from me, and I felt the tears start, even as the vampire pheromones and watching them play whipped my libido high. *This was so wrong.*

Ivy flowed around him to get between us. Standing with her legs wide, she ran her hands over him between his suit coat and shirt. She threw her head back, and a laugh of delight came from her, shocking me. "I can feel your scars!" she giggled, turning it into a soft, desire-filled sound of deviltry at the end. She was Ivy, but she wasn't. Playful, sensual, and domineering, this was a side of her she hadn't wanted to show me. This was Ivy doing what she did best.

Both captivated and repulsed, I couldn't look away as she bent her lips to his neck and his eyes closed. He exhaled, his hands trembling as he grasped her wrists and held them down.

"Tonight?" Ivy whispered, loud enough for me to hear. And DeLavine opened his eyes, smiling wickedly as he met my gaze.

"Bring her."

"Alone," she countered, pulling her hands from his grip to explore his inner thigh. "What I want to do would kill her." She laughed, ending with an eager moan. The playful sound of desire turned my stomach. This was probably what she had been in those years she wouldn't talk about, and she was returning to it to keep me safe.

God, how did I get to this place where my friends sell themselves to keep me alive?

Ivy shifted, doing something I couldn't see to make DeLavine's eyes widen. Peter hissed, and I wasn't surprised to find a jealous, sullen expression on his face. The woman behind him was running her fingers over him in distraction, but it didn't appear to be helping.

"Innocence can be exhilarating," Ivy murmured. "But experience? There's a reason Piscary indulges me," she said, the syllables as certain and warm as summer rain to make my pulse quicken. "Would you like to know . . . why? Not many do."

DeLavine smiled. "Piscary will not be pleased."

"Piscary is in prison," she said, pouting. "And I'm lonely."

The pheromones they were kicking out had tingles of passion pulsing through me. I was either going to climax where I stood or vomit. Ivy had left Skimmer and followed me here to escape her past, and now she was returning to it to save my life. I was going to unwittingly kill her. I made her bite me, and now she was whoring herself to keep me safe. She thought I was going to save her, but I was going to kill her.

All but forgotten, Peter stirred. "Please, DeLavine," he said sullenly, and I despaired at the filth I was wallowing in, the system that Ivy had worked within her entire life. "She knows the spells," Peter continued. "I hurt so badly."

DeLavine let go of my will. My pulse beat wildly, and with his support ripped away, my muscles gave a massive spasm and went limp. Barely conscious, I crumpled.

"For you, Peter," I heard from above me as I worked my arms under me so I could push my face off the floor. Dizzy, I wedged myself into a seated position. The undead vampire was ignoring me, his gaze tracking the perimeter of the room. Ivy had unwrapped herself from him and was standing at the curtained window, her head bowed as she tried to bring herself down. Guilt hit me, and I took a breath that was almost a cry.

"There are a few things I want from this," DeLavine was

saying, having apparently forgotten me lying on the floor. "Peter wants his last sight to be of the setting sun."

"That can be accommodated," Ivy said softly. Her voice was still husky, and I ignored the memory of hearing it whisper in my ear. Head down, I crawled to Jenks, checking his pulse and pulling back his eyelids to see if his eyes dilated. He was okay, and I slumped against the front of the couch, content to stay on the floor. Ivy wouldn't look at me, and quite frankly, I didn't want her to. How could . . . How could I ever repay her for this?

"Accommodated?" DeLavine scooped up Rex and looked into her green eyes. The cat looked away first. "There is no accommodate. Do it."

"Yes, DeLavine." Ivy turned, and I stifled a shudder at the thinnest brown rim to her eyes. They were almost fully dilated, and just standing there breathing, she looked like she wanted to pin someone to the floor and have at it.

Peter looked ticked that Ivy was taking something from his mentor that he wanted, and Peter's future scion was frightened as she saw her future, turned into nothing more than a source of blood and memory. When Peter died, she would have a shell of the man she fell in love with. She knew it, but she wanted it all the same.

"I'm concerned about possible damage to his facial structure," DeLavine said, gently setting Rex down and going to Peter. Not a hint of his blood lust showed, but I could feel it, shimmering under his voice. "Auto crashes can be extremely disfiguring, and Peter has suffered so many indignities already."

From the floor, I watched DeLavine run a finger down Peter's jawline, the touch both possessive and distant. It was nauseating. Peter's temper eased, his manner softening.

"Yes, DeLavine," Ivy said. "The charms will minimize that."

Oh, yeah. That's why they had come to the motel. "I, uh—" I jerked when everyone's eyes fell on me. "I need a swab of Peter's mouth so I can sensitize the disguise charm to him."

Ivy's hunger was chilling. Recognizing my fear, she pushed herself into motion, going into the kitchen and my spelling supplies strewn all over creation. Nick backpedaled out of her way. Head down, she shuffled about, striding back to Peter with a cellophane-wrapped cotton swab. I would have at least watched to be sure Peter gave a gloppy enough sample, but DeLavine was moving again.

I pulled myself into a ball as he headed for me. Fingers grasping, I fumbled for Ivy's sword, pulling it awkwardly out from where Jenks had let it fall. *This was wrong, so wrong.*

DeLavine gave me a raised eyebrow glance, then dismissed me as he picked up the artifact, sitting alone and vulnerable on the bedside table. He had looked at me, but it had been different. He had seen me, calculated the risk, and dismissed me, but this time he'd looked at me as a possible threat and not just a walking sack of blood. I wondered what had changed.

"This is it?" he murmured, casually moving out of the sword's easy reach.

My fingers tightened on the hilt, but I didn't think it was the blade that had him watching me while seeming not to.

Ivy came closer, the open cellophane-wrapped swab in her grip. She seemed to have regained control, only a remnant of her runaway hunger perceptible in her subtlest movements. "It will be destroyed with Peter," she said, but DeLavine wasn't listening, focused entirely on the ugly statue perched on the tips of his fingers.

"Such a wonder," he mused aloud. "So many lives ended forever because of it. It should have been destroyed when it was unearthed, but someone got greedy—and now they're dead. I am . . . wiser than that. If I can't have it, no one will." DeLavine took the thumb of his free hand and pierced the tip of his index finger. "Peter?"

"Yes, DeLavine?"

I held my breath as a drop of blood welled. With a careful attention, the undead vampire smeared it onto the statue. A shudder passed over me as it soaked in to leave a dark stain.

"Make sure," DeLavine said softly, "that this gets destroyed." He looked at me and smiled to show his long canines.

"Yes, DeLavine."

With a confident satisfaction, DeLavine set the marked statue down. My lips curled as it seemed to me that the pain etched in the figure's face was deeper. Turning with an exaggerated slowness, the undead vampire sent his gaze across the room, landing on Nick scrunched in the corner of the kitchen. "This is repulsive," he said, and suddenly the room was. "A dirty little hole stinking of emotion. We'll stay somewhere else. Peter, we are leaving. Audrey will make the arrangements to get you where you need to be come sunset."

Audrey, I thought, glancing at the woman. So she had a name. I shifted my feet so he wouldn't step on them, and he made his casual way to the door, snagging his coat on the way. Peter slowly rose, Audrey helping him with a professional grip that wouldn't hurt her back. The ailing vampire met my eyes, clearly wanting to talk to me, but DeLavine took his other arm in a show of concern born from memory, not love, and escorted him to the door.

Ivy opened it for them, and DeLavine hesitated while Peter and Audrey continued out.

My grip tightened on the hilt, but I could do nothing when the vampire bent to whisper in Ivy's ear, his hand curving about her waist possessively. My pulse pounded as she looked at the floor. Damn it, this wasn't right. She nodded, and I felt as if I had sold her to him.

The door shut behind him, and her shoulders slumped.

Twenty-nine

"Ivy—"
  "Shut up."

I dropped the sword and pulled my knees to my chin to make room when she knelt beside Jenks. With her vampire strength, she yanked him upright to lean against the couch, giving him a shake. "Jenks!" she demanded. "Open your eyes. I didn't hit you that hard."

He didn't respond, his head lolling and blond hair falling about his angular features.

"Ivy, I'm sorry," I said, my pulse quickening in guilt. "You . . . Oh God, tell him you changed your mind. We'll figure something out."

Close beside me, Ivy gave me an unreadable look, her hands on Jenks's shoulders, her oval face empty of emotion. "I wouldn't have offered if I wasn't prepared to follow through."

"Ivy—"

"Shut up!" she shouted, startling me. "I want to do it, okay? I can't touch *anything* without killing it, so I'm going to go back to things that are *already dead!* I'm doing this for me, not you! I'm going to enjoy myself, so just *shut the hell up, Rachel!*"

Face hot, my mouth fell open. It had never occurred to me she might want to. "I . . . I thought you only shared blood with people you—"

"Yeah, I tried that, didn't I. It didn't work. If I can't have you, I may as well go back to the way I was. Shut. Up."

I shut up. I didn't know what to think. Was she saying that to make me feel less guilty, or was she serious? She had damn well looked like she knew what she was doing, wrapped around DeLavine like that. I couldn't believe she really meant it. Not after her confession only an hour old. Apparently we were both going places we didn't want to—me forward and her back. "Ivy?" I said, but she wouldn't look at me.

"Jenks," she said, spots of color showing on her cheeks. "Wake up."

His breathing quickened, and it was no surprise when his smooth features scrunched in hurt. Eyes still closed, he reached for his head. Nick had come out of the kitchen, standing to look like a fifth wheel beside the TV, arms crossed over his faded T-shirt. Rex was having a field day, purring and rubbing on everyone, clearly happy we were on her level.

"Ow," Jenks said when his fingertips found the bump, and his eyes flew open. "You hit me!" he shouted, and Ivy let go. He fell against the couch, anger in his green eyes until he saw me beside him, probably looking as bad as I felt. His gaze shot to the empty table, then searched until he found the statue. "Holy crap, what did I miss?" he said.

"Sorry." Ivy stood and offered him a hand up. "He would have killed you."

So she hit him and risked giving him a concussion? Yeah, that made sense.

His gaze went to me, and my breath caught at the fear in it. "Are you all right? Did he touch you?"

"Of course he touched me," I said, getting to my feet and wavering until I found my balance. "He's an undead vampire. They can't look without touching. They can't not touch. I'm a freaking vampire candy cane and they all want a lick."

"Damn it all to hell!" Jenks rose, touching the back of his head when it probably protested at the quick motion. "Stupid pixy. Stupid green-assed, moss-wipe, thumb up my ass pixy! You knocked me out cold, Ivy!"

"Jenks," I protested, "leave her alone." But he wasn't mad at her, he was mad at himself.

"Tagged by a whiny little vamp," he said, gesturing. "Rache, take this sword and stick it in me. Just go and stick it in me. I'm a back-drafted, crumpled-winged, dust-caked, dew-assed excuse of a backup. Worthless as a pixy condom. Taken down by my own partner. Just tape my ass shut and let me fart out my mouth."

I blinked, impressed. Rex was twining about my feet, and needing some comfort, I picked her up. Immediately she jumped to the couch and bounced to Jenks, stretching against his leg. The pixy yelped when she flexed her claws into him, and the kitten skittered under the bed.

"Look! She drew blood. Rache! Your damn orange cat scratched me. I'm bleeding!"

"Rex!" Jax shouted, coming out from behind the top of the curtain. "Dad, you scared her! Rex, are you okay?" He darted under the bed after her.

"That is so unsafe," I muttered. Tired, I hobbled to the kitchen to get away from Jenks, who had collapsed onto the bed and was holding his leg as if Rex had hit a femoral vein. I jerked to a stop before I ran into Nick. "Hi, Nick," I muttered, hitting the *k* with an excess amount of force. "Get out of my way. I have a lot to do before I kill Peter and Ivy goes on her *big date.*"

His long face worried, he took a breath to say something. I wasn't going to listen. I owed him nothing. Feeling like I was eighty years old, I shambled around him.

"I can help," he said, and I dropped into one of those nasty kitchen chairs, put my elbows on the table and slumped forward. I was tired, hungry, and ticked. I had completely lost control of my life. It wasn't a simple snag and drag anymore. No, now I had to save the world from my former boyfriend and my roommate from herself. *What the hell. Why not?*

Ivy had gotten my bags from where she dropped them by the front door. Silent and clearly embarrassed, she set them on the table, making a show of putting Peter's swab before me. Jenks had apparently decided he wasn't bleeding to death, and with his very lack of movement, pulled my attention to him.

Standing, he first looked at the artifact, then flicked his gaze at Nick. I nodded, understanding. With a casual slowness, Jenks picked up the artifact and limped forward. My eyes were on Nick from around the curtain my fallen curls made.

My stomach caved in when Nick watched Jenks without appearing to. He wanted it. He still wanted to snatch it from us and sell it to the highest bidder, even if it would mean I'd have to go into hiding to keep the Weres from tracking me down and killing me for it. Whether he would or not was still unanswered, but he was considering it. *Son of a bitch.*

The vamp-bloodied artifact was set thumping down in front of me, and Jenks pulled the bags closer to indulge his pixy curiosity. "Catnip?" he said, pulling it out and opening it.

"It's for Rex," Ivy volunteered, suddenly sounding shy, of all things.

A grin flashed over Jenks, and he made a soft trill of a whistle. Immediately Jax buzzed out from under the bed. "Catnip!" the small pixy shouted, grabbing a handful and darting away.

"Oh, hey! Fudge!" Jenks exclaimed, finding the half-pound box I had bought to replace what he'd lost. "Is this mine?" he asked, green eyes alight.

I nodded, trying to stifle my anger at Nick. Jenks enthusiastically leaned against the counter and opened the box. Bypassing the plastic knife, he broke off about a third of it and took a huge bite. Ivy watched, appalled, and I shrugged. His mouth moving as he hummed, Jenks finished unpacking the sacks. I was half dead, Ivy was whoring herself to keep me safe, but Jenks was okay as long as he had chocolate.

It was getting tight in the tiny kitchen, but I didn't want either of them to leave. I felt cold and vulnerable, and the closeness was helping me distance myself from the play DeLavine had made for me. Inside I was shaking for what Ivy was doing for me—what she was falling back into—and if they left, it would start to show in my fingers.

"Rachel?" Nick said from the outskirts. "Can I help?"

Ivy bristled, but I stretched across the table and handed him a swab. "I need a sample," I said. "It's an illegal charm, but I didn't think you'd mind."

Face tight with frustration, he took it, turning away when he ran the cotton around the inside of his mouth. I remembered what DeLavine had said about so many people having marked me and squelched a feeling of shame. I didn't belong to anyone. But seeing Nick unable to enter the comfort I had found among my friends, I felt my Inderlander roots hard and strong.

Nick didn't understand. He never would. I'd been stupid thinking I could find anything lasting with him, and he had proved it by having no problem selling slivers of me to Al.

I wouldn't look at him when Nick handed me the swab, safely back in its cellophane wrapper. He moved as if to speak and I blurted to Ivy, "Piscary won't mind you helping Peter, will he?" Eyes down, I wrote Nick's name on the packet with a squeaky, big black marker.

"No." The sound of water trickling into the coffeemaker blurred her voice. "Piscary doesn't care one way or the other. Peter isn't important to him. To anyone. To anyone but his scion, anyway. It's likely that he'll simply fade from DeLavine's awareness when he's distracted by more exciting things."

Like you? I thought, but I didn't say it aloud.

Ivy turned, her black hair swinging to show her earrings. "I'm making coffee," she said. "Do you want some?"

Not if it was laced with Brimstone. Crap on toast, I was tired. "Please," I said, feeling Nick's gaze heavy on me.

"Jenks?" she offered, getting a tiny hotel mug down from the bare cupboard.

Jenks looked appraisingly into the box of fudge, hesitating before he closed it and set it aside. "No thanks," he said, starting to mess with my spelling supplies.

"Rachel," Nick tried again. "Can I sketch a pentagram for you or something?"

Ivy's head came up, and I moved my fingers to tell her I could handle it. "No," I said shortly, pulling my demon book closer and opening it up. My eyes lifted to the artifact, wondering if Nick had had the opportunity to switch it out with a fake, but I didn't think so. And there couldn't be two such ugly things.

"Ray-ray—" Nick tried again, and Ivy slammed the cupboard.

"What the hell do you want?" she said virulently, brown eyes fixed on him.

"I want to help Rachel," he shot back, stiff and a little afraid.

Jenks snorted, crumpling up the empty bag and throwing it away. "You can help Rachel by dropping dead."

"That's still an option," said Ivy.

I didn't have time or the energy to deal with this. "I need quiet," I said, feeling my blood pressure rise. "That's all I need. That's it. Just quiet."

Nick stepped back, his arms crossing over his faded shirt to make him look alone. "Okay. I'll . . ." He hesitated, gaze flicking to Ivy and Jenks beside me, taking up all the room so he couldn't come in. His held breath slowly escaped him, and not having finished his thought, he walked away, his movements full of frustration. Slumping into the chair Peter had been sitting in, he stretched his long legs out and ran his hand through his hair, staring at nothing.

I would not feel bad for him. He had sold me out. The only reason I hadn't walked off from this was because the Weres would hound me forever if they didn't see the thing destroyed, and for that I needed Nick. And I needed him cooperative.

Jenks pulled a chair from under the kitchen table and sat beside me. I blinked in surprise when I realized he had correctly put everything into three piles. "Do you need any help?" he asked, and Ivy snickered.

"Help from a pixy?" she scoffed, and Jenks bristled.

"Actually," I said before he could start swearing at her, "could you get Nick out of here?" I didn't want him to see the transference curse. God knows who he would sell it to. He couldn't invoke it without my or demon blood, but he could probably get some from Al in exchange for my underwear size.

A nasty smile curved over Jenks, but it was Ivy who put her palm aggressively on the table and said, "I'm doing it. I want to talk to him."

I looked up, wondering, but she had turned away. "Come on, crap for brains," she said, grabbing her purse in passing and heading for the door. "Rachel forgot something, and since I don't know anything about ley line magic, you're coming with me to make sure I get the right thing. Anyone else want anything while I'm out?"

Nick's face went defiant, and I simpered, knowing it was petty but unable to stop myself. "Watch out for the Weres," I said. Maybe that had been mean, but I was mean. Just ask the kids I kept chasing out of my graveyard. They could play hide-and-seek somewhere else.

"I'm out of toothbrushes," Jenks said, going to putter with the coffeemaker.

Ivy waited for Nick to shrug into the fabric coat that had been stashed in his truck. "You can use those more than once," she said, as I'd already told him, and Jenks shuddered.

Clearly aware he was being gotten rid of, Nick yanked the door open and walked out. Ivy gave me a wicked, closed-lipped smile and followed him. "I'm not afraid of you," Nick said as the door shut and my stress level dropped about six points.

"Here's your coffee," Jenks said, setting it down in front of me.

He poured me coffee? I looked at it, then up at him. "Is there Brimstone in it?"

Jenks plopped into the chair beside mine. "Ivy told me to put some in, but I thought you were well enough to decide."

My blood pressure went right back up, and remembering

my reflection in the store window, I hesitated, wondering if I was being wise or stupid. Brimstone would keep me alert for hours while I made whatever charms I needed, simultaneously increasing my blood count to pretty near normal. When I fell asleep, I'd wake refreshed, hungry, and feeling almost as well as before I was bitten. Without it, I'd be spelling while fatigued. My legs would shake every time I stood, and my sleep would end with me waking up feeling like crap.

But using black magic or illegal drugs to simply to make my life easier was a lie of convenience—one that would delude me into believing I had the right to flaunt the rules, that I lived above them. *I will not turn into Trent.*

I exhaled in a long puff. "I'm not going to do it," I said, and he nodded, his green eyes creased with worry. Though he clearly disagreed, he accepted my decision, which made me feel better immediately. I was in charge of my life. Me. *Ri-i-i-i-ight.*

"Which spell first?" Jenks asked, extending a hand for Jax when the pixy flitted to us. His wing was bent and he was leaking dust from it, but neither Jenks nor I said anything. It was nice seeing the little pixy taking an interest in what his dad thought was important—even if he was out here only because Rex had scored on him.

I tapped the pages, nervous. "You didn't lose the bone statue with your fudge, did you?"

A smile curved over Jenks. "Nope." Jax rose to the overhanging light as his dad went to his growing pile of bags beside the TV. I'd never seen a man who could outshop me, but Jenks was a master. I tried not to watch when he bent to shuffle about, striding quickly back to the kitchen with the twin boxes. He set them on the table, and pixy dust sifted over us while he opened them up. The first one was that godawful carved totem, and leaving it to stare at me, he opened the second. "Not a scratch," he said, green eyes giving away his satisfaction.

I picked up the wolf statue, feeling the weight and coldness of bone. It wasn't a bad choice for moving the Were curse to. Focus going distant, I remembered Nick's greed, and my eyes went to Jenks's totem. "Hey, uh, has Nick seen this?" I said, indicating the wolf statue.

Jenks sniffed in disgust, leaning to balance his chair on two legs. "I haven't shown it to him, but he's probably pawed through my stuff."

An idea was sifting through my mind, but I refused to feel guilty for not trusting Nick. "Hey, this is a really neat statue," I said, setting down the wolf and picking up the totem. "Matalina is going to love it. I should have gotten one. It'd look great in Mr. Fish's bowl."

Jenks let the chair fall to four legs. "Mr. Fish's bowl?" he said quizzically, and I darted a glance at the motel room door. Jenks's expression went knowing, then angry; he might be interior-decorating challenged, but he was not a stupid man. "You're worried about . . ."

I made a small noise, not wanting him to say aloud I was worried about Nick stealing the little wolf statue, so clearly the better choice for a demon curse. But they were both made out of bone, so . . .

"Yeah," Jenks said suddenly, taking the totem from me and setting it in the middle of the table. "I'll pick one up for you the next time I go out."

There had only been the one in the case, but seeing his understanding, I took a slow breath and reached for my recipe. Pencil in hand, I bowed my head over it and tucked a curl behind an ear. Fool me once, shame on you. Fool me twice, and you can kiss your ass good-bye.

Thirty

Motions steady, I massaged my stuck index finger for the blood needed to invoke the last inertia-dampening spell. My finger was starting to hurt after all the charms I'd invoked. It wasn't as if I could draw a vial of my blood and dole it out by eyedropper. If the blood didn't come right from the body, the enzymes that quickened the spell would break down and the spell wouldn't invoke. There were a lot of charms on the table, this second pair of inertia-dampening spells being a quick, guilty addition.

The blood wasn't coming, so I painfully squeezed until a beaded drop of red formed. It plopped onto the first half of the charm, then I squeezed again until the next plop hit the second amulet. The blood soaked in with an eerie swiftness, sending the scent of burnt amber to stain the stale motel room air. What I would have given for a window that opened.

Burnt amber, not redwood, proof it was demon magic. God, what was I doing?

I glanced over the quiet, dusky room, the light leaking in around the closed curtains telling me it was nearing noon. Apart from a nap around midnight, I'd been up all morning. Someone had obviously slipped me some Brimstone. *Damn roommates, anyway.*

Rubbing my thumb and finger together, I smeared the remnants of blood into nothing, then stretched to put the matched, invoked charms with the rest, beside Jenks. He was sitting across from me, his head slumped onto the table while he slept. Doppelganger charm for Peter, doppelganger charm for Nick, regular disguise charm for Jenks. *And two sets of inertia-dampening amulets,* I thought, gentling the newest in with the rest. After meeting Peter, I was changing the plan. No one knew it but me.

The clatter of the amulets didn't wake Jenks, and I sat back, exhaling long and slow. I was weary from fatigue, but I wasn't done yet. I still had a curse to twist.

Pulling myself upright, I reached for my bag, moving carefully so I wouldn't disturb Jenks. He'd sat watch over me while I slept, forgoing his usual midnight nap, and was exhausted. Rex was purring on his lap under the table, and Jenks's smooth, outstretched hand nearly touched the cup-sized minitank of saltwater containing the sea monkeys he'd bought somewhere along the way. "They're the perfect pets, Rache," he had said, eyes bright with anticipation with what his kids would say, and I hoped we all lived long enough to worry about how we were going to get them home.

I smiled at his youthful face looking roguishly innocent while he slept. He was such an odd mix, young, but a tried-and-true father, provider, protector—and almost at the end of his life.

My throat tightened and I blinked rapidly. I was going to miss him. Jax could never take his place. If there was a charm or spell to lengthen his life, I'd use it and damn the cost. My hand reached to push his hair back from his eyes, then dropped before it touched him. Everyone dies. The living find a way to assuage the loss and go on.

Depressed, I cleared a spot on the table. With the extra sea salt Jenks had gotten with his new pets, I carefully traced three plate-sized circles, interlacing them to make seven distinct spaces formed by three arcs from each circle. I glanced over the dusky room before retrieving the focus from my bag, which had been at my feet all night, safe from Nick.

Jenks was sleeping at the table, Ivy was sleeping in the back room, having returned from her "date" shortly after sunrise, and Nick and Jax were outside making sure the air bag wouldn't engage when Jenks ran the Mack truck into it tonight. And the NOS. Mustn't forget the NOS that Nick had in his nasty truck, which would be rigged to explode on impact. I'd have no better time than now to do this. I'd like to say that I had waited this long so it would be quiet and I'd be undisturbed. The reality was, I was scared. The statue's power came from a demon curse, and it would take a demonic curse to move it. A demon curse. *What would my dad say?*

"What the hell," I whispered, grimacing. I was going to kill Peter. What was a little demonic-curse imbalance compared to that?

Stomach knotting, I placed the statue into the first circle, stifling a shudder and wiping my fingers free of the slimy feel of the ancient bone. Jenks had watched me do this earlier, so I knew what came next, but unbeknownst to everyone but him, it had been a dry run using the wolf statue. I'd lit the candles but hadn't invoked the curse. The little wolf with its fake curse had been sitting on the table all night, Nick carefully avoiding looking at it.

Another glance at the light leaking around the curtains, and I rose, going to Jenks's things piled carelessly by the TV. I plucked the totem from his belongings, feeling guilty though I had already asked to use it. Nervous, I placed his carved totem with the stylized wolf on top in the second circle. In the third, I placed a lock of my hair, twisted and knotted.

My stomach clenched. How many times had my father told me never to knot my hair even in fun? It was bad. Tying hair into knots made a very strong bond to a person, especially when you knotted your own hair. What happened to the bit of hair I placed in the third circle would happen to me. Conversely, what I said or did would be reflected in the circle. It wasn't a symbol of my will, it *was* my will. That it was sitting in a circle to twist a curse made me ill.

Though that might be from the Brimstone, I thought, not putting it past Jenks, even though he'd agreed with my decision to stop taking it. At least it had been medicinal grade this time, and I wasn't dealing with the roller-coaster moods.

"Okay," I whispered, hiking my chair closer to the table. I glanced at Jenks, then got my colored candles from my bag, the soft crackle of the matching colored tissue paper they were wrapped in soothing. I had used white candles the first time, picked up by Ivy out "shopping" with Nick, a bitter touch of honesty to the lie our lives had become.

I set them down and wiped my palms on my jeans, nervous. I'd lit candles from my will only once before—mere hours ago, actually—but since my hearth—the pilot light on my kitchen stove—was five hundred miles south of there, I'd have to use my will.

My thoughts drifted to Big Al standing in my kitchen, lecturing me on how to set candles with their place names. He had used a red taper lit from his hearth, and it would probably please him that I'd learned how to light candles with ley line energy. I had Ceri to thank for that, since it was mostly a modified ley line charm she used to heat water. Lighting them from my will wasn't nearly as power-retentive as using hearth fire, but it was close.

"Ley line," I whispered, focus blurring as I reached for the line I'd found halfway across the town. It felt different from the line in my backyard, wilder, and with the steady, slow pulselike change and characteristic fluidity of water.

The influx of energy poured through me, and I closed my eyes, my trembling foot the only indication of the torrent of energy filling my chi. It took all of a heartbeat, feeling like forever, and when the force balanced, I felt overly full, uncomfortable.

Jaw clenched, I tossed my red frizz out of my eyes and scraped a bit of wax off the bottom of the white candle, holding it to the back of my teeth with my tongue. *"In fidem recipere,"* I said, to fix the candle in the narrow space where the circle holding the totem and the circle holding the knot of my hair bisected. My thumb and first finger pinched the wick, and I slowly separated them, willing a spot of heat to grow between them as I thought the words *consimilis calefa-cio,* setting into motion a complex, white ley line charm to heat water.

Okay, so it heated the moisture between my fingers until the wick burst into flame, but it worked. And the wax I'd scraped off on my teeth was the focal object, so I didn't set the kitchen on fire. My attention flicked to the small burn mark on the table. Yeah, I was learning.

I gazed, fascinated, when the wick first glowed, then caught as the wax melted from the virgin wick and the flame took. *One down, two to go.*

The black candle was next, and after I scratched the white wax off my teeth, I replaced it with a bit of the black candle before I set it in the space connecting the totem and the statue circles. *"Traiectio,"* I breathed, lighting this one as well.

The third candle was gold, to match my aura, and I placed it in the space between the statue and my knot of hair. *"Ob-signare,"* I said, lighting the candle with a studied thought.

My pulse increased. This was as far as I'd gone earlier that morning under Jenks's eye. I brought my head up, see-ing his breathing shifting the hair about his small nose. God, he had a small nose, and his ears were cute.

Stop it, Rachel, I berated myself. I wanted to finish this be-fore I set the smoke alarm off. I pulled a gray taper from my bag, setting it in the very center of the three circles, where they all bisected. This was the one that scared me. The first candle had been set with protection, the second with the word for transference, and the third with the word that would seal the curse so it couldn't unravel. If the gray candle lit itself at the end, then I had successfully twisted the curse and I was officially an intentional practitioner of the dark arts.

God, please forgive me. It's for a good reason.

In the glow of my three candles, I massaged my finger, forcing out a welling of blood. My bleeding finger scribed a symbol I didn't know the meaning of, then I wiped the re-mainder on the candle. I felt as if my will left me with that simple drop of blood, smeared on the faded laminate before the gray pillar of wax given meaning from my intent.

Shaking, I pulled my hand out of the three circles. I scooted my chair back and stood so that when the circles formed, I wouldn't accidentally break them by having my legs in the lower halves. I gave a final look at the three lit candles and the one marked with my blood. The table glowed in candlelight, and I wiped my hands on my jeans.

"Rhombus," I whispered, then touched the nearest circle with my finger to close all three.

I jerked when the ever-after flowed out of me and a haze of black aura rose to envelop the candles, totem, statue, and my knot of hair. I'd never set bisecting circles before, and where they existed together, the gold of my aura was clearer, making glittering arcs among the black smut. Though small, the circles were impenetrable by everything but me since I was the one who had set them. But sticking my finger into the circle to influence what was inside would break the circle, and if I had made them large enough for me to fit in, my soul would be in danger of being transferred along with the original curse.

It was my knot of hair that made this possible. It was my bridge inside. The black candle would go out when the power was moved from the statue to the totem; the white candle would go out to protect and prevent any part of me from being sucked into the new artifact along with the old artifact's power that I would be channeling; and the gold candle would go out when the transfer was complete, sealing it so it couldn't unravel by itself.

My body resonated with the power of the unfamiliar line. It wasn't unpleasant at all, and I wished it was. Grimacing, I reached out my will. *"Animum recipere."*

I held my breath against the rising strength and the taste of ash flowing into me from the focus, overwhelming my sense of self until I was everything it was. My vision blurred and I wavered on my feet. I couldn't see, though my eyes were open.

It sang to me, it lured me, filling me as if twisting my

bones and muscles. It would make me everything I wanted, everything that was promised but that I continually denied myself. I felt the wind in my face and the earth under my paws. The sound of the spinning earth filled my ears, and the scintillating scent of time was in my nose. It coursed in a torrent too fast to be realized. It was what made a Were—and it hurt. It hurt my soul that I couldn't be this free.

Hunched, I struggled to keep my breathing even so I wouldn't wake Jenks. I could be everything if I accepted it fully, took it entirely into me. And it made promises, making me long for it. If I'd had any doubt that Nick had done a switch, they were set to rest now.

But I wasn't a Were. I could understand the lure since I had run with as wolf, fought as a wolf, and existed for a short time with the wind bringing me messages. But I wasn't a wolf. I was a witch, and the lure wasn't enough for me to break my circle and take it as mine forever, destroying me in the process.

"Negare," I whispered, shocked when the word came from me. I had meant to say no. I had meant to say no! But it had come out of me in Latin. *Damn it, what was happening to me?*

Pulse pounding and feeling out of control, I saw the white candle go out. I stiffened as I felt everything in me being poured into the cheap carved bit of bone. I clutched at myself, holding myself together as the demon curse left me, taking with it the ache and lure. The extinguished white candle of protection kept me intact, holding me so that only the curse left, and absolutely nothing more or less went with it.

The black candle went out, and I jerked. Not breathing, I watched the three circles, knowing the transfer was complete and the curse almost set anew. I could feel the energy in the totem, swirling, looking for a lessening of my will so it could pour out and be free. I fixed my eyes on the gold candle, praying.

It went out as the gray candle lit, and I slumped in relief. It was done.

Eyes closing, I reached for the back of the chair. I had done it. For better or worse, I was the first demon magic practitioner this side of the ley lines. Well, there was Ceri, but she couldn't invoke them.

Fingers shaking, I smeared the salt circle to break it. My aura touched it, and the line energy flowed out of the circle and into me. I let go of the line, and my head bowed. I had all of three seconds before reality balanced itself, reaching out to bitch-slap me a good one.

I gritted my teeth so I wouldn't gasp. Stumbling backward, I reached for the wall, hitting the cupboards and sliding to the floor when I didn't find it fast enough. Panic jerked through me. I knew this was going to happen—had been expecting it. I would survive.

I couldn't breathe, and I hung my head and pretended it was all right as the black soaked in, coating me in another layer, molding to my sense of self and changing it. My demon marks throbbed, and I scrunched my eyes shut and listened to my pulse thunder. *I accept this,* I thought, and the band about my chest loosened. I took a gasping breath that sounded like a sob.

Tears were leaking out, and I realized someone had a hold on my shoulder as I sat with my back against the cupboards. "Jenks?" I burbled. I felt a moment of despair as I decided it didn't hurt as much this time. I was becoming used to it. Damn it, I didn't want this to become easy. It should hurt. It should scare me so badly that I never wanted to do it again.

"You okay?" he said, and I nodded, not looking up from his knees so he crunched before me. He had nice knees. "Are you sure?" he asked again, and I shook my head no.

His breath came and went, and I didn't move, trying to realign my thinking. I was a demon curse practitioner. I was a dealer in the black arts. I didn't want to be. I didn't want this.

I brought my head up. Relief tricked through me as I saw only concern, not disgust, in his worried face. I pulled my knees to my chest and held them, breathing slowly. His hand was still on my shoulder, and I wiped my eyes. "Thanks,"

I said, gathering myself to get up. "I think I'm all right now. It hit me hard is all."

His green eyes were narrowed in concern. "The imbalance?"

I stared at him, then decided he must have been listening the night Ceri explained it to me. "Yeah."

He stood and extended a hand to help me rise. "I never felt anything when I got big."

My heart clenched, and I pulled my hand from his warm one after I found my feet. "Maybe you'll get hit with it when I untwist the curse and you get small again," I lied.

Jenks's lips were tight with anger. "You hurt like that when you turned into a wolf too. I told you I'd take the black for becoming big. It's mine."

"I don't know how to give it to you," I said, depressed. "And even if I did, I wouldn't."

"Rachel, that's not fair," he said, his voice rising.

"Just shut up and say thank you," I said, remembering him saying the same thing to me when he agreed to become big so nasty-wasty vampires wouldn't bite me.

"Thank you," he said, knowing exactly what I was saying. We helped each other out. Keeping track of who was saving whom's ass was a waste of time.

Depressed, I shuffled to the table, thinking the circles and extinguished candles—all but the gray one—looked like something you'd see on a teenage witch's dresser. Pulse slowing, I plucked the extinguished candles from where they sat, rolling them up in their white, black, and gold tissue paper before snapping a rubber band around them and dropping them in my bag. That little box with the magnetic chalk would have been a nice place to keep them.

While Jenks pretended interest in his sea monkeys, I put my knotted hair on a saucer and set the burning gray candle to it. The ring of hair flared up, curled in on itself, and died. Feeling safer, I blew the candle out, then maneuvered around Jenks to wash the ash down the sink. I wanted all evidence of this gone as fast as possible.

"Sorry for waking you up," I said. Reaching for the salt, I rubbed the blood symbol off the table with a paste of it.

Jenks straightened from where he'd been leaning over his pets. His eyes were worried. "Did you know you look really scary when you do ley line magic?"

A sliver of fear took me. "How?" I asked, conscious of my two demon marks, weighing heavily on my wrist and the underside of my foot.

Dropping his eyes, Jenks shrugged. "You look tired, older. Like you've done it so many times that you don't care anymore. It's almost as if you have a second aura, and when you do ley line magic, it becomes dominant."

My lips curved down and I went to wash my fingers. "A second aura?" *That sounded absolutely fabulous. Maybe it was because I was my own familiar?*

He nodded. "Pixies are sensitive to auras. You really damaged yours with that last curse." Jenks took a breath. "I hate Nick. You're hurting yourself to help him, and he doesn't even care. He sold you out. Rache, if he ever hurts you again—"

"Jenks, I . . ." I fumbled. I put a hand on his shoulder, and this time he didn't flinch. "If I'm going to be able to walk away from this, I have to do it. This is for me, not him."

Jenks pulled back, looking over the empty room. "Yeah, I know."

I felt odd as he went to the table and looked at the remnants of the demon curse. "That's the real one?" he said, not touching it.

Pushing myself into motion, I picked up the totem. It felt heavier, though I knew it was an illusion. "Matalina is going to love it," I said, handing it to him. "Thanks for letting me borrow it. I don't need it anymore."

Jenks's eyes widened as it settled into his grip. "You want me to hold the real one?"

"He's going to try to steal it," I said, thinking I'd been stupid to trust Nick in the first place. "If you have it, he'll get the wrong one."

Depressed, I hefted the old statue. It felt dead inside, like a chunk of plastic. "I'll keep this one with me along with the wolf statue," I said, dropping the statue into my bag.

The front door opened, spilling light over the unmade beds. Jenks turned smoothly to the door, but I jumped when Nick came in, dirty and smelling of grease. Jax was on his shoulders, immediately abandoning him to see how his new pets were doing.

My hand slid across the table, brushing the salt circle into my hand and dropping it into the sink. I wondered how bad it smelled of extinguished candle, burned hair, and burnt amber.

There was a thump from the back bedroom, and Ivy came out in her bathrobe, hair in disarray, and hunched like a bridge troll. Snarling at Nick about the noise, and with a hand over her face, she limped past Jenks and me to vanish into the bathroom. Immediately the shower went on. The clean scent of oranges slipped under the door with the steam. I didn't want to know what she'd done last night to be limping today. I didn't.

Guilt-strewn and weary, I sat at the table. Jax found the ounce-sized container of sea monkey food, and Jenks stopped him, explaining he couldn't feed them since they hadn't hatched yet. Jax belligerently pointed out two bouncers, naming them Jin and Jen. The small pixy started to glow, which attracted the brine shrimp, and Jax had a fit of delight when they bounced closer. I couldn't help but smile. It was still on me when I turned, finding Nick awkwardly waiting for me. My smile faded, and he clenched his jaw.

"The truck is set, Ray-ray," he said with a false cheerfulness. "It will look like a defect when the air bag doesn't work." He winced. "I, uh, couldn't let a truck run into me—even if I knew I was going to wake up alive."

"Trust is the difference between you and us Inderlanders," Jenks said loudly, popping the lid to the sea monkey food. Jax grabbed a handful the size of a pinhead and dropped it in with encouraging words, enticing Jin and Jen to the surface with a bright glow. This was a hell of a lot safer pet for a pixy than the kitten, and I wondered if that was why Jenks had bought them.

I stifled a sigh, turning it into a yawn. I knew Nick wasn't keen on his truck being the sacrificial vehicle, but it wasn't as if he would be able to drive it again. He was going to be playing dead for the rest of his life. *Coward.*

"Thanks, Nick," I said, leaning away with crossed arms and preparing for a fight. "Now would you go out there and hook it back up? I'm riding with Peter. If I'm going to kill him, I'm not going to let that poor boy die alone."

Thirty-one

Ivy stood just outside the bathroom, wrapped in a white motel towel, short black hair dripping from thin spikes. "You aren't going to be riding with Peter, Rachel. No fucking way!"

I pressed my lips together and fought to not back up. *Okay, so she does swear, but only when extremely pissed.*

Jenks had retreated to the living room, looking like he wished he had never barged in on Ivy in the shower, terrified into playing the tattletale when I told him he was going to be running into me right along with Peter. Nick stood beside him in his grease-stained overalls, and they gave the impression of two boys who had jumped in the creek wearing their good go-to-church clothes five minutes before Pa hitched up the horse.

"Nick," I said, and he started. "We have four hours before we meet Audrey and Peter." *Four hours. Maybe I could get some sleep.* "Can you have the air bag fixed by then? I'd feel better if I had it to supplement the inertia-dampening curse."

"Ivy's right," he said, and I frowned. "There's no reason for you to risk your life."

Ivy laughed bitterly. "She isn't. Rachel, you are *not* getting in Nick's truck."

I turned to my spells on the table, pulse quickening. Her pupils were dilating, but it was in anger, not hunger. I knew this game of arguing with a vampire. "Everything is set," I said. "I made a second pair of inertia-dampening amulets for me, so there's no problem."

Ivy pointed, unaware I could see the new long scratch on the soft part of her arm running from her wrist to her elbow. "It's *not* going to *happen, Rachel!*"

"It will work," I said. "It's only a joke spell." *Curse, actually, but why bring* that *up?*

Jenks sat on the edge of the bed, white-faced. "Don't ask me to do this."

Nick shuffled nervously, looking like a garage repair guy in his blue overalls. Frustrated, I rubbed my temples. "The Weres won't believe I let Nick run off with it and we're trying to catch him," I said. "Especially if there happens to be an accident. I'm not stupid enough to let Nick swipe the artifact, and they know it."

There had been a spike of pleasure saying that. He would look back on the incident when it was over and know I had been thumbing my nose at him. But nervousness returned when I caught sight of Ivy. Scooping up Rex, I sat in a kitchen chair. "It's no big deal," I said, fingers moving to lull her into staying. "The charms will keep me safe. You can follow in the van, and we'll say we're on the way to the drop site in two vehicles. Telling them Nick ran off with it will only get them going after him themselves. They might catch him." *Not that I really cared.*

Ivy shook her head. "This is asinine. I've already got it worked out. Peter and crap for brains trade places. We tell the Weres Nick ran off with it and that Jenks went pixy-native to try and catch him. Jax takes his place on your shoulder, and while under a disguise, Jenks runs the Mack truck over Peter by 'accident' while we try to catch him. Truck explodes. Fake statue is destroyed. Peter gets carted to the morgue or the hospital, where we can pull his plug if we need to. Weres go away—we go for a beer. I spent hours coming up with this. Why are you screwing it up, Rachel?"

Rex jumped off my lap, back nails gouging as she skittered

to hide behind Jenks's ankles. I stood, angry. "I'm not screwing it up! And I'm going to ride with Peter! I'm not going to let him die alone," I said, coming out with what was really bothering me.

Ivy huffed, clutching the towel higher about her. "You're alone when you die, even if you're surrounded by hundreds."

Her arm was oozing to stain the white towel, and only now realizing it, she flushed. Angry, I rounded on her. "Have you *ever* been there when someone dies?" I asked, shaking. "Have you ever held their hand while their strength left them? Have you ever felt the gratitude in their touch that you were there when they stopped breathing? Have you!"

Ivy's face went white.

"I'm *killing him,* Ivy! It is my decision. And I'm going to be there so I understand what it means." I caught my breath, hating myself when my eyes filled. "I have to be there so I know if it was a good thing when it's all done."

Ivy went still as a pity born in understanding reached her eyes. "Rachel, I'm sorry. . . ."

Clutching my arms around myself, I bowed my head so I couldn't see anyone. Ivy stood in her towel and made a wet spot on the floor as she dripped. The scent of the citrus shampoo she used became pronounced, and the silence grew awkward.

From across the room, Nick shifted his weight and took a breath.

"Shut up," Ivy snarled, hitching her towel higher. "This doesn't concern you." Her gaze went to my stitches, and I lifted my chin. I wasn't bound to her. I could do anything I damn well pleased.

Jenks was pale. "I can't do it," he said from the bed. "I can't hit you with a truck."

"See?" Ivy said, catching her towel when she gestured. "He's not going to do it. I don't want you to do it. You aren't doing it!" She started for her room, Nick moving out of her way.

"This is a better plan!" I exclaimed, heading after her. "I'll be fine!"

"Fine?" She lurched to a stop, spinning. "That Mack truck is going to roll over Nick's little blue Ford like it's a cupcake! And you're not going to be in it. The run is off."

"It's not off! This is how we're going to do it!"

Ivy turned. Her eyes were full black. A shiver of fear took me, rocking me to a halt. But I wasn't going to let Peter die alone. I gathered my nerve, and Nick stepped forward.

"I'll do it," he said, his eyes flicking from Ivy to me. "I'll drive the Mack truck."

Ivy's anger hesitated, and I ran my eyes over him in surprise. "No," she said flatly. "Absolutely not. You're going with Audrey and staying out of it. I don't trust you."

Nick clasped his hands, then let them go. "Rachel's right. This is a better plan. They won't be watching Audrey's motel room. After Peter switches places with me, I can leave under a regular disguise charm, cross the bridge, get the truck. Hell, it's DeLavine's truck. Audrey can give me the key."

"No!" Ivy shouted. "I won't let shit for brains run over you. It isn't going to happen!"

I rubbed my temples, thinking that actually this was a lot easier than what we'd originally planned. "Ivy—"

"No!"

Nick made a frustrated noise, gesturing at nothing. "I'm not going to kill Rachel!" he exclaimed. "I love her, but if the only way to make her safe is to run her over with a Mack truck, then I, by God, am going to be the one to do it!"

Ivy looked at him as if she had eaten a pile of crap—or maybe she was looking at him as if he was a pile of crap. "You don't know the meaning of love—Nick."

I was shaking inside. Having Nick run into me instead of Jenks wasn't what I had planned, but it would work. Swallowing, I turned to the kitchen. He could use the regular disguise charm already made up. *Oh God. What was I doing?*

Ivy took a deep breath. "Rachel. I don't trust him."

"When did you ever?" I sat at the table before everyone saw me shake. "I'll be fine. Putting me with Peter will ensure they believe the statue burned with the truck. This is the best plan we have. I don't want to have to do this again if they realize that the statue wasn't destroyed."

Nick shifted from foot to foot and ran a hand over his stubble. "I'll fix the air bag," he said, apparently deciding I was going to get my way. "And the NOS," he added.

Suddenly I was a lot more nervous. "Are they watching?" I asked, meaning the Weres across the street.

Jenks made a soft chirp of a whistle, and Jax came out of hiding to land on his shoulder.

"Yeah," Nick said, head down. "But from the conversation Jax has been catching, they think I'm modifying the NOS tanks in case I need to leave in a hurry." He swallowed to make his Adam's apple move. "I rigged it to explode on impact, but I'll disengage that too. I'll set up a button for you to push after you get out."

Jenks looked at Ivy, then stood up, heading for the door. "We've got four hours. I'll make sure it's not going to explode until you want it to," he said.

Nick's expression clouded. "I know what I'm doing."

"Jax?" Shoulders hunched, Jenks never slowed down on his way to the door. "Come on. You should know how to rig a radio signal."

I felt better knowing Jenks was good with explosives too. Nick jiggled on his feet, looking as if he wanted to give me a hug but knew better, then followed Jenks out. The door opened, and I saw three street Weres across the way, yawning as they leaned against their little tricked-out car with wax paper cups of coffee in their grips. It had been cold this morning, but they looked warm enough now that the sun was high, and sun glinted on their bare shoulders and multiple tattoos.

Ivy scowled at them before looking at Nick's retreating back. "If Rachel gets hurt, you won't have to worry about Weres killing you because I'll find you first, little thief."

My gut clenched. She would go along with it. It was done. I was going to be with Peter when Jenks plowed into us. "I'll be fine," I said, feeling my pulse quicken. "Between the air bag and the charm, it will be like I'm riding in God's arms."

The door closed behind Nick, Jenks, and Jax, the slice of afternoon sun vanishing as if it had never existed. Ivy turned, bare feet silent as she limped to her room. "What if God wants you home early?"

Thirty-two

A witch, a vampire, and a pixy walk into a bar, I thought as I led the way into the Squirrel's End. It was early, and the sun had yet to set when the door swung shut behind Jenks, sealing us in the warm air smelling faintly of smoke. Immediately Nick yanked it open to come in behind us. *And there's the punch line.*

Ivy's lips were pressed tight as she took in the low-ceilinged room, scanning it for Audrey and Peter. It was Friday night, and already busy. From across the room, Becky, our waitress from before, recognized us and waved. Ivy responded with an empty look, making the woman go uncertain. "There," Ivy said, nodding to an empty table in the darkest corner.

I unzipped my coat and shook my new bracelet from Kisten down. "You're an Inderland ambassador," I said. "Make an effort."

Ivy turned to me, her sharply defined eyebrows high. Jenks snickered as she forced the edges of her lips to curl upward. She had put on some makeup, seeing as we were out here for a last supper kind a thing, and she looked more predatorial than usual in her leather pants, clingy shirt, and boots. She and Jenks had ridden over in Kisten's Corvette since she would *not* get in the van with me, and she smoothed a hand over her short hair to make sure every strand was in place. Drops of gold glittered from her lobes, and I wondered why she was wearing them.

It was obvious she wasn't happy about Nick driving the truck into me, but her logic told her my emotionally charged modifications wouldn't only make it more believable, but logistically easier. Relying on Nick had us both worried, but sometimes intuition had to take a backseat. That was when I usually got in trouble.

"They aren't here yet," she said, showing how worried she was by stating the obvious.

Jenks adjusted the collar of his jacket to hide his tension with a smooth casualness. "We're early," he said. Unlike Ivy, he was handling the stress well. He smiled at the women turning to look at him, and there were quite a few jostling their tablemates' elbows and pointing him out. Running my eyes over Jenks, I could see why.

He was still an eyeful at six-foot-four, especially now that he was acting his size. He had on his aviator jacket, and with his sunglasses and one of the Were's caps turned inside out, he looked good—damn good in an individualistic, innocent sort of way.

"Ah, why don't we go sit?" I suggested, becoming uncomfortable at the giggles. *Whoo-hoo! The Inderland nymphos are here! Who brought the pistachio pudding?*

We pushed into motion, and Ivy snagged Nick's elbow. "Get some water for Rachel and an orange juice for me," she said, her white fingers gripping him tighter than was polite or necessary. "Just orange juice. I don't want anything in it. Understand?"

Nick jerked out of her hold. He never would have managed it if she hadn't let him. Frowning, he shook his cloth coat out and went to the bar. He knew he was being gotten rid of.

Nick fit in well here, and it wasn't just the human/Inderland thing. The bar was replete with skinny women in skimpy outfits, chunky women in skimpy outfits, women who never let their glass hit the table and looked old before they should in skimpy outfits, and men in fleece shirts and jeans who looked desperate. Facial hair optional. *Oh yeah, this was a great place to eat before I bit the big one.*

Maybe I was a little depressed.

A woman in a red dress cut too low for her hips waved to Jenks. She was standing by the karaoke machine, and I rolled my eyes when it started playing "American Woman." Jenks grinned, heading off in that direction until Ivy dragged him backward to the table.

The woman at the machine pouted. Ivy fixed a look on her, whereupon the woman went ashen. Her girlfriend got scared and pulled her to the bar as if Ivy was going to drain the both of them. Irritated at their ignorance, I hiked my bag higher and plodded after Ivy and Jenks.

My fingers were starting to sweat, but I couldn't let go of my shoulder bag. Inside it was the defunct focus and the wolf statue. The real focus was sandwiched between Jenks's silk boxers at the motel, though only Jenks and I knew it. I'd have told Ivy, but leaving it unattended didn't fit in with her plan, and I wasn't up to arguing with her. Nick wanted the focus. I had to believe he'd steal anything I was protecting. *God, please prove me wrong?*

In my bag with the two fakes was half of my inertia-dampening curse. Nick had the other half and would be putting it on the grille of the Mack truck. When they got close, they would take effect and muffle my motions. Nick had his own inertia-dampening curse along with a normal disguise charm and the two illegal charms to make him into Peter's doppelganger and vice versa. I wouldn't dare use them in Cincinnati, where bouncers wore spell-check amulets as a matter of course, but I could get away with it here. Small-town life clearly had advantages, but having to educate the locals would get tedious.

Ivy was the first to the table, predictably taking the chair with her back to the wall. Jenks took the one next to her, and I reluctantly sat with my back to the room, scooting my chair in with a thump that was unheard over the music. Depressed, I gazed at the wall behind Ivy. *Swell. I was going to have to look at a stuffed mink nailed to the wall all night.*

The hair on the back of my neck prickled, and I turned

when Ivy's eyes jerked to the door. Our Were escort had arrived, looking more out of place than we did. I wondered how long Walter would be able to hold all three packs together once the "focus" was destroyed. Seconds, maybe? Brett was with them, bruised and moving slow. Walter must have farmed him out to the street pack as punishment. Clearly he was at the bottom of their social ladder and taking a lot of abuse. *Not my fault,* I thought. At least he was alive.

They settled at the bar, and I gave Brett a sarcastic "kiss-kiss" bunny ear gesture before I turned to sit properly. Watching the humans around them stiffen and mutter, I was glad my little party of freethinking sexual gamers had already been accepted.

Jenks's casual tracking of someone behind me gave me warning, and I leaned away when Becky bustled forward. She stood a step farther back than usual, but after Ivy's stellar welcome, I didn't blame her. It was noisy, and I wished they'd turn the music down. I couldn't hear a thing over the electronic pop music. Must have been retros night at the old Squirrel's End.

"Welcome back," she said, looking sincere though nervous. "What can I get you? Twenty-five bucks gets you a wristband and all the beer on tap you can drink."

Damn. Either it was really good beer or the locals could slam it.

Ivy wasn't listening and Jenks was making eyes at one of the women playing pool. She looked like Matalina with the cue in her hand and her little filmy skirt that barely covered her butt when she leaned over to take a shot. Disgusted, I tapped his shin. *What was it with men?*

Jenks jumped, and I smiled sweetly at him. "Could we have a plate of fries?" I asked, thinking that to ask them to put chili on it would get us thrown out.

"You betcha. Anything else?"

Eyeing her over his sunglasses, Jenks became sex incarnate. "What's on the desert menu, Becky? I need something . . . sweet."

Ivy raised one eyebrow and slowly turned her attention to him. We exchanged looks as the matronly woman grew flustered, not at what he said, but at how he'd said it.

"Peach cobbler?" Becky encouraged. "Made it yesterday, so the top is still crunchy."

Jenks carefully slid an arm behind Ivy. Without a show of emotion, she grabbed his wrist and set it on the table. "Put some ice cream and caramel on that, and you've got a deal," he offered, and Ivy gave him an irritated look. "What?" he said with a shit-eating grin. "I'm going to need all the sugar I can get to keep up with you two ladies tonight."

Becky's plucked eyebrows rose higher. "Anything else?"

"How about one of those drinks with the cherries on little swords?" Jenks asked. "I like those swords. Can you put a cherry on a sword for each of us?" His smile grew seductive, and he bent toward Becky, hiding his wrist. I think Ivy had bruised it. "I like to share," he said. "And if these two aren't happy when the sun comes up, I'm going to be a dead man."

The woman's eyes darted between Ivy and me. Ivy's lip quirked once, then steeled her features to a severe emptiness. Playing up to them, I cracked my knuckles in warning.

"Ooooh, hit me baby," Jenks said, moving suggestively where he sat.

"That's my job, sweetie," Ivy purred, pulling him close and tucking her head into the hollow between his shoulder and ear. Her hand was a stiff claw upon his pristine neck, and I saw a flicker of concern in Jenks before he realized she was playing and was nowhere close to losing it. "I'm the bad vamp this time," she purred. "She's the good witch."

Ivy drew her hand back to give him a tart slap on the face, but Jenks was faster, catching her wrist. Eyes sultry, he kissed her fingertips.

"Mmmm," Ivy said, her dark eyelashes fluttering against her pale cheeks and her lips parting. "You know what I like, pixy dust."

Becky's face reddened. "Just the cobbler?" she stammered. "And the drink?"

Ivy nodded, her free hand wrapping around Jenks's and her tongue coming out to lick his fingertips. Jenks froze, truly surprised. The woman took a breath and walked away, her steps unheard over the noise. Great. Now I probably wouldn't get my fries.

Jenks reclaimed his hand, a faint flush on his face. "Four spoons!" he shouted after her.

My breath escaped me in a hiss. "You two are awful!" I said, frowning at Ivy as she shifted away from Jenks, a satisfied-cat smile on her face.

"Maybe," Ivy agreed, "but the Weres were watching us, not Audrey and Peter."

I stiffened, seeing Ivy mentally tick item number two off her list. We had moved that much closer to the end of this, and the first of the butterflies rose in me.

"Jenks tastes like oak leaves smell," Ivy said, ignoring his fluster as he tapped the table in rhythm with the karaoke machine.

Jenks squirmed, looking all of eighteen. "Don't tell Matalina about that, okay?"

Ivy said nothing, and I forced myself to the back of my chair. What was keeping Nick? Maybe he'd seen the nice display of low-class Inderlander at our table and decided to stay at the bar. Or perhaps he didn't want to cross the room and draw the Weres' attention to himself. Regardless, I could use that water.

Slowly Ivy's tension started to filter back, unusual for her. For all my nervousness, Jenks and I were handling this better than she was, and I could understand why. Every run was personal to me. Ivy, though, wasn't used to having the outcome of a run mean this much to her. She didn't have the patterns of behavior to cope, and it showed around her eyes.

"It'll be okay," I said, stifling the urge to reach across the table and pat her hand. The memory of her fingers gripping my waist, the rush of her teeth in me, lifted through my thoughts, and I stifled a shiver of adrenaline.

"What?" Ivy said belligerently, her eyes flashing black.

"It'll work," I said, putting my hand under the table so I wouldn't touch my stitches.

She frowned, the rim of brown growing about her eyes. "A Mack truck driven by your ex-boyfriend is going to run over you, and you say everything is going to be okay?"

Well, when she put it like that . . .

Jenks snorted, shifting his chair a little farther from Ivy. "Crap for brains is back."

I turned in my seat, almost glad to see Nick. He had a glass of water with a slice of lemon and two drinks of differing shades of orange. One had a carrot stick in it, and he put the other before Ivy as he eased into the chair beside me. I resettled my bag on my lap and tried to make it look like I wasn't concerned about it.

Ivy curved her fingers about her drink. "That had better not have alcohol in it," she said, looking at Nick's drink. Jenks reached to take it, and Nick jerked it away, all but spilling it.

"You aren't drinking anything if you're aiming a truck at Rachel," the large pixy said.

Bothered, I grabbed the glass and brought it to my nose. Before Nick could protest, I took a sip, almost spitting it out. "What in hell is that?" I exclaimed, running my tongue around the inside of my mouth. It was mealy, but sweet.

"It's a Virgin Bloody Rabbit." Sullen, Nick pulled it closer. "There's no alcohol in it."

Bloody Rabbit? It was a Virgin Bloody Mary made with carrot juice. "These are better made from tomato juice," I said, and Nick blanched.

Jenks tapped his fingers on the table, smiling when Becky stopped at our table and set down a plate of ice cream and pastry along with his four-cherry drink and the requested number of spoons. No fries. Big surprise. "Thanks, Becky," Jenks called after her over the music, and her neck went red.

Ivy took one of the spoons and delicately scooped a dollop of ice cream, placing it succinctly into her mouth. She pushed it away as if done, saying, "Peter is in the bathroom."

My heart gave a thump. *Check.*

Nick took a shaky breath. I wouldn't look at him, pretending interest in plucking the cherry with the longest stem out of Jenks's drink. Nick stood, and Ivy reached across the table to grab his wrist. He froze, and my eyes went from his still swollen masculine fingers to Ivy's face. Her eyes were black, a severe anger shining from behind them.

"If you don't show up on that bridge," she said, lips hardly moving. "I swear I'll find you. And if you hurt her, I'll make you a shadow, begging me to bleed you every night for the rest of your pathetic life." Looking like a wraith, she inhaled, taking away the warmth of the room. "Believe it."

I sent my eyes up the faded flannel of his shirt to find him ashen and afraid. For the first time, he was afraid. I was too. Hell, even Jenks had drawn away from her.

He jerked from her. Clearly shaken, he stepped out of her easy reach. "Rachel—"

"Good-bye, Nick," I said flatly, feeling my blood pressure rise. I still didn't understand how he could think that selling Al information about me, even harmless information, wasn't a betrayal of everything we had shared.

I didn't watch him leave. Eyes lowered, I took a sword-pierced cherry. The sweet mush was bland in my mouth. Swallowing, I set the red plastic sword beside Jenks for him to take home to his kids. "I'm tired of this," I whispered, but I don't think anyone heard me.

Jenks took a scoop of the cobbler, watching me with his intent green eyes. "You going to be okay?" he asked around his full mouth.

Picking up a spoon, I held the plate so I could wrangle an even bigger bite of ice cream. "Just dandy." *Why was I eating? I wasn't hungry.*

The music finally died, and in the renewed sound of chatter, Ivy held a napkin to her mouth and muttered, "I don't like this. I don't like it at all. I don't like Nick. I don't trust Nick. And if he doesn't show up with that truck to do his part, I'm going to kill him."

"I'll help," Jenks offered, carefully cutting the remaining ice cream in two and claiming the largest half.

"Okay, I made a mistake in trusting him. Can we move on to something else?" I said, scraping the lion's share of caramel to my side of the plate. *God help me, but I had been stupid. Stay with your own kind, Rachel. Not that your track record there is much better.* "But I do trust his greed," I added, and Jenks's eyebrows rose.

Shifting my shoulder, I touched my bag on my lap. "He wants the statue. He's going to show, if only to try and steal it back after all is said and done."

Ivy crossed her arms in front of her and seethed.

Jenks cocked his head in thought and ate another bite of cobbler. "You want me to have Jax shadow him?" he asked, and I shook my head.

"It might be too cold," I said. "He can sit this one out."

"He's doing well with low-temp excursions," Jenks said around his full mouth, then swallowed. "I'm proud of him." A satisfied smile hovered in his eyes. "He can read now," he added softly. "He's been working hard at it. He's serious about taking after his old man."

My smile faltered at the reasons for the lessons. Jenks didn't have many more battles left to fight. Ivy steadied herself, visibly forcing herself to be cheerful.

"That's great," she said, but I could hear her stress. "What grade level is he at?"

Jenks pushed his plate away. "Tink's titties, I don't know. Enough to get by."

I sent my attention to the bathroom door when Nick came out, his head down, clearly worried. I exhaled in a slow puff, leaning back into my chair. "Oh that's just swell," I said sourly. "Something's wrong with the charms."

Triangular face worried, Jenks followed my gaze, saying nothing. Ivy didn't look at all, and waited for it as Nick sat down before his Virgin Bloody Rabbit and took a gulp.

"My shoes are too tight," he whispered, fingers shaking.

Mouth open, I stared. It hadn't been Nick's voice. "Peter?"

I breathed, shocked. My eyes jerked from him to Ivy and Jenks. "My God. Can I cook, or can I cook!"

Ivy's breath slipped from her in a slow sound. *Check* I thought, seeing her mentally cross off the next item on her list.

Grinning, Jenks started to eat again, this time working on my half of the ice cream.

I tried not to look at Peter, but it was hard not to. The vampire sat beside me, his arms resting on the table as if tired, the barest tremble in his fingers, which were a shade shorter than Nick's, and thin, not swollen. The two men had exchanged clothes along with identities, and it was eerie how complete the change was. Only in the eyes could I see a clear difference. Peter had a haze from the painkiller he had taken so he could walk upright. Just as well I'd be driving.

"No wonder those things are illegal," Ivy said, hiding her words behind her glass of juice.

My worry deepened when Jenks added, "His aura is the same."

"Shit," I whispered, my stomach knotting. "I forgot about that."

Jenks finished the ice cream and pushed the plate away with a little sigh. "I wouldn't worry about it," he said. "Weres can't use the ever-after. They can't see auras."

Embarrassed, I hunched over my drink. "You can. And you can't use the ever-after."

He grinned. "That's because pixies *are* ever-after. We're magic, baby. Just ask Matalina."

Ivy snickered. She took a cherry, and Jenks put her sword with mine when she casually handed it to him.

"You know," I said, "you can buy a box of those for a buck fifty in any grocery store."

Jenks shrugged. "Where's the fun in that?"

Watching the banter, Peter smiled, making my heart ache when I remembered Nick looking at me like that. "I wish I had the chance to know you before all this," he said softly. "You fit well together. Like a vampire camarilla, but without the jealousy and politics. A real family."

My good mood died. Jenks played with his fork to get it to balance on its tines, and Ivy became very interested in the Weres at the bar.

Peter blinked rapidly, a nervous reaction I'd never seen in Nick. "I'm sorry," he said. "Did I say something—"

Ivy interrupted him. "Peter, we've got about an hour until Nick gets into place with that bridge traffic. Do you want something to eat?"

I gathered myself to look for Becky, yelping when Jenks kicked me under the table. I glared at him until he said, "You don't like Nick. Nick can get his own food."

Feeling stupid, I slumped in my chair. "Right." So I tried not to fidget as Peter took the next five minutes to get Becky's attention. From the corner of my sight I watched Nick leave the bathroom, looking like the ailing vampire who was sitting beside me, trying to attract anyone in an apron. Hell, Nick even walked like Peter, slow and pained. It was creepy. He was good at this.

Professional thief, I reminded myself as I gripped my bag to assure myself it was still in my possession. How I could have been so blind? But I knew my ignorance had been born out of my need for that damned acceptance I hungered after almost as badly as Ivy lusted after blood. We weren't as un-alike as it seemed when you got right down to it.

The jitters started when Nick passed out of my sight. I turned my attention to Ivy, reading his progress across the bar by where her eyes went. "He's good," Ivy said, sipping her juice. "Audrey didn't recognize him until he opened his mouth and said hi."

"Did the Weres smell him?" I asked, and she shook her head.

Beside me, Peter gritted his teeth, and I was glad he'd had the opportunity to say good-bye to Audrey properly. He was a good person. It wasn't fair. Maybe he could bring the memory of suffering and compassion into his undead existence, but I doubted it. They never did.

Ivy tapped her fingers on the table, and Jenks heaved a sigh. "They're gone," Ivy said.

I put the flat of my arm on the table, forcing my foot to not jiggle. All that was left was waiting for Nick's phone call that he was in place.

Check.

Thirty-three

So this is what it feels like to be a murderer, I thought, taking a tighter grip of the wheel of Nick's truck, squinting from the low sun. I was nervous, sweaty, shaky, and I wanted to throw up. *Oh yeah. I can see why people get off on this.*

Beside me in Nick's jeans and cloth coat, Peter watched the passing view as we drove to the bridge, half of Nick's inertia-dampening curse fixed to the bumper. Peter's left hand cradled the defunct statue with DeLavine's blood smear on it. His right hand, looking slightly smaller than Nick's, was holding the handle of the door. I was pretty sure it was nerves since he didn't know the door had a tendency to fly open when you went over a bump.

Nick's truck was old. It rattled when it shook. The shocks were bad but the brakes were excellent. And with the NOS, it could be startlingly fast. Just what every successful thief needs.

Silent, we endured the stop-and-go traffic to get onto the bridge, my attention on Ivy and Jenks behind us as much as on the cars ahead of me jockeying to get on the bridge. It had been Ivy's idea to do this on the bridge. The stiff wind would hamper the Weres' sense of smell, and the bridge itself would prevent a helicopter ambulance and slow things down. But most of all, we needed a stretch of several miles without a shoulder to minimize Were interference after the crash. The five-mile bridge gave us that along with a nice margin to actually run into each other. The goal was the bridge apex, but a mile either way would work.

My eyes flicked to the rearview mirror, but I didn't feel any better seeing Ivy and Jenks in Kisten's Corvette running as a buffer between us and the Weres from the bar. "Put your seat belt on," I said. I thought it was stupid, like dragging the saddle behind you when you went looking for your horse fleeing the burning barn, but I didn't want to get pulled over for failure to wear a belt and have it all come crashing down when the cop realized Nick's newly flash-painted truck was the same one that had fled the scene of a crash yesterday.

The click was loud when Peter fastened his belt. We were going to be run over by a Mack truck. I didn't think it would make a difference if he had on his seat belt or not.

Oh God. What was I doing?

The traffic light finally turned green, and I pulled onto the bridge, headed for St. Ignace on the other side of the straits. I gripped the wheel tighter, stomach knotting. The bridge was a mess. The two northbound lanes were closed off, making traffic two-way on the southbound. Midway down the span there were big machines and powerful lights to turn the coming night to day as the workers tried to meet their pretourist-season deadline. They had missed it. Red cones separated the two lanes, allowing traffic to easily switch to the other side when needed. The bridge was an incredible five miles long, and every foot of it had needed repair.

Peter exhaled as we accelerated to a steady forty miles an hour, the opposing traffic doing the same an unnerving three feet away. Past the vacant northbound lane and thick girders, I could see the islands, gray and smudged from the distance. We were really high up, and I felt a moment of quickly stifled fear. Despite the stories, witches couldn't fly. 'Least not without a staff of charmed redwood that cost more than the Concord.

"Peter?" I said, not liking the silence.

"I'm fine," he said, his grip tensing on the statue. His voice was cross, sounding nothing like Nick. I couldn't help my awkward smile of understanding, remembering Ivy bothering me with the same question. My stomach gave a lurch.

"I wasn't going to ask how you were doing," I said, fiddling with the two charms about my neck. One was for pain that wouldn't cover the hurt caused by being hit, the other was to keep my head from meeting the dash. Peter had refused both.

My eyes lifted to the rearview mirror to see that Ivy and Jenks were still behind us. "Do you want me to turn the lights on?" I asked. It was our agreed upon signal to abort the plan. I wanted him to say yes. I didn't want to do this. The statue didn't matter right now. Peter did. We could find another way.

"No."

The sun was setting past him, and I squinted at him. "Peter . . ."

"I've heard it all," he said, his voice rough as he kept his stiff position. "Please don't. It comes down to one thing. I'm dying. I've been doing it for a long time, and it hurts. I stopped living three years ago when the medicine and charms quit working and the pain took everything away. There's nothing left of me *but* hurting. I fought for two years with the thought that I was a coward for wanting to end the pain, but there is nothing left."

I snuck a glance at him, shocking myself when I saw Nick sitting there, his jaw clenched and his brown eyes hard. It sounded like it was a story he had told too many times. As I watched, his shoulders slumped and he let go of the door. "This lingering isn't fair to Audrey," he said. "She deserves someone strong, able to stand beside her and meet her bite for bite in the passion she's aching to show me."

I couldn't let that go without saying something. "And becoming an undead is fair to her?" I said, making his jaw clench again. "Peter, I've seen the undead. That won't be you!"

"I know!" he exclaimed, then softer, "I know, but it's all I've got left to give her."

The whirl of air under the tires rose above the sound of

the engine as we went over the first of the grates designed to lighten the bridge's load.

"She knows it won't be me," Peter said, his voice calm. He seemed to want to talk, and I would listen. I owed him that.

He met my gaze and smiled a scared little-boy smile. "She promised me she'll be happy. I used to be able to dance with such passion that it could drive her wild. I want to dance again with her. I will remember her. I will remember the love."

"But you won't feel it," I whispered.

"She'll feel love for the both of us," Peter said firmly, his eyes on the passing bridgework. "And in time, I'll be able to fake it for her."

This was not happening. "Peter—" I reached forward to turn on the lights, and he stopped me with a shaking hand on my wrist.

"Don't," he said. "I'm already dead. You're only helping me move forward."

I could not believe this. I didn't *want* to believe it. "Peter, there's so much you haven't done. That you might do. There are new medicines every day. I know someone who can help you." *Trent could help him,* I thought, then cursed myself. *What in hell was I thinking?*

"I've had all the medicines," Peter said softly. "Legal and otherwise. I've heard the lies, I've believed the promises, but there's nothing left to believe in but death. I'm moved around like a table lamp, Rachel." His voice faltered. "You don't understand because you aren't done living yet. But I'm done, and when you're done . . . you just know."

The car ahead of me flashed its brake lights and I took my foot off the accelerator. "But a lamp can light a room," I protested, my will weakening.

"Not when the bulb is broken." His elbow was on the windowsill and his head was in his cupped hand. The setting sun became flashes on him as the girders holding the bridge arched up. "Maybe by dying I can be fixed," he said over the rumble of a passing truck. "Maybe I can do some good when I'm dead. I'm not good for anything alive."

I swallowed hard. He wouldn't do anything after he died, unless it met his needs.

"It's going to be okay," Peter said. "I'm not scared of death. I'm scared of dying. Not dying, but how I'm going to die." He laughed, but it was tinged with bitterness. "DeLavine told me that being born and dying are the only two things we do perfectly. There's a hundred percent success rate. I can't do it wrong."

"That sounds funny coming from a dead man," I said, my breath catching when a big truck went past, shaking the grate we were on. *This was wrong. This was so wrong.*

Peter pulled his elbow from the window and looked at me. "He said how I feel when I die is the one thing I have control over. I can be afraid, or I can go boldly. I want to do it bravely—even if it hurts. I'm tired of hurting, but I can take a little more."

I was starting to shake, though the air from the setting sun coming in was warm and my window was down. His soul would be gone forever. The spark of creativity and compassion—gone.

"Can . . . can I ask you something?" I ventured. The oncoming traffic had grown thin, and I prayed that they hadn't shut down the southbound lane for some reason. It was probably just Nick driving slow so we would meet somewhere in the middle as planned.

"What?"

His voice was tired and weary, and the sound of lost hope in it knotted my stomach tighter. "When Ivy bit me," I said, darting a glance at him, "some of my aura went to her. She was taking my aura along with my blood. Not my soul, just my aura. The virus needs blood to stay active, but is it more than that?"

His expression was unreadable, and I rushed forward with the rest of it while I still had time. "Maybe the mind needs an aura to protect it," I said. "Maybe the still-living mind needs the illusion of a soul about it, or it will try to get the body to kill itself so that the soul, the mind, and the body will be back in balance."

Peter looked at me from Nick's face, and I saw him for what he was: a frightened man who was stepping into a new world with no safety net, both extremely powerful and tragically fragile, reliant upon someone else to keep his mind and body together after his soul was gone.

He didn't say anything, telling me I was right. My breath quickened and I licked my lips. Vampires take auras as their own to fool their mind that a soul still bathed it. It would explain why Ivy's father risked his own death to provide her mother with his blood and his alone. He bathed her mind in his aura, his soul, in the hopes that she would remember what love was. And perhaps, in the instant of the act, she did.

I finally understood. Exhilarated, I stared at the road ahead, not seeing it. My heart was pounding and I felt light-headed.

"That's why Audrey insists on being my scion," he said softly, "even though it's going to be very hard on her."

I wanted to stop. I wanted to stop right there in the middle of the freaking bridge and figure this out. Peter looked miserable, and I wondered how long he had agonized over remaining as he was and causing her pain, or becoming an undead and causing her a pain of another kind. "Does Ivy know?" I asked. "About the auras?"

He nodded, his eyes lighting briefly upon my stitches. "Of course."

"Peter, this is . . . is—" I said, bewildered. "Why are you hiding this from everyone?"

He ran a hand over his face, the angry gesture so reminiscent of Nick that it shocked me. "Would you have let Ivy take your blood if you knew she was taking your aura, the light from your soul?" he asked suddenly, his eyes fixing on mine vehemently.

I glanced from the road, blurting, "Yes. Yes, I would have. Peter, it's beautiful. It brings something right to it."

His expression went from anger to surprise, and he said, "Ivy is a very lucky woman."

Feeling my chest clench, I blinked rapidly. I wouldn't cry. I was frustrated and confused. I was going to kill Peter in less than three miles. I was on a train I couldn't stop. I didn't need to cry, I needed to understand.

"Not everyone sees it like that," he said, the shadows of the passing girders falling on him. "You're truly odd, Rachel Morgan. I don't understand you at all. I wish I had time to. Maybe after I'm dead. I'll take you dancing and we can talk. I promise I won't bite you."

I can't do this. "I'm turning the lights on." Jaw clenched, I leaned to reach the knob. He wasn't done yet. There was more for him to learn. More he could tell me before he dropped his thread of consciousness forever.

Peter didn't move as I pulled the knob. I leaned into the seat, my face going cold when the dash remained dark. I pushed the knob in and pulled it back out. "They aren't working," I said as a car passed us. I pushed it in and tried again. "Why aren't they working, damn it!"

"I asked Jenks to disengage them."

"Son of a bitch!" I shouted, hitting the dash and hurting my hand through the pain amulet. "That damn son of a bitch!" Tears started leaking out, and I twisted in the seat, desperate to stop this.

Peter took my shoulder, pinching me. "Rachel!" he exclaimed, his guilt-ridden expression looking at me from Nick's face tearing at me. "Please," he begged. "I wanted to end it this way because it would help someone. I'm hoping that because I'm helping you, God will take me even without my soul. Please—don't stop."

I was crying now. I couldn't help it. I kept my foot on the accelerator, maintaining that same fifteen feet between me and the next car. He wanted to die, and I was going to help him whether I agreed with it or not. "It doesn't work that way, Peter," I said, my voice high. "They did a study on it. Without the mind to chaperone it, the soul has nothing to hold it together and it falls apart. Peter, there will be nothing left. It will be as if you never existed—"

He looked down the road. His face paled in the amber glow. "Oh God. There he is."

I took a breath, holding it. "Peter," I said, desperate. I couldn't turn back. I couldn't slow down. I had to do this. The shadows from the girders seemed to flash faster. "Peter!"

"I'm scared."

I looked over the cars to the white truck heading for us. I could see Nick, Peter's doppelganger disguise gone and the legal one in place. Hand fumbling, I found Peter's. It was damp with sweat, and he clutched it with the strength of a frightened child. "I'll be here," I said, breathless and unable to look from the looming truck. *What was I doing?*

"Please don't let me burn when the tanks explode? Please, Rachel?"

My head hurt. I couldn't breathe. "I won't let you burn," I said, tears making my face cold. "I'll stay with you, Peter. I promise. I'll hold your hand. I'll stay until you go, I'll be there when you leave so you won't be forgotten." I was babbling. I didn't care. "I won't forget you, Peter. I'll remember you."

"Tell Audrey that I love her, even if I don't remember why."

The last car between us was gone. I took a breath and held it. My eyes were fixed on the truck's tires. They shifted. "Peter!"

It happened fast.

The truck veered across the temporary line. My feet slammed into the breaks, self-preservation taking control. I stiffened my arm, clenching the wheel and Peter's hand both.

Nick's truck swerved. It loomed before us, the flat panel of the side taking up the entire world. He was trying to get entirely across the lane and miss me. I spun the wheel, teeth gritted and terrified. He was trying to miss me. He was trying to hit the passenger side only.

The truck smashed into us like a wrecking ball. My head jerked forward, and I gasped before the inertia-dampening curse took hold. I couldn't breathe as the air bag hit my face like a wet pillow, hurting. Relief filled me, then guilt that I was safe while Peter. *Oh God, Peter . . .*

Heart pounding, I felt as if I was wrapped in muzzy cotton. I couldn't move. I couldn't see. But I could hear. The sound of squealing tires was swallowed by the terrifying shriek of twisting metal. I managed a breath, a ragged gasp in my throat. My stomach lurched, and the world spun as the momentum swung us around.

Pushing at the oil-scented plastic, I forced it away. We were still spinning, and terror shocked through me as the Mack truck plowed into the temporary guardrail and into the empty northbound lanes. Our vehicle shook as we hit something and came to a spine-wrenching halt.

I pushed the bag down, fighting it, shaking, blinking in the sound of nothing. It was smeared with red, and I looked at my hands. They were red. I was bleeding. Blood slicked them where my nails had cut through my palms. *Yes,* I thought numbly, seeing the gray sky and dark water. *That's what the hands of a murderer should look like.*

Heat from the engine washed over me, pulled from the breeze on the bridge. Safety glass covered the seat and me. Blinking, I peered out the shattered front window. Peter's side of the truck was smashed into a pylon. There would be no getting him out that way. We had been knocked clean into the empty northbound lane. I could see the islands past Peter and the guardrail they were repairing. Something . . . something had ripped the hood off Nick's blue truck. I could see the engine, steaming and twisted. Shit, it was almost in the front seat with me along with the front window.

A man was shouting. I could hear people and car doors shutting. I turned to Peter. *Oh, hell.*

I tried to move, shocked when my foot caught, panicking until I decided it wasn't moving because it was stuck, not because it was broken. It was wedged between the console and the front of the seat. My jeans were turning a wet black from the calf down. I think I had a cut somewhere. My eyes traveled numbly down my leg. It was my calf. I think I'd cut my calf.

"Lady!" a man said as he rushed up to my window, gripping the empty frame with a thick hand, a wedding ring on his finger. "Lady, are you okay?"

Peachy, I thought, blinking at him. I tried to say something but my mouth wasn't working. An ugly sound came out of me, chilling.

"Don't move. I called the ambulance. I don't think you're supposed to move." His eyes went to Peter beside me, and he turned away. I heard the sound of retching.

"Peter," I whispered, my chest hurting. I couldn't breathe deeply, so keeping my breaths shallow, I struggled with my seat belt. It came undone, and while people shouted and gathered like ants on a caterpillar, I pulled my foot free. Nothing hurt yet. I was sure that would change.

"Peter," I said again, touching his face. His eyes were closed but he was breathing. Blood seeped from a ragged cut over his eye. I undid his seat belt, and his eyelids fluttered.

"Rachel?" he said, his face scrunching up in hurt. "Am I dead yet?"

"No, sweetheart," I said, touching his face. Sometimes the transition from living to dead goes in a heartbeat, but not with this much damage, and not with the sun still up. He was going to take a long nap to wake hungry and whole. I managed a smile for him, taking my pain amulet off and draping it over him. My chest hurt, but I didn't feel anything, numb inside and out.

Peter looked so white, his blood pooling in his lap. "Listen," I said, adjusting his coat with my red fingers so I couldn't see the wreckage of his chest. "Your legs look okay, and your arms. You have a cut above your eye. I think your chest is crushed. In about a week you can take me dancing."

"Out," he whispered. "Get out and blow up the truck. Damn it, I can't even die right. I didn't want to burn." He started crying, the tears making a clear track down his bloodied face. "I didn't want to have to burn. . . ."

I didn't think he was going to survive this even if the

ambulance got to him in time. "I'm not going to burn you. I promise." *I'm going to be sick. That's all there is to it.*

"I'm scared," he whimpered, his breath gurgling from his lungs filling with blood. I prayed he wouldn't start coughing.

Broken chips of safety glass sliding, I pulled myself closer, gently holding his shattered body to me. "The sun is shining," I said, eyes clenching shut as memories of my dad flooded back. "Just like you wanted. Can you feel it? It won't be long. I'll be here."

"Thank you," he said, the words terrifyingly liquid. "Thank you for trying to turn the lights on. That makes me feel as if I was worth saving."

My throat closed. "You are worth saving," I said, tears spilling over as I rocked him gently. He tried to breathe, the sound ugly. It was pain given a voice, and it struck through me. His body shuddered, and I held him closer though I was sure it hurt him. Tears fell, hot as they landed on my arm. There was noise all around us, but no one could touch us. We were forever set apart.

His body suddenly realized it was dying, and with an adrenaline-induced strength, it struggled to remain alive. Clutching his head to my chest, I held him firmly against the massive tremor I knew was coming. I sobbed when it shook him as if he were trying to dislodge his body from his soul. *I hated this. I hated it. I had lived it before. Why did I have to live it again?*

Peter stopped moving and went still.

Rocking him now for me, not him, I shook with sobs that hurt my ribs. *Please, please let this have been the right thing to do.*

But it didn't feel right.

Thirty-four

"**R**achel!" Jenks cried, and I realized he was with me. His hands were warm and clean, not sticky like mine—and after struggling with the door to the truck, he reached inside the window to unlatch it. I let my grip on Peter loosen as it opened. My leg, twisted behind me, felt kind of cold, and I looked at, going woozy. There was a dark, wet stain on my jeans, and my brand-new running shoe now had a red stripe. *Maybe my leg was hurt more than I thought?*

"Get Peter out," I whispered. "Ow. Ow, hey!" I exclaimed when Jenks dragged me across the seat and away from Peter. His arms went around me in a cradle, and with me getting Peter's blood all over him, he carried me to a clear space on the cold pavement.

"Up," I whispered, cold and light-headed. "Don't lay me down. Don't hit the button before you get him out. You hear me, Jenks. Get him out!"

He nodded, and I asked, "Where's the truck driver?" remembering not to call him Nick.

"Some lady in a lab coat is looking at him."

Fumbling, I pulled my half of the inertia-dampening charm from around my neck. I slipped it to Jenks, and he replaced it with the remote to ignite the NOS. Palming it, I watched him nudge the amulet through the nearby road grate, destroying half the evidence that we were committing insurance fraud. *David would have kittens.*

"Wait until I get back before hitting that, will you?" he

muttered, his eyes darting to my closed grip. Not waiting for an answer, he loped to the truck shouting for two men in the crowd to help him, and a woman descended upon me.

"Get off!" I exclaimed, pushing, and the narrow-faced woman in a purple lab coat fell away. *How had she gotten there so fast? The coming ambulance wasn't even a noise yet.*

"I'm Dr. Lynch," she said tightly, frowning at the blood I'd left on her lab coat. "Just what I need. You look like you're a worse PITA patient than me."

"PITA?" I asked, slapping at her when she took my shoulders and tried to lay me down.

She pulled back, frowning. "Pain in the ass," she explained. "I need to take your blood pressure and pulse supine, but after that you can sit up until you pass out, for all I care."

I tried to see around her to Jenks, but he was inside the truck with Peter. "Deal," I said.

Her eyes went to my leg, wet from the calf down. "Think you can put pressure on that?"

I nodded, starting to feel sick. This was going to hurt. Holding my breath against the wash of pain, I let her take my shoulders and ease me down. Knee bent, I clamped my hand to the part of my leg that hurt the most, making it hurt more. While she took her God-given sweet time, I listened to the sounds of panic and stared at the darkening sky framed by the bridge's cables, holding my ribs and trying not to look like they hurt lest she wanted to poke them too. I thought of my pain amulet, praying it had eased Peter when nothing else had. I deserved to hurt.

She muttered at me to hold still when I turned my head to look at the passing traffic. A black convertible was parked just inside the closed northbound lane. *Hers?*

I jerked at the ugly ripping sound and the sudden draft on my leg. "Hey!" I shouted, putting my hurt palms against the pavement and levering myself up. I held my breath as my sight grayed at the pain, then got mad when I realized she had cut my jeans up the seam to my knee. "Damn it, those were fifty bucks!" I exclaimed, and she gave me a cold look.

"I thought that would get you up," she said, moving my bloody hand back to my leg and taking my blood pressure and pulse a second time.

I could tell she was a high-blood living vampire despite her trying to hide it in the old way, and I felt safe with her. Her blood lust would be carefully in check while she worked on me. That's the way living vamps were. Children and the injured were sacred.

Still mad about my jeans, I took a shallow breath, staring at the chaos lit by the orangey yellow glare of the setting sun. "Let's see it," she said, and I released my hold on my leg.

Worried, I peered down. It didn't look bad from a bleeding-to-death standpoint—just a slight oozing and what looked like a huge bruise in the making—but it hurt like hell. Saying nothing, Dr. Lynch opened her tackle box and broke the seal on a small bottle. "Relax, it's water," she said when I stiffened as she went to pour it on me.

She had to hold my leg still with an iron grip as she poked and prodded, cleaning it while muttering about torn arterioles and them being a bitch to stop bleeding but that I'd survive. My three-year-old tetanus shot seemed to satisfy her, but my stomach was in knots when she finally decided I had been tortured enough and slipped a stretchy white pressure bandage over it.

Someone was directing traffic to keep the rubberneckers moving and the bridge open. Two cars of Weres had stopped to "help," worrying me. I wanted them to see the statue rolling around on the floor of the front seat, but having them this close was a double-edged sword.

Slowly I tucked the remote to blow the NOS under my good leg and out of sight. The wind through the straits pushed my hair out of my eyes, and as I looked at the faces pressed against the windows as they passed, I started to laugh, hurting my ribs. "I'm okay," I said when the woman gave me a sharp look. "I'm not going into shock. I'm alive."

"And it looks like you're going to stay that way," she said, taking both my hands and setting them so they hung past the shelf of my lap. "Aren't you the lucky one?"

She poured more water on my hands to get the grit off, then set them palm up on my lap to make a wet spot. Disgusted, I watched her pluck a second packet from her tackle box and rip it open. The scent of antiseptic rose, whipped away from the wind. Again I jumped and ow'ed as she brushed the grit and glass from my hands, earning another "wimp" look from her.

More people had stopped, and Nick's truck's paint job was showing where the metal had crumpled. Jenks was inside with Peter. They were trying to get him out. Weres had gathered at the outskirts, some in jeeps, some in high-end cars, and some in little street racers. I felt the remote under my leg, wanting to use it and finish this run. I wanted to go home.

Nick. "Where's the guy who hit us?" I said, scanning the faces and not seeing him.

"He's fine apart from a damaged knee," she said as she finished and I pulled my hands close to inspect the little crescent moons from my nails cutting my palms. "It might need surgery at some point, but he'll live." Her deeply brown eyes flicked to my dental-floss stitches. "Your gnomon is with him," she finished, and I blinked. *Gnomon? What in hell was that?*

"She's keeping him occupied until the I.S. gets here to take his statement," she added, and my eyes widened. The woman meant Ivy. She thought I was Ivy's scion, and gnomon was the flipside of the relationship. It made sense—a gnomon was the thingy on a sundial that casts a shadow. I was about to tell her Ivy wasn't my gnomon, then didn't. I didn't care what she thought.

"The I.S.?" I said with a sigh, starting to worry now that it looked like I was going to survive. Motions quick, she fixed a big bandage over each palm. I hadn't forgotten about the I.S., but if Nick's truck wasn't burning before they arrived, it was going to be a lot harder to get rid of that defunct statue.

Her attention followed mine to the truck, her shoulders

stiffening when Jenks and two men pulled Peter's broken body out. I expected her to get angry they were moving him, surprised that she was messing with the living and not him, obviously the worse off—until she leaned close with her little penlight and flashed it in my eyes, saying, "You cried for Peter. No one ever cries for us."

I pulled out of her grip, shocked. "You know . . ."

She moved, and I panicked. With vampire quickness she was atop me, knees to either side of my thighs, pinning me against the barrier. Her one hand was behind my neck holding me unmoving, the other held that light as if it was a dagger pointed at my eye. She was inches away, her closeness going unnoticed or considered okay by way of her official-looking lab coat.

"I'm here because DeLavine told me to come. He wanted to make sure you survived."

I took a breath, then another. She was so close, I could see the soft imperfections in her cheek and neck where she had been professionally stitched. I didn't move, wishing I wasn't so damn interesting to the undead. What in hell was their problem?

"I'd tell him to leave you alone," she said, her breath lost in the wind, "because I think you'd kill him if he tried to hunt you, but it would make him interested, not simply—concerned."

"Thanks," I said, heart pounding. *God help me, I would never understand vampires.*

Slowly she lowered the penlight and got off. "Good reflexes. No head trauma. Your lungs sound clear. Don't let them cart you off to Emergency. You don't need it, and it will only jack up your insurance," she said, switching from scary-ass vampire to professional health provider in seconds. "I'm done here. You want a pain amulet?"

I shook my head, guilt for being alive cascading through me when Jenks and two men set Peter gently on the ground apart from everyone. Jenks crouched to close his eyes and the other two men backed away, frightened and respectful.

The woman's face blanked. "I wasn't here, okay?" she said. "You bandaged your own damn leg. I don't want to be subpoenaed. I wasn't here."

"You got it."

And she was gone, the purple lab coat flapping about her calves as she lost herself in the crush of growing turmoil surrounding the single spot of stillness that was Peter, alone on the pavement, broken and bloody.

Feeling the adrenaline crash, I met Jenks's gaze. He sank to the pavement beside me so he could see Peter from the corner of his eye. Respect for the dead. He handed me my shoulder bag and I put it on my lap, hiding the remote to blow the NOS. "Push it," he said.

There were sirens in the distance. They weren't approaching quickly, but that would change when they reached the bridge and the closed northbound lanes. Behind Jenks was Nick's truck, a twisted chunk of metal with wheels and no hood. It was hard to believe I had survived it.

The Weres were starting to edge in, clearly wanting to swipe the statue. No one was within that golden circle of twenty feet or between the truck and the questionable safety of the temporary railing and a possible fall. Jenks leaned closer, and with him protecting my face with his body, I clenched my eyes shut and pushed the button.

Nothing happened.

I opened one eye and looked at Jenks. His expression was horrified, and I pushed the button again.

"Let me try," he said, snatching it away and pushing it himself. The little bit of plastic made a happy clickity-click sound, but there was no big ba-da-boom after it.

"Jenks!" I exclaimed barely above a whisper. "Did you *fix* this too?"

"It's not my fault!" he said, green eyes wide. "I rigged it myself. The NOS should have blown. Damn friggen moss-wipe remote. I should have had Jax do it. I can't solder with that stupid-ass iron Nick had. I must have fused the fairy fucking thing."

"Jenks!" I admonished, thinking that was the worst thing I'd ever heard him say. Starting to get one of those "Oh crap" feelings, I looked at the Weres. As soon as official people started poking around in there, that statue would be gone and my life with it when they realized it was a fake. "Can you fix it?" I asked, my stomach knotting.

"Five minutes with an iron I don't have in a private space that doesn't exist on a bridge six hundred feet above the water surrounded by two hundred good Samaritans who don't know crap. Sure. You bet. Hell, maybe it's just the battery."

This wasn't good. I sat and stewed while Jenks took out the battery and shocked himself on his tongue. While he swore and danced from the mild zing, I pulled my knees to my chest to get up, wincing at the dull throb in my leg. Ivy and Nick were still beside the flat panel of the Mack truck, Nick looking nothing like himself under his legal disguise charm. The wind coming up through the grating they stood on sent her hair flying. She gestured with a small movement, and I gave her a lost look. Her lips pressed together and she rounded on Nick.

Nick's head was down, and it stayed that way as she put her hands on her hips and shot unheard questions at him. Blood soaked one of his pant legs and he looked pale. That he was hurt would make it easier to get him to the hospital where the vampire doctor waited, ready to pronounce him dead of a complication, mix up the paperwork, and shuffle him both out the back door and out of my life forever. Peter would be moved to the vamp wing underground until his body repaired itself. Everything was perfect. But the damn truck wasn't exploding.

"What are our options?" I asked Jenks, taking the remote and dropping it into my bag.

"It might be the switch on the tanks," he said. "If Jax was here—"

"He's not."

Jenks took my elbow when I swayed. "Can you blow it with your ley line magic?"

"You mean like with me lighting candles?" Hiking up my shoulder bag, I shook my head. "Can't tap a line over water. And I don't have a familiar to connect through to a land line." My mind jumped to Rex. *Maybe I ought to remedy that. This is getting old.*

"Nick might."

A shiver went through me, remembering when I channeled Trent's ability to tap a line last year to make a protection circle. I had hurt him. I didn't care if I hurt Nick right now—I just wanted to finish this run—but the question might be academic; I didn't know if Nick *had* a familiar. "Let's go ask," I said, lurching into motion.

My chest hurt, and as I gripped it with my arms, I forced a slow breath into me and tried to pull myself upright. It wasn't worth the effort to look unhurt, so I gave up, hunching over and breathing shallowly. The wind sluicing through the straits had a chill in it, and the setting sun was lost behind the clouds. It was going to get cold very quickly. Relegating Jax to cat-sitting duties at the motel had been a good idea.

Ivy heard my footsteps on the grating and turned with a frown she reserved only for me, a mix of anger and worry. She was ticked. Big surprise there.

"Rachel," Nick breathed, holding out his hands as if I would take them. I stopped, and his hands fell.

"I wouldn't touch a strange man like that," I said, reminding him that he was still under a disguise. "Especially one that just hit me."

His eyes flicked to my dental-floss stitches, and my face warmed. He saw me stiffen, then forced his face smooth. Though he looked nothing like himself, I could tell it was him. Not only was there his voice, but I could see Nick in little mannerisms that only an ex-lover might notice: the twitch of a muscle, the curve of a finger—the glint of annoyance in his eye.

"My God," he said again, softer. "That was the hardest thing I've ever done. Are you okay? Are you sure you're not hurt?"

Hardest thing he'd ever done? I thought bitterly, the entire right side of my body sticky with Peter's blood. All he had done was hit me with a truck. I had held Peter while he died, knowing it was wrong but the only thing that would be right.

"The remote doesn't work, Nick," I said shortly, watching for his tells. "You know anything about that?"

Eyes wide in an emotion I couldn't read, he looked at my bag, telling me he'd seen me put the remote in it. "What do you mean, it doesn't work? It's got to work!"

He reached for it, and I grunted when Jenks yanked me back. My sneakers fumbled for purchase on the metal mesh. In a blink Ivy was between us. The nearby people were getting nervous—thinking we were going to take justice into our own hands—and the Weres watched, evaluating whether this was a scam or a real accident. Peter's body was lying on the pavement, looking like Nick. Someone had covered him with a coat, and a part of me hunched into itself and cried.

"Don't touch me," I all but hissed, hurting but ready to slug Nick. "You did this, didn't you? You think you're going to get that empty artifact and sell it to them. You'll be in hiding, so they'll come after me when they find out it's not real. It's not going to happen. I won't let you. This is *my* life you're screwing over, not just yours."

Nick shook his head. "That's not it. You've got to believe me, Ray-ray."

Shaking from adrenaline, I turned sideways. I didn't like having my back to the truck with the empty focus in it. Ivy had been watching it—along with Nick—but there were too many Weres lurking as accident witnesses for my liking. "Have a good life, Nick," I said. "Don't include me in it." Ivy and Jenks flanked me, and we walked away. *What was I going to do?*

"I hope you're happy as Ivy's shadow," he said loudly, his voice full of a vitriolic hatred that he'd probably been denying since Ivy first asked me to be her scion.

I turned, my bandaged hand atop my neck hiding my

stitches. "We aren't . . . I'm not—" *He had just blown our cover. Son of a bitch . . .*

Three official-looking cars pulled up using the unopened northbound lane, their rear-window lights flashing amber and blue: two FIB, one I.S. The truck wasn't burning yet. *Shit on crap, could it get any worse?*

Looking like himself even with the disguise, Nick slumped against the panel of the white Mack truck and held his bleeding knee. His mocking gaze flicked to the cars behind us, their doors slamming shut and loud orders being given to secure the vehicle and get the rubberneckers moving. Three officers headed for us.

"You're rat piss," Jenks said suddenly to Nick. "No, you're the guy who puts rat piss on his breakfast cereal. We save your worthless human ass, and this is how you thank her? If you come back, I'll kill you myself. You're a foul pile of fairy crap that won't grow stones."

Nick's face went ugly. "I stole a statue," he said. "She killed someone and twisted a demon curse to hide that she still has it. I'd say I'm better than a foul, demon-marked witch."

I sputtered, pulse pounding as I felt myself go light-headed. *Damn him!*

Ivy leapt at Nick. Jenks yanked her back, using her shifting momentum to swing himself into Nick. Hands made into fists, Jenks punched him solidly on his jaw.

I took a gasping breath, and the I.S. guys turned their walk into a run. Angry, but with a modicum of restraint compared to Jenks, I got in Nick's face. "You sorry-assed bastard!" I shouted, spitting hair out of my mouth. "*You* ran into *us*!"

I wanted to say more, but Nick pushed himself at me. Jenks was still holding him, and all three of us went down. Instinct kept my hands before my face, and the bandages on my palms were the only thing that saved my skin. Pain shot through my ribs and hands as I hit the grating. The cold metal pressed into my leg where my jeans were torn.

"Get off her!" Ivy snarled. She yanked Nick up and away,

and suddenly I could breathe again I looked up in time to see him spin into Jenks. Like a choreographed dance, Jenks cocked his fist and this time connected right under his jaw. Nick's eyes rolled up and he crumpled.

"Damn, that felt good," the pixy said, shaking his hand as a thick I.S. officer grabbed his shoulders. "You know how long I've wanted to do that?" he said, letting the men drag him off. "Being big is good."

Shaking so hard I felt I might fall apart, I got up, bobbing my head at the FIB officer's unheard questions and obediently going where he directed me, but I lost it when a hand closed on my arm.

"Rachel, no!" Ivy shouted, and I turned my spin-and-kick into a spin-and-hair-toss. Adrenaline cleared my thoughts, and I took a painfully deep breath. The man released me, knowing I had almost landed one on him. His mustache bunched and his eyebrows were high, questioning, as he looked at me with new eyes.

"He killed him!" I shouted for the benefit of the watching Weres and starting to cry like a distraught girlfriend. "He killed him! He's dead!"

The sad reality was the tears leaking from me weren't that hard to dredge up. How could Nick say that to me even in anger? A foul, demon-marked witch. He had called me a foul demon-marked witch. My sense of betrayal rose higher, cementing my anger.

Jenks wiggled out of the grip of the two men holding him, and as they shouted and tried to catch him, he darted for my bag on the pavement. Grinning, he tucked my phone and my wallet inside before shaking everything down. I wasn't sure, but I think the remote went through the grating, and I breathed easier.

An I.S. officer grabbed him, cuffing him before shoving him back into our little group. The man shuffled through my bag before returning it to me. I thought it better to let the stone-faced guy have his way than bring up my rights.

"Thanks," I muttered to Jenks, feeling my ribs ache as

I looped the strap over my shoulder. I looked at Nick's wrecked truck as we passed. The artifact was still there, thanks to an excited FIB guy in a brown suit keeping everyone back.

"My pleasure," he said, limping.

"I meant for hitting him."

"So did I."

The I.S. officer at my elbow frowned, but when he saw the covered body, he seemed to ease. Jenks had punched Nick, not done anything permanent. *Like killing him.* "Ma'am," the officer said. "I'd ask you to stay away from the other party until we get this sorted out."

Party. Yeah, this was one big joke. "Yes, sir," I said, then stiffened when he slipped one of those plastic-coated charmed-silver wraps on my wrist and tightened it with a slick motion.

Damn it all to hell. "Hey!" I protested, feeling abused as Jenks and Ivy exchanged tired looks. "I'm fine! I'm not going to hurt anyone. I can't even do ley line magic." *Not on this bridge anyway.* The officer shook his head, and I felt trapped, the weight of Kisten's bracelet caught between my skin and the restraint. "Can I sit with . . . with my boyfriend?" I managed a warble in my voice, and the beefy man put a comforting hand on my shoulder.

"Yes, ma'am," he said, his voice softening. "They're taking him to the hospital to pronounce him. You can ride with him if you want. I'm sorry. He looked like a nice guy."

Plan A for getting the wacko witch off the accident scene. Right out of the handbook. "Thank you," I said, wiping my eyes.

"You were the driver, ma'am?" he asked as we walked, and when I nodded, he added, "May I see your license?"

Aw, shit. "Yes, sir," I said, fumbling in my bag for it. In five minutes the Cincinnati branch of the I.S. would be telling him all about me. We halted at the back of a black I.S. blazer, the tailgate down to show an open kennel. *There was a dog out here?* Behind me, I heard Ivy and Jenks telling the officers with them that they were my roommates. *Oh God. Ivy's Brimstone. I probably smelled like an addict. Accident. Points. What if they took my license?*

The officer before me squinted to see my license in the fading light, smiling when he looked up. "I'll have this right back to you, Ms. Morgan. Then you can go with your boyfriend and get yourself looked at." Eyebrows high, he glanced at my bandaged hands and ripped jeans before nodding to Jenks and Ivy and trotting away to leave us with two officers.

"Thank you," I said to no one. Exhausted, I leaned against the truck. Jenks had been cuffed to the truck, and the two FIB guys moved a short distance, close enough to intervene if necessary but clearly waiting for more I.S. personnel to handle our interrogation. Holding my elbows with my scraped hands, I watched my life swirl down the crapper.

Rubberneckers passed with an infuriating slowness, faces pressed against the windows as they struggled to see in the deepening dusk. My new jeans were ripped almost to the knee. The truck refused to burn. A fourth Were pack wearing military dress uniforms had joined the three already here, all of them edging the limits of the FIB and I.S. officers keeping them back. Had I forgotten anything? Oh yeah. I had helped kill someone, and it was going to turn around and bite me on the ass. I didn't want to go to jail. Unlike Takata, I looked awful in orange.

"Damn it," Ivy said, licking a thumb and trying to rub out the new scrape on her leather pants. "These were my favorite pair."

My gaze went to the truck. The knot in my stomach grew tighter. Leaning, I reclined against the Blazer's tailgate and silently fumed as I categorized the arriving Inderlanders into their jobs, pulled in from their scattered locations.

The willowy blond witch was probably their extraction specialist, not only comforting information from distraught victims but from testosterone-laden bucks who wouldn't talk to anyone unless it might get her into bed with them. Then there was the guy too fat to do real street work but who had a mustache, so he *had* to be important. He'd be good at keeping angry people apart and would tell me he could get me a deal if I was willing to spill. The dog team was at the Mack truck since he was the one who had crossed the yellow line, but I was sure he'd get to the pickup soon, then probably make a little visit over here.

I looked for, and finally found, the officer who was slightly off and took his job too seriously to be safe. This was the guy that no one trusted and even fewer liked, usually a witch or Were, too young to be a fat man with a mustache but too gun-happy to be a data guy. He was walking around the broken pickup, hiking up his belt with his weapon and looking at the girders as if they might hold a sniper ready to take us all out. *And don't forget the I.S. detective,* I thought. I didn't see him or her, but since someone had died, one would show up soon.

FIB officers were everywhere, taking their measurements and pictures. Seeing them in control of the site kind of threw me, but remembering the intensive data the Cincinnati FIB had shared with me during a murder investigation, I probably shouldn't have been surprised.

Ivy slumped against the side of the I.S. vehicle, arms crossed and thoroughly ticked. She stared at the ambulance Nick was in as if she could kill him by her gaze alone. Me? I was more worried about how we were going to get that truck burning. I was getting the feeling it wasn't going to happen. A heavy wrecker was inching its way into place, rollers moving with a sedate laziness. Apparently they wanted to get it off the bridge before the news crews showed up.

Slipping out of his cuffs, Jenks levered himself to sit beside me on the tailgate, a pained grunt coming from him. "You okay?" I asked, though clearly he wasn't.

"Bruise," he said, eyes fixed to Nick's blue truck. With an obnoxious beeping, the wrecker backed up to it.

"Here," I said, pulling my bag around and starting to rummage. "I've got an amulet. Ivy never takes any of my amulets, and I'm not used to you being big enough to use them."

"Why aren't you using it?" he said, stretching his shoulder with a pained look.

"I have no right to," I said, my throat closing when I glanced at Peter. I was glad he wasn't trying to convince me otherwise, and I hardly felt the prick of the finger stick for the blood to invoke it. Ivy shifted, telling me she had noticed the fresh blood despite the wind, but she was the last vamp I had anything to be worried about. Usually.

"Thanks," he said as he draped it over his head in obvious relief. "I wonder if there's any way you can make tiny amulets? I'm going to miss these."

"It's worth a try," I said, thinking that unless that truck spontaneously combusted from Ivy's glare, I'd have about a week to find out. Once the Weres realized the artifact was fake, they'd be knocking on my door. Assuming I didn't land in jail. I felt as if we were three kids standing outside the principal's office. Not that I had any experience in that area. Much.

Nick's truck went atop the wrecker in a horrendous noise of whining winches and complaining hydraulic machinery. The garage guy moved slowly, his dirty blue overalls and cap pulled down low, pressing levers and buttons seemingly at random. The overzealous I.S. guy was telling him to hustle and get his vehicle out of the way before the first news van arrived.

The driver walked with a limp, almost unnoticed amid the FIB and I.S. uniforms, and I thought it rude they made the old man move faster than he comfortably could.

Someone had moved one of the massive construction lights to illuminate the area, and as the distant generators rumbled to life a quarter mile away, a soft glow swelled into a harsh glare, washing out the gray of the fading sunset. Slowly the background rumble became unnoticed. Mind whirling for an idea, I dropped the spent finger stick in my shoulder bag and sighed.

I froze, fingers brushing the familiar objects in my bag. Something was missing besides the remote. Shocked, I stared into the dark fabric bag, tilting it so the growing light would illuminate what it could. The sight of my things scattered on the grating when Nick knocked me down passed through my mind. "It's gone," I said, feeling unreal. I looked up, meeting first Jenks's and then Ivy's wondering gaze as she pulled herself away from the vehicle.

"The wolf statue is gone!" I said, trying to decide if I should laugh or curse that I had been right in not trusting Nick. "The bastard took it. He knocked me down and took it!" I had been right to leave the totem shoved between Jenks's silk underwear and his dozen toothbrushes. Damn it, I'd have been happy to have been wrong this one time.

"Piss on my daisies . . ." Jenks said. "That's why he picked a fight."

Ivy's bewildered face cleared in understanding. At least she thought she understood. "Excuse me," she said, pushing herself away from the I.S. vehicle.

"Ivy, wait," I said, wishing I'd told her what I had done, though it wasn't as if I could shout that Nick had a fake. I pushed from the tailgate. Pain shot through me, reminding me I had just been hit by a truck. "Ivy!" I shouted, and an I.S. guy headed after her.

"Won't take but a moment!" she called over her shoulder. She stormed across the closed lanes, uniforms coming from all over to head her off. I moved to follow, immediately finding my elbow in the grip of one of the mustache guys. Images of court dates and jail cells kept me still as the first man to touch Ivy went down when she stiff-armed him in the jaw.

A call went up, and I watched with a sinking sensation, remembering when she and Jenks had taken out an entire floor of FIB officers. But it was I.S. runners this time. "Maybe we should have told her," I said, and Jenks smirked, rubbing his wrist where his cuffs had been.

"She needs to blow off some steam," he said, then whispered, "Holy crap. Look."

His green eyes were brilliant in the mercury light hammering down on us, and my jaw dropped when I followed his gaze to the wrecker. The brighter light made obvious what the shadows had hid before. The garage guy's hands were spotlessly clean, and the dark stain on the knee of his blue overalls was too wet to be oil.

"Nick," I breathed, not knowing how he got his hair that dirty white so fast. He was still wearing my disguise amulet, but with the overalls and cap, he was unrecognizable.

Jenks stood beside me, whispering, "What in Tink's garden of sin is he doing?"

I shook my head, seeing the Weres watching him too. *Double damn, I think they knew it was him.* "He thinks he has the focus," I said. "He's trying to get the original too."

"Leaving us holding the bag?" Jenks finished in disgust. "What a slug's ass. If he doesn't go to the hospital and die on paper, then we have a dead vamp to explain and will be brought up on insurance fraud. Rache, I'm too pretty to go to jail!"

Face cold, I turned to Jenks, my stomach in knots. "We have to stop him."

He nodded, and I cupped my hands to my mouth. "Ivy!" I shouted. "The wrecker!"

It wasn't the smartest thing to do, but it got results. Ivy took one look and realized it was Nick. Crying out, she slugged the last I.S. agent and took off running, only to be brought down by a lucky snag by a previously felled officer. She sprawled, cuffs on her in two seconds flat.

Jenks flowed into motion, distracting the surrounding FIB officers. Thinking this was going to look great on my ré-sumé, I sidestepped them and ran for the wrecker. People were shouting, and someone had probably pulled a weapon as I heard, "Stop, or I'll use force!"

Force my ass, I thought. If they shot me, I'd sue their bright little badges from here to the Turn. I didn't have anything stronger than a pain amulet. I'd been searched, and they knew it.

It was right about then that Nick realized I was coming for him. Clearly frightened, he jerked the door open. A cry went up when his engine revved, loud over the generators. There was a piercing whistle, and the leader of the unknown military faction waved his hand above his head as if in direction. Horns started to blow when three street racers stopped in traffic and Weres got out. Grim-faced, they closed in. They weren't happy. Neither was I.

"Stop him!" came a bark of a demand, and I picked up my pace. I was going to get to Nick first, or whoever beat me to him was going to get my foot in their gut. He had hurt and betrayed me, leaving me to clean up his mess and take his fall. Twice. Not this time.

My gaze was fixed fervently on the truck as it lurched, almost stalling, but a flash of pixy dust jerked me to a stop. "Jax?" I exclaimed, shocked.

"Ms. Morgan," the adolescent pixy said, hovering before my nose with an amulet as big as he was, his eyes bright and his wings red in excitement. "Nick wanted me to tell you he's sorry and he loves you. He really does."

"Jax!" I said, blinking as even the sparkles from his dust faded. My eyes went to the truck. The wheels were smoking as Nick tried to get the heavy vehicle moving. With a lurch, the wheels caught. My face went cold as I realized it was headed right for me. I watched him fight the huge wheel, arms stiff and fear in his eyes, struggling to turn it.

"Rachel, get out of the way!" Ivy screamed over the rumble of the engine.

I froze as the wheels turned, missing me, the tires taking the weight compressing dangerously. Jenks crashed into me, knocking me farther out of the way. Stifling a gasp, I hit the pavement for the *third* time in the last hour. The truck roared past in a frightening noise and a breeze of diesel fumes. A crack followed by a boom shook my insides, the sound rolling over my back like a wave. Jenks held my head down and a second boom followed the first.

What in hell was that? Heart pounding, I pushed Jenks off me and lifted my head. The wrecker was careening out of control, the tires blown out. Someone had shot out his tires?

I scrambled up when the wrecker with Nick's truck swerved wildly to avoid the scattering news crews. Tires squealing and gears grinding, the brakes burned as he locked them. Momentum kept the vehicle moving—careening into the temporary railing.

"Nick!" I screamed when the wrecker crashed through it like toast. With a shocking silence, it was gone.

Heart in my throat, I hobbled to the edge, too hurt to stand upright. Jenks was behind me, and he yanked me back when I reached the crumbling edge. The wind gusted up from the distant water, blowing my hair out of my eyes. I looked down, dizzy.

Hand to my stomach, I started to hyperventilate. My sight grew gray, and I pushed Jenks's hand off me. "I'm okay," I mumbled, but there wasn't anything to see. Six hundred feet makes even a wrecker small.

Nick had been in it. *God help me.*

"Easy, Rache," Jenks said, easing me back and making me sit.

"Nick," I mumbled, forcing my eyes wide as the cold pavement met my rear. I wasn't going to pass out. Damn it, I wasn't! I looked at the edge, the roadway cracked to show the metal embedded in it, threatening to give way where the truck's weight had hit it hard. Shiny shoes clustered around me, belonging to the officers peering down. At the edges of the excited crowd were the Weres. They were dressed in suits, leather, and military uniforms, but the look on their faces was the same. Disbelief and shock. It was gone.

The crackle of a radio intruded, coming from the I.S. officer swearing softly as he peered over the edge. "This is Ralph," he said, thumbing the button. "We have two trucks off the bridge and a body in the water. Smile everyone. We're going to make the evening news."

I missed what was said back, lost in the hiss of bad reception and the thundering of my heart as I tried to fit it into my head. *He had gone over the bridge. Nick had gone off the bridge.*

"Yup," the man said. "Confirm a commercial vehicle towing a pickup truck off the bridge and a body in the water. Better get the boat out here. Anybody got Marshal's number?"

He listened to the response, then clipped it to his belt. Hands on his hips, he stared down. Soft swear words dropped from him like the gray smoke from his cigarette, mixing with the faint scent of incense. Ralph was a living vamp, the first local I'd seen apart from the one who had bandaged my leg. I wondered whose neck he didn't bite to get stuck with a job up here, so far from the bustle of the city they thrived on.

I pulled my head up. "Will he be all right?" I asked, and Ralph glanced at me, surprised.

"Lady," he said, noticing me, "he died of a heart attack before he hit the water. And if that didn't get him, he died on impact. At this height, it's like hitting a brick wall."

I blinked, trying to take that in. *A brick wall.* It would be the second brick wall Nick hit today. My focus blurred, the sight of Jax and that amulet filling my memory. What if . . .

"The body?" I insisted, and he turned, impatient. "When can they retrieve the body?"

"They'll never find it," he said. "The current will take it, moving it out into Lake Huron faster than green corn through a tourist. He's gone. The only way he would have survived was if he was dead already. Damn, I'm glad I'm not the one who has to talk to the next of kin. I bet he's got three kids and a wife."

I hunched over, the reality of what had happened sinking in. God bless it, I was twice the fool. Nick hadn't died going over the edge. This had been a scam right from when I told him he couldn't have the statue—and I had walked right into it.

"His name was Nick," I whispered, and the I.S. officer spun from the drop, surprise on his age-lined face. Ivy and Jenks stiffened. I was blowing our cover, but we were going to be questioned before too long, and I wanted our stories to be the same. "Nick Sparagmos," I added, thinking fast. "He was helping us with a piece of art I was contracted to recover. I'm an independent runner out of Cincinnati and this was a run." *The truth is good.*

"He wasn't supposed to be here," I continued as Ivy's tension pulled her shoulders tight. "But when that guy hit us and killed Peter . . ." I took a breath, the heartache real. "Peter was only supposed to make sure it got to the right people okay. He wasn't supposed to get hurt. The people we recovered it from . . . I think the accident was their attempt to get it back before we handed it over. Nick came out with the wrecker to make sure they didn't get it. The artifact was still on the truck. He was going to get it out of here, but someone shot the tires out. Oh God, he went right over the edge." *And a little lie mixed in with the truth keeps me showering alone.*

Jenks put a hand on my shoulder and gave it a squeeze to tell me he understood. Peter had been killed in the pickup truck in an accident to satisfy the insurance company. Nick had died when he went over the edge to satisfy the Weres. That Nick was the driver of the Mack truck as well wouldn't even be considered, the driver's absence explained as a hit and run. If anyone got curious and found out the truck belonged to DeLavine, he'd be the one slapped with the illegal early termination lawsuit from the insurance company, not me.

It sounded good to me. I was going to stick with it.

I could almost feel the worry ease out of Jenks, but Ivy was still a knot of tension, not knowing that Nick had gotten away with absolutely nothing.

The I.S. officer who had taken my license ambled up to the man before me. "Hi, Ralph. You got out here quick." He turned to me, camaraderie in the witch's eyes as he handed me my license back. "Ms. Morgan, what are you doing this far out of the Hollows?"

"Cincinnati?" Ralph looked at me in surprise. "You mean Rachel Morgan?" His gaze went to Ivy. "You're Piscary's girl. What are you doing this far north?"

"Getting my partner's boyfriend killed," she said, and the man took her ugly look as dark humor. Officer Ralph already had his cuff key out and was getting them off her, frowning when he realized Jenks wasn't in his. I held up my wrist with my little black strap, and he snipped it off with a special pair of clippers on his key chain. I wanted one of those.

"Where are you staying?" Ralph asked as Ivy rubbed her freed wrists. "I'm going to want to talk to you before you go home."

Ivy explained while I stared at the water. Nick wasn't dead, and the shock of seeing him go over the edge was evolving into a nasty feeling of satisfaction. I had beat him. I had beat Nick at his own game. Knees shaking, I stumbled away. Ivy hurriedly finished up with Ralph, and with her on one side and Jenks on the other, I started to chuckle. I didn't know how we were going to get to the room. Three of us wouldn't fit in Kisten's Corvette very well.

"Tink's daisies," Jenks whispered to Ivy behind my back. "She's lost it."

"I'm fine," I said, cursing myself and laughing. "He's fine. The crazy bastard is fine."

Jenks exchanged a sorrowful glance at Ivy. "Rache," he said softly. "You heard the man. I read the place mat about how many people they lost building the bridge. He wouldn't survive hitting the water. And even if he did, he'd be unconscious and drown. Nick is gone."

We passed the news crews, and I took a shallow breath, finding comfort in that my ribs hurt. I was alive, and I was going to stay that way. "Nick knew that too," I admitted in the dimmer light. "And yeah, he's gone, but he's not dead."

Jenks took a breath to protest, and I interrupted.

"Jax was here," I said, and Jenks pulled us all to a stop in the middle of the closed northbound lane. People swirled around us, but we were forgotten.

"Jax!" Jenks exclaimed, yanked into silence by Ivy.

"Shut up," she snarled.

"He had an inertia-dampening amulet," I said, and Jenks's face went from hope to a heartbreaking look of understanding. "Jax was here to fly it down to the water before the tow truck hit."

"And the NOS," I continued as Jenks paled. "It never exploded. He used the charges to blow the tires, knowing the truck was heavy enough to go through the temporary railing."

Ivy's face was empty, but her eyes were starting to go black with anger.

Shaking my head, I looked away before she scared me. "I'll give Marshal a call, but I bet he's missing some equipment. I never looked to see what Nick had in that truck locker he's got. He's swimming out of here, and I bet Jax is with him."

A pained sound came from Jenks, and I wished I could have said it wasn't true. Feeling his pain, I met his eyes. They showed a deep betrayal he would never talk about. Jenks had taught Jax all he could in the last few days with the idea that the pixy would take his place. And Jax had taken that and used it to burn us. With Nick.

"I'm sorry, Jenks," I said, but he turned away, shoulders hunched and looking old.

Ivy tried to tuck a strand of too-short hair behind her ear. "I'm sorry too, Jenks, but we have a big problem. As soon as Nick gets himself safely settled as a nonentity, he's going to sell that thing and all hell is going to break loose between the vamps and the Weres."

Something in me hardened, and the last of my feelings for Nick died. I smiled at Ivy without showing my teeth, hiking my bag farther up my bruised shoulder. "He won't sell it."

"And why not?" she asked, snarky.

"Because he doesn't have the real one." I looked for Kisten's Corvette, finding it standing by a pylon. Maybe we could splurge and move to the Holiday Inn tonight. I could use a hot tub. "I didn't move the curse to the wolf statue," I added, remembering I was in the middle of a thought. "I moved it to the totem Jenks was going to give Matalina."

Ivy stared at us, reading in Jenks's lack of response that she was the only one who hadn't known. He was staring at nothing, pain still etched in his posture that his son had just buried in the dirt everything he cared about. "When were you going to tell me?" she accused, blush coloring her cheeks. She looked good when she was mad, and I smiled. A real one this time.

"What," I said, "and risk spending the next two days trying to convince you to change your plan?" She huffed, and I touched her arm. "I tried to tell you," I said. "But you stormed off like you were an avenging angel."

Ivy eyed my fingers on her arm, and I pulled them away, hesitating a bare instant.

"Nick's an ass," I said. "But he's smart. If I had told you, you would have acted differently and he would have known."

"But you told Jenks," she said.

"It's hiding in his jockey shorts!" I said in exasperation, not wanting to talk about it anymore. "God, Ivy. I'm not going to mess with Jenks's underwear unless he knows about it."

Ivy pouted. The six-foot sexy vampire in scraped black leather crossed her arms before her and pouted. "I'm probably going to have to do more community service for hitting all those I.S. officers," she grumbled. "Thanks a hell of a lot."

I slumped, hearing forgiveness in her words. "At least he didn't get it," I offered, and Ivy threw a hand in the air and tried to look disgusted, but I could tell she was relieved.

Jenks found a thin smile, his gaze going to Kisten's Corvette. "Can I drive?" he asked.

Lips pressed, Ivy frowned. "We're not going to all fit in that. Maybe we can bum a ride from Ralph. Give me a moment, okay?"

"We can fit," Jenks said. "I'll move the seat back and Rachel can sit on my lap."

Ivy went one way and Jenks went the other. My protest froze when I found a point of stillness in the swirling mess of reporters, officers, and watchers. My lips parted. It was Brett, standing on a cement barrier so he could look over the crowd. He was watching me, and when our eyes met, he touched the brim of his cap in salute. There was a rip in it where the emblem had been removed, and with a significant motion he took it off and let it fall. Turning away, he started to walk for the Mackinaw City end of the bridge. And he was gone.

I realized he thought I had done it, and went cold. He thought I'd blown out the tires of the wrecker and killed Nick for trying to do a double run on me. Damn. I didn't know if that kind of reputation would save my life or get me killed.

"Rache?" Jenks returned from pushing the passenger's seat back as far as it would go. "What is it?"

I put a hand to my cold face and met his worried eyes. "Nothing." Determined to figure it out later, I sent my thoughts instead to the bath I was going to take. I had beaten Nick at his own game. The question was, would I survive it?

Thirty-five

My boot heel slipped on the uneven sidewalk, and the sound of me catching my step was dull in the air heavy from the evening's rain. The faint twinge in my leg reminded me that it wasn't quite right yet. The sun was long gone, and clouds made the night darker than it ought to be, close and warm. I splashed through a puddle, in too good a mood to care if my ankles got wet. Pizza dough was rising in my kitchen, and I had a grocery sack of toppings.

Lunch was going to be early tonight; Ivy had a run, and Kisten was taking me to a movie and I didn't want to fill up on popcorn. Passing under a lamp-lit, pollution-stunted maple, I reached to touch its leaves in passing, smiling at the green softness brushing my skin. They were damp, and I let my hand stay wet and cool in the night air. The street was quiet. The only human family living there was inside watching TV, and everyone else was at work or school. The hum of Cincinnati was far away and distant, the rumble of sleeping lions.

I adjusted the strap of my new canvas grocery bag, thinking that in the time we'd been gone, spring had shifted into high gear. It was almost a year since I'd quit the I.S. "And I'm alive," I whispered to the world. I was alive and doing well. No, I was doing great.

A soft clearing of a throat zinged through me, but I managed not to jerk or alter my pace. It had come from across the street, and I searched the shadows until I found a well-muscled Were in jeans and a dress shirt. He had been shadowing me all week. It was Brett.

I forced my jaw to unclench and gave him a respectful nod, receiving a snappy salute in return. Free arm swinging, I continued down the street, hitting the puddles that were in my way. Brett wouldn't bother me. That he was looking for the focus had occurred to me—either wanting to confirm that it was truly gone, or use it to buy his way back into Walter's good graces if it wasn't—but I didn't think so. It looked like he was going loner when he dropped his cap on the Mackinac Bridge and walked away. But he was just watching now. David had done the same for months before he finally made his presence known. When unsure of their rank, Weres were patient and wary. He'd come to me when he was ready.

And I was in far too good a mood to worry about it. I was so glad to be home. My stitches were out and the scars were thin lines easily hidden. My limp was fading, and thanks to that curse I used to Were, I had absolutely no freckles. The soft air slipped easily in and out of my lungs as I walked, and I felt sassy. Sassy and badass in my vamp-made boots and Jenks's aviator jacket. I was wearing the cap Jenks had stolen from the island Weres, and it added a nice bit of bad girl. The guy behind the counter at the corner store had thought I was cute.

I passed my covered car in the open garage and my mood faltered. The I.S. had suspended my license. It just wasn't fair. I had saved them a dump truck of political hassle, and did I get even a thank-you? No. They took my license.

Not wanting to lose my good mood, I forced my brow smooth. The I.S. had publicly announced on the back page of the Community Section of the paper that I was cleared of all suspicion of any wrongdoing in the accidental deaths that had taken place on the bridge. But behind closed doors some undead vamp had given me a hard time for trying to handle such a powerful artifact instead of bringing it to them. He didn't back off until Jenks threatened to cut off his balls and give them to me to make a magic bola. You gotta love friends like that.

The undead vampire didn't get me to confess that I'd meant to kill Peter, and that cheesed him off to no end. He had been beautifully dangerous, with snow-white hair and sharp features, and even though he whipped me up to the point where I would have had his baby, he couldn't scare me into forgetting I had rights. Not after I'd survived Piscary—who didn't care about them. The entire nationwide I.S. was pissed at me, believing the focus had gone over the edge with Nick instead of being turned over to them.

There was a continuous twenty-four-hour search going on for the artifact on the bottom of the straits. The locals thought they were stupid since the current had put it in Lake Huron shortly after the truck hit the water, and I thought they were stupid because the real artifact was hidden in Jenks's living room. With their official stand being what it was, the I.S. couldn't lock me up, but with the added points after the accident with Peter, they *could* suspend my license. My choices were riding the bus for six months or gritting my teeth and taking driver's ed. God no. I'd be the oldest one in the class.

My mood tarnishing, I took the church's stairs two at a time, and felt my leg protest. I pulled the heavy wooden door open, slipped inside and breathed deeply, relishing the scent of tomato paste and bacon. The pizza dough was probably ready, and Kisten's sauce had been simmering for the better part of the day. He had kept me company in the kitchen all afternoon while I finished restocking my charm cupboard. Even helped me clean my mess.

I shut the door with hardly a thump. All the windows in the church were open to let in the moist night. I couldn't wait to get into the garden tomorrow, and even had a few seeds I wanted to try out. Ivy was laughing at me and the stack of seed catalogs that somehow found me despite my address change, but I'd caught her looking at one.

Tucking a stray curl behind my ear, I wondered if I might

splurge for the ten-dollar-a-seed packet of black orchids she'd been eyeing. They were wickedly hard to get and even more difficult to grow, but with Jenks's help, who knew?

Slipping off my wet boots and coat, I left them by the door and padded in my socks through the peaceful sanctuary. The hush of a passing car came in through the high transom windows above the stained-glass windows. The pixies had worked for hours chiseling the old paint off and oiling the hinges so I could open them with the long pole I'd found in the belfry stairway. There were no screens, which was why the lights were off. There were no pixies either. My desk was again my desk. *Thank all that was holy.*

My wandering attention touched on the potted plants Jenks had left behind on my desk, and I jerked to a halt, seeing a pair of green eyes under the chair, catching the light. Slowly my breath slipped from me. "Darn cat," I whispered, thinking Rex was going to scare the life out of me if she didn't break my heart first. I crouched to try to coax her to me, but Rex didn't move, didn't blink, didn't even twitch her beautiful tail.

Rex didn't like me much. She liked Ivy just fine. She loved the garden, the graveyard, and the pixies that lived in it, but not me. The little ball of orange fluff would sleep on Ivy's bed, purr under her chair during breakfast for tidbits, and sit on her lap, but she only stared at me with large, unblinking eyes. I couldn't help but feel hurt. I think she was still waiting for me to turn back into a wolf. The sound of Kisten and Ivy's voices intruded over the slow jazz. Hiking the canvas bag higher, I awkwardly inched closer to Rex, hand held out.

Ivy and I had been home a week, and we were all still in emotional limbo. Three seconds after Ivy and I walked in the door, Kisten looked at my dental floss stitches, breathed deeply, and knew what had happened. In an instant, Ivy had gone from happy-to-be-home to depressed. Her face full of an aching emptiness, she'd dropped her bags and took off on her bike to get it "checked over."

Just as well. Kisten and I had a long, painful discussion where he both sorrowed after and admired my new scars. It felt good to confess to someone that Ivy had scared the crap out of me, and even better when he agreed that in time she might forget her own fear and try to find a blood balance with me.

Since then he'd been his usual self. Almost. There was a sly hesitancy in his touch now, as if he was holding himself to a limit of action to see if I would change it. The unhappy result was the mix of danger and security that I loved in him was gone. Not wanting to interfere in anything Ivy and I might find, he had put me in charge of moving our relationship forward.

I didn't like being in charge. I liked the heart pounding rush of being lured into making decisions that might turn bad on me. Realizing as much was depressing. It seemed that Ivy and Jenks were right that not only was I an adrenaline junkie, but I needed a sensation of danger to get turned on.

Thinking about it now, my mood thoroughly soured, I crouched beside my desk, arm extended to try to get the stupid cat to like me. Her neck stretched out and she sniffed my fingers, but wouldn't bump her head under my hand as she would Ivy's. Giving up, I stood and headed for the back of the church, following the sound of Kisten's masculine rumble. I took a breath to call out and tell them I was there, but my feet stilled when I realized they were talking about me.

"Well, you did bite her," Kisten said, his voice both lightly accusing and coaxing.

"I bit her," Ivy admitted, her voice a whisper.

"And you didn't bind her," he prompted.

"No." I heard the creak of her chair as she repositioned herself, guilt making her shift.

"She wants to know what comes next," Kisten said with a rude laugh. "Hell, I want to know myself."

"Nothing," Ivy said shortly. "It's not going to happen again."

I licked my lips, thinking I should back out of the hallway

and come in making more noise, but I couldn't move, staring at the worn wood by the archway to the living room.

Kisten sighed. "That's not fair. You strung her along until she called your bluff, and now you won't go forward, and she can't go back. Look at her," he said, and I imagined him gesturing at nothing. "She wants to find a blood balance. God, Ivy, isn't that what you wanted?"

Ivy's breath came harsh. "I could have killed her!" she exclaimed, and I jumped. "I lost control just like always and almost killed her. She let me do it because she trusted me." Her words were now muffled. "She understood everything and she didn't stop me."

"You're scared," Kisten accused, and my eyes widened at his gall.

But Ivy took it in stride as she laughed sarcastically. "You think?"

"No," he insisted, "I mean you're scared. You're afraid to try to find a balance you can both live with, because if you try and can't, she leaves and you've got nothing."

"That's not it," she said flatly, and I nodded. That was part of it, but not all.

Kisten leaned forward; I could hear the chair creak. "You think you don't deserve anything good," he said, and my face went cold, wondering if there was more to this than I had thought. "Afraid you're going to ruin every decent thing you get, so you're going to stick with this shitty half relationship instead of seeing where it might go."

"It's not a half relationship," Ivy protested.

He touched the truth, I thought. *But that's not what keeps her silent.*

"Compared to what you might have, it is," he said, and I heard someone get up and move. "She's straight, and you're not," Kisten added, and my pulse quickened. His voice was now coming from where Ivy sat. "She sees a deep platonic relationship, and you *know* that even if you start one, you'll eventually delude yourself into believing it's deeper. She'll be your friend when what you want is a lover. And one night in a moment of blood passion, you're going to make a mistake in a very concrete way and she'll be gone."

"Shut up!" she shouted, and I heard a slap, perhaps of a hand meeting someone's grip.

Kisten laughed gently, ending it with a sigh of understanding. "I got it right that time."

His liquid voice, gray with truth, sent a shiver through me. *Back up,* I told myself. *Back up and go play with the cat.* I could hear my heartbeat in the silence. From the disc player, the song ended.

"Are you going to share blood with her again?"

It was a gentle, hesitant inquiry, and Ivy took a noisy breath. "I can't."

"Mind if I do?"

Oh God. This time I did move, pulling the canvas bag tight to me. Kisten already had my body. If we shared blood, it would be too much for Ivy's pride. Something would break.

"Bastard," Ivy said, pulling my retreat to a halt.

"You know how I feel about her," he said. "I'm not going to walk away because of your asinine hang-ups about blood."

My lips parted at his bitter accusation, and Ivy's breath hissed. "Hang-ups?" she said vehemently. "Mixing sex with bloodletting is the only way I can keep from losing control with someone I love, Kisten! I thought I was better, but *obviously* I'm not!"

It had been bitter and accusing, but Kisten's voice was harsh with his own frustration. "I don't understand, Ivy," he said, and I heard him move away from her. "I never did. Blood is blood. Love is love. You aren't a whore if you take someone's blood when you don't like them, and you aren't a whore for wanting someone you don't like to take your blood."

"This is where I am, Kisten," she said. "I'm not touching her, and neither are you."

My pulse pounded, and I heard in his heavy exhalation the sound of an old argument that had no answer. "Rachel's worth fighting for," he said softly. "If she asks me, I won't say no."

I closed my eyes, seeing where this was heading.

"And because you're a man," Ivy said bitterly, "she won't have a problem when the blood turns to sex, will she."

"Probably not." It was confident, and my eyes opened.

"Damn you," she whispered, sounding broken. "I hate you."

Kisten was silent, and then I heard the soft sound of a kiss. "You love me."

Mouth dry, I stood in the hallway, afraid to move in the silence the last sound track had left.

"Ivy?" Kisten coaxed. "I won't lure her from you, but I won't sit by and pretend I'm a stone either. Just talk to her. She knows where your feelings are, and she still has the room next to yours, not an apartment across the city. Maybe . . ."

My eyes closed in the swirl of conflicting feelings. The image of me sharing a room with Ivy flitted through my mind, shocking me. Of me slipping between those silken sheets and sliding up to her back, smelling her hair, feeling her turn over and seeing her easy smile four inches from mine. I knew how her eyes would be lidded and heavy with sleep, the soft sound of welcome she would make. *What in hell was I doing?*

"She's rash," Kisten said, "impulsive, and the most caring person I have ever met. She told me what happened, but she doesn't think anything less of you, or herself, even when it went wrong."

"Shut up," Ivy whispered, pain and self-reproach in her voice.

"You opened the door," he accused, making her come to grips with what we had done. "And if you don't walk her through it, she'll find someone who will. I don't have to ask your permission. And unless you tell me right now that someday you're going to try to find a blood balance with her, I will if she asks me."

I shivered, jerking when a soft brush on my leg made me jump. It was Rex, but I was little more to her than something to brush up against as she headed to the living room, following the sound of Ivy's distress.

"I can't!" Ivy exclaimed, and I jumped. "Piscary . . ." She took a gasping breath. "Piscary will step in and he'll make me hurt her, maybe kill her."

"*That's* an excuse," he hammered on her. "The truth is that you're scared."

I stood in the hallway and trembled, feeling the tension rise in the unseen room. But Kisten's voice was gentle now that he'd gotten her to admit her feelings. "You should tell her that," he continued softly.

Ivy sniffed, half in sorrow, half in bitter amusement. "I just did. She's in the hall."

I sucked in my breath and jerked upright.

"Shit," Kisten said, his voice panicked. "Rachel?"

Pulling up my shoulders, I raised my chin and went into the kitchen. Kisten scuffed to a halt in the hall, and tension slammed into me. His lanky build, wide shoulders, and my favorite red silk shirt took up the archway. He had on boots, and they looked good peeping from under his jeans. His bracelet felt heavy on me, and I twisted it, wondering if I should take it off.

"Rachel, I didn't know you were there," he said, his face creased. "I'm sorry. You aren't a toy that I have to ask Ivy's permission to play with."

I kept my back to him, shoulders stiff while I opened the canvas sack and took things out. Leaving the cheese, mushrooms, and the pineapple where they were, I strode to the pantry, hanging my grocery bag up on the hook I'd nailed in yesterday. Images of Ivy's comfortable room, of Kisten's face, his body, the way he felt under my fingers, the way he made me feel, all flashed through me. Pace stilted, I went to the stove and took the lid off the sauce. Steam billowed up, the rising scent of tomato making the wisps of my hair drift. I stirred without seeing as he came up behind me. "Rachel?"

My breath came out, and I held the next one. I was so confused.

Softly—almost not there—Kisten put a hand on my shoulder. Tension slipped from me, and sensing it, he leaned until his body pressed against my back. His arms went around me, imprisoning me, and my motions to stir the pot stilled. "She knew the moment I came in," I said.

"Probably," he whispered into my ear.

I wondered where Ivy was—if she had stayed in the living room or fled the church entirely, shamed that she had needs and fears like the rest of us. Kisten took the spoon from me, setting it between the burners before turning me around. I pulled my eyes to his, not surprised to see them narrow with concern. The glow from the overhead light shimmered on his day-old stubble, and I touched it because I could. His arms were about my waist, and he gave a tug, settling me closer into him. "What she can't say to your face, she'll say when she knows you're listening," he said. "It's a bad habit she picked up in therapy."

I had already figured that one out, and bobbed my head. "This is a mess," I said, miserable as I looked over his shoulder to the dark hallway. "I never should have—"

My words cut off when Kisten pulled me closer. Arms about his waist and my head against his chest, I breathed deeply the scent of leather and silk, relaxing into him. "Yes," he whispered. "You should have." He pushed me back until I could see his eyes. "I won't ask," he said earnestly. "If it happens, it happens. I like things the way they are." His expression grew sly. "I'd like it better if things changed, but when change is too quick, the strong break."

My eyes on the archway, I stood and held him, not wanting to let go. I could hear Ivy in the living room, trying to find a way to make a graceful entrance. The warmth of his body was soothing, and I held my breath against the thought of his teeth sinking into me. I knew exactly how good it would feel. *What was I going to do about that?*

Kisten's head came up an instant before the peal of the

front doorbell echoed through the church. "I got it!" Ivy shouted, and Kisten and I pulled apart before her boots made a soft brush down the hall. The light flicked on in the hallway, and I heard the beginnings of a low conversation. The mushrooms needed cutting, and Kisten joined me as I washed my hands. We jostled for space at the sink, bumping hips as he pushed me into a better mood.

"Cut them at an angle," he admonished when I reached for the cutting board. He had his hands in the flour bag, then clapped them once over the sink before putting himself at the center island counter and the ball of dough he had set to rise under a piece of linen.

"It makes a difference?" Still melancholy, I moved my stuff to the opposite side of the counter so I could watch him. "David?" I shouted, eating the first mushroom slice. It was probably him, seeing as I'd asked him to come over.

A low noise escaped Kisten, and I smiled. He looked good over there. A brush of flour made a domestic smear on his shirt, and he had rolled up his sleeves to show his lightly tanned arms. Seeing him gently handling the dough and watching me at the same time, I realized the thrill was back—the delicious danger of what-if. He had told Ivy he wasn't going to walk away from me; I was on dangerous ground. Again.

God save me. I thought in disgust. *Could I* be *any more stupid?* My life was so messed up. How could I just stand here and cut mushrooms as if everything was normal? But compared to last week, maybe this *was* normal.

My attention came up when David walked in ahead of Ivy, his slight build looking blocky before her sleek grace. "Hi, David," I said, trying to clear my mind. "Full moon tonight."

He nodded, saying nothing as he took in Kisten casually pulling the dough into a circle. "I can't stay," he said, realizing we were making lunch. "I have a few appointments, but you said it was urgent?" He smiled at Kisten. "Hi, Kisten. How's the boat?"

"Still afloat," he said, eyebrows rising as he took in David's expensive suit. He was working, and he looked the part despite the heavy stubble the full moon made worse.

"It won't take long," I said, slicing the last mushroom. "I've got something I want you to take a look at. Picked it up on vacation, and I want your opinion."

His eyes went wondering, but he unbuttoned his long leather duster. "Now?"

"Full moon," I said cryptically, sliding the sliced mushrooms into my smallest spell pot and quashing the faint worry that I was breaking rule number two by mixing food prep and spell prep, but they were just the right size to hold toppings. Ivy quietly went to the fridge, getting out the cheese, cooked hamburger, and the bacon left over from breakfast. I tried to meet her eyes to tell her we were okay, but she wouldn't look at me.

Angry, I slammed the knife down, careful to keep my fingers out of the way. *Silly little vamp, afraid of her feelings.*

Kisten sighed, his eyes on the disk of dough he had tossed professionally into the air, "Someday, I'm going to get you two ladies together."

"I don't do threesomes," I said snidely.

David jerked, but Kisten's eyes went sultry and pensive, even as he caught the dough. "That's not what I was talking about, but okay."

Ivy's cheeks were red, and David froze as he took in the sudden tension. "Uh," the Were said, half out of his coat. "Maybe this isn't a good time."

I dredged up a smile. "No," I said. "It's just everyday normal crap. We're used to it."

David finished taking off his coat, frowning. "I'm not," he muttered.

I went to the sink and leaned toward the window, thinking David was a bit of a prude. "Jenks!" I shouted into the dusky garden, alight with pixy children tormenting moths. It was beautiful, and I almost lost myself in the sifting bands of falling color.

A clatter of wings was my only warning, and I jerked away

when Jenks vaulted through the pixy hole in the screen. "David!" he called out, looking great in his casual gardening clothes of green and black. Hovering at eye level, he brought the scent of damp earth into the kitchen. "Thank Tink's little red shoes you're here," he said, pulling up two feet when Rex appeared in the doorway, her eyes big and her ears pricked. "Matalina is about ready to dewing me. You gotta get this thing out of my living room. My kids keep touching it. Making it move."

I felt myself blanch. "It's moving now?"

Ivy and Kisten exchanged worried looks, and David sighed, putting his hands into his pockets as if trying to divorce himself from what was coming. He wasn't that much older than me, but at that moment he looked like the only adult in a room full of adolescents. "What is it, Rachel?" he said, sounding tired.

Suddenly nervous, I took a breath to tell him, then changed my mind. "Could you . . . could you just take a look at it?" I said, wincing.

Jenks landed on the windowsill and leaned casually against the frame. He looked like Brad Pitt gone sexy farmer, and I smiled. Two weeks ago he would have stood with his hands on his hips. This was better, and might explain Matalina's blissful state lately.

"I'll have the boys bring it up," Jenks said, tossing his hair out of his eyes. "We've got a sling for it. Won't take but a tick, David."

He zipped back out the window, and while David looked at his watch and moved from foot to foot, I pushed the window all the way up, struggling with the rain-swollen frame. The screen popped out, and the air suddenly seemed a lot fresher.

"This doesn't have anything to do with the Were sentry at the end of the block, does it?" David asked wryly.

Whoops. I turned, my eyes going immediately to Ivy, sitting before her computer. I hadn't told her Brett was shadowing me, knowing she'd throw a hissy. *Like I couldn't handle one Were who was scared of me?* Sure enough, she was frowning. "You saw him, huh?" I said, putting my back to her and moving the sauce to Kisten.

David shifted his weight and glanced at Kisten as he non-chalantly spread it thinly on the dough. "I saw him," David said. "Smelled him, and nearly dropped my cell phone down the sewer calling you to ask if you wanted me to, ah, ask him to go away until he . . . mmmm."

I waited in the new silence broken by shrill pixy whistles coming from the garden. David's face was red when he swung his head back up and rubbed a hand across his stubble.

"What?" I said warily.

David looked discomfited. "He, ah . . ." A quick glance at Ivy, and he blurted, "He gave me a bunny kiss from across the street."

Ivy's lips parted. Eyes wide, her gaze touched on Kisten, then me. "Excuse me?"

"You know." He made a peace sign and bent his fingers twice in quick succession. "Kiss, kiss? Isn't that a vampire . . . thing?"

Kisten laughed, the warm sound making me feel good. "Rachel," he said, sifting the cheese over the red sauce. "What did you do to make him leave his pack and follow you all the way down here? By the looks of it, I'd say he's trying to insinuate himself into your pack."

"Brett didn't leave. I think they kicked him out," I said, then hesitated. "You knew he was there, too?" I asked, and he shrugged, eating a piece of bacon. I ate one too, considering for the first time that perhaps Brett was looking for a new pack. I had saved his life. Sort of.

Jenks came in the open window, making circles around Rex until the cat chittered in distress. Laughing, Jenks led her into the hall as five of his kids wafted over the sill, toting what looked like a pair of black lace panties cradling the statue.

"Those are mine!" Ivy shrieked, standing up and darting to the sink. "Jenks!"

The pixies scattered. The statue wrapped in the black silk fell into her hand.

"These are mine!" she said again, red with anger and embarrassment as she pulled them off the statue and shoved them in her pocket. "Damn it, Jenks! Stay out of my room!"

Jenks flew in just under the ceiling. Rex padded in under him, her steps light and her eyes bright. "Holy crap!" he exclaimed, making circles around Ivy, wreathing her in a glittering band of gold. "How did your panties end up in my living room?"

Matalina zipped in, her green silk dress furling and her eyes apologetic. Immediately, Jenks joined her. I don't know if it was his joy of reuniting with Matalina or his stint at being human-sized, but he was a lot faster. With her was Jhan, a solemn, serious-minded pixy who had recently been excused from sentry duties in order to learn how to read. I didn't want to think about why.

Ivy dropped the new focus onto the counter beside the pizza, clearly in a huff as she backed away and sat sullenly in her chair, her boots on the table and her ankles crossed. David came closer, and this time I couldn't stop my shudder. Jenks was right. It had shifted again.

"Good God," David said, hunched to put it at eye level. "What is it?"

I bent my knees, crouching to come even with him, the focus between us. It didn't look like the same totem that I had put in Jenks's suitcase. The closer we had gotten to the full moon, the more it looked like the original statue, until now it was identical except for a quicksilver sheen hovering just above the surface like an aura.

Ivy was wiping her fingers off on her pants, and she quit when she saw my attention on them. I couldn't blame her. The thing gave me the willies.

Kisten added the last of the meat, pushing the pizza aside and putting his elbows on the counter, an odd look on him as he saw it for the first time. "That has got to be the ugliest thing in creation," he said, touching his torn earlobe in an unconscious show of unease.

Matalina nodded, a pensive look on her beautiful features. "It's not coming back in my house," she said, her clear voice determined. "It's not. Jenks, I love you, but if it comes back in my house, I'm moving into the desk and you can sleep with your dragonfly!"

Jenks hunched and made noises of placation, and I met the small woman's eyes with a smile. If all went well, David would be taking it off our hands.

"David," I said, pulling myself straight.

"Uh-huh . . ." he murmured, still staring at it.

"Have you ever heard of the focus?"

At that, a fearful expression flashed across his rugged features, worrying me. Taking a step forward, I slid the pizza stone off the counter. "I couldn't just give it to them," I said, opening the oven door and squinting in the heat that made my hair drift up. "The vampires would slaughter them. What kind of a runner would I be if I let them get wiped out like that?"

"So you brought it here?" he stammered. "The focus? To Cincinnati?"

I slid the stone into the oven and closed it, leaning back to take advantage of the heat slipping past the shut door. David's breath was shallow and the scent of musk rose.

"Rachel," he said, eyes riveted to it. "You know what this is, right? I mean . . . Oh my God, it's real." Tension pulling his small frame tight, he straightened. His attention went to Kisten, solemn behind the counter, to Jenks standing beside Matalina, to Ivy, snapping a fingernail on the rivet on her boot. "You hold it?" he said, looking panicked. "It's yours?"

Running my fingers through the hair at the back of my head, I nodded. "I, uh, guess."

Kisten jerked into motion. "Whoops," he said, reaching. "He's going down!"

"David!" I exclaimed, shocked when the small man's knees buckled.

I stretched for him, but Kisten had already slipped an arm under his shoulders. While Ivy fiddled with the rivet on her boot with a nail in feigned unconcern, Kisten lowered him into a chair. I edged the vampire out of the way, kneeling. "David?" I said, patting his cheeks. "David!"

Immediately his eyes fluttered. "I'm okay," he said, pushing me away before he was fully conscious. "I'm all right!" Taking a breath, he opened his eyes. His lips were pressed tightly together and he was clearly disgusted at himself. "Where . . . did you get it?" he said, his head down. "The stories say it's cursed. If it wasn't a gift, you're cursed."

"I don't believe in curses . . . like that," Ivy said.

Fear slid through me. I believed in curses; Nick had stolen it—Nick had fallen off the Mackinac Bridge. *No, he had jumped.* "Someone sent it to me," I said. "Everyone who knew I had it thinks it went over the bridge. No one knows I've got it."

At that, he pulled himself upright. "Just that loner out there," he said, shifting his feet but staying seated. He glanced at Kisten, who was at the sink, washing the topping bowls as if this was all normal.

"He doesn't know," I said, wincing when Ivy went to set the timer on the stove. *Crap, I'd forgotten to again.* "I think Kisten's right that he might be trying to get into our pack, seeing as I trounced him." I frowned, not believing that he was digging for information and would go back to Walter after the insult of being given to the street pack.

Nodding, David's gaze returned to the focus. "I got notification that you won another alpha contest," he said, clearly distracted. "Are you okay?"

Jenks lifted off the table, making glittering sparkles around me and bringing Rex to my feet when he landed on my shoulder. "She did great!" he said, ignoring the small cat. "You should have seen her. Rachel used the Were charm. She came out the size of a real wolf but had hair like a red setter." He flitted up, moving to Ivy. "Such a *pretty puppy* she was," he crooned, safely on Ivy's shoulder. "Soft fuzzy ears . . . little black paws."

"Shut up, Jenks."

"And the *cutest* little tail you've ever seen on a witch!"

"Put a cork in it!" I said, lunging for him. Fighting Pam hadn't been a fair contest, and I wondered who had credited me with the win at the Were registry. Brett maybe?

Laughing, Jenks zipped up and out of my reach. Ivy smiled softly, never moving except for putting her feet on the floor where they belonged. She looked proud of me, I think.

"Red wolf," David murmured, as if it was curious but not important. He had scooted his chair to the table and was reaching to the statue. Breath held, he touched it, and the carved bone gave way under his pressure like a balloon. He pulled back, an odd sound slipping from him.

Nervous, I sat down kitty-corner to him, the statue between us. "When I moved the curse to it, it looked like a totem pole, but every day it looked more like it did when we first got it, until now it looks like this. Again."

David licked his lips, dragging his attention from it for a brief second to meet my eyes, then back to the statue. Something had shifted in him. The fear was gone. It wasn't avarice in his gaze, but wonder. His fingers curled under, a mere inch from touching it, and he shuddered.

That was enough for me. I glanced at Ivy, and when she nodded, I turned to Jenks. He stood beside Mr. Fish and his tank of sea monkeys on the windowsill, his ankles crossed and his arms over his chest, but I still saw him as six-foot-four. Feeling my gaze on him, he nodded.

"Will you hold it for me?" I asked.

David jerked his hand away and spun in his chair. "Me? Why me?"

Jenks lifted smoothly into the air in a clatter of wings and landed next to it. "Because if I don't get that freaky thing out of my living room, Matalina is going to leave me."

My eyebrows rose, and Ivy snickered. Matalina had almost pinned Jenks to the flour canister when we had walked in, crying and laughing to have him home again. It had been hard on her, so hard. I'd never ask him to leave again.

"You're the only Were I trust to hold it," I said. "For

crying out loud, David, I'm your alpha. Who else am I going to give it to?"

He looked at it, then back to me. "Rachel, I can't. This is too much."

Flustered, I moved my chair beside him. "It's not a gift. It's a burden." Steeling myself, I pulled the statue closer. "Something this powerful can't go back into hiding once it's in the open," I said, looking at its ugly curves. I thought I saw a tear in its eye—I wasn't sure. "Even if accepting it might cause everything I care about to go down the crapper. If we ignore it, it's going to bite us on our asses, but if we meet it head on, maybe we can come out better than when we went in."

Kisten laughed, and in front of her computer, Ivy froze. By her suddenly closed expression, I realized that what I had said could also be applied to her and myself. I tried to catch her gaze, but she wouldn't look up, fiddling with the same rivet on her boot. From the corner of my sight Jenks's wings drooped as he watched us.

Oblivious, David stared at the statue. "Okay," he said, not reaching for it. "I'll . . . I'll take it, but it's yours." His brown eyes were wide and his shoulders were tense. "It's not mine."

"Deal." Pleased to have gotten rid of it, I took a happy breath. Jenks, too, puffed out his air. Matalina hadn't been happy with it being in their living room. It was sort of like bringing a marlin home from vacation. Or maybe a moose head.

The pizza had a bubble starting to rise, and Kisten opened the oven to stick a toothpick through the dough to release the hot air under it. The odor of tomato sauce and pepperoni billowed out, the scent of security and contentment. My tension eased, and David picked the focus up.

"I, ah, I think I'll take this home before I finish my appointments," he said, hefting it. "It feels . . . Damn, I could do anything with it."

Ivy put her feet on the floor and stood. "Just don't go starting a war," she grumbled, heading out to the hall. "I've got a box you can put that in."

David set it back on the table. "Thanks." Face creasing in worry, he edged it closer in a show of possession—not greed, but of protection. A smile came over Kisten as he saw it too.

"You, ah, sure the vampires won't be after it?" the small man said, and Kisten pulled out a chair and sat in it backward.

"No one knows you have it, and as long as you don't start rallying the Weres to you, they won't," he said, draping his arms over the top of his chair. "The only one that might know about it would be Piscary." He glanced at the empty hallway. "By way of Ivy," he said softly. "But she's very closed with her thoughts. He would have to dig for it." Kisten's look went worried. "He doesn't have any reason to think it's surfaced, but word gets around."

David put his hands into his pockets. "Maybe I should hide it in my cat box."

"You have a cat?" I asked. "I'd put you as a dog person."

His gaze darted over the kitchen when Ivy came in and put a small cardboard box on the table. Jenks landed on it and started tugging at the tape holding it. "It belonged to an old girlfriend," David said. "You want it?"

Ivy went to flick Jenks away to open the box herself, then changed her mind. "No," she said as she sat and forced her hands into her lap. "Do you want ours?"

"Hey!" Jenks shouted as the tape gave way and he flew back from the momentum. "Rex is *my* cat. Stop trying to give her away."

"Yours?" David said, surprised. "I thought she was Rachel's."

Embarrassed, I shrugged with one shoulder. "She doesn't like me," I said, pretending to check on the pizza.

Jenks landed on my shoulder in a soft show of support. "I think she's waiting for you to turn back into a wolf, Rache," he teased.

I went to brush him off, then stopped. A ribbon of memory pulled through me—of how he had treated me when he was big—and I made a soft "Mmmm" instead. "Have you seen her stare at me?" I turned, seeing her doing it now. "See?" I said, pointing at her in the middle of the threshold, her ears pricked and a curious, unafraid look on her sweet, kitten face.

David pulled the scarf from the collar of his duster and wrapped the focus up. "You should make her your familiar," he said. "She'd like you then."

"No fairy crap way!" Jenks shouted, wings a blur as he went to hold the box open for David. "Rachel isn't going to draw any ever-after through Rex. She'll fry her little kitty brain."

Might be an improvement, I thought sourly. "It doesn't work that way. She has to choose me. And he's right. I'd probably fry her little kitty brain. I fried Nick's."

A shudder rippled over David. The entire kitchen seemed to go still, and I looked worriedly at Ivy and Kisten. "You okay?" I said when they met my blank stare with my own.

"Moon just rose," David said, wiping a hand across his dark stubble. "It's full. Sorry. Sometimes it hits hard. I'm cool."

I gave him a once-over, thinking he looked different. There was a smoother grace, a new tension to him—like he could hear the clock before it ticked. I yanked open the drawer for the pizza cutter, shuffling around. "You sure you can't stay for some lunch?" I asked.

There was the skitter of cat claws on the linoleum, then David gasped. "Oh my God," he breathed on the exhale. "Look at it."

"Holy crap!" Jenks exclaimed, and Ivy took an audible breath.

I turned, pizza cutter in hand. My eyebrows rose and I blinked. "Whoa."

The cursed thing had turned completely silver, malleable like liquid. It looked entirely like a wolf now too, lips pulled from her muzzle and silver saliva dripping down to melt into the fur at the base. And it was her. Somehow I knew it. A shudder went through me as I thought I might hear something but wasn't sure. "You know what?" I said, my voice shaky as I looked at it in its box, cushioned by David's scarf. "You can have it. I don't want it back. Really."

David swallowed. "Rachel, we're friends and everything, but no. There is no way in hell I'm taking that thing into my apartment."

"It's not going back into my house!" Jenks said. "No freakin' way! Listen to it! It's making my teeth hurt. I already get misery once a month from twenty-three females, and I'm not putting up with it from some weird-ass Were statue on the full moon. Rachel, cover it up or something. Tink's tampons, can't you all hear that?"

I picked the box up, and the hair on my arms rose. Stifling a shudder, I opened the freezer and shoved it between the cold-burned waffles and the banana bread that tasted like asparagus that my mom had brought over. The fridge was stainless steel. It might help.

The phone rang and Ivy jumped up, heading for the living room as Jenks hovered over the sink and shed golden sparkles. "Better?" I said when I closed the freezer, and he sneezed, nodding as the last glitters fell.

Ivy appeared in the archway with the phone, her eyes black, and clearly ticked, to judge by her wire-tight stance. "What do you want, crap for brains?"

Nick.

Jenks jerked three feet into the air. I was sure my eyes were full of pity, but Jenks shook his head, not wanting to talk to his son. That Nick had romanced his son from him for a life of crime was far worse than anything Nick had ever done to me.

Not knowing what I was feeling, I held my hand out. Ivy hesitated, and my eyes narrowed. Grimacing, she slapped the phone into my palm. "If he comes here, I'll kill him," she muttered. "I mean it. I'll drive him up to Mackinaw and throw him over for real."

"Take a number," I said when she sat in her spot before her computer. Clearing my throat, I put the receiver to my ear. "Hello-o-o-o-o, Nick," I said, hitting the *k* hard. "You're the world's biggest jerk for what you did to Jax. You ever show your scrawny face in Cincinnati again, and I'm going to shove a broomstick up your ass and set it on fire. You got that?"

"Rachel," he said, sounding frantic. "It's not real!"

I glanced at the fridge, putting my hand over the receiver. "He says he's got the fake one," I said, simpering. Kisten snorted, and suddenly smug, I turned back to Nick. "What?" I said, my voice light and flowery. "Didn't your statue go silvery, Nickie da-a-a-arling?"

"You know damn well it didn't," he said, voice harsh. "Don't mess with me, Rachel. I need it. I *earned* it. I promised—"

"Nick," I soothed, but he was still talking. "Nick!" I said louder. "Listen to me."

Finally there was silence but for the hiss and buzz of the line. I looked over the kitchen, warm with the scent of pizza and the companionship of my friends. The new picture of Jenks and me that I'd stuck to the fridge caught my eye. His arm was over my shoulder, and we were both squinting from the sun. Ivy wasn't in it, but she had taken it, and her presence was as strong as the bridge behind us. The picture seemed to say it all.

So I lived in a church with pixies and a vampire who wanted to bite me but was afraid to. So I dated her old boyfriend who was likely going to spend his free time convincing me he was a better choice, when he wasn't angling for a threesome. And yeah, I was alpha of a pack and the only curse I could Were with was black, but that didn't mean I was going to. No one *knew* I had a Were artifact in my freezer that could set off a vamp/Were power struggle. My soul was coated with darkness from saving the world, but I had a hundred years to get rid of it. And so what if Nick might be smarter than me? I had friends. Good ones.

"Tag, darling," I said into the receiver. "You lose."

I hit the off button mid-protest. Tossing the phone to Ivy, I smiled.

Dead Witch Walking

Kim Harrison

Forty years ago a genetically engineered virus killed half of the world's human population and exposed the creatures of dreams and nightmares that had, until then, lived in secret alongside humanity.

Rachel Morgan is a runner with the Inderland Services, apprehending criminals throughout modern-day Cincinnati. She is also a witch.

Used to confronting criminal vampires, dark witches and homicidal werewolves, Rachel's latest assignments – apprehending cable-stealing magic students and tax-evading leprechauns – have prompted her to break her thirty-year contract with the I.S. and start her own runner agency. But no one quits the I.S.

Marked for death, Rachel is a dead witch walking unless she can appease her former employers and pay off her contract by exposing the city's most prominent citizen as a drug lord. But making an enemy of the ambiguous Trent Kalamack proves even more deadly than leaving the I.S.

ISBN-13: 978-0-00-723609-1
ISBN-10: 0-00-723609-3

The Good, the Bad and the Undead

Kim Harrison

During the last few months, former bounty-hunter Rachel Morgan has been rather busy. Having escaped relatively unscathed from her corrupt former employers, she's acquired a vampiric room-mate – called Ivy, faced were-wolf assassins; battled shape-shifting demons, found the time to pick up a boyfriend (even if he is only human), and has opened her very own runner agency.

But cohabiting with a vampire, however reformed, has its dangers. Ivy's evil vampire ex-boyfriend has decided that he wants her back, and views Rachel as a tasty side-dish. To make matters worse, Rachel's demon mark is the ulti-mate vamp-aphrodisiac – one that works both ways.

The stakes are high, and if Rachel is to save herself and her room mate she must challenge the criminal master vam-pire and confront dark secrets she's kept hidden even from herself.

ISBN-13: 978-0-00-723611-4
ISBN-10: 0-00-723611-5

Every Which Way But Dead

Kim Harrison

If you make a deal with the devil, can you still save your soul?

To avoid becoming the love-slave of a depraved criminal vampire, bounty-hunter and witch, Rachel Morgan, is cornered into a deal that could promise her an eternity of suffering.

But eternal damnation is not Rachel's only worry. Her vampire roommate, Ivy, has rediscovered her taste for blood and is struggling to keep their relationship platonic, her boyfriend, Nick, has disappeared – perhaps indefinitely, and she's being stalked by an irate pack of werewolves. And then there's also the small matter of the turf war raging in Cincinnati's underworld; one that Rachel began and will have to navigate safely before she has the smallest hope of preserving her own future.

ISBN-13: 978-0-00-723612-1
ISBN-10: 0-00-723612-3

What's next?

Tell us the name of an author you love

| Kim Harrison | Go ▶ |

and we'll find your next great book.